T.C. O'Connor

by Eoghain Connor Darragh*

---

* The given name Eoghain is an Irish variation of Ian and it is
pronounced the same way.

i

Dedication: Susan Beth,
best friend for a lifetime.

Acknowledgements

Virginia Slep, Group Leader of many Creative Writing Workshops, for her constructive criticism, patience, dedication, adherence to writing principles and willingness to compromise on writing principles, hard work, organizational skills, and demonstrating how to write very, very well with numerous examples.

Marilyn McGrath, Author and creative writing teacher, for encouragement and advice.

Claire Elizabeth, Meghan Eileen, Tara Katherine, Susan Beth, Helen Rose Olma, James William for believing, promoting, and teaching me to write.

Susan B. McGrath and Meghan E. McGrath for constructive reading of the review copy.

Many thanks for the constructive criticism graciously provided by all of the participants in the LLARC Creative Writing Workshop including (to name just a few alphabetically) Rosalie Beith, Irving Erlichman, Karin Flynn, Stephen Garanin, Irene Gerwick, Ken Greenberg, Marilyn Hicks, Nora Hussey, Ruth Harriet Jacobs, Mary Brandt Kerr, Richard Leone, MaryJo Libertino, Chuck McWilliams, Susan Mills, Margaret Mulcahy, Bonny Musinsky, Melvin Norris, Al Persson, Eileen Power, Shirley Reiss, Rosemary Rimkus, Robert Russo, Patricia Sullivan, Joseph Tennyson.

On a less serious but still auspicious note, thanks to Alvin J. Sturdley for enlightenment.

Author's Note

Chapters. Upon the advice of editors and agents, the narrative is told in many short chapters (two to less than ten pages) spread over eight parts.

Titles. In accordance with the suggestion of well-published literary experts, the title of each chapter is a teaser and the theme for the following paragraphs.

Names. For the convenience of both the reader and the author, there is an appendix containing the **Index of the Initial Occurrence of a Name**. Locating the first time a character or place appears in the story can be helpful.

Genre. The suspense novel is a murder mystery. It is about Ted O'Connor's struggle to become worthy of friendship and trust. Ever since childhood, his lack of good judgement got him into the kind of trouble that put his future in jeopardy. Upon occasion, loyal friends and relatives were able to come to his rescue. At other times, he could not escape the costs of his misguided behavior.

Theodore Christopher O'Connor is the narrator of his story. He has spun a well-written yarn and poignant drama. The events are described and the personalities are revealed in a fashion that holds the reader's interest from beginning to end. Please take the time to savor the passages in **T.C. O'Connor** with no sense of urgency but with full appreciation for Ted's life journey.

Page by page. There are stories within the story in Mr. O'Connor's narrative. To skip over any one of the tales would be to miss intriguing aspects of his life and good character. By the author's design, the reader's anticipation for the ending is constructed page by every single page in the flow of Ted's struggle to salvage self-respect and reputation.

Please be sure to give a copy of **T.C. O'Connor** to friends and relatives as a birthday gift or for most any other special occasion.

Eoghain Connor Darragh

Contents

Part I

Rough Beginnings

Present fears are less than horrible imaginings.

- William Shakespeare, Macbeth

Chapter 1 . Unwelcome visitors interrupted an activity to be relished.

§ June 2019 §

A police cruiser crawled past our residence on Elm Avenue. The patrolman behind the wheel turned the car around at the corner, came back, and parked across the street. The two uniformed occupants got out. They stood by their car watching our house for signs of life.

They exchanged a few words before crossing the street onto our front yard. The sergeant motioned for the patrolman to climb the stairs to the porch. The young man waited at the door for his superior to join him before ringing the bell.

The call to answer the door rang out in the garage where my attention was focused on a cherished hobby. I enjoy restoring classic cars to pristine condition. It is an activity to be relished, not to be interrupted.

My Saturday morning's enterprise was just two hours old on the first nice weekend in June of 2019. I was anxious to start taking advantage of the good weather between the days when it was too cold and the days when it would become too hot and humid to be laboring in my uninsulated workshop.

I was engrossed in a job that seemed to be coming together pretty nicely. I knew the interruption could prove to be a monkey wrench thrown into the works literally as well as figuratively. I was inclined to ignore the summons to our front door.

Whoever was there would not be for me. The bell would not be ringing for my wife either. Her friends and associates knew she was out of town on business. My friends and coworkers would come looking for me in the garage if no one answered after the second ring.

An impromptu visitor on a Saturday morning would most likely be looking for the younger of our two daughters, who was not at home. The older one was a college student just returned for the summer. She was in the house but would be inclined to ignore something not likely to concern her.

Our two children were well-liked, well-adjusted young women with very different personalities. The gregarious, younger girl had friends and classmates coming and going all of the time. The older one was more reserved. It was rare for her to have an unannounced visitor.

I was on my back on a mechanics creeper under a classic '58 Chevy when the buzzer connected to the front doorbell reverberated in my ears. The linkage for a new clutch was dangling in my face.

The visitors had evidently not noticed the bright lights shining from our barn-like garage where mechanical repairs were in progress on a pair of vintage automobiles. I was toiling on the more challenging of the current projects.

Perhaps, whoever was at the door would give up and go away.

Chapter 2 . It was I who would have to answer the door.

Our unexpected visitors rang the chimes twice and more quickly a third and fourth time. Evidently, it would be up to me to discover whatever could be so urgent.

Summer vacation had just gotten underway for the fifteen-year-old girl. Our college-aged daughter was in the house but probably still in her pajamas. If you will pardon the sarcasm, Diane was not about to get out of bed to answer the door at the early hour of ten o'clock even on such a beautiful spring day.

Diane was working part-time selling clothes in an Anthropologie store. We were pleased that she had a job but not particularly happy with her lack of industry around the house. The coed was home for the summer after her sophomore year. Her final exams for the semester had been completed in early May.

The almost grown-up daughter did not go to work until the middle of the afternoon. It was a bit of a drive for her to get to the mall in the city, which meant she did not return home until late. Her commuting schedule served as a sufficient excuse for the young woman to sleep in every day. She was usually not dressed before noon.

It was a struggle to push myself and the mechanics creeper out from under the car. The casters squealed on the concrete and the rigid board slid hesitantly backward until I was free of the front bumper.

I managed to roll over onto my hands and knees and pull myself up. I had been up and down, on and off the cold floor for over an hour already. My hands hurt from threading bolts and turning wrenches. My muscles were sore and my joints had stiffened. My back creaked and my knees grumbled.

And I was loving it. What could be better than bringing back to life such a mechanical classic as a vintage Chevrolet?

When I posed that question to Diane's little sister, I hate to tell you that she had a ready answer. Eileen said, "How about a root canal?"

If only she were here to display some of her quick wit for whomever was ringing the doorbell but she was not. It was I who would have to answer the door. I hobbled along the side of the house in the direction of the front yard. The unpleasant sound of the buzzer was still screeching in my ears.

I had installed a device that was loud enough for me to hear no matter what I was working on. I wanted an audio signal that would penetrate background noise generated by power tools, running engines, and ventilation fans. The discordant squawk was effective. However, it was also a mistake.

Several years ago, just a week after I had done the wiring for the relay from the front doorbell, the screech pierced the air in the garage. It shocked my eardrums. I was working under the hood of my wife's car. The harsh sound startled me.

I straightened up and banged my head on the overhanging steel frame. A wrench slipped out of my hands. The hex nuts and the bracket for attaching the exhaust manifold to the engine block scattered across the floor.

The scene was comical enough to be funny if it were not so annoying. After retrieving the tool and the parts, I had to restart the process of aligning the components.

That was a long time ago. I still intend to fix the problem. It would not be hard to swap out the buzzer for a more melodious but still loud signal that a visitor was at the front door. However, there are too many items on the to-do list for me to take the time to fix something that is not truly broken.

On that Saturday morning in June, when I heard the doorbell again and then once more, I quickened my pace along the driveway and around the corner onto the early spring's, yet-to-be-mowed grass in our front yard.

The two police officers on the porch turned to observe my approach. I stopped in the middle of the lawn when I saw them there and felt their glare.

Chapter 3 . Hard edge was for affect.

A sudden chill of apprehension swept over me. A knot tightened in the pit of my stomach. The reaction was not entirely reasonable. Anxiety at the sight of a uniform should not have such an effect on me anymore.

My wayward years, when I was frequently in some kind of trouble, were in the distant past. My turned-over new leaf might have had a few dog-eared corners. Perhaps, I was guilty of roughhousing during a ball game or failing to hold up my end for an obligation at home. However, there has been nothing worthy of any interest to the police. Indeed, I have not touched a drop since my first Alcoholic Anonymous meeting over seven years ago.

Recent activities that might arouse any suspicion of criminal activity could not be connected to me. Or, so I thought. Perhaps, something from years ago might have just come to light. But, I couldn't think what it might be.

Prior to taking the sobriety oath, I considered the police to be adversaries. Quite the reverse was true after I entered recovery.

I learned to accept that, for the most part, officers in the Batavia Police Department were conscientious public servants who would rather be keeping the peace than enforcing it. I believed they were genuinely concerned about the well-being of their neighbors in our small town.

There were good reasons for me to appreciate the police beyond the gratitude that might be felt by most of the other residents of Batavia. My personal recovery from addiction had been aided in no small part by their interventions.

There was, however, an exception to the rule that the policemen were nice and friendly neighbors. Indeed, my sudden bout of anxiety was exasperated by the sight of the more senior of the two men on our front porch.

Sgt. Robert Ryan and I had a history from years ago. I was acquainted with him both in his capacity as an officer of the law and during off-duty recreational activities.

Our baseball team in Batavia competed under the auspices of the Amateur Athletic Union. We were a talented bunch and Ryan was a decent outfielder. To have him in the lineup was generally a good thing. However, he was difficult to placate when a play did not go his way whether it was called correctly or not.

The people who knew Sgt. Ryan best learned to stay out of the way when they found him to be in a surly mood. No one needed to remind me of his quick temper.

He lost control on the one occasion he had to arrest me for disorderly conduct. The obstreperous policeman became abusive when I was not fully cooperative with his attempt to take me into custody. The handcuffs were already affixed when he administered a few licks to the head and torso that left me with bad bruises and a black eye.

It was time for me to leave the old memory behind. My professed new attitude was that the hard edge to the man's personal skills had to be more show than substance. At least, that's what I told myself.

An essential component of the recovery process is to forgive and move on. Because I believe in the principle, I was trying to forget how unprofessional Ryan had been. Evidently, I was not quite there yet.

Chapter 4 . The curmudgeon held sway.

Hello, gentlemen, what can I do for you?" I called out to the sergeant and the patrolman standing on our front porch. The question was meant to be taken as a friendly greeting.

"Ah, Theodore Christopher O'Connor, there you are. I'm Sgt. Ryan. You know Officer White. We need to talk to you." The police sergeant yelled back in a rather snarky tone.

For him to tell me their names was rather odd. His attitude evoked the bad memories of our age-old encounters. I held my place on the lawn too uneasy to proceed. I just stood there about thirty feet short of the porch stairs.

Both of the policemen knew my family and me well enough to drop by to chat about anything that might come up. Robert Ryan had been a member of the police department for many years. The younger man's name was William White. His big sister used to babysit for our two children.

Although more antagonist than friend, Bob Ryan had been to our house at least a few times over the years. Billy White grew up in the neighborhood. He and his sister attended the same elementary school and high school as our two children.

We did not see much of Billy for a long while after he graduated and went off to college but we did not lose track of him. His mother kept us informed. She told us how disappointed she was when he left the university and joined the service after his sophomore year. She made him promise to keep working toward a degree.

Diane asked Billy's mother for his address and they exchanged a few letters. Although I was not privy to the quantity of their correspondence, I was aware that

10

Diane was always happy to get a letter from her soldier friend. She did tell me that Billy was stationed at a base near Seoul for part of his enlistment.

When he returned to Batavia at the end of his two years, young Mr. White's name appeared in the local newspaper. He had been hired by the Batavia Police Department and sent to the school for police cadets in the city. The picture of the graduating class was on the front page with the caption that William White and Angela Dunning would be joining the BPD full time.

I tried to counter the police officer's unfriendly words with a cheerful reply. "I know who you boys are, Bob. We all remember the times when I was a too-frequent visitor in your lockup. Billy, you grew up just down the street."

Sgt. Ryan became defensive. "It has been a while since we've seen you. I just didn't know if you would recognize us."

Officer White didn't say anything. He stood back shifting uneasily from one foot to the other.

"That's ridiculous, Bob. Just because I'm senile does not mean I've forgotten your names," I said with a laugh in another attempt to lighten the mood.

"Of course, Mr. O'Connor, we did not mean to imply that we thought you had Alzheimer's or anything like that," Ryan replied. He completely missed, I believe intentionally missed, the irony in my answer.

"OK, I understand," I said even though I didn't. "What brings you to our front porch?"

"We will get to that in a moment. What took you so long to answer the door?" he asked.

The lack of civility in his manner and the unpleasant memories of our past were getting to me. I did not want to feel the resentment but Sgt. Ryan had a way of testing my resolve.

The ranking officer at the front door was evidently annoyed that they had been kept waiting. It was, after all, fairly obvious that someone was in the house. The music blaring from the open upstairs window and through the closed front door was hard to miss.

I remained standing in the yard looking up at the policemen unsure of what to do. I tried again to ease the tension.

"C'mon, Bob, don't be so stuffy. Formality is not needed in a conversation between neighbors and teammates."

Billy White seemed to agree with my wish for a more pleasant tone to the conversation. He nodded at me from where he was standing back out of the shorter, solidly built sergeant's field of view.

The cantankerous, contemptuous curmudgeon snarled over a curled lip, "You're wrong, Mr. O'Connor. Playing it by the book is exactly what's needed." Sgt. Ryan's belligerent response left a chilling silence hanging in the air.

"Why are you here?" I just stood on the lawn looking up at them with my arms crossed.

"As I said, we need to talk to you, Mr. O'Connor," Sgt. Ryan repeated.

"You can still call me Ted like you always have, Bob," I said to the humorless Ryan. "What's going on?"

"We have been wondering about where you have been, Mr. O'Connor, and what you have been up to." Evidently, he thought the circumstances did not allow for first names.

Chapter 5 . There was space for a garage.

All of the teachers and students knew everyone else by name in the local elementary school. The environment had been working well in kindergarten for our oldest daughter by the time she started first grade in September of 2005. The atmosphere of pleasant familiarity continued throughout both of our children's grade-school years and beyond at the one high school in Batavia.

When our two were small, Margaret White was their preferred babysitter. She was two grades ahead of her brother William who was a few years further along than Diane. William's nickname was Billy. Young Margaret insisted on Margaret. They lived with their mother Julie and stepfather John Anderson a few doors down on our side of Elm Avenue. The White children's surname came from their mother's previous relationship.

As a young lad, Billy White would come over and hang around the backyard and the garage when Diane was toiling somewhat reluctantly as my workshop assistant. I liked the boy. He was respectful and would voluntarily pitch in with the chores. Diane would perk up while he was there. Billy was clearly sweet on the pretty neighborhood girl and she liked the attention of the older boy.

"Hey, Diane, what do you think of that guy? He really likes you," I teased after we got to the side door into the house. Billy was still within earshot on his way home.

"No, Daddy. Don't say that. He is way older," she flustered. It was in the summer of 2007 shortly before Diane would be going into the third grade.

I didn't know if he was still close enough to hear but I'm sure my observation would have made Billy squirm too. Is it not an eternal truth that grade-school children are self-conscious about any association with the opposite sex?

In the fall just two months later, I caught sight of Billy carrying Diane's books on their way to school. When our third grader noticed me noticing them, she snatched her books back and looked the other way.

It would have been the perfect opportunity for her father to inflict a bit of razzing when she got home that afternoon. However, I got outmaneuvered.

Diane's mother stood up for her. She said, "That would be really mean." She threatened me with dire consequences if I dared to even bring it up. So, of course, I didn't mention it.

The garage was part of our plans for the place when we bought the house in January of 1998 before the children were born. The large, open space at the end of the driveway was one of the reasons we made an offer.

We call the building our garage but it is more like a small-size barn. The thirty-by-forty foot structure has large sliding doors on barn hinges for the double-wide entrance. It can hold as many as half a dozen vehicles. There are a workbench and tool racks at the back and a second story with more space up above.

The corner office on the second floor at the back of the building is mostly for my wife. It is the only square footage with adequate insulation. The natural-gas furnace and the air conditioning are sufficiently powerful to keep it comfortable throughout the year.

My wife finds the setting to be a useful hideaway for concentrating on tasks that she brings home from work. The lavatory on the second story is attached to the office space with another door to the hallway.

I did a good job with the placement of the large windows on the two outside walls in the office. The views overlook the trees in our backyard. We enjoy watching the new life hatching in the branches in the spring and the glistening winter wonderland on the tree limbs in December and January.

The woods and stream across the back of the property provide a picturesque separation between our property and the houses on the next street over. The water attracts geese and other in-season wildlife for us to observe and enjoy from the upstairs' office windows.

We have a large backyard. Only the closer half between house and woods has to be maintained. The garage is on one side of the property. A good piece of the rest of the backyard is staked out for our garden. We try to keep the grass in the remainder healthy and trimmed. It's where the badminton net is set up during the summer.

There are a flat-screen television, upholstered furniture, and a wet bar in the front half of the second floor of the garage. The open area can be nice during the spring and fall but the extra family room is too costly to cool or heat in the summer and winter. Someday, I will put in the insulation needed for year-round enjoyment. However, on my do-it-yourself schedule, it may be a while.

The garage is an improvement on our property that I am quite proud of. Always the handyman since old enough to hold a hammer, I came up with the basic design and built the place mostly by myself.

My wife played a significant role in drawing up the floor plans. We like to remind ourselves that it took us just a little over two years from pouring the foundation in August after closing on the purchase in January of 1998. The last brush stroke of paint was applied in October of the year 2000.

Chapter 6 . Construction and automotive repair were instinctive.

My talent for construction originated with my maternal grandfather's remodeling company. The old man put me to work after school and during the summers. I was not yet nine years old between the second and third grades in the summer of 1980 when Grandpa started paying me to help out on one of his jobs. It didn't really qualify as genuine experience yet but I did take to it immediately.

The regular construction workers enjoyed having me around. For the first few years until I got a little older, they found it to be gratifying to tutor an apprentice who took pride in the work. I showed respect for them and for what they could do. I was a student of the trade and I took to heart essential maxims like, "Measure twice and cut once."

They got a kick out of my enthusiasm. Their teasing would be good natured each time I naively agreed to a task beyond my abilities. Yet, they did not hesitate to challenge me.

As a teenager, I began to detect something of an edge to their razzing. The boss's fair-haired grandson was no longer as easy for them to accept as one of the boys. The arrogance of youth probably did not help. In my mind, I could do everything as well as any of them even though I couldn't, at least not yet.

My inclination to be a student of the construction process may have rankled a few of the old timers. I wanted to know the physics and engineering principles that guided the fabrication process. For example, was it whim or structural integrity that dictated 16 inches or 24 inches on-center for the studs in the walls and joists under the eaves?

I asked questions that the senior construction workers couldn't answer. They may have detected a bit of disdain in my attitude when they were not interested in the technical materials that I brought home from the library.

One of the benefits of construction work is appreciation for the need for physical strength. A middle-aged member of the crew introduced my teenaged self to weight training and aerobic exercise as a way to become tougher on the job and in life.

The man was there such a short time that I did not get to know him very well not even well enough to know his real name.

"What happened to Stretch?" I asked.

Grandpa said, "I fired him." He would not tell me why.

The brief episode is worth mentioning because it had a lasting influence. Anaerobic and aerobic exercises became an important part of my life. While never an Adonis, I grew up to be strong and fit. I still go to the gym several times a week or at least as often as I can.

While the men and the only two women on my grandfather's crew were all business on the job, there was a downside that did not serve me all that well in the long run. They did not set a good example with their talk and drinking when the day was done.

The women could be as profane as any of the guys. They probably had to be that way in order to hold their own in such a politically incorrect atmosphere.

Early on, Grandfather did what was right to shield me from the bad influences. As I got older, he loosened up quite a lot. I think he realized that stuff would go on behind his back no matter how much he tried to protect me from seeing the vulgar.

"I've got to trust you to know what is right and to stay out of trouble," he reminded me many more times than once.

"I know. I won't do anything foolish."

"Just come to me if you have any problems. I'll cover for you."

Grandfather knew the curiosity of a youth in his early teens worked against his protective measures. He must have figured I would find out about bad stuff eventually anyway. My weakness was the need to appear mature among the guys.

In the end, I saw things and heard a few tales not too appropriate for someone of my tender age. While I do not believe any of the prurient stories did me any lasting harm, the occasional taste of alcoholic beverages was a foreshadowing of bad things to come.

The goofing off was only a small part of my learning experience with the construction crew. They taught me to do wiring and plumbing. The lessons included how to sweat joints for water supply lines and to connect the bathroom and kitchen drainpipes. It surprised me to learn that the black pipe for natural gas was easier to install than the plumbing for the water lines.

By my mid-teens, I could do all of the electrical work and the plumbing needed for the construction of a house. I was ready to take the exam for the journeyman plumber's license by the time I was old enough to drive. I even learned how to hang wallpaper although I hated it. To get it right took too much attention to detail.

The experience with Grandfather's construction company explains how I was able to design and build our barn-like garage and do it really well. My expertise with auto repair came from a different source.

My father was a master mechanic. He knew as much about automobiles as his father-in-law knew about construction. In fact, that was how he met my mother. He was repairing one of the construction company's vehicles when she came to pick it up.

"As soon as she saw me, she latched on and never let go," is how he tells it. Mother just snorts when she hears him repeat the joke.

It was the good fortune of my youth to learn trades from both grandfather and father. They were impressed by my achievements. They were proud to have me follow in their footsteps. I could do residential construction, automotive mechanics, or both.

My avocation for the two different occupations had a doubling effect on the motivation for the barn-like garage on Elm Avenue. First, I savored doing the construction and, second, I needed a place to work on vintage cars. It certainly helped that my wife liked the idea of the extra family room and office space upstairs.

The restoration work in my new automotive workshop was a challenging and expensive hobby that gave me a real sense of satisfaction. It could also pay off handsomely when a buyer took an interest in the restoration of a particularly valuable classic vehicle. In addition to auto mechanics, my father taught his son how to do a fair appraisal of the finished product.

Restoration of antiques was not a business interest of mine. That is, I did not solicit or accept repair jobs. I did not have the facilities or the desire to do such work especially not on a promised schedule for fixing someone else's vintage vehicle.

When I happened upon an old car that might have some potential, I read what I could find about the history of the make and model. If there was something curious about the technology of the antique that caught my interest, I would examine it carefully for hidden defects before bringing the vehicle home to bring it back to life.

I tried not to be too obsessive but the job was not done until I had the machine running like new. When the project was finished to my satisfaction, I sold it or donated it to a charitable cause. Although making a little money on the deal was nice if it happened, the reason for releasing the title when I finished a job was to make room for the next project.

I liked making a vehicle run well but not the finishing work. It was a lot like hanging wallpaper in my Grandfather's construction business, too much effort to get it right. Also, body work was time consuming. I could assemble and attach replacement fenders, bumpers, and the other parts on the car but that was as far as I would go.

When the vehicle was ready for painting or if rust had to be removed and dents repaired, I passed it off to Vince's Body Shop. Vincenzo Pepé Vannutelli actually bought a couple of my restorations to display in his private collection. The wealthy eccentric was a bit of a celebrity in the town of Batavia.

By concentrating on just the mechanical aspects of the job, I had enough time to cycle two or three projects through my garage from spring through fall.

Restoration work is a nice hobby that does not get old for me. It is also a lifelong interest that I share with my father. He enjoys coming over to kibitz or lend a hand. After all, I inherited the love for automotive mechanics from him.

Chapter 7 . The sergeant was unpleasant; The patrolman was polite.

The uniformed policemen must have had a reason for showing up on my doorstep but it was a mystery to me. Sgt. Ryan did not offer an explanation. I figured it would not be up to Officer White, the junior man on the team.

The standoff was not getting us anywhere. I thought about turning around, walking away, and going back to the task at hand in the garage. I did the opposite. I approached the policemen instead.

I started up the five steps from the front sidewalk onto the porch. Sgt. Ryan moved forward to block my way before I could get level with him. It was a menacing gesture.

I squeezed past the burly obstruction and moved away to my right toward the wooden chairs and table on our broad front porch. I turned to face the two policemen and reminded them, "The reason you have not been seeing much of me is I have been staying out of trouble. I've been sober for over seven years."

"If you say so," Ryan scoffed at my assertion.

"Look, I admit I had difficulties in the past. You might remember, Billy, that your sister was a babysitter in our home back when I was confined in the city jail."

"Yes, sir. I remember." Billy looked directly at me for the first time that morning.

He had been well liked in high school. His sister Margaret and Billy played mixed doubles for Batavia High. They took first place in several competitions when she was a senior. Billy was two years younger than Margaret. As I recall, William White got a partial scholarship to play tennis at Holy Cross in Worcester.

21

"Jail time was a wake-up call. I got help and I have not touched a drop ever since," I said.

"Interesting to hear you say that, Mr. O'Connor. Tell me. How do you explain what we found? Did you take a few nips here on your porch?" Ryan pointed to the railing by the bushes next to the porch. "Well, show it to him, Officer White." Ryan barked at his uneasy partner.

Billy was holding a clear plastic bag containing an empty bottle with the Jim Beam label. I was well acquainted with both an evidence bag and a fifth of bourbon.

"I have no idea how that got here. It is certainly not mine."

Both men were looking at me. Ryan was sure I was lying. I think Billy wanted to believe me but he had seen enough in the past that he might have had his doubts. He had a pained expression on his face. I had to look away.

"Well, maybe so, maybe not. But your sobriety is not why we came to see you," Ryan muttered in a condescending tone.

Just then, I caught sight of Eileen over Ryan's right shoulder. She was just coming into view from around the corner.

Our house was the fourth on Elm Avenue from the intersection with Columbia Street. She and her friend Nicole were walking in our direction.

When Eileen spotted us, she grabbed Nicole's arm and the two of them hurried back around the corner out of sight. I pretended not to notice. Neither of the policemen picked up on my reaction to the appearance of the two girls.

"What do you want?" It was impossible to keep all indications of annoyance out of my voice.

"We are investigating a recent incident in town, Mr. O'Connor," Officer White said.

"What does that have to do with us?" I quaked. "I mean with me?" I lamented to myself, why did I say us? Did our daughter's reaction to the sight of the police make me wonder if she or Diane had been up to something?

Chapter 8 . The second police car was an ominous sign.

Diane opened the front door and stood there watching from behind the glass storm door. The commotion on the porch had roused Eileen's big sister from her late slumber. The music could still be heard but the noise was no longer shaking the rafters. She had turned the volume down on her player.

Officer Ryan noticed Diane's appearance in the doorway right away. "Can we go inside and have a look around?" he asked in a demanding voice.

"I don't think so. You can tell me what you want right here." I instinctively resisted.

"Would you prefer to come with us to answer a few questions at the station?" Ryan threatened.

"No. Tell me what you are looking for."

Ryan increased the pressure. "We can get a warrant and take you downtown and search your house. Is that what you want?"

"You have no justification for a warrant," I snapped back.

Another of our small town's several police cars rolled slowly up the street and pulled into our driveway. The dark blue cruiser that had transported Ryan and White to our neighborhood was still parked across the street.

The ominous look of the patrol cars was a bit of an irony. In my opinion, unmarked vehicles were an affectation for the Batavia City Police Department. There was no reason for stealth when keeping the peace in our sleepy village.

Petty theft was about all the police had to contend with. On rare occasions, a report of abusive behavior would appear on the police blotter printed in our town's newspaper. However, Batavia had almost no serious crime.

Rush hour was not much of an issue either. With three traffic circles and maybe half a dozen stoplights, the per-year rate of serious auto accidents was in the single digits. The principal thoroughfares in and out of the adjacent metropolitan area skirted around Batavia as if intentionally avoiding our quiet community.

The police force was correspondingly small in number. The town employed about a dozen full-time and part-time officers in addition to a few administrative staffers. Robert Ryan was one of three who held the dual distinction of police officer and department detective.

Sgt. Ryan had been on the force as long as anyone in the department. It was widely held that he harbored some resentment when an outsider was hired to be the new police chief a few years ago.

Given our history, I was relieved that he didn't get the job. I was also surprised because Ryan was dedicated and competent even though hot headed at times. As it turned out, a curmudgeon for the chief of police was exactly what the search committee wanted to avoid. I know because I was a member.

I was appointed by the mayor and approved by city council partly because my troubled history gave me a certain perspective that was otherwise absent from the committee meetings. The council respected the fact that I had become an exemplary citizen with my work in the schools. My community-service requirements had included supervising youth recreational activities. I was hooked on the satisfaction that it gave me. It became a lifelong activity.

Because I did not know if I could be fair, I recused myself from the interviewing session with Sgt. Ryan. However, I wondered all along if he suspected me of sabotaging his candidacy. The fact is I did my best to do nothing to diminish his chances for the job. In the end, the committee decided to declare a unanimous selection and to keep secret how each member voted. I hope that the details will remain hidden permanently.

"Excuse me, Sergeant," Billy finally spoke up. "I'd like to ask Mr. O'Connor something. Maybe it would help."

Ryan was clearly not happy about the interruption. "Good cop, bad cop," he sneered at Officer White. He was staring daggers at the young policeman.

At first, Billy looked unsure of himself but he stiffened and went ahead anyway. "Mr. O'Connor, we have some evidence that you were at Hennigan's at about the time of some trouble there last night. We are hoping you can help us find out what happened." His manner was polite and respectful.

He continued, "The sergeant and I do not want to create a big scene here at your residence and cause trouble for you or for ourselves." Officer White turned to look right at Sgt. Ryan. "Or, for ourselves," he repeated.

The older man was silent. Perhaps, there had been complaints from others about his rude treatment of civilians. Billy was a smart kid. The addendum to his comment that they did not want to cause trouble for themselves might have been designed to temper Ryan's behavior.

White turned back to me. "Did you stop for gas at Hennigan's last evening, Mr. O'Connor?"

"Yes, Officer White, I was there but I saw nothing unusual but . . . Um." I hesitated.

Chapter 9 . There was no attendant in the convenience store.

Hennigan's was the only filling station in Batavia that stayed open past seven o'clock in the evening. It was owned and operated by Matthew Hennigan.

In addition to the fuel pumps out front, there was a glittering convenience store on the property where you could pick up a few grocery items outside of regular hours for the supermarket. I had stopped for gas at Hennigan's the previous evening.

My hesitant response was all Ryan needed for him to resume his interrogation. He demanded, "Nothing unusual but what?" He stepped closer to bark in my face.

The affront forced me to stumble backwards. "Come to think of it. The lights were on but no one was there," I explained.

"You don't see that as unusual?" He feigned surprise. Sgt. Ryan was certainly aware of the casual attitude about security in Batavia and at Hennigan's in particular.

"No, no. Of course, leaving the place unattended like that is probably unwise. But, it has happened before. He does not want his employees to do it but Hennigan himself will leave the place unlocked while he runs over to the deli to pick up a sandwich. I just figured whoever was on duty stepped out for a lavatory break or something."

"Did you check to see if he was next door at Nora Package Liquors?" Billy asked.

It was an obvious question. Nora's is adjacent to Hennigan's. The buildings are attached. It is just a few steps from the main entrance to the liquor store, up the sidewalk, and into the front of the service station.

There is also a plate glass door that serves as a side entrance directly into Nora Package Liquors from

Hennigan's convenience store. Without going down the aisle on the far left in Hennigan's, the view into Nora's would be very limited.

It is an odd fact in Batavia that the logistics of the two establishments make it so convenient for drivers to refuel and purchase alcohol at the same stop. Nora's is not a bar but the store has plenty of cold beer for sale.

I answered Officer White's question. "No. I never go in there."

"I've known you to be a frequent customer of hundreds of liquor stores," Ryan exaggerated.

"What I meant is I never go in there anymore. I have not been inside Nora's in years."

"The bottle of bourbon that we are holding here in your front yard has the liquor store's price tag on it."

"I've already told you I have no idea how it got here."

"Please, Mr. O'Connor, what did you see and do at Hennigan's last night?" Officer White tried to stay in the conversation with a moderating tone.

"I paid for the gas with a credit card at the pump like I always do. I decided to go into Hennigan's for popcorn and a soft drink. Matt keeps the popper going all day and I find it hard to resist. He makes really tasty popcorn."

"Yeah, yeah. We don't need the commercial. What else?" Sgt. Ryan would not soften his acerbic questioning.

"I waited around for a while. When no one showed up, I helped myself to a bag of popcorn and left the store."

"Are you confessing to larceny, Mr. O'Connor?" Ryan asked.

"Um, Sergeant, the popcorn at Hennigan's is complimentary for their customers," Billy interjected before I could defend myself.

Ryan fired more visual daggers at Officer White.

"Yes, that's right. Thanks, Billy." I was glad to have his help. I also knew that Ryan was well aware of Hennigan's generosity. He had certainly enjoyed the free popcorn snacks himself on many occasions.

"You said you searched the place while you were waiting around. How hard did you look for someone? It would have been right neighborly to make sure nothing was wrong." Ryan's belligerence was becoming tiresome as well as unnerving. Evidently, there would be no relief from his harsh interrogation strategy.

"No, I don't think I said I searched the place. I did not go further than the front part of the store. I called out, 'Is anybody home? Is anybody here?' but there was no response. So, after a while, I just left."

"Did you see anyone at all?" Billy asked.

"No. I wanted to get back home to our teenagers."

Billy gave me a look. "Diane is almost twenty," he said in a quiet voice.

"Yes, I know, Billy. Our oldest daughter is an adult now."

Chapter 10 . Neighbors witnessed the commotion.

Out of the corner of my eye, I caught sight of two people lingering on the sidewalk in front of our house. Neighbors, Roger and James, were returning from their two-mile, daily morning walk to Starbucks.

The two of them brought over a coffee cake as a welcoming gift when my wife and I moved in. They had been living in the house next door for eight or ten years. We did not have children yet.

The next-door neighbors kept to themselves at first. It took the exchange of many pleasantries and several summers of tending their garden and getting the mail from the box on their porch when they were out of town for us to become better acquainted.

Watching over each other's property became a reciprocal arrangement. We were glad to do it although, I have to say, their garden took a lot more work than anything we ever cultivated. Of course, we couldn't complain. We partook of the bounty when their fruits and vegetables were ready for the harvest.

We gradually became friends. During turbulent times in my life, the two of them were supportive of my wife and helped me with my troubles. They were sympathetic and nonjudgmental. I loved them for that. They provided a watchful, reassuring presence for raising children on Elm Avenue.

Roger and James got married as soon as the prohibition was declared unconstitutional in July of 2015. We attended their wedding. Our two daughters came with us.

At the very moment when we witnessed their vows, my African American wife whispered to me, "At one time, it was illegal for you and me to get married in many parts of this country."

"Hardly anyone gives us a second thought anymore," I mused.

"I'm not so sure," she said.

I believe the presence and comportment of Roger and James were significant reasons for the evolution of our neighborhood into a tolerant, even welcoming place for unusual families. If the people who lived on our street could learn to accept the two of them, they could make us feel at home too.

While our mixed-race family did not mesh very well with the mores of the times, the two men living next door had endured even greater small-minded bigotry than any of the slights inflicted on us or upon our beautiful children. Consequently, they could appreciate more than most the difficulties that might befall me on that Saturday morning with a police officer, who had intolerance issues, confronting me on our front porch.

Most days, at the end of their walk, our next-door neighbors went right into their house. However, on that Saturday morning, they did not pass me by. They were clearly concerned about my predicament.

Roger peered into the driver's side window to speak to the man behind the wheel of the patrol car in our driveway.

James approached the porch. He stopped halfway across the lawn from the sidewalk. He stood there with his muscular arms folded across his chest watching as if ready to rush to my defense. The burly, ruddy-faced man was an imposing presence in our front yard.

A small crowd was gathering on the sidewalk next to the patrol car across the street. Oh, great I thought. We might as well have all of Batavia watching me. One of them stood out from the rest. I recognized all of the others as from the neighborhood but his face was hidden within the shadow of a hooded sweatshirt.

I did not appreciate their attention at the time. However, it turned out later that the group included valuable witnesses for my defense.

"Look, O'Connor," Sgt. Ryan snarled. "Matthew Hennigan was found dead in the convenience store at his gas station this morning. Elliot Shaw discovered his body when he got there to open for business. Hennigan had been shot in the head."

"Whooh!" It felt like a kick to the stomach. I fumbled for one of our wooden-slat chairs on the porch and sat down.

"Oh, no. Not Mr. Hennigan," Roger cried out in a loud, trembling voice from the driveway.

Sgt. Ryan said, "Hennigan's body was on the floor behind the counter for the popcorn maker. What were you thinking when you left him there?"

Chapter 11 . This time was different.

Sgt. Ryan boosted his questioning to full accusatory mode. "You know what I think happened? You know what I know happened?" He growled at me. "You swiped a fifth of bourbon from inside the door at Nora's. We found the empty bottle."

The hefty policeman leaning over me was intimidating. His face was screwed up in an ugly red contortion.

"Matthew Hennigan saw you and threatened to expose you for the hypocritical sot and the thief that you are. You followed him into the service station and shot him. You turned off the lights and released the lock on the door and got the hell out of there."

"No, none of that is true," I replied in as firm a voice as I could muster from my seated position under his hulking frame.

Ryan pressed on. "What you didn't know is Elliot Shaw saw you do it or you would have shot him too. He was there out of sight watching you."

"You are spouting total nonsense. I already told you what happened." I managed to get out of the chair and stand up to the antagonizing voice.

"Theodore Christopher O'Connor, you are under arrest for the murder of Matthew Hennigan. Cuff him, Billy."

Sgt. Ryan stepped back and took an attack-ready stance. It occurred to me, from the steely glint in his eyes, that he hoped I would put up a fight. It would be evidence in support of his concocted story.

"You're wrong. The lights were still on and the door was unlocked just the way I found it when I left. You've got the wrong man." My voice was trembling. I could not help it.

Officer White stepped forward with handcuffs at the ready. He took hold of my arm and turned me around. Although Billy and I were both aware that he was no match for me, I did not try to resist. It would not have been helpful.

Officer White started to say, "You have the right to …" but he was interrupted.

Diane charged out of the house before the young officer could get the restraints attached to my wrists. The storm door made contact with Billy's shoulder. It was not more than an unintentional bump. It was hardly enough for him to notice.

Diane grabbed his arm and shouted, "Billy, you leave my father alone."

Sgt. Ryan jumped forward and shoved Diane into the door frame. He pushed her up against the rough siding face first. The impact drew blood. I could see the abrasions on her forehead, right cheek, and chin.

Blood spurted from a split lip and ran down her neck. She put a hand on the wall and looked back at me with an expression of fear and anger. The pleading in her eyes gave meaning to the words, "It made my blood boil!"

Her knees buckled and she twisted toward me. A bright red stain was spreading across the front of her light blue sweatshirt. Heavy drops splattered onto the wooden floor. Diane lost her balance and started to fall. Officer White dropped the handcuffs and tried to catch her. He was not quick enough.

Diane hit the deck with a thud. She screeched in pain. The sound cut through me to the soul. Billy dropped to his knees next to her and lifted her head in his hands.

"You fucking idiot," I shouted at Robert Ryan. The rage swelled up from my chest and burned into my face. My left hook caught him on the chin and my right cross to the jaw knocked him cold.

The two police officers were already out of the car in our driveway. They came running up the stairs and pushed me against the wall. I offered no resistance. In a moment, my wrists were in cuffs behind my back.

Officer Louis Thompson was a new man on the force. He was the driver of the second car. He had chauffeured the police chief, Jennifer Hepburn, to our house. He escorted me roughly down the steps and across the lawn toward their vehicle.

Chief Hepburn took charge immediately. "Mr. O'Connor, you are under arrest for murder and for assaulting a police officer. You have the right to remain silent. Anything you say ..."

I cut her off. "I did not assault him. I was defending my daughter. That son of a bitch assaulted my daughter. I did not assault him. It was self-defense. Arresting me is a travesty. I was defending my daughter from that idiot. You should arrest him." I am sure the entire neighborhood, probably all of Batavia, could hear every word of my full-blown tirade.

Chief Hepburn completed the Miranda warning but I was not listening. Diane was getting up off the floor with Billy's assistance. She stood sobbing onto his shoulder.

"Diane are you all right," I called to her from the lawn en route to the police cruiser. "Officer White, take Diane to the emergency room. Get her some medical attention."

Sgt. Robert Ryan was sitting up against the porch railing with his head in his hands and his back to me. He turned in my direction at the sound of my voice. He looked dazed as if he did not know where he was. It appeared the man could not focus well enough to see me.

Whether Ryan needed medical attention was of little concern to me at that moment. I didn't give a damn. He had brutally attacked my daughter. In all of my previous run-ins with the law, I had never before resorted to my ruffian skills against a police officer but this time was different.

Chapter 12 . Daughters are resolute defenders.

Our oldest child struggled to her feet with help from the young police officer. She wobbled a bit and grabbed the railing to steady herself. Diane regained her balance, pushed Billy White away, and started down the porch steps after me.

She was holding the policeman's white handkerchief under her chin. It was stained red with blood. "I'm all right, Dad. I don't need to go to the ER. Should I call Mom?"

"Yes, of course. Tell her I didn't do it."

"She knows that, Dad," Diane declared. She continued moving toward me and she was closing fast.

"Go back inside and call Elmer Wrightson," I ordered but she did not stop.

With a firm grip on each arm, the police chief and the patrolman were escorting me toward their car in the driveway. They were facing forward, away from Diane. She appeared to be charging right at them. Oh, no, I thought. Could the situation get any worse?

"Stop, Diane. Go back in the house," I repeated but she kept coming. I feared she was about to join her father in jail, arrested for assaulting a police officer.

A hand pushed my head down. Officer Thompson shoved me into the rear seat of the cruiser. I twisted back around to see that Diane was not trying to tackle one of them. Rather, she was rushing forward to intercept her little sister.

Eileen had reappeared from around the corner and up the street. She was running full speed back toward our house. Diane grabbed her inches before her clenched fist could make contact with the small of Thompson's back.

He would have felt it. It would have been painful. I had taught both of our girls how to throw an effective punch. The wild look in Eileen's eyes made clear the teenager's intent to come to her father's rescue.

Diane and Eileen tumbled backward in a heap onto the lawn. James was there to help them struggle to their feet. Roger was standing by.

"It's OK. It's OK," I lied to the four of them. "Thanks, James. My attorney will have this straightened out in no time."

They stood there for a moment looking at me in disbelief. Diane had her arm around Eileen whispering into her taller, little sister's ear.

They glanced over their shoulders at me as they stumbled toward the porch, up the steps, and into the house. Such amazing women for daughters! I could only sit and watch with tears in my eyes and with a feeling of inadequacy.

I was certain that Diane would put in a call to Attorney Wrightson right away. I was not as confident that he would rush to my aid.

Both of our children had become acquainted with Elmer Wrightson from the years he spent consoling and counseling our family. He had provided me with legal representation and had been a great help to all of us during the degenerate period of my life.

I knew at the time that my wife and childhood friend had become quite close but I was both too arrogant and too disinterested to take their relationship seriously.

It was only after I had finally straightened out that I fully understood how devoted they had become to each other. Elmer Wrightson and the self-sacrificing woman struggling to be a part of my life had started making plans for a future together.

It took years of effort and dogged adherence to the rules for me gradually to regain my wife's trust. I believe that her affection for me never wavered. However, the woman had gotten to the point where she was ready to give up and settle for a more stable life for herself and our children.

Elmer Wrightson never meant more to my wife than someone she could be comfortable with. For him, however, it was different. He had become completely committed to the idea of a relationship with her. He was deeply disappointed when she declined to start a new life with him.

My wife and I would reconcile but Wrightson and his wife never did. He tried but could not get her to forgive him. She refused to take him back. As they say, it was fortunate that she never wanted children.

Elmer's wife moved away and out of his life forever. He hated me for that but remained loyal to my family and even to me. It is hard to explain or even to understand. Friendships are complicated.

After years of frustration, I had made something of myself as a mechanic, a teacher, and a good father. However, on this particular Saturday morning in June, misfortune had struck again.

The neighborhood crowd including the individual in the hoodie watched Officer Thompson drive away with me in the back of the police car. He took me to the station and booked me on charges of murder and assaulting a police officer. Exactly why they needed to get my fingerprints again was annoying but I was in no position to complain.

It had been over seven years since the last time I was arrested but it was still a familiar ritual with one significant difference. On every previous occasion, my arrest was justified at least to some extent.

In the past, my transgressions were relatively minor. The incidents included disorderly conduct, public intoxication, defacing private property, and illegal possession of a controlled substance. This time, I stood accused of a very serious crime.

During my troubled years, Elmer Wrightson came to my aid each time I needed him. However, he had grown increasingly disgusted with me. I had failed too many times to live up to my repeated promises to straighten out.

He arranged for bail and negotiated plea bargains but he couldn't fix me. I disappointed him and my wife and my family over and over. I relapsed after two different rehab programs that Wrightson found for me.

It finally became too much for him. My attorney and life-long friend had given up. Consequently, I was afraid that he might decline to represent me when Diane called to tell him I had been arrested again.

Chapter 13 . My assignment was to be welcoming, his to be loyal.

Elmer Wrightson and I had known each other since grade school. Our friendship grew at Batavia High to the point where we looked out for each other. He was the oldest of four children in one of the few African American families in our town. There were two sisters in the middle and the youngest was another boy who was just a baby.

They moved to Batavia when his mother was transferred here to be the bank manager at the new branch office of TDBank. His father got a job teaching at Hoover Elementary School.

There were two kindergarten-through-eighth-grade schools in Batavia. The Wrightson children joined me at Wilson Elementary School even though they lived much closer to Hoover.

Elmer joined my class halfway through the fourth grade. He told me that they were not allowed to attend the same school where their father was a teacher. It was not until much later that I learned the superintendent never imposed such a rule on any of the white families.

The teacher asked me to be Elmer's "welcoming buddy." It caught me by surprise because I was always in trouble. She was strict, organized, and totally without favorites as far as any of us could tell. From her point of view, my new assignment must have made sense for the sake of discipline and academic progress for all of us in her classroom.

I knew everybody, spoke to everybody, and refused to join in any cliquish behavior. I wonder now if the teacher hoped the responsibility would force me to get more serious about my schoolwork.

Elmer was quiet, studious, and intelligent enough to appreciate the humor in my mischievous behavior without getting sucked in. We became friends. I believe it was a mutually beneficial relationship.

For me, our quiet camaraderie included chatting about academic topics that Elmer found interesting. Upon occasion, I could be caught up by his enthusiasm for learning in spite of myself.

For him, our friendship meant there was never any doubt that he would be accepted and included in my large circle of friends and associates.

Elmer always knew he would go to college. At different times, he was going to study mathematics or history or physics. The civics class we took in our junior year in high school got him talking about political science. It became an interest that stuck with him.

The counselors at Batavia High helped us with college applications. More accurately, they offered Elmer encouragement and cajoled me into filling out the forms. We got acceptance letters from the same university. Elmer pressured me to go with him but I was not interested.

After graduation, I got a job with my grandfather's construction business. It would not be steady work. Capricious weather in the winter months would disrupt the most carefully laid plans for the outdoor projects. Also, there were occasional lapses between jobs.

When I was not busy hammering nails or doing the plumbing or wiring on a house, I helped out at the Batavia Service Center where I enjoyed the automotive mechanics more than the construction work anyway.

Grandfather paid me better than the boss at the auto repair shop. So, I always went back whenever he summoned me.

While my attendance and performance on both jobs were pretty good, my main interest as a high-school graduate was to enjoy life. I liked the money for what it could provide. There seemed to be no barriers to frivolous spending on cars and a motorcycle, drinking, partying, trips into the city on days off, and whatever I fancied at any given moment.

The owner of the Batavia Service Center had a real name but everyone just called him Clutch. The man had a way with a manual transmission that was impressive. No matter how worn or abused, the gears would slide smoothly together again when he was done.

Some years ago, Clutch had teamed up with Robert Ryan to organize an AAU baseball club in Batavia. Ryan was a patrolman on the police force at that time. They persuaded Matthew Hennigan to become one of the principal sponsors.

The Amateur Athletic Union or just AAU was the umbrella organization that provided the rules, a list of certified officials for our games, and a competition schedule with other teams in the area.

The AAU team in Batavia was pleased to have me join the club. I had been a decent pitcher and good infielder in high school. Both my earned-run average and my slugging percentage were the best on the team at Batavia High. To be fair, of course, it must be said that extra-base hits do not necessarily equate to consistency at the plate. I struck out more than anyone else. Also, I wonder if my record for grounding into three double plays in a single high-school game still stands.

Chapter 14 . Superiors knew education was important.

One evening after work, I stopped at Allen's Diner where they have a great Italian sausage hot dog on the menu. Clutch was there in a booth by himself when I walked in. It was early in the spring the year after my graduation from Batavia High.

He motioned for me to join him. A moment later, Grandfather slid into the seat next to me. I was trapped on the inside across from Clutch. There was no escape.

"Is everything all right?" I asked. "Am I in trouble?"

It was clear I had been setup. They were there to gang up on me. I am pretty sure my mother or perhaps both of my parents had something to do with it.

Grandfather answered, "No, no. The quality of your work is not the question. I think Clutch and I both appreciate your contributions on the job."

Clutch said, "I am pretty much in agreement with your grandfather on that."

"Pretty much?" I asked.

"Well, there is something more you could do. It would be nice if you would assume some responsibility to look around and see if someone needs help after you finish your work on a car."

"What do you mean?"

"Help the other guys if they are struggling with a difficult job."

I knew right away what Clutch was referring to. Early that afternoon, Mark Steiger, one of the long-time employees at the service center, was not getting the timing right on the car in the bay next to where I was on another job. I kept thinking, if he would tighten down the carburetor before snapping the cap back on, it would stop slipping when he revved the engine but he wasn't seeing it.

Steiger was a good mechanic. I learned a lot from him. However, I was also aware that he was prone to the occasional wrong diagnosis. He could get stuck spinning his wheels on a problem. If he would just take a step back and think about it for a minute, he might see that he had been taking the wrong approach.

The timing issue was getting him frustrated for about a quarter of an hour. Clutch took notice. He came in from the counter in the lobby and looked over Mark's shoulder for a minute. Before long, the problem was fixed. From where I was standing with the paperwork for my completed job, it appeared that the solution was exactly what I expected. When Clutch walked back out to the lobby, he glanced my way and shrugged.

That evening in Allen's Diner, I said to Clutch, "I'm just the kid in the shop. The older guys don't want me telling them what to do."

"Are you worried about hurting someone's pride when you could be helping them out and saving time and money for the garage?" Clutch asked.

"Well, yeah. Mark Steiger must be fifty years old," I exclaimed. "He is a laid-back guy but he doesn't want me butting in."

"You're partly right and partly wrong. He is easy going which is why he would not take offense if you pitched in to help out on one of his jobs. In fact, he would appreciate it." Clutch corrected me.

"OK," I said but I was still not comfortable with the idea.

"You know what is more disturbing to poor old Mark? It is failing to get a job done right. Why not step in and point out what he is missing whenever you can?"

"All right, I'll try to be more helpful. I actually heard what was wrong from where I was working in the bay next to him in the garage today. I guess I should have said something to him."

"Yes, you should have. But, as your grandfather said, your performance on the job is not what we wanted to talk to you about."

"That's right. I like having you on board. I'm noticing that you are quick about finding the right way to finish a task in the construction business. It's the same as what Clutch was just saying about your work in the auto repair shop."

"Thank you."

"You're welcome. Remember the wiring on the house we are just finishing at the end of the cul-de-sac off Walnut Street?"

"Yeah, sure."

"When you got there last Thursday, you ignored the way the foreman had laid out the wiring for the lights and wall sockets in the bedrooms. By pulling two, or was it three, circuits in through the garage, you saved a couple of hundred feet of 12-guage. Not only that, your approach meant the job got done by the end of the day."

"It was three circuits and I spliced in the wiring for the hallway in addition to the bedrooms as well," I boasted. "I am glad you noticed."

"Of course, I noticed. We'd still be there if you had not fixed the plan," Grandfather replied.

"So, what do my bosses want with me? Why are we here?"

Clutch answered, "You are too smart and talented to not go to college. Even a future in construction or automotive repair would benefit from a college degree."

"Have you been talking to my Mother?"

Both of them smiled. Neither answered the question. Clutch had a bachelor's degree. Grandfather, the much older man, had a more informal education. He never went to college but no one ever questioned his intelligence. He loved to read and he learned on the job.

"What about the AAU baseball team?" I was slow to take them seriously.

Grandfather's retort was quick. "Getting an education is not to be taken lightly. The Amateur Athletic Union will have to get along without you."

"You just think about it, Ted. I've got to get some groceries on the way home." Clutch looked over at Grandfather. "Have we made our point?"

"Yeah, I hope so. There is not a lot to say about it. Someone as smart as you are, Ted, should have the benefit of a college education. It becomes more important in this world every year."

"Well said," Clutch agreed.

"I have to get going too," Grandfather said. "We really mean it, Ted. Your aimless lifestyle is not going to get you anywhere in life. As much as we enjoy having you work with us, we know that getting an education is in your best interests."

"I hear you," I sighed.

"See you at the house with your folks on Sunday."

"Listen to your grandfather." Clutch started to leave but stopped and said, "By the way, Ted, Mark Steiger is a bit older than 50. He's 61 and he is talking about retiring to their mobile home in Lakeland, Florida, within the next year or so."

The two men followed each other out the front entrance to Allen's Diner. It had taken just eight months for both well-meaning bosses to become disgusted with my lack of ambition. They needed to tell me that I could do better.

The following fall, I joined Elmer at the University. My lazy and fun-filled gap year was over. It had been a time of aimless nights and weekends interrupted by a little hard work remodeling houses and repairing cars. I had graduated from high school in June and, fifteen months later, I showed up late for freshman orientation in September.

Chapter 15 . College athletics were a distraction.

My undergraduate career commenced at the same university where Elmer Wrightson's outstanding scholastic performance was already well recognized. He would go on to graduate with highest honors and I would not in spite of his best efforts.

Elmer was certain he could help me develop the scholarship necessary for academic success but it was a huge challenge. He would encourage me to work harder and I tried to take him seriously. Unfortunately, I failed to muster the discipline necessary for the task.

I remember Elmer admonishing me, "You need to get started on the term paper for English Lit."

"OK. See you in the library this afternoon after class," I agreed but the good intentions were soon forgotten.

On another occasion, he queried, "Where are your books? Where is your backpack today?"

True to form, I had a smart-aleck reply. "Carrying books around is an unreasonable encumbrance for a man of my stature."

"You jerk." Elmer laughed but he did not really think it was funny. It was clear he was not happy with me.

It was not like I wanted to fail. Rather, I was stuck with a talent for procrastination to a fault. Last minute cramming for tests and overnight composition of term papers were more than enough for decent grades at Batavia High. Why shouldn't it be that way in college? I was determined to get by with minimal effort.

I told Elmer, "If you get 71 percent on an exam and 70 percent is passing, then you wasted time studying."

He got the joke but did not appreciate the attitude. No one but myself could be blamed for such foolishness.

The lack of ambition was entirely my own doing. Elmer was destined to be disappointed by my failings.

Ever since middle school, my grandparents and parents preached the importance of an education. They told me to make school a priority in my life. They were self-motivated themselves and thought I should be too. However, they declined to force me to study.

It was my mistake to misinterpret their mild reactions to poor academic reports. The lack of stern reprimands did not actually imply they were satisfied with good enough. Of course, they did not approve of my personal achievement gap but I refused to grasp the significance of their warnings.

Many friends appreciated my wit and good humor but the teachers were not impressed by the absence of any enthusiasm for doing the work. I was not purposefully disrespectful but my boastful attitude was frequently taken the wrong way. In spite of their disapproval, I was able to shrug off the teachers' reprimands.

Disciplinary issues were a different matter. My parents would get cross with me when they were called in for discussions regarding unruly behavior but Grandpa and Dad would also find my antics to be entertaining.

I did not learn how to be a good student. Consequently, the academic skills needed for college were lacking. Worse than that, the maturity to recognize the need for change was slow to come. Even so, my good friend did not give up on me.

Elmer persisted as long as there was hope. "You have the brains to do well," he told me. "You're smarter than I am." He continued to offer encouragement but he had to leave me behind.

Elmer Wrightson graduated Phi-Beta-Kappa in four years. I did not make it through the sophomore-level, university courses.

There were too many hours lost during the day in the campus coffee shop and at night in the local pub for me to qualify as a serious student. Day or night, I could be found in the athletics center playing pick-up basketball or outside playing baseball. I even learned to play squash and soccer. I found the money to pay for a few martial arts lessons which included boxing techniques for self-defense.

The intramural sports program gave me the chance to make many friends and to be a star athlete in a delusional sort of way. Many hours in the weight room three times a week paid off in terms of the build and strength needed to be competitive in most any sport. To be combative came naturally.

I made the practice squad as a walk-on tight end for the defense on the varsity football team. The assistant head coach actually talked to me about what it would take to secure a scholarship position.

He knew about my academic difficulties because he had already checked the records. The coaches obtained the right to look at my transcript when I signed up to be on the team.

He suggested, "Go play football in the program at the community college in Socorro and get your grades up."

He told me that a "B+ to A- average in a full load of courses for two semesters and a recommendation from the head coach at the junior college would go a long way toward winning an athletic scholarship. You have the talent to compete for a position on our team."

I believe the man was sincere and well-meaning but I was not really interested. My first love was baseball. It was not the brutality of football that put me off. I just didn't care for the game.

I told the assistant football coach at the University, "I will think about it. Thank you for the advice."

I tried to walk-on with the baseball team in the spring but did not make it. Baseball takes luck along with skill. I struck out and hit a feeble grounder to second base in the two at-bats that I got in front of the coaches who mattered.

At the end of the second afternoon, one of the assistants broke the bad news, "We have so much good talent vying for just seven positions that we have to cut you loose."

He tried to be nice about it. "I am sure you could be an asset here if only we could take a couple more players. Thank you for trying out."

That was the end of organized sports for me. I continued working out in the weight room with some of the football players and doing their skill-training drills in the off-season program. However, my enthusiasm was on the wane.

My interest in varsity athletics at the University was displaced by the socializing advantages of the intramural programs. It was a more enjoyable and less burdensome alternative.

For me, university life was all about the extra-curricular events and student parties. Scholarship was just not important to me. At least, not back then.

Chapter 16 . College life should be cherished.

My time at the University was not a failure in all respects. There was a very attractive black woman at the desk in the Math Lab when I went for help with an overdue Calculus assignment.

It was my sophomore year and this was my second try to make it through the freshman mathematics course but it was my first visit to the Math Lab. I am not sure what motivated me on that day. A classmate was heading over there and I went along.

The math tutor took a few minutes to look over my notes. She did not indulge in any dreaded criticism of a student who lets himself get behind. She treated me with respect and a dollop of good cheer.

"Do you not know how to differentiate x^3?" she asked.

"Yes, of course, I do," I stammered.

The beautiful coed smiled. Her dark sparkling eyes were looking right at me. She was stunning.

To be at a loss for a clever comment was a humbling experience. I was not prepared for the effect she had on me. I leaned forward to read her nametag.

"It's Lydia Kingston," she said. "I told them to put 'Mathematics Tutor Extraordinaire' under my name. I don't know why they didn't."

"It must have been an oversight." It was a witty retort that would have been great had my voice not cracked and squeaked.

"Of course." Lydia Kingston smiled. "Now, let's see if I am sufficiently extraordinary to help such a clever man as yourself."

"I would appreciate it."

"Look right here." She pointed to a spot where I had written two question marks. "Simplify the expression and the calculation will fall right out." She wrote corrections in a beautiful script.

"I knew that."

"Did ja?" The supreme beauty gave me a bright smile.

"Yes, I think so." I could feel the red creeping up my neck onto my face. No one can put me off my game. How could she?

"You just spotted a careless mistake," I stammered.

"Oh, of course." She was looking right at me again. We made eye contact. The moment taught me the meaning of "she took my breath away." Worse than that, I was struck dumb. What could Lydia Kingston be thinking of such a befuddled student as I?

I tried inner counseling to regain composure. I told myself no need to be nervous. She is just a college student with a campus job. My cognitive trickery wasn't working. Somehow, Ms. Kingston could make me feel sheepish and be nice to me simultaneously.

With a bemused expression, my amazing tutor pointed to another calculation. "What about here?"

I managed to mumble an explanation of what I thought it should be before admitting, "Well, I guess I don't really understand it."

"That's OK. Let's see if we can figure it out." Lydia Kingston pretended not to notice my embarrassment.

To be availing myself of the tutoring service for the very first time after a year of struggling with the concepts was not something to be proud of. The professor's teaching assistants for the calculus class had urged me to go. Other students recommended it. Now, there was a more compelling reason to kick myself for not getting around to it much sooner.

A tutor who could make a difference in my academic success was also a woman I really wanted to get to know. I came back the next day for more help and the day after that with no new questions.

"Why are you wasting my time?" Lydia Kingston demanded.

"I just wanted to see you again." I was forced to admit.

"Well, Ted, why not ask me out on a proper date or are you too cheap to buy me a soda?"

Ms. Kingston's cheeky response turned my knees to rubber. I could hardly believe my good fortune.

We saw a lot of each other after that. I was very much taken with the beautiful, brilliant Lydia Kingston. She became a soulmate to be treasured forever. I was in love.

We were inseparable. Meals together nearly every day. Socializing with mutual friends. She even took me to church on a couple of Sundays.

Six weeks after we met, however, there was a serious glitch that I nearly allowed to destroy our relationship. I put the best thing that ever happened to me in jeopardy.

Chapter 17 . The true friend is not jealous.

I spotted Lydia at a table with another man in the cafeteria where she and I always ate together. By the look of the wrappings in front of them, they were about finished but I wasn't late. Without letting me know, Lydia had come to lunch early with someone else.

I ducked to the other side of the food court where I could get a better view of him, a Caucasian as white as myself. I was at Lydia's back where she could not see me.

She reached across and patted his arm. A moment later, Lydia grasped his hand the way she would sometimes show affection for me. It was a clear indication of a close relationship.

Suddenly, they stood up from the table. Lydia turned my way and caught sight of me. She smiled and waved as if nothing was amiss.

I replied with a weak nod of the head. I stumbled several steps backward and turned sideways. She shrugged and walked the other way with her male friend toward the exit.

"Isn't that your girlfriend?" I was startled by the voice of a mutual acquaintance. I no longer remember her name only that I had enjoyed her company at a party the previous weekend.

"Yes, it was. I mean yes she is."

The girl laughed. "I'm just getting some lunch. Care to join me?"

I agreed. I picked up some items and found the table where she was sitting. I took the chair across from her but didn't feel like eating. Nothing tasted good.

Lydia had introduced me to the girl a few weeks earlier. They lived on the same floor in the red-brick dormitory next to the cafeteria.

She was cheerful. She tried hard. But, I could not get into the conversation.

After about 15 minutes, she was finished eating. She said, "You were a lot more chatty at the party on Saturday."

"I know. I'm sorry. I'm just preoccupied with other things at the moment."

"I can tell. Pining away does not become you."

"I guess I am not hiding it very well. I like her a lot but we have not made any commitments to each other. So, I guess I should not be angry if she has another boyfriend besides me."

"Look, Lydia is vivacious. She has a great youthful figure right now. She is articulate and friendly. What did you expect from her?"

The stereotypical condescending comments rankled me. "Lydia Kingston is a wonderful, decent woman," I snapped back.

"Sure, she is. Perhaps, you and I can get together another time." She got up to leave.

"I would like that," I said without knowing if I meant it.

I sat at the table mulling over my situation and the racist overtones in the conversation with Lydia's pseudo friend. I decided there was nothing to do but confront my damaged feelings.

I crossed over to the next building, went up the stairs, and knocked on the door to Lydia's room.

"You must be Ted O'Connor." The young man who had been at lunch with her answered the door. He was wearing pants but no shirt. His hair was wet as if he had just gotten out of the shower.

I refused his hand and turned to flee back toward the stairs only to find Lydia right in my face. She was carrying a suitcase from the same stairwell.

"I brought your stuff up from the car while you were showering," she said to him.

"Thanks," he said.

"I see you have met my cousin," she said to me.

"Um, not quite," the new guy said. He was standing barefoot in the hall outside Lydia's door.

"Well then, allow me. Timmy, this is my boyfriend Theodore O'Connor. Ted, this is my cousin Timothy Kingston. He is a senior in high school and he is staying with me for the tour of the University for prospective students who might want to attend our beloved institution."

Of course, I had to challenge Lydia's story. "Your cousin? The man you hold hands with at lunch and who showers in your dorm room is your cousin?"

The two of them stood there looking at me. Timothy was amused. Lydia did not seem to be. I avoided her eyes and looked down at the floor.

After an awkward moment, Timothy said, "Lydia, you know how my big sister says I am clueless about a lot of things? Well, I believe she would agree that I have this one right. Your boyfriend has not been made aware of the white folks in your family."

"I wouldn't have thought it would matter to him," Lydia said.

She turned to me. "If you must know. Our grandfathers are the twin brothers Aaron and Jacob Kingston, the proprietors of Kingston General Store in Savanah,

Georgia. Their father was an English American and their mother a Welsh immigrant."

"Oh, I did not know any of that."

"Why should you care?"

I rose to the challenge. "Whenever I see you with another man, I will always feel at least a twinge of jealousy no matter what."

"Is that so?"

"Yes, it is."

"I would have thought it would be more than a twinge." Lydia's irritation was gone.

"Nope, just a little." I got her back.

"While we're at it, let me tell you that Timmy has twin younger brothers Gabriel and Daniel Kingston. His sister Janet Bread is two years older. The reason for different surnames is a story for another time."

"Such things happen," I said.

"Oops, Ted, you have jumped to the wrong conclusion," Timothy said. "It was unusual in their day, but my parents kept their own last names when they got married. When my older sister Janet was born, they gave her my father's last name. When I was born, they decided, if girls got his name, boys would get her name. Sorry it is so confusing."

"Fortunately for you, my situation is simpler. As you already know, I am an only child," Lydia condescended.

"Thanks, Lydia, but I think I can handle the lineage. The story you would have me believe is your second cousins are Janet Bread and Timothy, Gabriel, and Daniel Kingston and all four have the same mother and father."

Lydia feigned a haughty response. "Good for you and you can believe it or not. It makes no difference to me."

Kingston Family Lineage

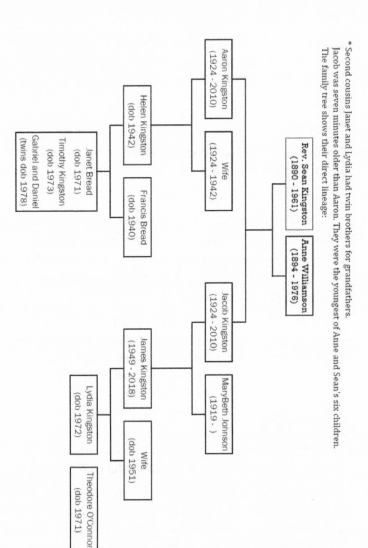

* Second cousins Janet and Lydia had twin brothers for grandfathers. Jacob was seven minutes older than Aaron. They were the youngest of Anne and Sean's six children. The family tree shows their direct lineage:

Aaron Kingston
(1924 - 2010)

Wife
(1924 - 1942)

Helen Kingston
(dob 1942)

Francis Bread
(dob 1940)

Janet Bread
(dob 1971)

Timothy Kingston
(dob 1973)

Gabriel and Daniel
(twins dob 1978)

Rev. Sean Kingston
(1890 - 1961)

Anne Williamson
(1894 - 1976)

Jacob Kingston
(1924 - 2010)

MaryBeth Johnson
(1919 -)

James Kingston
(1949 - 2018)

Wife
(dob 1951)

Lydia Kingston
(dob 1972)

Theodore O'Connor
(dob 1971)

Chapter 18 . Scholastic achievement is elusive.

With Ms. Kingston's assistance and insistence, I started scoring in the 80's and even higher on the mathematics exams. As our friendship grew, she decided to take an interest in my other classes as well.

For no particularly good reason, I had checked the box for science and engineering on the form when I first enrolled at the University. Perhaps, it was because Elmer Wrightson was studying political science and I had to be different.

The curriculum for my chosen field included a block of required liberal arts courses and a Chemistry class in addition to the Calculus sequence. Lydia could explain the concepts from the science lectures along with tutoring me in mathematics. However, writing reports for the experiments in the Chemistry laboratory was up to me. I insisted I could handle the English and Western Civilization classes on my own which was true but unrealistic for a person with very little self-motivation.

The best part about studying with Lydia was spending time with her. Actually, for me, it was the only part of my academic life that I valued.

During the day, when Lydia was in class, I was participating in intramural sports. When she was studying for her upper-division courses in the evening, I was usually in the campus pub with friends. When Lydia had free time, it was nice to have her help me with my studies but we also had fun together.

During one long weekend, we drove to Monticello in Charlottesville because she wanted to see it. In fact, I also found the historical implications to be interesting.

On another occasion, we drove to an afternoon Orioles game in Camden Yards, took an evening cruise on the

Inner Harbor, and enjoyed a four-day weekend in Baltimore.

It was a very nice break from school for Lydia and for me. The more time I spent with the beautiful Ms. Kinston, the more I appreciated her values, her intellect, her good nature, everything about her.

Lydia Kingston was a fun-loving, serious student. Elmer Wrightson was just serious. He had far more of a studies-come-first attitude than I could muster.

She got her degree and accepted a graduate assistantship at Columbia University. Elmer graduated and went to law school at Boston College.

"When I am ready, Lydia, I will make you proud."

"You already do." She was never critical but Lydia knew I was not a serious student. She just liked me for who I was.

My brilliant college sweetheart saw enough in me to believe that I would grow up to be a better man. She was right back then. But, the full measure of respectability was a long time coming. In fact, it took more than a decade for me to enter recovery from a lack of ambition and from alcoholism and drugs.

Chapter 19 . To return home was both a relief and a letdown.

At the end of my first year when I was packing up to go back to Batavia for the summer, the dean of students at the University sent me an e-mail message. It was a summons to meet him in his office.

"Mr. O'Connor, you do not appear to be ready for college." He said, "Go home. Get a job. We will welcome you back here in a year or two."

When I insisted that I would do better in my sophomore year, he relented. He reluctantly agreed to probation with the warning that I had to work harder.

The dean encouraged me to believe that I had the potential. He said, "You can be successful but you must incorporate much more academic discipline into your life every day."

I left his office with good intentions but my thinking was misguided. I still believed a little more time with the books when convenient should be enough. Success in the classroom need not interfere with enjoying the carefree nature of life on a university campus.

My second year was better but not by a lot. The improvement was notable largely due to Ms. Lydia Kingston's assistance. However, after nearly two years of half-hearted efforts my academic record was still considered too inadequate for me to continue. I had not accumulated enough credit to be counted as a second-semester sophomore.

The same man called me back to his office. "If you had the level of interest in English and history that you have shown in mathematics, you could be a real student. Your work in Chemistry shows improvement but it is spotty. According to Dr. Brody, some of your test scores were very good but half your lab reports were never turned in."

Walter Brody was my Chemistry professor. His lectures were well prepared and easy to follow. The laboratory assistants were quite good too but I was not.

Lydia was helping me with the Chemistry homework as well as with my Calculus assignments. Due to her efforts, I was doing well in math and passing the science course.

In the latter case, Dr. Brody could teach me the Chemistry theory with an assist from Lydia but I just couldn't be bothered with the time-consuming work in the Chemistry laboratory.

The dean sent me home. I did not tell him about Lydia and Elmer, my tutor and my enforcer. They continued at the University for one more year without me before embarking on their respective graduate programs.

I knocked around back in Batavia without too much ambition, just waiting for life to happen. Living in the basement apartment of my parents' house was not a particularly good omen.

The two friends who had my best interests at heart were sorry that I could not make a go of it with the course work. They were also resigned to my lack of enthusiasm for academic success.

After completing her undergraduate work, Lydia went home to Savanah for the summer before entering the business program at Columbia University in August of 1994. I drove to Manhattan to see her almost every weekend that fall and winter.

"You don't have to be a college graduate to be somebody," she told me. We made plans to get married after she got her MBA.

Part II

Failings and Tribulation

Tell us what the world has been to you in the dark places and in the light.

– Toni Morrison

Chapter 20 . My fate was poor judgement.

Grandfather was easing into retirement that spring when I was chucked out of the University. He was closing down his construction business but Clutch took me back at the Batavia Service Center.

It was full-time work and the pay was better than before. I found automotive repair to be gratifying because I was good at it. Unfortunately, my personal weakness could drag me down. The drinking problem was getting worse.

The frequent hangovers had a negative effect on my punctuality. I got laid off and got called back. I failed to show up for work and got fired. I apologized and Clutch rehired me again.

It wasn't that he was soft hearted although the man was decent and kind to everybody. The reason Clutch kept me on the job was I could fix the cars and get it right. Also, I was nearly always sober during the day.

The first time I was arrested for drunken and disorderly conduct, the judge delivered a stern lecture and let me out the next morning. Lydia did not know about that event.

The next time, there was no hiding a thirty-day incarceration for fighting and smashing furniture in Harry's Pub. I had registered my vehement displeasure with the bartender's ruling that there would be no exception for me when I asked for yet another long after the last call. The proprietor called the police.

Lydia skipped classes at Columbia and drove straight through from Manhattan to Batavia to find me beaten-up and behind bars. Her tears in the visiting room really shook me up but it was not enough to have a lasting effect.

She was also furious that the arresting officer had used a bit more force than necessary. My wrists were already handcuffed behind my back when Officer Ryan felt obliged to retaliate for my lawless behavior and effort to resist. He let loose with a punch to the gut and a couple of smacks across the side of my head. The tell-tale black eye was reportedly just an accident.

Ms. Kingston considered quitting school and moving to Batavia to take care of me but, of course, the suggestion made no sense. Maturity and respectability were qualities I had to learn for myself. She returned to New York and pressed on with her course work.

When she came back to see me on the last day of my stay behind bars, Lydia said, "Knowing you were in jail made it really difficult to concentrate in the classroom."

My promises convinced her that I had learned a lesson and there would be no more serious, over-the-top drinking. She was sure I would stay out of trouble because she believed in me.

Ms. Kingston returned to New York the next day confident or maybe just hoping that there would be no more ridiculously bad behavior. I was also sure that I could keep my life under control. Unfortunately, it was not long before I betrayed both of us.

The problem with my well-intentioned promises was they were based on a delusional conviction. I believed I could handle one or two drinks and quit for the evening. I thought I could control my thirst for another and another but I was wrong. The need was more powerful than my resolve.

Chapter 21 . The saloon was not helpful.

After completing the MBA program at Columbia University, Lydia moved to Batavia to be close to me. She found a furnished efficiency apartment on Central Boulevard and spent the summer studying for the Uniform Certified Public Accountant Examination, the CPA exam. I gave her my full attention and support.

She told me, "It is really a big help when you cook for me. Take-out is great too. I have just one request. Please don't take this as a criticism but Taco Bell once a week might be often enough."

"What?" I pretended to be offended.

"Seriously, Ted, thank you. Uninterrupted study time is very valuable."

Her appreciation was all the motivation I needed to come up with more ways to help. Without her knowledge, I picked up a sheaf of her hand-written notes and made about forty flash cards. I selected items that seemed to be important from lines she had highlighted on the pages.

The idea seemed a bit silly after I had done it. So, without saying anything, I hid my newly minted flash cards on top of the refrigerator in her kitchen and put Lydia's study pages back on the table.

"Hey, I was looking for those notes. What were you doing with them?" Lydia caught me before I could pull my hand away.

I stammered, "Oh, nothing. I was just looking at them."

Lydia grimaced. "Don't fool around with my notes." She turned back to the text in front of her without any interest in hearing excuses. She muttered mostly to herself, "I have everything organized in my own way. So, stay out of ... Oh, whatever."

"Do you mean I better stay out of your way?" I asked.

My feelings were hurt although the slight should not have been taken personally. I knew the irritation with me was just a reflection of frustration and exhaustion.

Lydia did not answer. My question did not penetrate her concentration shield.

"See you later," I said.

"OK, good."

I decided that several drinks in the saloon would restore a reasonable level of good humor. It didn't work. I could not enjoy the next few hours at Harry's Pub. I spent the time worrying about Lydia. She seemed so tired and discouraged.

I was a bit plastered by the time I got back to her apartment. She jumped when I came in.

"Are you OK?" I slurred.

"I must have dozed off for a minute."

"Go to bed. You'll do better with some sleep," is what I tried to say.

"Are you drunk? Where are you going?" Her questions were really accusations.

"I um go-en home ta-a bed."

"You can't drive back to your folks' house in your condition."

"Maybe I'll ju-us walk. G-bye," I staggered toward her and leaned in for a kiss.

"Ooh, your breath! Stay away from me. You can sleep it off here on the couch."

My grasp missed the chair back where she sat and I teetered toward the table. Lydia stood, grabbed my arm hard, and guided me toward the couch.

"Owe, you're hurting me," I whined.

"Good. Lie down. You can sleep it off here." She repeated. Lydia was not very happy with me.

"Thanks," I remember saying when she pulled off my shoes. I have no recollection of the blanket that I found over my shoulders when I came to in the morning.

Lydia was back at her kitchen table with a mug of coffee in front of her and a textbook in her hands.

She looked up when I groaned and tried to sit up. "You certainly made a fool of yourself last night," she admonished.

"Sorry," I gasped and coughed.

"Do you want some coffee? I've already had breakfast but I could make more toast and scramble some eggs."

"Coffee would be great."

"Look, I am sorry I was short with you last night. You weren't hurting my notes. I was just tired and feeling discouraged. I feel like I drove you to drink." Lydia was trying to blame herself for my weakness.

"Lydia, it is never your fault if I drink too much," I said. "Besides, no offense taken. I can see how hard you are working and I should never mess with your notes."

"You weren't mad at me?"

"Nothing you do can ever make me mad at you. I love you too much."

Lydia laughed. "We'll see about that," she said. "You did not answer about the eggs and toast."

"Food does not sound very good to me right now."

"I imagine not." Lydia handed me a mug of black coffee and leaned over to give me a very brief buzz on the lips. "Whew, you stink worse this morning than you did last night."

"Sorry," I apologized again. "I better get to work. What time is it?"

"You're already pretty late. I hope Clutch doesn't fire you."

"That won't happen. I'm too important." I took pride in my boastful attitude.

Lydia smiled but did not say anything.

I went back to the basement apartment at my folks' house to shower and change clothes before heading over to explain myself to Clutch at the Batavia Service Center.

Chapter 22 . Preparation for an exam demands dedication.

When I got back to her place that afternoon, Lydia was hard at work at the table as if she had not moved all day.

"How are you doing?" I asked.

"Oh, I don't know. There is so much material to cover and no end in sight." Lydia burst into tears. "I am not making any progress," she wailed.

"Don't say that. You're doing great. No one can write an exam that the brilliant Lydia Kingston can't pass with flying colors."

"Thanks." She grabbed Kleenex from the half empty box on the table and blew her nose. She took another and dabbed at her eyes. "I am just feeling really discouraged. There is so much material to cover. Did I say that already?" Lydia's eyes glistened when she looked up at me.

"Maybe you need a break. Let's go out for something to eat."

"No, I've been nibbling all day. All sorts of junk food. I am going to be so fat by the time I am ready that I will have to waddle into the room for the exam." She made a face and puffed out her cheeks.

My smile and encouraging words did little to cheer her up. She looked down at the books on the table and sighed. A few tears splashed onto the page. The sight hit me to the quick.

"Hey, I know what will help." I retrieved my home-made flash cards from where I had stashed them on top of the refrigerator.

I started asking the questions but Lydia couldn't answer. She was giggling too much at my bumbling attempt to pitch in with hand-made study materials.

"Hey, those aren't bad questions," she exclaimed after I had read a few of my personal favorites. The smile through her tears was more like the Lydia I knew and loved.

My idea turned out to be the right medicine for Lydia Kingston. My girlfriend and I worked with flash cards for half an hour in the morning and again in the evening every day until the exam.

Lydia had already written some flash cards to test herself even before she saw my creations. With me to do the quizzing, she made up many more cards. She gave me guidelines and rules for creating even more questions and answers directly from the references stacked up on her kitchen table.

When the day finally came, my prediction was spot on.

"Maybe not with flying colors," she said. "But, it was not that bad."

Lydia's efforts to prepare for the CPA exam were impressive. To make her life a little easier, I even did some of her laundry. I was in love with Lydia Kingston and she seemed to appreciate me.

Her respect actually scared me a little. "Does it bother you that I am not much of a student?"

"Are you feeling insecure?" Lydia laughed at me.

"Perhaps a little. You are so smart and such a good student, I'm afraid you will become bored with me."

She immediately got serious. "Are you breaking up with me because I'm smart?" Her voice trembled.

"No! I never said that. My commitment to you is forever. I'm worried that you will tire of me. I just hope you know what you are getting into."

"You may not be a man of letters but you are not dumb. You are sweet and kind and funny and intelligent. You are intellectually curious about all sorts of things. You are just the kind of man I have always dreamed about."

"Wow, I hardly know what to say. It was love at first sight for me."

"Of course it was." The feisty woman regained her attitude. "How could it not be? I love you too."

"Until death do us part?"

"Don't press your luck."

§ December 1996 §

We got married in December of 1996 and rented an apartment for a year while looking for something to buy. After weeks of deliberations and drawing up plans for improvements, we decided the house on Elm Avenue had enough potential to be right for us.

We moved into our home on Elm Avenue in January of 1998, one month after our first anniversary. Lydia and I started work on the barn-like garage as soon as the ground had thawed sufficiently for digging the foundation.

Chapter 23 . The firm came to Batavia.

When he got his law degree in the spring of 1997, Elmer was offered a position as an associate with a large firm in Philadelphia. It was the same company where he had served as a highly paid intern between his second and third years at Boston College Law School. The firm would give him an office in City Center and put him on full salary while he prepared for the bar exam.

He turned them down. He chose instead to return to Batavia to be close to his ailing parents and to be a positive influence for his little brother. The youngest in the family was in need of mentoring to get through the last two years of high school.

Elmer studied on his own and, of course, passed the exam on the first try. He got married in October to his girlfriend from high school. She had remained in Batavia after graduation and they reconnected when he moved back. I was honored to return the favor as his best man.

It was a marvelous weekend. As newlyweds recently relieved of the pressures required for organizing the same gala for ourselves, Lydia and I could relax and enjoy the festivities.

It was the first time my wife felt free to take a break from her new job. She had been at her company's headquarters in New York City for nearly two weeks out of every month since the beginning of the year.

The timing was just right. Lydia was at home with limited travel requirements for the remainder of the year. She borrowed vacation time from future accruals and we took a week-long second honeymoon. It turned out that we were a little late for the leaves in Vermont but the colors were still beautiful.

Back in Batavia, life settled into a happy camaraderie for Lydia and me. She went to work each day in the small office space that Cardinal Energy Services leased for her in a building on the corner of Virginia Street and Central Boulevard. I returned to my job as an auto mechanic at the Batavia Service Center.

I took a couple of days off to help Elmer and his wife get settled in an apartment. Their place was also on Virginia Street but it was a mile away on the edge of town. The four of us did a few things together. We met for dinner at a nice restaurant in the city. We saw a play and went out for a drink.

Lydia and I kept a watchful eye on our wonderful college friend as the newlyweds became accustomed to their life together. We offered good counsel as only a naïve, one-year married couple can.

Ours was not a perfect couple-to-couple friendship. It's hard to say exactly what was wrong. The three of us had always been entirely at ease together. However, I think, Lydia did not believe his new wife was quite right for our beloved Elmer, maybe not good enough for him. I knew he had always been smitten with her and he still was. It was her devotion to him that seemed questionable.

"I wonder how long a one-sided commitment can endure," Lydia said just to me.

Attorney Elmer Wrightson set up a much-appreciated private practice in our small town. Before long, he had hired a couple of associates.

The law firm needed office space not commonly found in Batavia. Elmer had to lease one unit, then a second and a third along the hallway on the second story over a contiguous string of store fronts on Central Boulevard.

He did not need me to tell him that the location was not entirely appropriate for a prestigious law firm but I told him anyway. He showed a bit of irritation with my repetitious comments about the unprofessional appearance of the offices occupied by Wrightson and Associates, PLLC.

I said, "I don't care if my criticism makes you mad. After all, what are friends for?"

The firm finally moved to an office building a few blocks away from the original store-front location. It was a big improvement. However, this time it was Elmer who was not too happy with the arrangement. Three years after the move, he came to me for my opinion as a friend and long-time resident of Batavia.

He asked me, "What do you think of the old bank building on Central Boulevard?"

The question came totally out of the blue. It caught me off guard.

"It's terrible. It is really shabby. It's a dump." My dismissive reaction showed little sensitivity for the sincerity of his question. Denigrating the idea did not go over very well.

Elmer got defensive. He said, "It may be run down but it is also cheap. It's available for not much more than back taxes."

"The place has changed hands so many times I've lost count." It was a struggle to be nice about the idea.

"Go check it out for me. Use your experience in construction to give the place a serious evaluation. Karen Sicarda has the listing. She is waiting to hear from you." Elmer handed me her card.

"Sicarda Realty? I've never heard of them."

"It's a small outfit. Not everyone wanted the listing."

"I can believe it."

"I would like your help, Ted. We are not finding satisfactory alternatives. One of our associates asked me today if I would consider moving out of town or even into the city."

I thought about saying that I already knew what my evaluation of the abandoned building would be. However, Elmer was so serious that I thought better of it.

My quick review of the property that afternoon did little to change my mind. Even the chain-link fence meant to prevent trespassing was in bad shape. There were places where it would be easy to breach but I didn't try.

The environs were too uninviting and maybe not safe. I could see boarded-up doors and there were pieces of plywood on the inside of the first-floor windows. Almost all were cracked or shattered.

When I called Elmer to tell him I didn't like it, he was quiet. "Elmer, are you there?"

"Yes, Ted, I'm here."

"Look, Elmer, it would cost three million dollars to fix the place."

"The realtor thinks maybe half of that."

"The property does not even have adequate parking."

"That's not true, Ted."

"Elmer, I was just there. You might be able to squeeze in a dozen spaces out front. Crowding in more than that would not give it the professional look you would want."

"It has underground parking."

"I didn't see an entrance."

"That's because it's all boarded up and you have not been inside."

"Oh," I said.

How did he know I had not been inside? He had talked to the realtor, of course.

"I'll call Ms. Sicarda this afternoon," I said.

"I would appreciate it." Elmer hung up.

The inside was dusty but not as filthy as I feared. The first floor had an open concept with just an enclave for the elevator shafts in the center.

Of the four elevators, only one had been in use for the previous tenant. The other three were covered with a decorative siding as if visitors would not recognize the shortcoming in the building.

Ms. Sicarda had gotten the power turned on but neither of us felt bold enough to try the one working elevator. We chose to take the stairs. The stairwell was not bad either. It had not collected the piles of trash that I expected.

We climbed to the second floor where there were offices and conference rooms on the outside of parallel hallways. Utility closets, storage rooms, and the lavatories were in the center between the two corridors. With a good bit of imagination, it was possible to envision it as well-appointed, professional office space.

It appeared that the previous tenant had kept the men's room in good working order. However, Karen and I decided it would be unwise to test the plumbing by flushing the urinals or commodes. I declined to join her when Karen took a peek in the women's room but she said it seemed to be in similarly decent condition.

"The upper floors are all pretty much the same. I suggest we go down to check out the garage space," Karen Sicarda said.

I agreed and we descended to the first floor. She pulled a flashlight from her shoulder bag and we continued down many stairs to a landing with a steel door marked

Garage Level I. I pushed it open to see that it was as large as the total footprint for the building.

"Level I? Is there another level?" I asked.

"As you can see there is another flight of stairs. Shall we?" Ms. Sicarda started down ahead of me or I would have declined.

We descended not nearly as many stairs to a landing with a steel door marked Garage Level II. I looked inside to see that it was the same space as on the first level.

"Karen, why are there even more stairs going down?"

"There is one more level of parking that I think you should see."

The steel door to the garage on the third below-ground landing was marked Executive Parking.

"There are half as many spaces on this level. The executive parking comes with its own entrance." Karen pointed toward the rear of the garage where I could see circular ramps in the corners marked Exit and Entrance.

We hiked back up to the ground level and strolled about for a while. Karen let her imagination create ideas for what the place could be like. We discussed how the area might be used as public space for seating, a restaurant, a café, and other things.

It occurred to me to check the adjacent pair of lavatories located on one side of the ground floor. The men's room was large with a good number of stalls. However, it was there where we found conditions to be in as bad shape as I had feared. Dirty and smelly.

"Is the women's room this bad?" I asked Karen.

"Worse," she said.

"It might be hard to find a plumbing company to take this on."

"For the right money, you can," she said.

"Maybe for a million dollars."

"Could be," Karen rolled her eyes at me. "Have you seen enough?" she asked.

"I think so."

"Good Elmer is waiting for us."

On the way over in her car, Karen explained the realtor's guidelines for the number of parking spaces needed for a professional building. The calculation depended on the type of occupant. The numbers varied for dentists, clinics for medical doctors, lawyers, and others. She also recited numbers for retail and restaurant businesses. The requirements had to accommodate the occupants and the expected flow of their patrons. From my rough count, the available spaces below the old bank building would be more than enough to cover Karen's estimates.

When we got to his office, I said, "I was wrong about the parking, Elmer. There is plenty. However, I was not wrong about saying it will take a lot of work."

"Understood."

"Karen does not think that it will cost as much as I fear it might. Of course, even educated guessing is not what counts. The proof will be in the estimates from the contractors."

"Of course."

"Karen said you have a couple of architectural firms in mind for drawing up plans. Once you settle on a set of options, you might want to ask a bevy of contractors to submit bids on the remodeling, the wiring, and the plumbing requirements that the designs call for."

"All of that sounds right to me," Elmer said

"There is something else that puzzles me. I know you need more space but the building is really large. It's seven stories tall."

"Part of the plan for financing the restoration includes tenants. Ms. Sicarda has already staked out a few rooms on the second floor."

"Ah, well," she stammered. "That's a little misleading, Elmer."

"Right, right, right," Elmer hastened to qualify his remark. "Karen does not prefer to be a tenant. She is pressing for part ownership."

"Good luck with that," I laughed. "Do you really want to be in business with this guy?" I joked.

Elmer ignored my light-hearted affront.

"So, Ted, is the place salvageable?" he asked.

"If you can accept that it will take a lot of work and months of delays before occupancy, make an offer with an engineering contingency."

"Sounds right," Karen said.

Elmer said, "Explain."

"The building seems sound to me but obviously I can make no guarantees regarding structural integrity based on a walk through. An engineering company has the equipment to test the load-bearing walls and pillars with sonar imaging and other devices to tell you if there are any serious deficiencies," I explained.

"OK," he agreed.

"You will probably want two engineering contingencies. One inspection would be for structural integrity. The second inspection should be done by a company that has the expertise to evaluate the elevator shafts."

"Do you have names?" Elmer asked.

I turned to Realtor Sicarda. "Karen, the state realtors' association should have a database of reliable engineering companies."

"That's true."

"It probably goes without saying to the two of you that the contingencies are not limited to the question of structural integrity but they have to spell out a dollar amount that would invalidate the contract."

"What do you mean?" Elmer asked.

"The offer should specify a dollar threshold for fixable problems. Your commitment to the sale will be enforceable if the estimate from a mutually acceptable contractor is within the specified amount."

"Yes, of course," Wrightson clearly did not need my tutorial on contractual contingencies.

He made a decision. "All right, let's do it. Get the paperwork going, Karen, and we will see what happens."

"Just out of curiosity, who will be making the offer?" I asked.

"Not Wrightson and Associates," Elmer answered. "I have formed and registered a real-estate investment company of which I am the principal owner. Depending on their level of interest, the partners in my law firm and you, Karen, will be offered a stake in the property."

Approximately eighteen months later, Wrightson and Associates, PLLC, moved into the top two floors of the newly renovated building on Central Boulevard.

"The Elise Monroe Office Building" was prominently displayed over the main entrance. Elmer had named the edifice after his maternal grandmother who had been an inspiration throughout his life.

Chapter 24 . Friends and family appreciate intelligent conversation.

When Elmer Wrightson first arrived back in Batavia with his law degree, our continuing friendship provided a degree of stability in my life. While I could be completely without any ambition in the eyes of my coworkers and with friends on the baseball field and in the saloons, he did not see me that way.

He was not willing to accept that I might be less than a man deserving of respect. He was civic minded and interested in world events so why shouldn't I be too? It was an attitude that could not be ignored.

My home life was more easy going. Lydia was focused and disciplined about her work and about our household and family obligations. She commanded and deserved the respect of her colleagues but my kind and generous wife put no pressure on me. I took it for granted that she did not need me to be anything better than I was.

Lydia and I saw a lot of my parents on the weekends. On just about any day of the week, when Lydia was out of town or had to be at work early, I found it convenient to drop by their house for breakfast. The coffee was great and the service was good too. After the children were born, they came with me to see Grandma and Grandpa on their way to childcare or to school.

My inclination to impose on my parents was not as bad as it might sound. Mornings at their house were for their benefit too. The folks enjoyed seeing me and their grandchildren. A few minutes at the breakfast table early in the morning with Mom and Dad before they and I hurried off to work was a good thing.

To their surprise and amusement, I started reading my parents' copy of the New York Times before breakfast in the mornings. When they caught me, Mother chided, "I didn't know you knew how to read."

Dad followed Mom's satirical words with a judgmental comment of his own. "If you studied like that in college, you might have been more successful," he said.

Reading the paper had another unplanned benefit. Elmer was as pleased as my parents. It meant I could hold my own with my good friend whenever I caught him for a free buffet lunch in the firm's conference room.

Of course, Lydia enjoyed talking to me about articles in the New York Times and to hear my interpretation of Elmer Wrightson's thoughts on the topics. It came naturally for the educated woman to appreciate an intelligent conversation with her life partner.

My interest in politics and public affairs was not new to me. In fact, my outgoing, somewhat aggressive personality made me an effective member of the debate team in high school. However, when the discipline imposed by the teachers went away with graduation, the motivation disappeared too. My parents' New York Times allowed me to rediscover what it was like to enjoy the respect that comes with being in the know.

During the first few years back in Batavia, life was both good and sometimes not so good. The good came in many forms including the intelligent, pleasant conversations with friends and family. The not so good was a life with no ambition and nowhere to go. I lifted weights, played pick-up basketball games, and competed as a member of the AAU baseball team.

I enjoyed the pushing and shoving required to settle some of the disputes on the court or in the field. The ruckus and the furor never got too serious. A good donnybrook gave us something to crow about in the sports bar after it was over.

Chapter 25 . Family life clamors for responsible parenthood.

It took Lydia and me a couple of years to decide we were ready for children. We knew we wanted to have a family but I had to demonstrate a greater level of maturity before Lydia was comfortable with the plan.

"Parenting is life changing," she told me.

"I know."

"I believe you know it. I am just reminding you that there will be times when our children's needs must come before your best friends."

Lydia's reference to your best friends struck me as a bit snide but I didn't say anything. The implication regarding my personal weaknesses for the good life was undeniable.

"Yes, of course." I agreed but the child-rearing commitment probably did not mean quite the same to me as it did to her.

Occasional bouts with the bottle created some friction at home and a few problems for me on the job. The lapses gave Lydia pause. However, after a time, my efforts were sufficient to satisfy my wife as well as myself that we would be good parents.

§ August 1999 §

Diane was born in August of 1999. We were delighted with such a wonderful addition to the family.

Our plans had always called for more than one but we decided to wait a while. Lydia was not ready for our second child until she was finally getting some relief from the demanding responsibilities at work.

§ October 2003 §

Eileen was born in October of 2003. Diane was already four years old.

For each child, Lydia put O'Connor in the space for the surname on their birth certificates. She said, "They are daughters for you to be proud of."

"How about you?" I asked. "You never changed your name."

"You can be proud of me too if you wish. However, I am your wife not your daughter," she replied.

Respect for Lydia, our life together, and parenthood helped me adhere to a degree of responsible behavior. Her influence and the needs of the children provided just enough motivation for me to strive to be the husband and father that Lydia, Diane, and Eileen deserved. For the next few years, my serious self did pay attention to the children and to my job.

I worked hard at the Batavia Service Center. Clutch noticed the improvement and delegated more responsibilities to me. On my better days, he would give me supervisory tasks for half a dozen full- and part-time mechanics. I discovered a sense of satisfaction in teaching new automotive technology to the teenagers.

Educating the eager-to-know youths at work was a good thing. Caring for and reading to our little children at home was even better. Both experiences got me thinking about my own ambitions.

The idea that I would consider education as a vocation would probably come as a shock to the faculty at Batavia High who had to suffer through my shenanigans as an erstwhile student but the interest was authentic.

Although I will never admit it to anyone who might scoff at the idea, the inkling had been there for a long time. Only I knew that it could be traced to the fourth-grade teacher who was disdainful of my tomfoolery while trusting me to look out for a new student in the classroom.

To begin work on teaching credentials, I signed up for courses at the community college in Socorro but I wound up dropping most of them. The instructors were fine and the classes were all right. They just took more work than I found the time for.

I did earn credit for a couple of history courses and for a class on elementary childhood psychology but my way forward was impossibly slow. The commitment to bettering myself was weighed down by the demands of my social life and an increasing need for the bottle.

In the meantime, my wife became a well-respected business manager for Cardinal Energy Services, Inc. Although their headquarters were located in New York City, Lydia insisted on keeping her office in Batavia. The arrangement was satisfactory because much of her work was on the road anyway.

Chapter 26 . Family life is phenomenal.

Lydia Kingston was successful in her professional life because she took her responsibilities at work very seriously. She was on the job even when fair weather and sunny skies might tempt others to take off early. As far as Lydia was concerned, there was no such thing as a snow day.

While her career was important, dedication to me and her family was my superwoman's first priority. My wife made time for the children. She listened to them and took their concerns seriously. She and I enjoyed each other's company at home and out for dinner, sometimes with and other times without our offspring.

Scheduling vacations was important and Lydia had a knack for good ideas. We were always able to get away for a week around the Fourth of July and for another ten days or so later in the summer.

A cabin on the shores of Lake Winnipesaukee was the family's favorite vacation destination for swimming, sailing, and relaxing on the deck with a book. Picnics on the pontoon boat were particularly nice.

We took the children on trips overseas, once to Copenhagen, another time to Barcelona, and twice to London. Lydia asked me what I thought about a vacation in France. We discussed plans for a trip to Paris at some undetermined time in the future.

For much of each summer, the children enjoyed their free time away from school just running around with their friends. Naturally, Lydia believed some structure was good too.

It was she who found sailing and basketball camps and other activities for the two of them. I held up my end by getting them wherever they were supposed to be when Lydia was out of town and when she was at home as well. In general, however, our daughters continued to demand very little supervision from me.

Diane loved to read and to talk on the phone. As a teenager, she began to earn a little spending money babysitting in the neighborhood. The parents who hired her were most appreciative when Diane took their children on outings to the library on Saturdays or on any morning during the summer.

Before starting the first grade, Eileen had play dates with children from her preschool program. Later on, she was always thinking of activities that would entertain herself and her friends. The little girl enjoyed a delightful excitement for living.

While they kept busy, I was happy to sit back and watch the two of them. My responsibilities were to be the neighborhood dad who was agreeable with everything nice, respectful children wanted to do. It was nice to sit back and watch and pour myself another beer.

Along with the professional advancements, there came additional demands on Lydia's time at Cardinal Energy Services. Both children were in school and my wife was intent on her duties at work. While the three of them were occupied with other things, I was free to do as I pleased. The occasional binge was an easy option for me.

There were always bottles of the two or three brands of lager that I preferred in the employee's refrigerator at the Batavia Service Center. I made sure of it. When the shelves were empty, my friends could count on me to replenish our supply with a quick side trip down the street to Nora's. We did not imbibe in the hard stuff very much on the job but there were bottles of vodka, rum, or bourbon on the shelf in the back storeroom for anytime that I considered to be a special occasion.

On most days, the guys would refuse more than a sip or two after hours at the garage. They preferred to head for home at the end of the day. If no one from work cared to linger, I could always rely on a friendly greeting at Harry's Pub.

On game days or when we had a practice session, the libations flowed freely at the park. For a few dollars, the visitors from out of town would share a joint after a game. If you asked for it, someone might even have a packet of cocaine hidden away.

I was certain that I could handle the beer and the bourbon. I also believed that I would not regret just a smidgen of the white powder once in a while. What's the harm if I always made it home at night and to work close enough to on time in the mornings?

The answer, of course, was the harm could be considerable. My irresponsible behavior led to increased tension at home. The arguments with Lydia became more frequent. There were intermittent estrangements between me and my wife and family.

Chapter 27 . Two events characterized hitting bottom.

Lydia said I was in denial. I justified my actions. I knew I could handle it all. Our children suffered when we argued. They were jerked around by the on-again, off-again hard feelings in our house but the problem seemed minor to me. Conviviality with cohorts after work and on weekends made it easy to forget unpleasantness at home.

Signs of slipping reliability started to show up at the garage. Rather than hand me the clip board with the day's commitments, Clutch was making the assignments himself. I could still do it but my trust factor had diminished among the other mechanics. I would give instructions or advice and they would go to Clutch to make sure what they heard from me was right. It was easy to put such sleights out of mind. A nip or two after hours at the auto-repair shop was a balm for any nagging difficulties.

My share of the repair jobs was done right. Unsatisfactory results can happen to anyone but, I believe, my record was better than most. I was becoming a high functioning alcoholic and a likely candidate for drug addiction.

It was not unusual for me to be the last to leave the park on a summer evening after a baseball game. I liked to sit back on a bench with the last beer in the cooler or for a few puffs on a weed and enjoy the night air.

I might nod off for a while before walking the half mile to our house on Elm Avenue. I could still get to work in the morning and, if you asked me, I was just fine doing my share at home.

I have vivid memories of the good things in our lives, especially the family vacations and trips to Europe. I do not remember much of the negative times. I was too muddled to retain the details.

It is not possible for me to chronicle all of the ups and downs during those years. However, there were two events, one in the summer of 2011 and the other in the spring of 2012, which characterized hitting bottom.

One night after a game early in August of 2011, the jab of a policeman's baton to my ribs woke me up. I flicked the burned-out roach from between my fingers into the dirt behind me but it was too late. They had already seen the evidence.

I denied any knowledge of the empty plastic baggie in the trash. Fortunately, the police decided not to press the issue even though it tested positive for cocaine. They arrested me for just simple possession. Only a few months had passed since the last time Attorney Wrightson had gotten me out of jail.

It was late the next afternoon after the police found me asleep on the park bench when I walked out of the city jail. Attorney Wrightson was there to greet me. He had won the argument for a sentence of community service. I was all smiles and appreciative but he was angry.

He had come through for me again but was not happy about it. He had bailed me out and negotiated plea deals more times than I cared to count. I had disappointed him and Lydia and my family over and over. I had relapsed after two different rehab programs that Attorney Wrightson had arranged for me.

Lydia did not hurry over to the station on that afternoon. She sent a hand-written note instead. Elmer handed it to me. Her words were so unsettling that they are still firmly etched in my memory.

> You have been the love of my life. We have started a beautiful family together. To be married to you was a dream that filled me with

joyful anticipation. It seems now, however, that it was only a pipe dream.

I had failed too many times to live up to my repeated promises to straighten out.

For nearly a week, I was relegated to the guest room or the couch in the den. I apologized again and worked hard on keeping better hours around the house and with the children. We agreed that there would be no drinking buddies in the house from Sunday evenings through Thursdays.

I listened to Lydia tell me that my family needed more from me. Once again, she heard my promises to do better. After a week of misery, she accepted me back into her good favors. I knew, if only subconsciously, that Lydia would relent, indeed had to relent, because an unpleasant home was too painful for her to endure for very long. It was not because I deserved another chance.

The second event that hastened my plunge to the bottom of the downward spiral unfolded the following spring in April of 2012.

Chapter 28 . My story was classic alcoholism.

The situation at home settled into a manageable level of equilibrium beginning the year Eileen entered the third grade and Diane started middle school.

Lydia complained that I was drinking too much and neglecting the children. I reacted with resentment. However, I knew she was right and I tried to be more conscientious. Lydia just sighed when I apologized. She was becoming resigned to how things were.

We could still be friends and go out together. Dinner and drinks were fine as long as I did not tip a few too many. When I did need one or two more than reasonable, which happened more than once, Lydia took the car and drove home without me.

The winter was uneventful for our family for the first few months of 2012. I was feeling bored and restless by early spring. One day after the first of April, I found Matthew Hennigan and Bob Ryan sitting at the bar in Harry's Pub when I walked in.

I was there to meet Lydia at the end of the day on a Friday afternoon. We liked to wrap up the week with fish and chips and a beer at Harry's when she was in town, especially if she had just returned from a business trip.

"Hey, Ted. Hang on a second," Matt said.

"Hello, Matt, Bob." I greeted them. "What's up?"

Matt answered, "The weather has been pretty nice this spring. We were just talking about getting some early practice sessions in before the AAU schedule gets started. Are you up for it?"

"Absolutely, Definitely." I replied. In fact, I was more than up for it. I was anxious for some relief from the preceding gloomy months.

"Ah, good," Ryan said with his usual lack of enthusiasm.

I said, "I need to grab that booth. Lydia and I are here to get something to eat and she just walked in. Count me in for whatever you come up with and thanks."

We did not get a very good turnout the following Wednesday afternoon. Not enough for a game but, as long as you have someone who can pitch, batting practice is an option.

I threw and threw and threw till my arm ached. The eleven guys who were there loved it. Bob Ryan sounded the only sour note. He hit the ball deep several times but he was still not happy. I struck him out three times.

Word must have gotten around a little better after the first practice session because a ton of players showed up on Friday. We had a great time playing ball and arguing strikes and balls, out or safe, and trapped or caught line drives.

Part of the reason for the good fellowship, of course, was Matt Hennigan brought a cooler stocked with cans of Miller High Life from the refrigerated shelves at Nora's. The turnout was so good and the day so warm that we ran dry earlier than expected.

It could have been that I was the one to suggest adjourning to Harry's Pub. In any case, the idea was met with a good deal of enthusiasm. Even Bob Ryan was enjoying himself when we got there. I know because he bought the first round at Harry's.

The good fellowship didn't last long. It never did with Ryan. I should have known better but I took the contrary view when he started to rehash a line drive that I hit down the right-field line. It was called fair but he disagreed. A couple of other guys at the bar counseled us to just let it go but we couldn't. Ryan reacted by storming out of the bar.

My way of cooling off was a little different. I ordered the ingredients for a boiler maker and enjoyed every drop. Unfortunately, when I slammed the empty glass down on the bar, it broke into smithereens. The bartender told me I had enough and asked me to leave.

He was actually a friend who always tried to look out for me but this time I failed to cooperate. I refused to go. When he insisted, I grabbed a chair and smashed it on the bar. I don't remember much after that. I did not know how I got there when I woke up late Saturday morning in the holding cell at the city jail.

More than 48 hours later, Attorney Wrightson showed up to spring me out once again. It was late in the day on Monday afternoon,

"Where have you been?" I asked. "I have been incarcerated the entire weekend. Didn't you get the word?"

"Yes, I did," he said.

"Just kidding, Elmer. I appreciate you getting me out again. I just wish they served beer at the afternoon parties in jail." I tried to laugh it off.

He did not see the humor. Elmer laid into me. "Do you really think this is funny? Your family deserves better from you. Your behavior has caused Lydia much more pain than she should have to endure. I'm through with you."

"No, no. It wasn't that bad." As usual, I tried to make excuses.

Wrightson would have none of it. He said, "The attorney fees, the fines, and the reparations have taken far too much of Lydia's resources. You are more of a burden than she should have to bear and you are an embarrassment to your children."

"What embarrassment? The kids don't ever see me drunk. They don't know if I ever have too much to drink. I am careful to shield them from any trouble I might get into. You know I am good to them." I was pleading with Elmer to agree.

"Oh, yeah. Sure," He sneered.

Now, I got angry. I shouted, "Eileen and Diane respect me. They do not know about any trouble that I might have gotten into. We never burden them with such problems."

"You don't think they hear about it at school?"

"What are you talking about?" I stepped backward and sank down onto a jailhouse step. "It was never as bad as people think."

"No, it is worse than what you think."

"I'll talk to the girls. They will understand."

"There is nothing you can say that could possibly help. Do you really not know that Diane and especially Eileen are brutalized by the hazing they get about the town drunk?" Attorney Wrightson's comment hit me like a verbal sledgehammer.

"I don't know what you are talking about."

"Don't you? What you really mean is you don't want to know. You have not bothered to pay attention to the harm you are doing to your own children. That makes it even worse old friend."

"OK, OK. You can stop now," I whimpered. "I know you are right. I'll do better. It won't happen again."

"For God's sake, I hope not. But, I don't believe it. I've heard it all before." Elmer Wrightson shook his head.

"Where is my wife? Why isn't she here?"

"She sent me because she said she couldn't get off work. But, I think she just did not want to face you again. You have disappointed her too many times."

"I'm sorry," I gulped.

"Are you really? You know feeling sorry for your self-centered self is not enough." Elmer's expression was full of disgust. "Find yourself another attorney." His words were a punch to the stomach that I had to know was well deserved.

"No, wait. What do you mean? You can't quit on me."

Elmer Wrightson did not answer. My friend since we first met in the fourth grade turned around, walked away, got into his car, and drove off without looking back. He did not offer to give me a ride home.

Chapter 29 . It was a bitter pill to swallow.

The painful conversation with Attorney Wrightson left me without transportation but it was not needed. To spend even one night let alone the weekend in jail means you are sober when you are released. A bit hungover perhaps but in possession of your ambulatory abilities.

I walked home. When I got there, I found a packed suitcase on the front porch with a note attached.

> You are not welcome here. Do not
> come in. Do not come back until you
> have straightened yourself out.

The message was in Lydia's handwriting.

I stuffed the note into my shirt pocket and went into the house anyway. I carried the suitcase across the living room and into the kitchen. No one was home. Lydia and the children were gone.

Just as well I thought. Maybe, I did not want to face them anyway. It was hard to think of anything I might say after the tongue lashing that I had just gotten from Elmer Wrightson.

I sat down at the kitchen table and pulled Lydia's folded-over note from my pocket. There was writing on the back. "Please don't be mad, Daddy." It was written in Eileen's neat child-like script.

It made me smile but it also hurt. The little girl was just eight years old and she was worried about my feelings when it was I who was the fool.

I thought the family might return at any minute and I had better not be there. I would come back after Lydia had a chance to cool off. My car was parked at the curb with the keys in the ignition. I threw the suitcase into the trunk and drove off.

I figured I might not be welcome at Harry's Pub for a while. So, I headed for a bar in Socorro on the long way around to my parents' house. I needed to brace myself before facing them. Also, I wanted something to anesthetize the hurt inflicted by Wrightson's harsh words. I sat at the bar by myself and ordered a draft. I looked around to see who else was there. None of my usual cronies cared to join me.

I had to flag down the bartender for another beer. He was somebody I recognized from previous visits. The man took his time with the pour. I had been at the bar a good hour but was served only two mugs of beer. It was clear he was pacing me. I figured it was time to go.

Mom and Dad were waiting for me when I got there. They knew I would be coming. Of course, they did. Where else could a waisted, forty-year-old inebriate go?

Mother was judgmental. "You know what? You have really fucked up your life." Her profane vocabulary was totally out of character.

She pulled cold cuts out of the refrigerator and put a loaf of bread on the table. "Make yourself something to eat." She handed me a glass of water. "Here. It's late. I'm going to bed." Mother left the kitchen. It was only about nine o'clock.

My father did not say much. "You can stay in the room in the basement for a while I guess." He seemed old and sadly resigned to what his adult son had become.

"Thanks, Dad." I did not say I'm sorry because I knew it would be taken as more empty words.

Dad broke the news, "Lydia has taken the children for a vacation in Paris."

"That cannot be true," I shouted. "Are you serious?"

Dad nodded.

They had gone without me. It was supposed to be our next European vacation. I strode to the bar in the family room and helped myself to a double bourbon on ice to ease the pain. I gulped it down and went back for another.

"Is more of what is destroying your life and your family really what you need?" There was an edge to his voice.

I put the bottle down without pouring and complained, "They should not have gone to Paris without me."

My father's answer was clear. "You're wrong. They had to go without you."

"What do you mean? I don't believe you."

He looked the other way and didn't answer. So, I made it a triple and clinked in more ice.

Dad and I sat in our favorite chairs in the living room. He turned on the television and used the remote to search for a baseball game. It seemed to be a good time to go for a third drink while I waited for him to find something.

"God damn it, Theodore, you've had enough. Sit down," he ordered with an angry shout. My father's voice was stern and not to be denied.

"OK," I agreed. I could not remember a time when he had used such blasphemous words with me or, for that matter, with anyone on any occasion.

"Just sit down and watch the game," he repeated.

I sat but I was still feeling sorry for myself.

"The trip to Paris was supposed to be for the whole family. We have been planning it together for years. Haven't you heard Lydia and me talking about it," I whined.

"I guess I have but ... " He stopped.

"But what?" I insisted.

"Why would they want you along? What would they do with you? How could they enjoy themselves with a stumbling drunk on their hands every evening?"

"That's harsh," I shouted. I stood up and glared at him. I could not control a gush of angry and sad tears. Either out of spite or to hide my face, I went back to the wet bar and made myself another drink. When I turned around again, my father was gone.

Dad had found a late-night game on the television. As I recall, the Dodgers were at home against the Padres but it might have been against the Pirates.

I may have enjoyed one or two more bourbons while I watched the game. What the hell. Everyone's deserted me anyway. I might as well make myself feel better.

I poured a cold Budweiser into a frosted glass and dropped a single shot of Jack Daniels into the beer. The libation hit the spot. The boiler maker was just what I needed.

Through bleary eyes, I watched the starter for the Dodgers give up several runs in the top of the sixth inning. The last thing I remember was Manager Don Mattingly signaling for a right-handed reliever on his way out to the mound.

Chapter 30 . The lifeline was intervention.

§ April 2012 §

The television was off when I came to the next morning. I was still in the chair in the living room. My father was standing over me. I don't know if it was he or my headache that woke me up. Dad handed me a mug of coffee and a bran muffin on a plate.

He told me, "Your mother left for work already."

"I guess I better get over to the garage," I muttered.

"No, they are not expecting you this morning. What you must do is come with me."

"Where are we going?"

"You'll see when we get there." He poured more coffee but refused to talk.

A quarter of an hour later, he said, "Let's go."

I slumped into the passenger seat of his Buick and leaned forward. I held my throbbing head in my hands.

"Put your seat belt on," he said.

"I'm not feeling good," I complained but I attempted to comply. A wave of nausea swept over me when I turned my head to reach for the buckle. I gulped down a few deep breaths and managed to suppress the retching turn of my gut before trying again. I leaned back and finally got myself strapped in.

Neither of us said anything more until my father turned off the engine. We were in a parking space on the street in front of the Congregational Church in Socorro, the dusty town thirty miles southwest of Batavia.

"Good, we're on time. Let's go," he said.

I tried to respond but my voice was too hoarse to talk. All that came out was sputtering and a cough.

Dad got out of the car and started down the sidewalk. When I managed to catch up, he handed me a water bottle.

After a couple of gulps, I could finally speak intelligibly. "On time for what?"

"This way," He said without answering my question.

Dad walked past the wide marble steps that reached up to the main entrance to the nave of the church where the worshippers prayed on Sundays. He led me toward a side entrance into the lower level of the building.

The two and a half mugs of coffee that he served me that morning and the water were beginning to help me feel a little better.

I followed along behind my father without saying anything more. We walked down a hall and hesitated in front of a men's room.

"You'd better stop in here." Even now, my father kept my basic needs in mind. He knew that my liquid intake would require some relief.

I nodded and made use of the facilities. Dad was waiting for me when I came out.

We continued on our way and entered one of the classrooms in the lower level of the church. A meeting of an Alcoholic Anonymous group was about to begin.

"What have you done? I don't need this," I growled at him in a low voice.

Dad ignored my objections. He motioned to a few empty places in the circle of ten or twelve chairs. With a firm grip on my arm, he guided me to one side of the room and sat down next to me.

Within a few minutes, every seat was taken. A man a few places to my left looked familiar but I couldn't place him.

Otherwise, I was not sure if I was acquainted with anyone else in the meeting.

The group leader turned out to be the professional-looking suit and tie seated directly across from me. He appeared to be in his early sixties. At his signal, the attendees began to introduce themselves.

Chapter 31 . Participant's story hit home.

A nervous, panicky feeling came over me when I realized that Dad was gone. A stranger was in the chair next to me.

My turn to speak came last. I said, "Pass."

Everyone looked at me with what I perceived to be a heavy dose of pity. They turned away again when the group leader spoke.

He explained, "All of you are here because you are alcoholics on the road to recovery. Some of you might suffer from drug dependencies as well. The purpose of our meetings is to offer each other support and to get help for ourselves. We make progress by sharing our stories with each other. Nothing that we hear can ever be repeated outside of this room. Confidentiality is an absolute necessity. Do you understand?" The group leader was looking at me.

I nodded.

"Do you agree?" he repeated more forcefully.

"Yes, yes, OK," I stammered. "But actually, I don't need to be here." I wanted to get up and walk out but I was frozen in place by the disapproving, doubtful looks from everyone around me.

"We can talk later if you wish. The meeting will last about an hour. For today, you can participate as much or as little as you like. Your ride will be back for you after the meeting."

"My ride?" I asked. How did he know about my ride? Had my father talked to this stranger behind my back about me?

He turned to the person on his left. She began to speak as if on cue. "My name is Dawn and I am an alcoholic," she drawled.

Dawn explained, "I am in my fourteenth year of recovery. The reason you have not seen me for the last month is I was visiting my grandchildren in Nashville. I still made it to a meeting every week while I was there. Actually, a couple of times, I attended more than one meeting. As I have mentioned before, there is a wonderful AA group at the Veterans Hospital in Nashville."

Everyone clapped and smiled. The group leader said, "Thank you, Dawn. Who would like to go next?"

Three or four others had something to stay. Andrea confessed that she had relapsed when her old boyfriend moved back in with her. But, she had thrown him out and she was determined to remain sober from now on. The people murmured encouragement.

A kindly, middle-aged woman said, "Come over for tea when you are having trouble Andrea and we can talk."

"I prefer a good cup of strong coffee," Andrea replied.

"I've got that too," she smiled.

There followed a brief period of silence. "Anyone else?" the group leader asked again. "We don't want to adjourn too early." He looked at me. "How about you?"

I squirmed in my chair and looked down at the floor.

"You know, I should say something." The voice of the familiar-looking man two chairs to my left came to my rescue.

"As you all know or at least most of you know, my name is Bill and I am an alcoholic and a drug addict. I have been attending this meeting longer than nearly every one of you even you, Dr. Rudy. You took over from Dr. Barbara eight or ten years ago. Am I right?"

"Just about," the group leader agreed.

"Today is a good time to tell my story again because I have just reached an important milestone. It was twenty years ago last week when I fell off the roof of my house and broke my back."

I suddenly knew why he looked familiar. I had met the man. He used to be a neighbor. Bill was Officer William White's biological father. I remembered the story about his accident. It was covered extensively in the local newspaper. It was serious. He nearly died.

Bill continued, "After the accident and surgery and physical therapy, the Percocet was a medically justified necessity. When the months dragged on into years, the pain killers turned into an addiction that I could not shake. But, it got to be more and more difficult to persuade the doctors to write prescriptions. Alcohol was a much more convenient substitute.

"Harry's Pub became my home away from home. In fact, if you needed to find me, that was the first place for you to look. One of my most loyal employees at my bank would come to get me when my lunch break extended beyond a couple of hours.

"I had to travel to board meetings in the city as part of my job at the bank. It could be pretty late when we finished work. So, I would have to stay over. Not all of the time but often enough.

"You could find pretty much whatever stuff you needed at a couple of sleazy bars in the city. Once I found a favorite supplier, I started staying the night at the Sonoma Hotel regardless of how late it was when the board meeting adjourned.

"The coke habit got to be very costly. I had to run up a tab. My supplier never threatened me but the implication was there. To keep the drugs coming, I had to pad my expense account and even borrow a little from the till at the bank from time to time. It was so easy that I got careless and the auditors discovered the discrepancies. They caught me.

"Alcoholism and drugs are not compatible with being a bank president or a husband and father. I lost my job and my wife."

Bill's voice broke and he paused. He pulled a handkerchief from his pocket and wiped his face. His shoulders heaved. It was hard for me to look. I turned away.

"If you asked me, I would have insisted that I loved my children but a cell mate disagreed. A reborn lifer who had turned righteous in the Federal penitentiary lectured me that mine was not true love. He simply asked me if I understood that parental love meant setting your own priorities aside for the sake of raising your kids. Of all the places where you would not expect a life lesson, mine was delivered in jail." Bill chuckled but his voice was trembling. He paused again.

The awkward silence began to feel uncomfortable to me. I glanced up at some of the others. No one else was squirming in their seat. I believe their patience with the speaker was proof of empathy for his story.

"Go on if you want to, Bill," the group leader said.

He gave a big sigh and continued, "I had hoped she would wait for me but my wife remarried while I was in prison. I can't be too bitter about it because he is a great guy. He became a wonderful father to my daughter and son which I was certainly not. Now, I show up for their special events, graduation and such, but I am really not needed." He shrugged. The smile was surely forced.

As his words sunk in, I felt a chill come over me. I was sure everyone there would notice the trembling and hear me breathing but no one looked my way.

Bill said, "The embezzlement conviction meant that I could never work in a bank again but I can't complain. I have made a good living with my lawn-care and landscape business. I have this group and all of you to thank for helping me get back on my feet and, more importantly, for helping me stay there.

"One more thing I should say is I appreciate your counselling, Dr. Rudy, on how to accept my role as a third parent." With that, he looked down and was quiet.

"Thank you, Bill," the group leader said. The applause was enthusiastic. Even I put my hands together.

I was shaken by Bill's comments. The words "third parent" echoed in my head. His story could easily have become mine.

I knew his children. They had indeed been blessed with a good stepfather. John Anderson was a very fine man. Did my children deserve as much? How close was Lydia to coming to such a conclusion?

Their mother was Julie Anderson. She took her new husband's name when they got married. The family lived just a few houses away from us on Elm Avenue. They were a valued part of our neighborhood. Bill's biological children were respectful and well behaved. Their daughter used to babysit for Diane and Eileen.

The group leader looked my way one more time.

"My name is Ted and maybe, I don't know if it's true, but maybe I do need to be here," I said. "I can't tell you my story right now, at least not yet."

"Good. See you next week." He adjourned the meeting.

It was the beginning of the end of my wayward life.

Dad was waiting for me in the car.

"Where did you go?" I asked.

"The meeting was for you. I could take you there but I was not welcome to stay and hear their stories," he explained.

"How did you know about it?"

"Lydia has been asking us for help for a while now. She took your mother and me to an Al-Anon meeting at the Congregational Church a long time ago. We have been attending meetings with Lydia on and off for a couple of years."

"She never told me."

"Perhaps, she did but you couldn't hear her."

"Have you always been so prescient?"

"Yes, of course," my father quipped. "Actually, not so much. We have depended on and needed the counselling at the meetings to teach us many things."

"About what?"

"About alcoholism and how to live with it," was all the explanation I got from my father.

I didn't say anything.

Dad said, "I will drive you to the meeting again next week."

"How did you know I lost my license?"

"Prescient, remember?" He chuckled. "Actually, I heard it from your mother. Maybe, she is the prescient one. Some afternoons, your mother goes to an Al-Anon meeting by herself in the church hall over at Saint Ann's."

I gasped and held my breath. I didn't want him to see me crying again. Indeed, I did not like the overwhelming feeling of sadness and remorse.

"I have a really tough question to ask, Dad."

"Go ahead," he sighed.

"Did anyone else go with Lydia and my children to Paris?"

"From what I have heard, Lydia was wondering if her cousin Janet Bread might accompany them or perhaps join them for a few days. But, that is not what you are asking. Is it?"

I shook my head.

"About six months ago, Lydia told your mother that she heard from an old boyfriend, someone she dated in high school. She has had other overtures as well but, as far as Lydia is concerned, there is nothing to any of it but talk. So, no. No one else went to Paris with your wife and family."

I could not hide the tears of relief.

"Lydia is loyal to you, Ted. But, to be blunt, the alternatives would be enough to worry me," my father warned.

Chapter 32 . Someone must stand in your way.

My father drove me back to their house. We had lunch together and chatted about old times.

"Your Mother said you would not be in much shape for work today. So, I called Clutch at the garage. They are expecting you back on the job first thing tomorrow."

"What did you tell him?"

"I said you were sick but I think they probably know you pretty well by now. Don't they?"

I did not answer the question. Finally, I said, "Dad, this is it. I am turning my life around today."

"Addiction is a tricky thing, Ted. They say it is not possible to go halfway."

"I think I know how it works. I have got to quit cold turkey."

"We would like to see it happen."

"I have to do it now before I lose everything. But, I am scared."

My father said, "Your mother and I will do whatever we can to help. I hope that you can still salvage your family."

We walked into the living room and sat down. I leaned back in my chair and looked around. There was something different in the familiar surroundings of my parents' home. Then, it came to me. The shelves over the wet bar in the family room were empty.

My parents had discarded the entire contents of their always well-stocked liquor cabinet. They were sacrificing their own pleasures for the benefit of their addicted son, physically an adult but still the child they could not abandon.

No one said much to me at the garage the next morning. I jumped right in and went to work on the backlog. The boss was at the counter in the lobby on the phone. He was talking to the few customers who might be inconvenienced by a delay. It was after ten o'clock when he came over to talk to me.

"Ted, I have reworked the schedule to make up for lost time. I explained we were shorthanded to concerned customers. Try to keep things going in here. I'll be back later. Melissa has the front counter."

About ten minutes later, I saw the boss lugging a box out of the office and around the counter where Melissa stood. He looked at her. She shrugged and smiled at him. They glanced my way but I could not get a read on their expressions. Clutch continued through the lobby and out to his car.

Just before noon, Melissa approached me and asked, "Can I get you anything?"

"Yes, please. Would you pick up something from the deli for everyone? I'll pay."

"Sure." It was not the sort of thing Melissa usually took on but she agreed.

"I called out in a loud voice, "Hey everybody, I appreciate how you covered for me yesterday. Order what you want from the deli. My treat. Can you call it in Melissa?" I dug a credit card out of my wallet and handed it to her.

Twenty minutes later, she walked across the street and returned with a large bag of chips and sandwiches. I went to the refrigerator for a soft drink and discovered my supply of beer was gone. I looked around to see that the vodka and rum bottles had disappeared too. The shelves at the back of the storeroom were empty. No wonder the box Clutch carried out to his car that morning was so heavy.

A strange silence hung over my comrades as we sat on benches at the back of the garage. Everyone had soft drinks with their sandwiches. I washed mine down with a bottle of water.

To say a beer at lunch was my usual beverage would not be entirely accurate. Two or three tall cans comprised my entire nourishment as often as not.

It crossed my mind that a quick trip to Nora's liquor store for a six-pack would not be such a bad thing. I might have gone for it if not for the embarrassment among coworkers. On the first day of my recovery, watchful eyes helped to keep me on the journey toward sobriety.

A few hours later, when everything seemed well in hand at the garage, I thought about taking the short walk over to Harry's Pub for a midafternoon libation. I stood out front of the garage looking down the street. The image of a favorite spot at the bar was in my mind but it was Clutch who was in my field of view, standing right in front of me.

"Are you going somewhere?" he said. It was an accusation more than a question.

"I will never touch another drop," I vowed.

"Good," Clutch replied and he walked back through the glass doors into the lobby.

I drove past Nora's and Hennigan's on my way home. There was a police car at one of the pumps at the filling station. Matthew Hennigan was standing next to the car. He was talking to the policeman behind the wheel. It was Officer Robert Ryan.

Before I could even consider dropping by Harry's Pub to see what was going on, Ryan whipped out behind me in his cruiser. He pulled me over with flashing lights and a short blast of his siren. He got out and approached the driver's side. I rolled down the window.

"What's going on? Mr. Theodore O'Connor? You staying out of trouble?"

"Bob, I will never touch another drop."

"Yeah. Sure, Ted. That damn well would be best but I'll believe it when I see it," he sneered. He started back toward his car. "You drive carefully now. Ya hear?"

My gut reaction to the disdain in his voice was redoubled determination. I thought to myself I'll show you.

As I drove off, I wondered could he possibly have intended to strengthen my resolve by taunting me like that. Had he been lingering at the service station just to catch me on my way by? It was a bit too much to believe that the hardened policeman could harbor such good intentions.

I do not know if the strength of my resolve would have been sufficient over the following few months if not for friends and family looking out for me. With their encouragement, I have been good to my word. I have not been inside Nora's or Harry's since that day.

Chapter 33 . Dining out was different.

H as she let you back in the house?" Clutch asked. It had been about a month since the beginning of my recovery.

"Not yet. But, we are making progress."

After a few weeks with my confidence growing stronger, Lydia and I began to do things together. Just with the children at first and then by ourselves.

We met for coffee at Allen's Diner and went out for lunch. I started coming to the house fairly regularly for dinner. At first, it was meals with the family mostly on the weekends but more and more I could be a father during the week.

The following fall, when the children were back in school, I took on more of the parenting responsibilities at the house on Elm Avenue. Lydia was capable of assuming the burdens of single parenthood. However, she did not want it to be that way. She believed it was important for the children to have a father in their lives.

"Even a defective father is better than none." Brutal honesty was the new norm.

"Ouch. I'm not that bad."

"Aren't you?"

Toward the end of the second month of living in my parents' house, we left Diane in charge and we went out for dinner at the Legal Sea Foods restaurant in the city. We had soft drinks with the Rhode Island style Calamari for an appetizer to share.

I do not remember what we ordered for our entrées but the new beginning for a nice dinner out with the fun-loving Lydia was a different experience. In the past, our favorite start to the evening included martinis for both of us, calamari or mussels, and another drink with the main course.

"And drinks with your dinner?" the waitress asked.

"Perrier, please." Lydia who loved to tip a glass of wine with her meal did not order an alcoholic beverage. Her response sounded as natural as if she always preferred sparkling water.

"Same," I said.

Later that evening, over Shirly Temples at our table in the restaurant, Lydia started talking about the trip she and our two daughters took to Paris.

She said that they were sorry I was not with them, that they missed me, that the children did not really understand why I was not there.

Lydia said, "Every day, Eileen would ask, 'Where's Daddy?' Most times, Diane would tell her, 'Daddy was too busy to come with us.' Those were Diane's words. I did not know how to explain it any better."

"I am sorry I wasn't there," I said.

"I was too. I kept remembering how nice it was when we were all together for the family trip to Copenhagen."

"A treasured memory for me too."

"Of course, I missed you in Paris but a nice vacation was something I just knew I had to do for myself and for my daughters."

I took a breath. You said, "my daughters?" I questioned the mother of our children.

"Yours too," Lydia conceded.

"They deserved better than what I was," I confessed.

My wife did not disagree.

She said, "They got to see many wonderful things in Paris. We toured Notre Dame Cathedral; We visited the Eifel Tower; We took a boat ride on the Seine and walked along the Champs Elysees to the Arc de Triomphe. Every minute of all that time, I wished you were with us but I was determined to enjoy the trip. I needed to get away from the downward spiral that was consuming our life."

"I understand." It was all I could get out from my aching chest.

"Do you? I want you to believe it and to believe in me and our daughters. I have missed you. Of course, I still love you. I am hopeful for the future."

I tried to say something but the tears choked off any words.

"Let's get out of here before you make a scene and embarrass yourself and me," Lydia laughed.

There were tears on her cheeks too but the saucy, fun loving woman was still there. A bit of hope was shining in her glistening eyes. Lydia was daring to believe that our family just might be coming out from under the cloud of gloom that had hovered over us for so long.

The next day I packed a few clothes in a suitcase and walked back into our house. I was scared to my soul that Lydia would tell me to go away but she did not.

She did not throw me out. For a few days that seemed like an eternity, I was still not welcome back in the bedroom until suddenly I was.

Chapter 34 . The good citizen is an asset to family and community.

Participation in AAU baseball games was put on hold. Socializing with cronies from Harry's Pub or with anyone who could pose a threat to my sobriety was to be severely limited. I might be allowed to resume some activities and reconnect with the best of my old friends someday but not for a while.

It was a strange feeling not knowing how to occupy myself. There was empty time to be filled after work and in the evenings. It was a problem that my mother and Lydia anticipated. They found things to keep me busy and involved.

The true adults at my side had the right idea. I was in no position to argue nor did I want to. I was happy to have them step forward to put something good into the holes in my life.

They presumed to design a curriculum for me at the community college. The time and focus required for adhering to the schedule kept me too busy to worry about aimless activities with friends. All idleness was swept away by reading and discussing material with family and ever watchful members of my AA group.

Mother accompanied me to many of my class meetings. She took an interest in the topics. I believe she enjoyed the learning experience herself.

Two years later, I had accumulated enough credits along with previous entries on my transcript to cross a significant threshold. My family was in the audience when I walked onto the stage to accept an associate degree in business.

It was not obvious to me at the time but Lydia was filling my schedule in much the same way as she had organized activities for our children. I wonder if the comparison occurred to her.

Not everything she and my folks tried to rope me into was successful. I was too restless to do well in the book club. But, other diversions did take hold.

Lydia introduced me to the idea that witnessing our children's activities was something a loving father might enjoy. She was right. As atonal as Eileen's clarinet might have been, I actually enjoyed her first recital.

Both daughters participated in athletic events that were scheduled with dizzying frequency. I even learned to appreciate a soccer game.

My father joined the team of good-intentioned meddlers in my life. He talked to the athletic director at Batavia High.

Starting in the fall, my stint as an assistant coach for the varsity basketball team was a saving grace. Diane was a talented shooting guard who could take the point almost as well as she could drive to the basket.

Having her father as one of the coaches turned out to be more embarrassing for me than it was for her. I could teach the fundamentals but I struggled to keep up with the girls on the court.

I put up a free-standing backboard and hoop over the paved area in front of the garage at home. I worked with both daughters on their ball-handling techniques under the new lighting system that I installed. It became a favorite gathering place for their neighborhood friends late into the evening. Sometimes, Lydia would have to hit the lights-out button to get everyone to go home. I had wisely wired a switch inside the back door to the house.

Chapter 35 . Teaching is the preeminent vocation.

Both of my parents encouraged me to take the education courses required for a teaching certificate. As soon as I had enough of the right credentials, I was hired to be the instructor for an auto-mechanics class in the after-school program for high school students.

"Are there any girls in your class?" Eileen's question had a judgmental tone but I was ready for her.

"Yes, I make an effort to recruit and encourage women. How about you? You should take my class. I could teach you to be a really good auto mechanic."

"No, not for me. I am studying to be a stay-at-home housewife," Eileen answered in a fake whisper loud enough to be sure her mother would hear.

I chuckled at Eileen's well-developed propensity for making mischief.

"The woman's place is in the home to do the cooking and cleaning," Eileen deadpanned.

Lydia called out from the next room, "No! Whose daughter are you? Do you not dare to dream?"

By the look on her face, Eileen was taken aback by how her mother phrased the question but it did not surprise me.

The occasion reminded me of something an independent young woman might want to know. The quote was in the textbook for my previous semester's English literature class. It was taken from a modern classic, which we happened to have on a shelf in the den. I knew just where to find it.

I beckoned for Eileen to follow me and pulled <u>Wouldn't Take Nothing for My Journey Now</u>, by Maya Angelou, from the shelf. There was a bookmark on the page,

> A person is the product of their dreams.
> So, make sure to dream great dreams.
> And then try to live your dream.

Eileen read the words quietly. She said, "Thanks, Dad. I like that you knew where to look for a great quote."

"To be married to Lydia Kingston has significant literary benefits," I explained.

She squeezed my arm and we joined the family in the dining room. It was time for dinner. Naturally, that evening when we were alone, I had to brag to Lydia about my literary prowess.

Night school and later my teaching assignment took much of my time but I was still able to keep my job at the garage. In fact, sobriety had a way of making me into a more reliable and, hence, more valuable employee.

As the one in charge of keeping the books, Melissa was only too happy to make use of my newly acquired skills in business by calling on me for help in the office. I found a little humor in the competition for my time between Melissa and her husband.

It was a friendly exchange when Clutch would stick his head in and shout, "Hey, Boss, send Ted back out here. Greasing wheels in the shop is more important than pushing paper in the office."

"OK, if you don't care if the bills get paid," she replied in a voice just as loud as his.

My talent for diagnosing a mechanical problem served me well in my job at the Batavia Service Center. It also made me a natural for teaching auto mechanics.

The curriculum I developed included many of the consequential developments in the 120-year history of the automobile. Naturally, there were students who offered resistance to the extra burden that I imposed but I insisted the material was part of what it meant to be a well-educated automobile mechanic.

My students needed to know that cars and trucks brought about a cultural shift in our country. The invention provided individuals with the independence to move about at will. Transportation and travel over long distances became commonplace for goods and for people.

The students of the trades in my evening classes at Batavia High learned about the mechanical, chemical, and electronic genius that created the internal combustion engine, battery power, and electric motors. The ingenuity gave us vehicles that can operate reliably both for short trips to nearby locations and for amazing endurance tests of a thousand miles or more.

The century-old development of the automobile made our lives easier and more productive. It was the source of significant economic benefits. It also created safety and environmental challenges that are as great as the innovations required for the invention itself.

I asked students in the trades program at Batavia High to think about the difference between the two problems. On the one hand, the research and development of the automobile are certainly accomplishments to be celebrated. On the other hand, the massive environmental effects could be so inconvenient that the obstacles are insurmountable. I preached in the classroom that it would be up to the new generation of innovators to decide if the United States had the will to overcome the apathy and political resistance.

While it was a priority in my classes for students to understand the impact the automobile had on the economy and on our way of living, it was also important for me to teach the greasy-hands history of the car, meaning the development of automotive repair.

The piston-driven crankshaft has been the fundamental mechanism in the gasoline engine since the very beginning. While the basic design of oscillations inside the engine block has endured for well over a century, the technology was fragile at the beginning.

The ubiquitous popularity of the automobile could not have happened without the discovery and implementation of significant developments in mechanical engineering and in the chemistry of the materials. Within just a few generations, there has been a steady flow of important improvements from pneumatic tires made of vulcanized rubber in the 1890's to the electronic controls in late-model vehicles.

The enthusiasm for learning in my classes contributed to my own motivation to teach well. While admittedly not true of every one of them, I could see excitement in many eyes. The good students were pleased to learn about a significant engineering development. They might even be surprised by the revelation of one key idea or another dating back only as far as their recent ancestors, a grandparent they might have known.

In my view, there was no better way to learn about the historical developments than to work on the restoration of vintage vehicles. I petitioned for and obtained funding for more tools and vehicles in need of repair. The students in the automotive repair classes at Batavia High can now hone their skills on a 1935 Packard V-8 and a 1948 six-cylinder Plymouth.

Auto mechanics is classified as a trade. It is not considered to be a profession. However, I like to preach to our future mechanics that tradesmen can still take pride in their work as much as any professional.

My avocation for vintage vehicles was both a hobby and an instructional tool. It also helped me as a professional mechanic.

My knowledge and experience meant that Clutch called on me to replace brake shoes and grind the inside surface of the drum whenever an old model car with such an increasingly obsolete braking system was on the docket. I could also pull a wheel and snap in new pads for disc brakes in half the proscribed time for the task.

The braking system provides a good illustration of the two requirements for being an expert mechanic. You should know both the greasy-hands history and the academic principles of automotive repair. On the one hand, you must be able to assemble brake shoes inside drums or new pads on discs. On the other hand, it is important to understand the forces and the dissipation of energy required to bring a multi-ton vehicle to a stop.

Chapter 36 . Reliability is its own reward.

Every so often, there would be a repair job for me to crow about at the Batavia Service Center. The diagnosis of an electrical short is an example of a story that I am particularly fond of retelling.

As we were closing up one evening, Clutch said, "Thank you for finding the short circuit in that Mercedes' electrical system. I was getting tired of hearing Mrs. Roberts complain and question our competence but who could blame her. How many times did she bring it back after we thought it was fixed but it wasn't?"

"Seven times before I looked at it. Never again after today," I chirped. "Her name is Mrs. Richards."

"Oh, yeah. Richards, of course. But, it was not seven times. Give me a break." Clutch laughed.

I started to add, "My Dad taught me to check for the obvious and sure enough the ..."

"I know, I know. You've bragged about it enough."

He wouldn't let me finish retelling the story of how I discovered the frayed tail-light wire that no one else had noticed in Richards' car.

"Good work, Daddy." At least, Eileen gave me a thumbs up when I explained it to her that evening. She came to ask me to proofread an essay for her history class but she stayed to listen to the whole story. Don't tell me that getting my help with her essay had anything to do with her sincere interest in my impressive diagnostic talents.

Business was expanding at the Batavia Service Center. The six mechanics, counting Clutch and me, were able to handle more jobs. We had the space to accept even more work but finding qualified help held us back.

I enjoyed working with others and making sure a job was done right. Clutch appreciated the greater throughput when I was on the job. However, he had become restless with the everyday workload at the Batavia Service Center. He decided we needed a greater variety of tasks.

Mellissa and Clutch solicited my assistance with a new business plan. Before long we were accepting the full range of mechanical-repair jobs. We even added engine overhaul to the list.

There might have been a little self-importance to my conviction that I was good for his business but it was only a touch of arrogance at worst. I just knew that Clutch's investments in new equipment could not have been justified without my contributions.

After I had continued to build respectability for a couple of years, Clutch took me aside for a serious conversation. He needed to make sure I understood my responsibilities to the Batavia Service Center.

He said, "Listen, Ted, the business is doing pretty well. Things have improved enough for us to upgrade some of our tools. However, I want you to know that the expenditures will be worth it only if we can rely on your contributions on the job. The junior mechanics can get a lot done but they need to know what to do."

"I understand," I replied. The pressure was on but it did not bother me. I had become confident that I could stay the course of a recovering alcoholic.

Clutch added emphasis. "I am not asking you. I am telling you that you must remain permanently sober and reliable."

"Count on it."

The investments at the Batavia Service Center included more powerful lifts in all of the first three bays. There were extra training days with experts brought in from Ford Motor Company and from BMW. Melissa upgraded the parts department and hired another member of the staff to monitor and maintain the inventory.

The foldable shop crane was a portable tripod that was always breaking down. I told Clutch, "We need something better than this piece of junk."

"I'm way ahead of you, Ted. We are going to install a permanent hoist in the second bay. It is an expensive upgrade but, as you said, we need it. The product should arrive sometime next week." Clutch showed me the invoice and watched me scrutinize the specifications.

"No installation on the order?" I asked.

"Steiger will put it together. He's done similar work in the past but you should stand by 'cause he'll need your help."

I commented, "I thought Mark was going to retire."

"He keeps threatening to but I guess he loves the work too much," Clutch said.

"It must be our good company," I opined.

"I'm sure it is," Clutch agreed with a laugh.

It turned out that my help was not required for the installation of the new hoist because I was not around to do my part. Mark Steiger came in one weekend and put it all together with the salesman's assistance.

When I got to work halfway through the morning on Monday, the contraption was already in use. The engine from a minivan was dangling over the open hood of the vehicle in the second bay.

Clutch did not say anything but it was clear he was not too pleased that I had not been there to help with the work.

"Tough weekend," I explained.

He was non-committal. "Put the old foldable shop crane somewhere in the rear of bay four until we figure out what to do with it."

"I can fix it again if we ever need it," I volunteered. "Do you want it on the ledge over the parts cabinet?"

"Just figure something out." Clutch snapped. He turned his back and walked away.

I went after him. "Clutch, I had to go to an AA meeting this morning."

"You leave early every Tuesday for AA meetings."

"We have been so busy here that I missed the last two in a row."

"And on Saturday when you agreed to help Mark?"

"Lydia's birthday."

"Ah, you don't want to mess that up." Clutch shrugged and we went about our business. He seemed to be placated and, indeed, that was the end of it.

There were many occasions when I was tempted to indulge in just one beer but I managed to be faithful to the pledge.

Clutch took notice and started giving me additional responsibilities at the garage. It was a gradual process during the third and fourth year of my recovery.

His growing confidence in me was gratifying. Still, it surprised me and pleased me when he created a new position and asked me to take the job.

"Can you be the shop supervisor for the Batavia Service Center?" Clutch asked. It was more an appointment than a request.

Part III

Immigration and Evasion

Beauty was not simply something to behold; it was something one could do.

– Toni Morrison

Chapter 37 . A classic vehicle arrived at the Batavia Service Center.

Early one morning in September of 2014 before we had a chance to raise the doors at the Batavia Service Center, a world-weary man of about 30 drove up in a 1948 Ford F-1 pickup truck. It was clearly in need of some serious work. The vehicle clunkered to a stop in front of the first bay next to the lobby.

I hit the button to roll the garage door up to the top and Clutch ducked out to have a look. He lifted the hood and stepped back from the full blast of the rumbling. The rhythmic thumping was alarming.

Clutch shouted, "Hey, man, shut it off. You really do not want to hear an engine banging like that."

"Yeah, I know," the driver answered. He switched off the engine and asked, "Can you fix it here?"

"I don't know about parts for such an antique," Clutch laughed. His cheerful response did not soften the man's sober expression.

The owner of the F-1 pickup evidently did not see any humor in his predicament. The three of us left the truck sitting in the drive and walked into the front lobby.

He said, "It doesn't need a lot of parts. Just machining on a lathe to return to round. It has thrown the rod off the back turn of the crank shaft."

"The engine does sound like a thrown rod. How do you know which one?"

"Oh, I know."

Clutch looked doubtful. "Well, we have to ask is it worth it?"

"It is to me. My family needs the truck. It might need a rod and main bearing shim. Can you find them?"

"Let me see what I can find out. Will you wait here in the lobby while I call around?"

"OK." He slumped into a chair in the waiting area by the front window. He looked haggard and glum. So down in the dumps, it was hard to know what to say to him. I just left him alone and went to work.

Other members of the crew were dribbling into the shop and looking for their assignments. Melissa handed me two clipboards with repair sheets on projects left over from the previous workday. I went into the shop and handed one of them off and kept one for myself. We had obligations to meet that day but nothing was as interesting as the heap of metal sitting outside in front of the first bay.

The six-cylinder flathead engine in the F-1 pickup used to be a staple in the Ford product line more than half a century ago. None of us in the shop had any hands-on experience with the classic machine. I had seen it, of course, but I had not worked on such an engine in my workshop at home on Elm Avenue. It had not been in any of my restoration projects.

Every mechanic at work that morning would have liked the chance to get their hands dirty under the vehicle's hood. Given my interest in vintage vehicles, I presumed it would come my way. However, Clutch took the job for himself. That did not stop me from sticking my nose in to see how it would go.

Clutch was hidden away in the office for over half an hour while the owner of the truck waited for the verdict. In the meantime, Melissa spoke to the man a couple of times and brought him a cup of coffee which he readily accepted.

I could not tell what he was thinking. Was he just hoping that it would run well enough for an antique auto show? The vehicle was over sixty years old. Perhaps, he wanted more. The worries showing on his face said serious problems had to be bothering him.

The boss finally came back out of the office. Naturally, I found a reason to join them in the lobby.

Clutch said, "Melissa, would you go over this with Mr. Hernandez?" He handed her a clipboard with several sheets attached. "I've got to check on a problem with the Dodge Dart that Dave is working on in the third bay. He can't seem to get the timing right. I'll come right back if there are any questions."

He spoke to the man, who had already risen from his chair. "Mr. Hernandez, we can fix it for you but you'll have to leave it here for a couple of weeks. Also, I'm afraid it won't be cheap."

Clutch nearly bumped into me on his way out of the lobby. He said, "Why are you in the waiting room? Have you nothing to do? This is a repair shop not a vintage vehicle museum." He started toward the door into the garage.

I blocked his path. "Are you going to let me in on this?" I pointed in the direction of the pickup still sitting in front of the first bay.

"Maybe. Maybe not. Now get out of my way and get back to work or you're fired."

"You can't fire me. I know too much," I chuckled at my very clever retort.

Clutch stepped around me and pulled open the door into the garage. "Melissa, fire Ted please. I have more important things to do."

With a bemused expression, Melissa said, "Get back to work, Ted."

I glanced at Mr. Hernandez and rolled my eyes in a fake show of disgust before defiantly moseying back to whatever more mundane task I was supposed to be doing.

The man looked confused by our antics. At least, the glum expression was gone.

Melissa took Hernandez by the elbow and guided him away from the front door. Two new arrivals were coming in for help.

"I'll be right with you," she said to them.

Melissa put the clipboard on the counter for Mr. Hernandez to see the numbers.

My stroll back out of the lobby was slow enough to hear him ask Melissa if he could do cleaning work for the garage to pay for the repairs to his truck.

"We don't really need the help right now," Melissa answered.

"OK, I understand." Hernandez sighed. He was halfway out the front entrance before turning back. "Can I leave the truck here a few days while I try to raise the money?"

"Let me talk to the boss," Melissa answered. She carried the clipboard with her into the garage. When at work, Clutch and his wife referred to each other as the boss even though all of us on the staff saw them as full and equal partners in the business.

Melissa handed the clipboard to Clutch and hurried right back to the lobby to deal with the newcomers. Clutch followed a minute later and I tagged along behind him.

He said, "Mr. Hernandez, Melissa told me about your offer to help out but we already have arrangements for a cleaning service."

"Sir, I could do the repairs myself but I don't have the tools."

He was clearly uneasy in front of the other two customers in the lobby's waiting area. They were so tuned in to the conversation, it seemed impolite to me. In fact, I wished I had not been there myself to see how discouraged the man looked.

To his credit, Clutch recognized the potential for embarrassment. He said, "Let's go into the office, Señor Hernandez.* Do you really believe you could overhaul that engine?" They moved around the counter and went through the door into the room where the paperwork was done for the business.

I looked at Melissa but she turned her head. I avoided eye contact with the customers in the room and returned once more to my job in the garage.

It seemed like a long time for Clutch to be talking to a customer. It had to be over an hour before he called to me from the doorway, "Ted, can you come in here for a few minutes?"

---

* According to the naming convention observed by their families in Mexico, Angel Carlos Hernandez y Rosado had a first name, a middle name, and two last names. His first last name was his father's first last name. His second last name was his mother's first last name.

The convention is the same for women until they marry. A woman keeps her first last name and takes her husband's first last name as her second last name. The conjunction 'y' meaning 'and' is replaced by the conjunction 'de' for 'of.'

The conjunction can be omitted. Using it is optional in all cases.

The centuries-old naming convention is patriarchal in the sense that the surnames on the father's side persist while they are lost after one generation on the mother's side.

There are no hard rules for first and middle given names. They are chosen to honor relatives or favorite saints or personalities.

"Sure. What do you need?" I followed him around the counter in the lobby and into the office.

"Ted, this is Angel Hernandez y Rosado. Angel, this is Ted O'Connor. Ted is the shop foreman here."

To hear my title felt good. It was the first time I had been introduced that way. "How do you do, Mr. Hernandez. Sorry I am out of business cards to hand you."

It was a pointed remark in front of the owner and it worked. About a week later, Theodore C. O'Connor, Shop Foreman, was emblazoned on a stack of cards in the desk-top racks for Clutch and Melissa on the counter in the lobby.

"Please, just call me Angel," the man said.

We shook hands.

Clutch continued, "Ted, can we let Mr. Hernandez use the fourth bay for a few days to work on his truck?"

"I guess so. We have not been using it lately. We could be but we are so shorthanded right now. How much help will you need, Mr. Hernandez?"

Clutch answered for him. "Angel tells me that he can do the repairs on the Ford F-1 by himself. He just needs the tools and the hoist."

"When does he start?" I asked Clutch who turned to Mr. Hernandez.

"Tomorrow morning, please," he said.

"OK. Come in when you are ready tomorrow and I will help you get started."

"Well, now, that may be where we have snookered you a bit, Ted. Angel likes to get started early," Clutch said. There was a tentative grin on his face. The expression was fair warning of something I might not like.

"How early?"

140

"I have a job in the evenings, Mr. O'Connor. I have to be there at four in the afternoon. So, I will need to be leaving here by three each day. Also, I have children I must look after."

Clutch added, "Ted, the F-1 pickup is the Hernandez family car and they need to get it back quickly. It is how they haul groceries home from the supermarket."

"Uh-huh. What are you guys trying to tell me? You have not answered the question. Mr. Hernandez, how early?"

"Four o'clock."

"No!" My immediate reaction was nearly a shout. "Not a minute before five," I said. Oops, I thought what have I just gotten flamboozled into?

"Oh, OK," Hernandez agreed. He acted disappointed over the starting time but I think he was also at least somewhat relieved.

Clutch and I followed him out of the office into the lobby.

"See you tomorrow morning," he said and started to leave but did not go.

"Yes. See you tomorrow," I said.

A long moment later, he said, "Mr. Clutch, tell Dave in bay three to take a link or two out of the timing chain in that Dodge sedan. I think it might be stretched out." With that, Mr. Hernandez hurried off down the street.

Clutch watched him go with his mouth agape. He said, "Ted, see if we have a new timing chain in the parts department." He walked back into the office laughing and shaking his head.

Chapter 38 . It can be hard to find a good mechanic.

After Hernandez left the shop, Clutch explained that the man was new in town and could not afford to spend a lot on repairs. He had just moved here from the city with his family for a janitorial job because that was all he could find.

Angel's employer had contracts for the after-hours cleaning of commercial buildings in Batavia. His wife was working as a maid at the Holiday Inn Express. They were expecting their fifth child in December.

"You're a good man, Clutch."

"I know but don't tell anybody. Now get back to work. I don't want to have to tell Ms. Reynolds that we could not get a simple brake job done when we've had her Lacrosse for two days already."

"It's a LeSabre."

"Whatever."

By the end of the day, the Dodge Dart had a new timing chain and its motor was purring more smoothly than a feline with catnip. Ms. Reynolds had picked up her car. We were ready for more challenging tasks.

One of the mechanics was having trouble with a Plymouth Horizon, which did not surprise me. I knew it could be tricky. I decided to wait till morning to lend a hand.

I went back to talk to the boss. "Why me, Clutch?" I asked.

"Why you what?"

"You know what I'm asking. Why do you want me to lose time working with Hernandez?"

"I thought you would catch on to that," he replied. "Angel Hernandez was working as a mechanic in Las Minitas, Sonora, Mexico, before he and his family immigrated to the United States."

"So, you want me to see if he is any good."

"You said yourself that we are shorthanded."

"Ah, I think I get it now. Without actually hiring him, we can check the man out to see how good he is," I ventured.

"You make it sound a bit crass but we are not doing him any harm. In fact, we're going out on a limb for him. We are giving Hernandez the only possible chance in the world for getting that rattle trap fixed, which is not a sure thing."

"Sorry if I sounded critical. I actually like the idea of working with Hernandez to see if he has what it takes before offering him a job. We've made our share of mistakes with hires who could screw up most any job."

"Yeah, remember that kid who couldn't inflate a tire."

"Be fair, Clutch. That was only because he glued the valve core open."

We both got a good chuckle out of that one.

Clutch got back on topic. "It is not just to see if he is a good mechanic. I've talked to him and I'm pretty sure Hernandez knows his way around a garage."

"What else?"

"Before offering him a job, we need to know what we might be getting into. Can he be trusted? Are there issues of legality? It would be good to find out why he left Mexico."

"You always do a criminal background check. It's just a good business practice."

"Mr. Hernandez asked me not to."

"Oh, he's got something to hide. That can't be good."

"I suspect Mr. Hernandez does not have valid papers for being here. He showed me his green card and it looked all right but who knows how he might have acquired it."

"Does he have a social security card?" I asked.

"Yes and we will be paying into it."

"But, the number might not be his." I finished the thought for Clutch. After a moment of thought, I said, "You know his wife must have a social security number. The Holiday Inn is not likely to be fooled by phony credentials."

"True enough."

"So, what do we know about Angel Hernandez?" I asked. "You must have asked him about his background."

"Of course. He said he understood the need for due diligence."

"Which means he had ready answers."

"Not so much. He was hesitant with details about his former employer. Finally, I made it clear he had to tell me what I needed to know to let him work here."

"You must have gotten something. You are letting him into the garage."

"Naw, I figure life's a risk. If I can let the likes of O'Connor into the garage, why not some Mexican refugee."

The smirk on Clutch's face told me he was pleased with his own attempt at a bit of humor.

He said, "Sorry, Ted. Just joking."

"I know."

"Here's my understanding of what Hernandez told me. The clientele at the garage where he worked in Mexico included some very shady characters. He overheard and witnessed more than they wanted him to know. It was hard not to see what was going on. It became clear the owners were complicit in running drugs. He refused to participate in the business, which made them uneasy about him. Two years ago, when it became clear that the safety of his family was at stake, he fled to the United States."

"It's a believable story," I said. "It would not have to be in Mexico. We hear about similar situations with organized crime in this country."

"That actually occurred to me too."

"So, we go with his story for the time being?" I asked.

"I guess so," Clutch gave his answer.

I looked out toward the bays in the garage and hesitated for a moment. "We have two problems with the current plan."

"Which are?"

"The fourth bay does not have a built-in hoist and our foldable shop crane is broken."

"I know. I told Mr. Hernandez he would have to fix it. But, move him to the second bay if you wish."

"I think I will. It would be easier to evaluate his work if he is not saddled with that clunky thing. The downside is I'll have to move to the fourth bay."

"I'd rather have you next to Hernandez in one or three but I'll leave that up to you. What's the other problem?"

"Who is paying for it?"

"That's another risk entirely. We are. If he turns out to be good and comes to work for us, it will be worth it. If not, we will get him to pay what he can and eat the rest."

"Can we find parts for a relic like that?"

"That's a third problem. Not new parts and not easily. There are plenty of sources for used parts. Ford made a lot of pickups in the late forties and fifties but it might be hard to find the models that meet the right specs."

"They are all in junkyards now," I said.

"Almost all," Clutch chuckled.

"Except the one sitting in front of our garage."

Clutch continued, "I started looking after Hernandez left and I found a flat head, six-cylinder engine at the salvage yard over in Socorro. Hernandez wants to overhaul the engine that he's got but it is in worse shape than he knows or cares to admit. I am going to tell him to take the Silverado and go over to Socorro to check it out. He can bring it back if he thinks it will work."

"Wow. You really are getting involved in this adventure. Sometimes you surprise me, Clutch, but I like it. It should be fun," I said.

"I agree. Given your love for antique cars, I figured you would enjoy seeing this one through."

When I got to the garage, the next morning, Angel Hernandez was waiting for me. It was not quite ten after five. I just couldn't get there any earlier but I did bring coffee from Dunkin Donuts for both of us. He seemed grateful.

I unlocked the building and turned on the lights. We pushed the Ford F-1 pickup into the second bay and the man went to work. I sat down in the lobby with my coffee and yesterday's New York Times.

Coincidently, there was an article in the Business Section about a company struggling to stay afloat. A whistleblower had reported finding evidence that some of their funding was provided by the drug trade in western Texas. Just the business that Angel Hernandez had run away from.

After a while, I decided what the hell. It did not seem right for our guest to be hard at work while I was taking it easy. I pulled the sheet on the Plymouth Horizon in the third bay and joined the man in the garage.

It was a fortuitous move because Clutch was pleased to find me working when he showed up shortly after 5:30 AM. It took me by surprise and made Angel quite anxious.

"What are you doing here? You have never been up at this hour in your life." I jeered.

"I know, right?" Clutch laughed. "I have an idea for the Ford F-1."

"Is everything all right?" Angel worried.

"Yeah, Angel. Everything is fine."

The anxiety on the man's face was as obvious as a backfiring engine.

Clutch noticed the reaction. "Look, Angel. We are as good as our word here. No one is going to pull the rug out from under you."

"OK," he whispered.

"Don't take the head off that block just yet, Angel. I have another idea that might help."

Clutch walked Angel out the front of the garage. He handed him a sheaf of notes on a clipboard and a paper map. Their conversation was not loud enough for me to make out everything they said over the garage noise.

"No, you don't have to do that." Angel raised his voice to object to whatever Clutch had said.

I could hear Clutch's answer. He said, "Let me explain again. This could turn out to be good for both of us."

"I can't accept it. How will I repay you?"

"We will figure something out. Look, it is your only chance to get the truck running. You know I am right. I have to insist." Clutch's decision was firm.

He slapped Angel on the shoulder and they stepped back toward the garage bay where I was pretending to be hard at work. Clutch went into the office to get something.

When he came out and started for his car, I asked, "What's going on?"

"Oh, sorry, Ted. I thought you could hear my proposal for Angel. In fact, you already know about it. I was just telling Angel about the motor in the salvage yard in Socorro. The two of you, talk about it among yourselves." Clutch gave me a hopeful look. "I've got to get back home. Melissa's going to think I ran away."

Chapter 39 . Children must be watched over.

"Mr. Clutch is getting me a new motor." Angel was incredulous.

"It's not going to be new, Angel. Nothing about a Ford F-1 pickup is new. It's an antique"

"The salvage yard manager at the salvage yard told Mr. Clutch that their pickup had very few miles on it before it was in an accident that twisted the frame beyond repair.

"Yeah, I know," Angel chuckled. He did not get the humor in Clutch's use of the phrase "talk among yourselves" but he did appreciate the truth in my comment about his old truck.

"The job has changed. You should not dismantle the engine that's in there. You want to lift it out in one piece," I told him.

"Yes, of course," he said. "The job might also be a lot easier than trying to fix what's wrong."

"Fixing what's in there might not even be possible."

"Oh, I've seen worse in the old country." Angel sounded like my immigrant grandparents talking about getting off the boat from Ireland.

"I agree that unbolting the engine mounts should be straightforward. Also, disconnecting the fuel lines and exhaust system should not be hard but the transmission is another matter."

"It's a manual transmission and Mr. Clutch said I should try to bring the transmission with the new motor from Socorro."

"There you go calling it new again," I chided.

Angel didn't say anything. I couldn't tell if he was offended but I didn't think so.

We had only been working another half an hour when Angel walked out into the parking area in front of the building. Both of our bay doors were open to the cool early morning air. I looked out to see where he had gone. He was talking to a woman by the entrance to the lobby.

He saw me and said, "I'll be right back. My wife is on her way to work."

I did not go out to meet her. I would have introduced myself but she was looking away as if anxious about something. Perhaps, the woman was in a hurry to get to her job.

A few minutes later, Angel returned to the garage through the lobby instead of directly from the driveway. In another ten minutes, I thought I heard him speaking to someone. I looked up to see that he was back at the door to the lobby.

By that time, the Plymouth seemed to be running pretty well. I decided to delegate the test drive to another mechanic. No point in leaving Mr. Hernandez alone even if only for a few minutes. I went back to the counter in the lobby to find out what else was on the day's docket.

I was startled by the quiet presence of four children sitting across the room in the corner of the waiting area. They appeared to be between the ages of three and ten. I knew who they were right away.

I went to the phone and got Eileen out of bed. It took her under half an hour to get to the garage all scrubbed and dressed for the day. What a great daughter!

Eileen took the children to Dunkin Donuts for milk and a sweet roll on my dime. She escorted them to school and hurried to get to her own classes a little bit late. Eileen had to carry the three-year-old the last two blocks to her day-care center on the way to the grade school.

Angel protested, of course. However, Eileen and I prevailed. She insisted that she would love to get to know the children.

Their father admonished them in Spanish. Eileen translated for me, "Christina, Junior, Miguel, and you too Elsa, do what Ms. O'Connor tells you."

Shortly after eight o'clock, Clutch was back at work. He came over to the second bay with a set of keys. The engine block from the F-1 was already hanging from the hoist. It dangled free of its mounts in the engine compartment between the front fenders.

"Thank you, sir." Angel took the keys and drove off in the Silverado. Clutch looked my way and shrugged as he walked past me on his way to the office.

Chapter 40 . Old fashioned methods are fascinating.

It was well into the afternoon and Angel had still not returned. I was beginning to worry but, if Clutch was concerned, he did not show it. It turned out that the boss was right.

The Silverado coasted to a stop in front of the garage a little after two o'clock. There was an engine sitting in the truck's bed. Angel had removed it himself from the wreck at the salvage yard in Socorro. They helped him load it up for the drive back to Batavia.

Mark Steiger drove in right behind him. He was returning from the test-drive for the Horizon that had my attention earlier in the day. The two stood admiring the engine in the Silverado. Mark helped Angel drag the foldable shop crane from the fourth bay and showed him the broken joint.

"This piece of junk is not worth your effort. Why not wait for a hoist that works?" Mark asked. "Ted should be finished with that GMC before the end of the day." He pointed to the Acadia that I was servicing.

Mark went into the office to finish the paperwork on the Plymouth Horizon. In the meantime, Angel not only got the portable hoist working but also had the engine up in the air out of the bed of the Silverado faster than Mark could wipe the surprised expression from his face. It was quite amusing to see the reaction.

The rest of the operation was a case of musical chairs. Mark pulled the Silverado forward leaving the engine from the salvage yard hanging from the tripod in the driveway. We helped Angel roll the gutless pickup under the replacement motor. He lowered it into place and attached the engine mounts.

Angel had to get back into the second bay to work on the remaining, tricky connections. We freed up the space by dropping the old blown engine into the now empty bed of the Silverado.

Two days later, the Ford truck sputtered and coughed to life. All that remained was a proper tune-up. Angel's approach was a bit old-fashioned.

He repeatedly removed the cap and loosened and twisted the carburetor. The growl of the engine improved with each iteration but he was not done yet.

Angel pulled a strobe from his own toolbox and focused the light on the fly wheel behind the fan belt. He had a neat trick for holding the device in place by clipping it to the top of the radiator. It looked like a custom-made clamp that he might have fabricated himself. Angel adjusted and readjusted the timing until the mark illuminated by the strobe was right where he wanted it.

"It's sounding pretty good," Clutch said.

We thought the job was done but Angel was evidently not completely satisfied because the visiting mechanic went over to the side of the paved area in front of the garage and pawed around in the scrub grass looking for something. When he turned to walk back, he had a pebble in his hands that he was rubbing clean with his fingers.

He placed it on the front left-side fender of the pickup and motioned for Mary Gallagher to get into the driver's seat. She was one of the two high-school seniors to whom Clutch had given summer jobs at the garage. Mary and a few others including myself and Clutch were standing around gawking at Angel's demonstration of mechanical know-how.

The youngster climbed in and revved the engine. Angel told her to hold it at a couple of hundred rpm while he watched for vibrations. It took several more tweaks before the pebble was completely still.

"All right, That's good." The smile on his face was brighter than the light from the strobe. Angel was satisfied.

Piston knock was imperceptible to the human ear. The engine was purring more quietly than I thought possible for such an antique. Angel called his thanks to the young woman behind the wheel and she switched off the ignition.

While his technique with the pebble for tuning the engine was effective and interesting to observe, there were technological advances at the Batavia Service Center that made tuning an engine more of a science than an art. I was pleased to find opportunities in the future to show Angel how to use some of our electronic equipment.

The following Saturday morning, Diane played with the Hernandez children at the park. Eileen relieved her at noon and brought the four children over to the garage at about four o'clock.

Their mother stepped off the bus and hurried over from the stop on Central Boulevard. She arrived just a few minutes after Eileen and the children. She came into the shop to thank me and Clutch for everything we had done for their family. Angel took her directly into the office with Melissa and Clutch while I kept working and Eileen played with the children in the lobby.

A bit later, I noticed Angel and his wife were in the lobby hugging the children and talking to Eileen. I stopped what I was doing and joined them.

"This is my wife, Iola Valdez de Hernandez," Angel said.* "Iola, this is Mr. O'Connor."

'Thank you for everything, Mr. O'Connor, and thank you for Eileen and Diane taking care of my children."

"Nice to meet you, Iola. You are very welcome and please call me Ted."

Angel said, "Iola, take the children outside while I talk to Mr. O'Connor and his daughter."

"No, Angel. I will talk to them about the children," she answered.

Angel was clearly startled by Iola's bold dissent but he started for the door anyway. "Come," he said. At the one word, the children followed.

Before he got out the door, Eileen spoke up, "Por favor, Señor y Señora Hernandez, I am studying Spanish in school and I am not doing very well. The teacher tells me I need practice. If you will allow your children to teach me to speak Spanish, mi hermano Diane and I will babysit for them after school and on Saturdays."

"Oh, sí, sí," Iola's oldest child exclaimed. The others squealed with delight.

When her parents hesitated, Christina continued, "You should say hermana, Eileen, not hermano. See Mama, we have to help Eileen."

The children snickered. Their parents gave in with the stipulation that we must come over for dinner.

---

* When Iola Alicia Valdez de Hernandez got married, she adhered to her family's naming convention by keeping her first last name and taking her husband's first last name as her second last name.

Chapter 41 . There was a job opening at the garage.

Angel Hernandez turned out to be a great asset in the repair shop at the Batavia Service Center. Even before he was finished with his pickup, he had pitched in to assist when an extra pair of hands were needed on one of our paying jobs. He hardly had to be asked. The man seemed to notice opportunities for him to be a valued guest in our garage.

The following week, Clutch offered Mr. Hernandez a full-time job. He jumped at the chance and we were rewarded with a superior mechanic from whom all of us could learn a few things. We also got a talented addition to our AAU baseball team.

Our opponents soon found it to be unwise to hit the ball anywhere up the middle. Hernandez could scoop up anything within a mile of his shortstop position and throw out the fleetest of foot before they got close to first base.

The guy could hit too. He quickly replaced me as the RBI leader on the team. Singles and doubles were soon raining down all over the outfield.

Angel had played professional baseball for a time in Mexico. He even had major league scouts stop over to watch him play but that was as far as it went. Family came first for Angel and Iola. Life was good for the extended Hernandez-Valdez clan in the Las Minitas community until it wasn't.

My Mexican friend gradually opened up about his family's former life in their homeland. He talked about how trouble managed to find just about everyone in their region of the country.

Late one afternoon, as we were closing up the garage, Angel seemed to need someone to listen. We were about to leave for home at the end of a productive day.

"You did good work today, Angel. We got a lot done. Clutch will be pleased when he gets back tomorrow."

Angel looked toward the setting sun and replied, "It is nice in this country. We miss home but there is no going back."

"I guess things were not too pleasant for you in Las Minitas," I said.

"No, not good at all." Angel held his breath for a moment before he said, "Iola's uncle was killed in a dispute with the leader of the Mendoza Cartel. We tried to go on as usual by keeping a low profile but there was no escaping the violence." There was a wistful tone to his voice.

"Those were rough times." I filled the silence.

"Very early one morning, we heard the horn go off in my truck. I ran out to shut it off. One of the patron's men was sitting behind the wheel. He told me, 'Mr. Mendoza wants to see you.'"

"That could not have been good. What did you do?"

"The man drove off in my truck. He had my keys. I hang the key ring on a hook by the door. He had been in my house."

"Your Ford truck?"

Angel nodded.

"How did you get it back?"

"I went back in the house. Iola was already packing clothes in our old suitcase and in boxes. 'We have to get out of here,' she said to me." He paused for a long time. "Those were bad times."

He stopped talking again. We just sat in silence on the low wall in front of the entrance to the lobby. I couldn't be sure if Angel had said all he wanted.

Finally, I asked, "Angel, do you want to come over to the house for a while?"

"No, I better get home. The children have things to do. Iola likes me to help with the baby."

I said, "You are a god father to those children, Angel."

We stood up and started moving toward the pickup.

Angel continued, "It was a long walk over to the patron's ranch. It took me more than two hours that morning. When I got there, my truck was out front. His protectors, who are always hanging around the place, told me that the patron did not have time for me. They said I should come back later. I didn't say anything. I just held out my hand and the man who took my truck threw the keys on the ground at my feet.

"By the time I got back to our house, Iola had the children and everything ready to go. We sat in the parlor just looking around at everything we had to leave behind. Iola would not cry. Not out loud anyway. She was determined like steel that we had to go. The children and I prayed with her. 'Please, God, a safe journey. Holy Mother Mary, watch over us.'"

"What about the children? How much did they understand?"

"Christina, our oldest, understood. She asked me, 'Will they chase us?' I did not answer because, of course, they would. I thought about how far we had to go to be free of them. Iola was thinking it too. 'Get the tractor from the barn and pull it up by the milk shed,' she told me."

"Were you trying to take the tractor too?"

"No, No," Angel chuckled at my question. "Parking the tractor where it would be seen was a good idea. It made it look like we were home because I never left it outside unless I was in the house for lunch or siesta or something."

"Were you a farmer too?"

"No, not really. We had a few acres where we grew some chili and corn. You asked a good question about the tractor. I hated leaving my old John Deere behind."

"Tell me about it."

"I picked the tractor up at a junk yard. It wouldn't start when I got it. I paid too much for it but I recognized it as the powerful model that the company didn't make anymore. It lived up to its reputation once I got it running."

"That was a shame to leave it behind," I concurred. "You did manage to hang onto the F-1." We were standing next to the pickup. I reached over and patted a waxed and polished front fender.

"Yes, I did," Angel smiled. "The whole family got into the truck with all of our things under a tarp in the bed and we headed toward Heroica Nogales."

"How far was that?"

"Far but we didn't go there. I stopped to fill up the truck in town. I knew the kid pumping gas was part of La Familia. I told him I was coming back to visit Mr. Mendoza in another day and I turned around and drove toward our house. At the next turn-off, I circled back toward Nogales.

"When we got north of town, we changed direction and drove to Ciudad Juarez instead. It was further away but Iola said going there would be enough to fool Mendoza's men if they did come looking for us. We never knew for sure but I imagine they did. I knew too much. Iola too.

"We crossed into the United States and applied for asylum in El Paso. The application is still under review.

I am supposed to check in with the immigration office every month."

"Iola too?"

"No, Iola is a citizen. She was born at Saint Mary's Hospital in Tucson, Arizona."

Chapter 42 . Immigrant life was a marvel.

For the next two and a half years, Angel Hernandez and his family were a part of our lives in the town of Batavia. During the summers, he joined us at the ballpark on Wednesday and Friday evenings. Iola and the children would show up with a picnic basket.

Their oldest two, Christina and Junior, wanted to be part of the fun. They retrieved bats from around home plate for both teams when a hitter got on base. They delivered baseballs to the umpire and ran after foul balls. They were the Batavia team's "bat boys" to use a gender specific term for both the girl and the boy.

Angel asked me to be the Godfather for their new baby boy whom they named Liam. A woman from the Holiday Inn Express was the Godmother.

It was an unexpected and humbling honor for me. Lydia, Diane, and Eileen attended the ceremony with me at Saint Ann's Catholic Church. It was a nice service.

At the end, there was a noisy reception filled with cheerful people laughing and talking. Although everyone tried to be friendly and inclusive, most of the chattering was in Spanish.

Eileen was in her glory jabbering away with what she told me was her garbled Spanglish. Diane was too reserved to say much even though she is probably a bit further along with the language than Eileen.

The girls talked to the Hernandez children at the reception. They were well acquainted after all the babysitting and trips to Dunkin Donuts. On the way home, Diane said, "Christina doesn't know how to drive."

"Is she old enough?" I wondered aloud.

"Yes, I think so. Or, maybe not," Diane said. "I told her I would teach her anyway and she said, 'OK, but don't tell my Dad.'"

Lydia squawked at her daughter, "Well don't tell me either. I don't want to hear about it."

Eileen said, "Diane, you have to teach me to drive before you teach Christina. Isn't that right, Dad?"

"Hell, no," I hollered.

Eileen's smirk was audible. She got me again.

Diane said, "Eileen, you are not old enough yet."

"I am very mature, Diane."

"Mature? News to me," Lydia teased her little girl.

"All you people who were born in the previous millennium simply cannot understand how capable we are," Eileen pontificated.

Diane just rolled her eyes.

On the evening before the Baptism, Lydia and I visited with Godmother Rosalie Ortega at the preparation meeting. Her parents immigrated from Mexico many years ago. She and Iola were about the same age. They looked out for each other at work.

When Iola started at the Holiday Inn Express, Rosalie had already been there a while. She explained the bus routes to Iola and they started riding to work together every day.

Rosalie said, "I told Iola that I used to drive but my car was broken down. The next day, her husband showed up at my house with his tools in their old truck."

I said, "Don't tell me, Rosalie. I can guess."

She laughed, "You're right. He had my jalopy running like a top in ten minutes."

"Naw, not even Angel Hernandez is that good."

"OK, maybe it was half an hour but my old four-door Mercury Sable has been running great ever since."

Angel Hernandez was a good man. His work ethic and devotion to family were something to be admired. I enjoyed working with him and I know that watching how the younger man lived had a positive effect on me.

Most days for the next several months, Angel would look pretty haggard when he got to work. "Your Godson can be trouble." He groaned.

"Yes, I've seen him. To be lively is good."

"I guess so," he said but it was a half-hearted answer. Exasperation was simmering below the surface.

"Send Liam over to our house. We can entertain him for a few hours."

"Thanks." The offer cheered him up.

My sobriety was something Angel took seriously. I knew he liked a glass of wine with dinner. He could down a few bottles of beer too. However, he never touched the stuff when I was around.

The liquor remained hidden away at his house when I was there. It was coffee or water on the infrequent occasions when he and I and perhaps one or two others from the shop went out for lunch.

"Angel understands," Iola told me one day at our house. "There is alcoholism in his family. Mine too. One of my uncles died of cirrhosis of the liver."

Unfortunately, it was a short-lived honor to work with Angel Hernandez and to know him and his family.

Chapter 43 . The pickup was at the garage.

A valued employee at the Batavia Service Center did not show up for work one morning in May of 2015. It had never happened before. I got worried and called Angel's home at about ten o'clock but no one answered.

"Do you think something is wrong?" Clutch was as concerned as I was.

"I hope not. I'll go over to the house on my lunch hour."

"That would be good. Thanks."

A neighbor, whom I had met before, was in the yard next door. He told me that the immigration police had been there that morning looking for Señor Hernandez but the family was not home.

When I got back to the garage, Angel's pickup was parked around the side of the shop but he was not there.

Two agents from Immigration and Customs Enforcement were in the lobby talking to Clutch. They asked me where they could find Angel Hernandez and his family. I admitted Angel and I were friends but I did not know where they were.

When I said I was Godfather to their youngest child, it was all they needed to hear. Their questioning turned into a grilling.

Clutch moved back out of their line of sight. He glared at me and shook his head. It was a signal to be more guarded with what I had to say. The two men clearly did not have Angel's best interests in mind.

Slow study that I may be, I stopped volunteering details. I insisted the Hernandez family were good people but I had no idea where they might have gone. I did not tell them that the pickup truck on the premises belonged to Mr. Hernandez.

The agents proceeded to lectured us in demeaning terms. "You know that we have a serious problem with illegal immigrants in this country."

"Yes, I've read that," I acknowledged with a shrug.

"Some people get themselves in real trouble by sheltering the illegals when they should be more cooperative with law enforcement."

"Yeah, I guess," I said.

"What do you mean guess? True Americans know their obligations."

Clutch jumped in. "Of course, of course. My employees are very patriotic about our civic duties as citizens of the United States."

The agents drove off and came back a few minutes later. They sat across the street in their car. I presumed they were watching for Hernandez. They finally gave up after waiting for nearly an hour. Before they left, the younger of the two came over to instruct us to contact them immediately if we heard from anyone in the family.

As soon as he was sure they were gone, Clutch told me that Diane was looking for me. She had arrived in Angel's truck and parked it there at the garage while I was out for lunch.

"Your daughter needs to talk to you." His expression was serious.

"OK, I better see what she wants." I turned to leave.

"Don't go home," Clutch cautioned. "Diane said to meet her at Allen's Diner. She said she would be there at two-thirty."

I tried to keep busy but the more I spun my wheels the more frayed my nerves. Finally, I snuck out the back door across the paved parking area where the jobs in our queue wait for parts.

I went out through the gate in the chain link fence into the alley and crossed the street. The large round clock over the window to the kitchen at Allen's Diner said 2:27 PM when I walked in.

Diane was in a booth off to the side away from the front windows. "Mr. Hernandez and his family are at our house," she said as soon as I sat down.

"All seven of them?"

She nodded.

"What happened?"

"Mr. Hernandez knocked on the back door right after you left the house. I was still in bed, of course," she said, with a wry smile on her face. "Eileen and I came downstairs to see what was going on."

"Are they OK? Iola and the children?"

"Yes, the whole family. I think they are all right but I don't understand what is happening. Who could be after them? They were hiding on our back porch."

"Did your Mother let them in?"

"They didn't want to come in. I couldn't follow what was going on. Do you know?"

"I might. Tell me what happened."

"Mom sent me to look out the front door to see if anyone was coming. No one was around. So, Mom told Eileen to take all of them up into the loft over the garage."

"How did they get to our house?"

"Mom asked Mr. Hernandez, 'Where is the truck? We should move it.' He handed her the keys."

I said, "I just saw it at the Service Center."

"I know. I put it there. As soon as he told Mom where it was parked, she gave me the keys and I ran down to the corner, jumped in, and drove it over there."

"Good."

"I went inside to look for you. The other mechanics saw me. Mary Gallagher was there too. Dave Green said you went to check on Mr. Hernandez."

"Mary's been coming in to help out one day a week as part of a work-study program at the junior college. What did you tell them?"

"Nothing. I went in the office and talked to Clutch. He said not to tell anyone about their whereabouts. He said he did not want to know either. I asked him what I should do with the keys. He took them and said he would write up a work order like the truck was there for repairs. I walked home and came back here in my car."

"Good."

"What should we do? Why are they hiding?"

"Someone complained about the family to Immigration and Customs Enforcement."

"Who would do that?"

"I don't know. Some useless bastard."

My daughter did not seem surprised or put off by my language.

"Go to work, Diane, as if nothing happened. I will call your mother from the garage and we will figure out a plan."

"Work can wait. I'm going back to the shop with you."

When Lydia answered the phone, I said, "Two ICE agents are looking for Angel Hernandez."

"The two men are here now."

"Are they in the house?"

"Yes, here in the kitchen. Do you know if the baby was baptized?"

It took me a minute before I realized that quick-thinking Lydia had improvised a coded message. Angel Hernandez was hiding at Godmother Rosalie Ortega's residence.

I played along. "Yeah, I think so. Why do you ask?"

"Maybe, they are at the church."

"I suppose that is possible."

"By the way, I can't pick you up today. I don't have the car." There was more hidden information in her words. Lydia had given Angel and Iola her car.

"OK, I can walk home after work today."

"We can go over to the supermarket on Virginia Street tomorrow afternoon," Lydia said.

"Sounds good." I hung up.

"What did Mom mean by that? Virginia Street is all residential and some professional buildings. Mom's office is over there."

Nothing wrong with Diane's hearing. She picked up every word from her chair next to where I was standing in the office.

"Your mother was talking to me in riddles, Diane. The ICE agents were there eaves dropping on our conversation. I believe I understand what she was trying to say. The Hernandez's have your mother's car. They will leave it near her office on Virginia Street. I suspect they are on the run. I think we have to help them. We can figure out how to make things right at another time. In the meantime, we have to get the pickup to them right away. They are at Ortega's house."

"I can drive it over there."

"You might be followed. I have another idea. Let's go talk to Mary Gallagher." The junior mechanic was changing the oil in a sedan in the fourth bay.

"Mary, would you deliver the old Ford truck to a friend's house?"

"Mr. Hernandez's F-1 pickup?" she lit up.

"Yes. Here's the address." I wrote the information for the Ortega's on a shop note pad.

Mary looked at it. "I know exactly where that is. My cousin lives in that part of town. I'll go as soon as I finish up here."

"No, you better go now. Park the truck around behind the house. Leave the keys in the visor like we always do and come right back. Diane will be coming to get you."

"OK. Shall we?" Mary said to Diane.

"You go ahead, Mary. Diane has a quick stop to make but she will catch up to you."

"This will be fun." Mary grabbed the keys and headed out the door.

"Not too much fun," I called after her. "Treat that antique gently, Mary. Both of you, drive carefully. No speeding either one of you."

As soon as the pickup was out of the driveway, I said, "Diane, just leave your car at the diner and take mine. It is less likely to arouse suspicion if you hang back and don't follow close behind Mary. If you are spotted, the ICE agents are more likely to follow you in my car than Mary in an old truck."

"If I see them, I'll just go home and call you from there."

"That's right or you can wonder around a bit first. Mary will have to figure something out if you don't show up."

Angel Hernandez, Iola, and their five children disappeared from our lives on that date.

Mary Gallagher walked over to her cousin's house and gave me a call at the shop. She is still mad at me and my daughter all these years later but the ICE agents followed Diane to a Dunkin Donuts in Socorro and the Hernandez family escaped the scourge of ICE's family-separation plan.

From time to time, I have checked in with Liam's Godmother who is still working at the Holiday Inn Express. About a year ago, Lydia came with me. We went in her car and Lydia drove.

Lydia called first and Rosalie said we were welcome to come right over that Sunday afternoon. It was nice to have Lydia with me because the conversation flowed more easily. We talked about the Hernandez family and how the children must be growing.

"How's the old Mercury running?" Lydia asked. It was not a topic that had occurred to me before.

"Oh, I don't know. I am taking the bus to work."

"What happened?"

"Remember Iola's daughter Christina?"

"Yes, of course, we do."

"Two days after Iola quit her job, Christina showed up at the Holiday Inn. She asked if she could borrow the car. She never brought it back."

"I always wondered how far they could get with the five children in a pick-up truck."

"I was happy to help any way I could," Rosalie said.

"We never hear from them, not a word since they left," I said.

"It is the same with me."

Rosalie Ortega and her husband visited with us on their back patio for a while longer. She served glasses of lemonade. We made vague plans for them to come to our house next time.

We said goodbye. Lydia took the wheel in her car and we drove off. She pulled an envelope from the breast pocket on her blouse and handed it to me.

"Rosalie said I should give this to you."

It was a photograph of a little boy of about four or five standing on a dusty road. There was no name and nothing to give away the location just a house in the background.

I said, "Someday we will travel to Las Minitas and try to track down the family through their cousins. I should know how they are doing. After all, I am Liam's Godfather."

Part IV

Trial and Negligence

It is never too late to be what you might have been.

– George Eliot

Chapter 44 . Trust is fragile; Friendship endures.

My friendship with Elmer Wrightson had been a wonderful treasure in my life but it had lost its luster. He had grown weary of the constant efforts to rescue me from myself. His respect for me had eroded away with my alcoholism and drug abuse. There was little left of our good fellowship well before I entered recovery.

In fact, his disdain was as bad as it could be. My years of irresponsible behavior and self-indulgence turned Elmer Wrightson from loyal friend into a man so alienated that he could entertain the thought of usurping my place with my wife and children. How close she came to giving up on me I do not really know. There may have been a time of serious doubt about our future together. I am eternally grateful that Lydia chose to stick with me in spite of it all.

After I turned the corner toward recovery, my parents kept Elmer informed of my progress. Lydia talked to him too. However, the emotional turmoil that I had put him through made it difficult for Elmer Wrightson to accept me back into his life. Consequently, my plea that he come to my aid in a time of crisis was an audacious presumption. I could only hope that his memory of the bad times had become less painful with the years.

He was always civil but not cordial when we bumped into each other around town. On one occasion, I told Elmer I had earned another year-sober coin and he congratulated me. I got a note on office stationery telling me Wrightson and Associates, PLLC, were pleased with my achievement. The coin was for my fourth AA anniversary.

I did not confront him about his relationship with Lydia and he never brought it up. I believe or, at least, I like to think that his wounds gradually healed with time. Just as my recovery had given me back a good measure of self-respect, perhaps he could find satisfaction from his exemplary dedication to the law.

More than once over the years, there had been stories in the big city newspapers about accomplishments attributed to Wrightson himself or to another member of his firm. The reputation of Wrightson and Associates had become a source of provincial pride in our small town.

Despite our past difficulties, I knew Attorney Wrightson was my best option in Batavia to help with the current crisis. More easily than anyone, he could step into the fray with the stature, dignity, and reputation that commanded respect. Without doubt, I would be best served by his representation in the face of murder and assault charges.

What I did not know as I sat in my cell on that fateful Saturday was could he bring himself to come to my aid once again. Indeed, I was getting worried as the hours dragged by. It was not until nearly three o'clock that I was escorted in handcuffs into the attorney-client conference room. Elmer Wrightson was there to see me. It was a huge relief.

He was all business. After he ordered the restraints removed, Attorney Wrightson began the conversation on a very serious note. "Ted, the police believe you killed Matthew Hennigan with malice of forethought."

"It is a ridiculous, unfounded accusation," I replied.

"Tell me about Friday night."

"You haven't asked me if I did it."

"It never crossed my mind."

The emotional impact of his reflexive affirmation of my character was powerful. It brought home a feeling of sadness for my failures and a powerful sense of relief that I was not alone.

"Thank you," I gulped.

"What I do not know, Ted, is why the police are so certain it was you."

"Neither do I."

"That is not a good answer, Ted. I need more from you. We only have a few minutes now but I will be back tomorrow afternoon to review all possible connections between you and Matthew Hennigan. So, think about it. We will be learning a lot about the District Attorney's case against you on Monday. We need to be prepared."

"On Monday? Will I be locked up until then?" I could not keep the quivering out of my voice.

"Yes, I'm afraid so. I called in a favor with the judge and met with her at one o'clock this afternoon. Naturally, the prosecution was there as well. I asked for you to be released on your own recognizance. The motion was met with vehement opposition by the DA's office."

"Why are they out to get me?"

"There is nothing here to be paranoid about. In cases of a capital offense, it would be unusual for a suspect to be released before the trial. In the face of the prosecution's objections, the judge had no choice but to deny the petition for your release."

"What do you mean before the trial? Will I be going to trial for a crime I did not, could not ever commit?"

Chapter 45 . On Saturday, they threw away the key.

There is no sugar coating the mess you are in, Ted. We must expect an indictment and trial. The lawyers in the District Attorney's office tend to listen to the police. The two institutions are generally on the same side. They shy away from any undue strain on their partnership. When the police make an arrest, attorneys in the prosecutor's office will try for a conviction. The problem in your case is exacerbated by the assault charge. You struck a police officer. If the DA did not come after you, their relationship with the police would be severely tested."

"He had it coming," I muttered.

"That makes very little difference. The men in blue rally around a stricken member of the brotherhood no matter how unpopular he might be. From their perspective, you inflicted humiliation on one of their own. As a result, the DA cannot be seen as going easy on you by agreeing to your release prior to the indictment."

"When will I be indicted?"

"A grand jury will be convened first thing on Monday. In a case like this, it is almost a foregone conclusion that they will return indictments for murder and assault."

"It is all very discouraging, Elmer. I am in jail for something I did not do. I don't know what to think."

"Let me tell you what to think. You are the victim of a mistake that will be corrected. To dwell on worst-case scenarios does no one any good."

"It's hard not to."

"I know. Try not to focus on the negatives. Rather, think about what we can do to make things right."

"I would never hurt the guy. He sponsored our AAU team and ran a good business in town."

"So, you and Hennigan were friends?"

"I didn't say that. We just tolerated each other."

"That might be just as good or even better. The prosecutor can argue that a personal slight turns friendship into hatred while emotions do not run as deep between acquaintances. Try to remember pertinent information and we will talk tomorrow."

"OK. I'll work on it. Can I take notes?"

"Yes, your family is here to see you. They have writing materials for you. I had them wait while I talked to you alone to let you know what is happening. They cannot stay long. I insisted on 45 minutes but the prison guards will be strict about the timing."

"Thank you."

"I think they brought dinner. I smelled something really good on the way in," Elmer smiled.

"Are you staying?"

"No, I can't. I have matters to attend to and I must get back to the office to make plans for your defense. I will come back to see you tomorrow after church. We have work to do. I want to be completely prepared at every moment in the sessions before the judge. A preliminary hearing has been scheduled for ten o'clock Monday morning by which time I will have seen the indictment."

"What happens after that?"

"It's hard to be sure. There might be a quick trial that is over in two weeks with a not-guilty verdict or you could be released on bond with a trial and a favorable decision some weeks into the future."

"Exonerated in both cases, right?"

"Absolutely. Listen, I have gotten authorization for your family to bring you a few items. In addition to pen and paper, you can have reading materials and things to eat. I will leave that up to them. Also, they can arrange for a priest or minister to say a prayer with you if you wish. Tomorrow is Sunday. I won't bother with any other non-essential matters for now. I have to remain focused. There are neighbors and witnesses to interview."

It was an intensely emotional gathering with Lydia, Diane, and Eileen after Wrightson left us alone. We got angry at such bad luck. We laughed and cried. We talked about good times in the past. We wondered how the Hernandez family and my Godson Liam were doing. We avoided talking about the serious trouble I was in.

Chapter 46 . On Sunday, the defense attorney heard my story.

The vicar from Elmer Wrightson's church visited me in my cell at noon on Sunday. He asked me to pray with him. He gave me a blessing. He did not stay long. There were two other prisoners for him to see.

Wrightson sent a message with the vicar. He wanted him to emphasize that we had work to do. Elmer would be there to see me at two o'clock.

The regular time for visiting the imprisoned in the Batavia jail was four o'clock in the afternoon and it had to be arranged in advance. Spiritual counseling was allowed only on Sunday notwithstanding the day of the week appropriate for a prisoner's particular religious observance. Consultations with your attorney could be scheduled at any time on any day.

Elmer Wrightson arrived at the promised hour and told me, "I asked the family not to come by to see you today because we have a lot to do to be ready for tomorrow. I called the house and spoke to Diane yesterday evening."

"How are they taking all of this?"

"They are doing very well under the circumstances. I believe your family will be a strength we can rely on."

Wrightson repeated what he had said to me on Saturday, "The District Attorney is convinced that they have a strong case against you."

"It just doesn't make any sense."

"It does to the prosecution. They will have witnesses to call and evidence to present. We have already heard about most of it but there will be more."

"Aren't they obligated to inform you of everything they've got?"

"According to the laws of our state, the District Attorney must make a full disclosure to the defense, which means names of witnesses and a list of the physical evidence. The information must be provided in a timely fashion. We should have everything prior to, during, or immediately after the preliminary hearing tomorrow morning. The judge could allow more time but only for a very good reason."

"What could they have that we do not already know?"

"That is what I need from you. So far, we have the names of some but possibly not all of the witnesses. We have a fair idea of what the witnesses will say in court but there could be surprises. No weapon has been found and there has been no match with the slugs taken from the body."

"Anything else besides the liquor bottle that was planted in my front yard?"

"The District Attorney obtained search warrants for your residence, for the Batavia Service Center, and for your locker and desk at the high school. They searched your house in my presence. It happened while your family was here with you yesterday afternoon. I knew it was coming but I did not tell you about it when I was here because the situation did not have to be any more distressing for you and the family than it already was."

"Unwanted hands rummaging through my private belongings. Lydia's things too. I feel sick. Did they go to the school and the repair shop?"

"No. They accept that you probably went directly home from the crime scene. So, they only searched your residence. The prosecutors are holding the other two warrants for a later time if deemed useful. They are aware that unfruitful searches weaken their case before a jury. They want to avoid the appearance of desperate fishing expeditions."

"If the liquor bottle was found at my house, the killer could have planted the gun there too."

"That is exactly why I had to be there. I had to be ready to explain a murder weapon. Fortunately, it was not there."

"The idea that it could have been is frightening."

"Understood. However, it is not a problem for us to worry about today. The prosecution has nothing that connects you to a murder weapon. The fact that the gun was not planted at your residence could mean that the killer did not want to part with the weapon. Whatever the reason, it doesn't matter now. We need to concentrate on issues that are of concern."

"OK."

"Start by telling me everything about Friday night. Do not leave out any details even if they seem inconsequential. After that I will ask you about your relationship with Matthew Hennigan. Anything you can say about Elliot Shaw might be helpful too."

"I gave Eileen a ride over to her friend Nicole's house at about seven o'clock. On the way back, I noticed the gas gauge was low. So, I pulled into Hennigan's and filled it up at a self-serve pump. I used a credit card to pay for the gas."

"How long did that take? I would like to pin down the timing as closely as possible."

"I dropped Eileen off before seven. She did not want to be late. I watched her go in. She turned and waved me away before closing the door. The clock on the dash said 6:54 PM when I drove off. It had to be just about seven o'clock when I got to the service station. I finished filling the tank no later than ten minutes after seven and walked into the store by quarter after."

"The time-stamp on your credit card receipt was 7:17 PM."

"OK, I guess I was not quite as fast as I remembered. I still think I entered the store before seven twenty."

"Why were you buying gas in the evening? Hennigan's is not the cheapest place."

"Diane had been using my car during the week because she said hers was not running right. It occurred to me that the real reason might have been her car was low on fuel. I was just being nice. She wanted my car again on the weekend."

"Go on."

"I decided to go in and grab a bag of popcorn from the popper that Matt always has running in his convenience store. You've probably noticed it."

"Yes, I have. Did you see anyone? Did anyone see you?"

"As I told Ryan and White when they came to the house the next morning, the lights were on but no one was around. They are the ones who told me Elliot Shaw saw me at Hennigan's that night but I didn't see him or anyone else."

"Go on."

"I was going to buy a soft drink to have with the popcorn but, with no one there to pay, I couldn't. After hanging around for maybe five minutes, I put the soda can back and left without getting anything."

"Could there have been a body on the floor that you did not see?"

"Absolutely not. There's no way. I looked down every aisle from the front of the store. I went around the center food counter and took a few steps toward the restroom and called out, 'Hello. Is anybody here?' There was no sound from the restroom. I got no response. The place was quiet."

"Could someone have been in the back room or in the men's room or hiding at the end of an aisle?"

"I suppose it's possible. More likely, Elliot Shaw would have gone next door to the liquor store."

"Tell me about Elliot Shaw."

"He works for Hennigan. He was probably on duty. Hennigan was usually there with him at night. I only know Elliot from his job at the convenience store and service station. He is not much for conversation at least not with me."

"Would you say he was sullen?"

"No. Just quiet. An ordinary service-station attendant and clerk in a store who does not engage with the customers."

"Any reason to mistrust Elliot Shaw?"

"No. He never shortchanged me or anything. Also, he never gave me a break either. It was full-price Elliot even if the coffee was stale."

"Good. Now, tell me about your prior interactions with Matthew Hennigan. You said you were not friends but you put up with each other. How did that work?"

"I didn't like him much but we were fine. There is not much to tell."

"What do you mean not much?"

"He came to the baseball games with the gang on Wednesday nights but wasn't very reliable. I understood that he had his business to attend to but he would say he was bringing some new equipment or refreshments or something and then not show up or arrive late. We would have to make do with whatever we had until he got there."

"What do you mean refreshments or something? I am not comfortable with vague answers."

"I don't remember anything else. Equipment and refreshments were the only things."

"What about interactions between the two of you in the past? Were there confrontations, trivial or not, that would cause the detectives in the Batavia Police Department to suspect that you might have intended to do harm to Mr. Hennigan?"

"There were arguments but nothing that should be construed as extremely serious. He was self-centered and I told him so. I lost my temper with him once for being totally inconsiderate of another human being. Mean and nasty is what it was and I let him know it."

"How did he take it?"

"Not well but it was soon forgotten. Also, I scolded him for not being a team player. Once, I yelled at him you gotta be here when you say you're coming. Maybe it was more than once."

"How many more than once?"

"Two or three times total. Look, it was clear that nothing I said would make any difference. So, I did not keep after him. Anyway, it was no big deal. It was about an AAU game. Nothing to kill him for. That's ridiculous."

"It may not seem ridiculous to a jury."

"Matt and I had disagreements from time to time. But, I couldn't avoid him completely, he was the principal sponsor for the team."

"Anything else you can tell me about Hennigan?"

"Come to think of it, now that he is gone, where will we get the money for team expenses?"

"Baseball games be damned! Least of your worries at the moment, Ted," Wrightson admonished. Making light of the subject did not sit well with my defense attorney.

"OK, sorry. I should not have said that." It was an inappropriate question for me to bring up given the circumstances. I was trying to get off the topic of my problems Matthew Hennigan.

"Did you touch anything at Hennigan's on Friday?"

"Well, sure. I opened a couple of doors to the refrigeration case to find a soft drink. I put it down at the popcorn maker. I put the drink back. If you are asking about fingerprints, mine could be anywhere in the front part of the store."

"Did you see anything unusual out in front at the service station or inside the convenience store?"

"Do you mean aside from the fact the station was open and no attendant was on duty?" My answer might have been taken as a little snippy. "No, there was nothing else unusual."

"Were there things about the gas station or the convenience store that you did not like?"

"Nothing serious. The place was generally pretty well kept. Everything in the convenience store was overpriced but that's par for the course."

"Did the way Hennigan treated you as a customer get under your skin?"

"You've already asked me about Hennigan."

The conversation was beginning to get to me. It was feeling more like an inquisition by my own lawyer than talking to a sympathetic supporter. Also, twenty-four hours in jail made me tired and irritable.

Wrightson acknowledged my discomfort. "Look, Ted, there is a reason we need to go over everything very,

very carefully. If some of my questions seem redundant, that's because they are. I want you to rethink every little detail in case something else comes to mind. I have to be prepared. I must not ever be surprised in the courtroom by hearing about something that you have not told me."

"I understand," I sighed. I added with emphasis, "I am telling you everything. There are no surprises."

"We have to go on, Ted."

"I know."

"Did you see anyone else, coming or going on Friday evening?"

"There was a car leaving when I pulled up. I did not pay any attention to it. It was just a gray sedan turning right onto the street."

"That might be something for us to follow up on. What about other customers at the pumps while you were there?"

"It seems to me that I heard traffic out front or in the parking lot for Nora's but nothing caught my interest. There could have been several cars with drivers paying at the pump. It was all completely ordinary. Nothing stood out."

"Did anyone come inside?"

"No. I'm sure not. I don't remember that there was anyone else around outside as close as the sidewalk but there were probably customers going into Nora's. Both establishments were lit up with bright lights inside and over the parking spots and the fuel pumps. They were open for business as usual except Hennigan's was unattended. The front door was unlocked when I arrived and I left it that way. I let the door close behind me and walked out to my car."

"Tell me more about the timing. You estimated that you entered Hennigan's store by seven twenty. How long were you in there?"

"Probably ten minutes and less than fifteen."

"You said that you looked down each of the six aisles and you waited around for someone to show up."

"So, maybe it was twenty minutes. I am certain I did not waste more of my time than that just waiting around in an empty convenience store."

"That puts the time at 7:30 or 7:40 when you returned to your car. Did you go anywhere after that?"

"Just straight home. I parked the car in the garage and went into the house."

"What time was that?"

"According to the calculations you just did, it was no later than seven forty-five. Sorry I can't do any better than that."

"Anybody see you?"

"Wait. Can we go back? Did I say I looked down all six aisles? There are just five aisles separated by four gondolas, a center aisle and two more narrow aisles on each side."

"I said six aisles, Ted. You didn't."

"Were you testing me?"

Elmer refused to confirm. He asked again, "Anyone see you when you got home?"

"Diane was there. She actually spoke to me. In fact, she was unusually attentive. Diane is becoming a young woman who is still at the awkward age between self-centered and mature enough to have a conversation with her father. I refrained from saying anything to her about leaving the gas tank on empty. I said goodnight and worked at the desk in the den for a while. I talked to Lydia on the phone and went to bed."

"Did you call Lydia or did she call you?"

"She called me. She was out of town at a conference. Normally, she would have returned already. Given my history, Lydia does not like to leave me alone for very long especially not on Friday or Saturday evenings. However, there was a dinner in Cincinnati on Friday that she thought she should attend."

"What time did she call?"

"Not long after I got home. Actually, I know that one. Friday was the last day of the conference. The cocktail party and dinner were scheduled early for the benefit of the attendees who wanted to get home for the weekend. As soon as the festivities concluded, Lydia called and talked to Diane at about seven. Diane reminded her that I was driving Eileen to a friend's house. Lydia called back at eight."

"Did she use a cell phone to reach you on your land line at home?"

"Yes, I don't carry a cell phone. I don't have much use for one."

The probing and questioning continued for another couple of hours or more. I believe Wrightson would have gone on even longer if not for my evident exhaustion.

"All right, Ted. If you think of anything else I should know, make a note and brief me on the details before the session starts on Monday." Elmer stood up as if to leave.

"When can you get me out of here?" I pleaded.

He sat back down. "The charges against you are grave. You might have to sit in here for a while. But, I will see what I can do."

"How long is a while?"

"It could go a couple of different ways. Let me start with the worst-case scenario. It is very common with a murder charge for the judge to decide that you cannot be released before the trial. The assault on a police officer adds to the seriousness of the matter."

"The son of a bitch was beating up Diane. I could not help myself. In fact, they should throw a father in jail if he did not defend his daughter. No father can let a thug beat up his daughter without taking action."

"We will use your argument with the judge. She has not yet heard the full description of a bully policeman striking a daughter in front of her father."

"The son of a bitch drew blood for Christ's sake."

"I understand, Ted. In fact, I am hopeful that the assault charge will be dismissed. However, dismissed or not, the altercation with the police will be used as proof of guilt before the jury. Vivid descriptions of the fight are in the news. There is no way we will be able to hide it."

"Wow! What bad luck." It suddenly occurred to me that bad conduct by a teacher is not appreciated in the schools. "What about my teaching position?"

"I called Principal Mansfield this afternoon and asked her not to rush to judgement. I presumed it would be all right with you if I talked to her about you but I didn't think we had much choice. I wanted her to hear it from me before she was surprised by a reporter."

"Thank you. How did she take it?"

"Oh, you know Lois Mansfield. Of course, she won't do anything drastic. She thanked me for letting her know."

"You have been busy. Thank you," I repeated.

"The situation at the school is a little touchy with me representing you and with my father and you both teaching in the same school district."

"Why is that?"

"Isn't it obvious, Ted? The question will be asked. Is Principal Mansfield showing favoritism with regard to your job because your lawyer's father asked her for a favor?"

"What about my job at the Batavia Service Center? They have put up with a lot from me over the years but it was all supposed to be in the past."

"Lydia said she would talk to Clutch. He and Melissa are not about to turn their backs on you. Aren't they almost family by now?"

"Yeah, you're right. You said confined until trial was the worst-case scenario."

"Other possibilities are not a whole lot better. You could be released on your own recognizance or on bail tomorrow. However, going free before trial is usually allowed because the judge is anticipating a significant delay before the proceedings begin. Prolonging the process will become more and more painful for yourself and your family as time goes by."

"I do have a right to a speedy trial."

"That's true. The rules of justice do not permit incarceration for an extended period before the trial. After all, you are innocent until proven guilty."

"You are right, Elmer. I hope to get all of this over with as soon as possible."

"Agreed. It is time for me to get back to work." Elmer Wrightson stood up again. "I still need to talk to you about the actions of the arresting officers at your house on Saturday morning. The particulars are important but they will have to wait till Monday. Our discussion will be time consuming because there were so many witnesses."

"Like who?"

"That's what I want to ask you. According to Diane, everyone on your block was there. The associates in my firm have been gathering names. They tell me everyone has something to say."

"Can they verify the police misconduct?"

"Don't worry about that. Diane said they are on your side. All your neighbors seem to like you but um ... well, ..." his voice trailed off.

"I didn't hear that. What did you say?"

"Nothing."

"Come on. You were about to say something."

"I thought better of the words in my head just in time to stop them from coming out of my mouth," Elmer smirked.

"OK, but I caught you. Now you have to tell me."

Elmer laughed. "No, I don't but I will. I was about to say, as unbelievable as it may seem, your neighbors think you're a great guy. Don't ask me to explain where they got that from."

"That's a good one, Elmer. However, you should know that I've turned over a new leaf since I last had a drink. Your father will tell you I am a responsible citizen and a good teacher."

"Yeah, yeah. I've heard all about it. The old guy always did like you even when you were a rotten, no good teenager and a bad influence on his impressionable, young son."

The mood had lightened up but I could not keep a few tears from rolling down my cheeks. I stood up and gave him a hug.

"Thank you. Elmer. I don't know how I will ever repay you."

"Oh, don't you worry about that. We'll think of something." He laughed. "I know. We'll garnishee your wages."

"Oh, no." I feigned a frightened reaction. My wages would be of little interest to the wealthy, well-established, well-respected Attorney Elmer Wrightson.

I took his arm and held him back when he turned toward the door. "Elmer, I have not been able to tell you this before but I am truly sorry about everything. If only ..."

He cut me off. "Listen, Ted. You don't need to say anything more. I'm sorry too. Lydia and I were never meant to be and we both knew it." He smiled and joked, "Besides, anyone who could put up with the likes of you could never be right for me."

Elmer laughed again. When he left the room, he took with him a great weight of regret and sadness from my shoulders. Unfortunately, worries about my perilous predicament lingered on.

Chapter 47 . Black and white shared ancestors.

After two long nights of fitful sleep in the city jail, two guards came to get me for the courtroom appearance on Monday morning. To have made it through the weekend gave me a weird sense of relief mixed with anxiety. I wanted to get things over with but I was fearful of the possibilities.

It would be my first session before the judge. I had hoped that Lydia would be there and she was. Diane and Eileen were sitting on her left. There was a familiar face on her other side. It took me a minute to recognize her. What was Janet Bread doing in Batavia?

Janet Bread and Lydia Kingston had twin brothers for grandparents. The women shared the same great-grandfather, the son of English immigrants. Sean Kingston was born in Savannah, Georgia, during the Reconstruction era after the Civil War.

At the age of sixteen, he traveled north to Trinity Divinity School. Toward the end of the nineteenth century, Reverend Kingston returned to Savannah to become a righteous minister. He preached against the evils of the Jim Crow laws to the dismay of his congregation in the all-white First Presbyterian Church where he met his wife.

Anne Williamson came to the United States as a child with her Welsh parents. Their twin sons Aaron and Jacob were Janet Bread's and Lydia Kingston's grandfathers, respectively.

The boys were raised in an austere household under the control of their strict father. As the youngest of six, they formed a close alliance and managed to fly under the radar until they were the last to leave the nest.

Aaron was the more rebellious of the two. He chafed under his Father's teachings regarding the correct behavior expected of a God-fearing young man. After a while, Rev. Kingston would have little to do with him.

While his twin brother flaunted the rules, Jacob managed to toe the line a little better and remained in his father's good graces.

Aaron courted a popular young woman in the church choir. They were headstrong teenagers who dared to sneak off for a picnic by the river just by themselves. Their rebellious behavior was scandalous in the community. Both families heaped harsh criticism on the young couple.

Aaron's shotgun wedding to his childhood sweetheart ended quickly and tragically. She died in childbirth and Aaron was left with a baby girl to raise on his own. Helen Kingston was Janet Bread's mother.

It was Janet's brother Timothy Kingston who threw me into a fit of jealousy back in college. What I saw was familial affection between cousins but I mistook it for something else. The incident occurred before I had met any of Lydia's family.

It took a bit of convincing for me to accept cousin Timmy's far-fetched story that his military mother Helen Kingston and his bohemian father Francis Bread decided Janet should have her father's surname and the boys, Timothy, Gabriel, and Daniel, would take Kingston for their last name.

Grandfather Aaron took over a run-down general store as a means of support. It is believed that the financing was provided by the family of Anne Williamson, the twin's mother.

It is not clear that Rev. Kingston was entirely at ease when his obedient son Jacob fell in love with and married their domestic servant MaryBeth Johnson the granddaughter of former Virginia slaves. However, his teachings had always been that all God's children were created equal. He treated MaryBeth with respect and acknowledged her as a member of the family. It was her influence that got the old man to accept Aaron and little Helen back into the fold.

Jacob and MaryBeth had several children in quick succession. They had to move in with her older brother to save money. Thus, Jacob's family was absorbed into the black community. The Aaron and Jacob branches of the Kingston genealogy became racially distinct. Jacob's and MaryBeth's youngest son James was Lydia's father.*

Before long, Jacob joined his brother at the general store. The two men became successful merchants with many patrons from the black community. Neither of the twins had very much schooling. However, probably due to their father's influence, both men appreciated the value of an education for their children.

Aaron's daughter left home to attend college in Syracuse where she met her husband-to-be Francis Bread. Janet Bread was the oldest of their four children. Lydia has fond memories of playing with Janet in their twin grandfathers' general store.

Helen Kingston went to law school and joined the military in time to see action in Afghanistan. She returned to the United States and was sent to the other side of the world to a military installation on the island of Guam. In a very short time, less than twenty years, she had attained senior rank in the United States Army.

Colonel Helen Kingston's daughter Janet Bread was now sitting next to her second cousin Lydia Kingston in the courtroom where I was the defendant.

---

* Turn to page 60, Chapter 17, for the Kingston Family Lineage or search Lineage.

Chapter 48 . On Monday, the defense moved for immediate dismissal.

The prosecution of the murder and assault charges against me began with a preliminary hearing on a gloomy Monday morning early in June of 2019. I was seated on Attorney Elmer Wrightson's left at the table for the defense.

"Who are those people?" I did not know either of the lawyers for the prosecution. The two men were discussing a file at the table across the aisle to our right.

Elmer answered, "The lead attorney is an assistant prosecutor for the state. His name is Morris Hofmann and I do not much care for his tactics. He will cut any corners that he can to get a conviction."

"Oh, great. Who is the guy talking to Hofmann?"

"That's John Yoder. He is new in the District Attorney's office. I don't know much about him. His background is a bit hazy. I asked one of our associates to look into his credentials. We like to know with whom we are dealing when we face someone in the courtroom but we haven't found much yet. Our best guess is he seems fine."

"All rise." The bailiff stated the case number and gave my name as the accused. "The Honorable Anne Fitzgerald presiding."

The judge made some preliminary statements.

When she paused to survey her courtroom, Attorney Wrightson spoke up, "Your Honor."

"Yes, Mr. Wrightson."

"The defense moves for immediate dismissal of all charges."

"Are you aware of the seriousness of the indictment?"

"Yes, I am Your Honor. However, there is no legally permissible evidence that links Mr. O'Connor to the scene of the crime or to the crime itself."

"That's preposterous. There is convincing evidence," Morris Hofmann interrupted.

"Mr. Hofmann can you wait to be recognized? Is there some reason you have decided that such an outburst is acceptable in my courtroom?" The judge came down hard on the prosecuting attorney. She was clearly annoyed with the man.

It seemed to me that Hofmann had gotten off on the wrong foot with Judge Fitzgerald. I kept my head down to hide the smirk on my face.

Wrightson said, "I repeat, Your honor. The evidence against Mr. O'Connor is not admissible."

"You do not need to be repetitious for my benefit, Mr. Wrightson. I am neither deaf nor senile."

Oh, great, I thought. Now the judge was as displeased with my attorney as she was with the prosecutor.

"Sorry, Your Honor." At least, Attorney Wrightson apologized while Hofmann gave no indication that the judge's rebuke bothered him in the least. He reacted with a dismissive attitude that she could not have missed.

"Tell me about the convincing evidence Mr. Hofmann," Judge Fitzgerald said.

"Sgt. Robert Ryan and Patrolman William White of the Batavia City Police were dispatched to Mr. O'Connor's residence on the first Saturday morning in June. They were sent there to investigate the murder of Matthew Hennigan who was shot at his place of business the previous evening. A witness had seen Mr. O'Connor at the scene around the time of the murder. Mr. O'Connor's reluctance to come to the door and his attempt to avoid contact with the police aroused suspicion."

"I was not avoiding contact with the police. I didn't even know who was there," I whispered to Wrightson who just nodded his head. He motioned for me to be still with his hand flat on the table in front of me. It was clear that the judge noticed and disapproved of the distraction.

Attorney Hofmann was not finished. "Officer Ryan immediately read Mr. O'Connor his rights and placed him under arrest. Mr. O'Connor reacted by assaulting Officer Ryan leaving him with a concussion. The details are corroborated by three other officers who were at Mr. O'Connor's residence at the time."

"Just a moment, please." Judge Fitzgerald held up her hand to stop Hofmann.

She said, "Mr. Wrightson, why do you believe the evidence supporting these charges is not admissible?"

"Your Honor, the truth is different from what Mr. Hofmann just told you. At best, his description of the events is misleading."

"It's all in Officer Ryan's report," Hofmann blurted out.

"Sit down, Mr. Hofmann," the judge shouted.

Attorney Wrightson continued, "Sgt. Ryan did not read Mr. O'Connor his rights before interrogating him. The reports from the other officers do not corroborate Sgt. Ryan's recounting of the incident. While there are no outright contradictions, there are differences that call some of the details into question."

"Explain."

"Sgt. Ryan and Officer White rang the bell at Mr. O'Connor's residence. Mr. O'Connor did not know it was the police at his front door until he got there. He was certainly not trying to avoid them. They had to wait for several minutes because Mr. O'Connor was out back in the garage and, at first, he thought his daughter would get the door."

"Be more specific. What does several minutes mean?" the judge asked.

"Approximately, six to eight minutes. Not more than ten including three minutes for Mr. O'Connor to wait for someone else to answer the door. I paced off the distance myself this morning."

"Go on."

"While they were waiting for someone to respond, Officers Ryan and White conducted an illegal search through the bushes around the front of the house. They reportedly found an empty whiskey bottle, genesis unknown. It was not a justified search."

In anticipation of another outburst from the prosecutor, the judge said, "I can see you straining at the bit, Mr. Hofmann. Hold your place. You will get your turn."

Wrightson held the floor for several more minutes. "Neither Sgt. Ryan nor Officer White read Mr. O'Connor his rights. In fact, without even letting on that he might be suspected of a crime, Sgt. Ryan began questioning him.

"The interrogation began immediately after Mr. O'Connor came around the corner of the house and saw the two officers on his front porch. After making unfounded accusations, Sgt. Ryan announced that he was placing Mr. O'Connor under arrest, which was very likely the police department's intention from the beginning. If so, they should have read him his rights immediately.

"Sgt. Ryan told Mr. O'Connor they were arresting him for the murder of Matthew Hennigan. It was only then that Officer White began to recite the Miranda warning. He was interrupted before saying anything of substance by

Mr. O'Connor's daughter. She came out the front door to proclaim fealty for her father.

"Sgt. Ryan instigated the confrontation with my client by striking his daughter. Mr. O'Connor's physical reaction did not constitute assault. Rather, it was spontaneous intervention to preempt further abusive treatment of his daughter by Sgt. Ryan. Moments later, Chief Jennifer Hepburn got involved. It was she who read the Miranda warning to Mr. O'Connor after the skirmish on his front porch was over."

"Why was the chief of police on the scene?"

"Chief Jennifer Hepburn and Officer Louis Thompson came to the O'Connor residence in a second police car. Their reasons for being there are not clear," Wrightson said.

"Mr. Hofmann, tell me what Chief Hepburn was doing there." Judge Fitzgerald needed an explanation.

The prosecuting attorney said, "Chief Hepburn's report does not indicate the reason she considered her presence to be necessary."

"An interesting omission that I would like to see resolved," the judge said.

"Yes, Your Honor," Hofmann answered.

Attorney Wrightson said, "I believe Chief Hepburn considered Sgt. Ryan's tendencies for rude behavior and misconduct to be problematic. She joined Sgt. Ryan at the scene to oversee his interactions with Mr. O'Connor. She brought Officer Thompson along as a witness. He stated that his role was entirely as backup but his report does not include further details."

Mr. Hofmann sputtered audibly.

"Mr. Wrightson, would you agree with the attorney for the prosecution that your speculation about Chief

Hepburn's motivation is inappropriate?" The judge's question could have been taken as an admonishment.

"Yes, Your Honor. I withdraw the comment regarding the reason for their visit. What I can say is Officer Louis Thompson and the chief of the Batavia Police department arrived in a second car while the Sgt. Ryan's interrogation of Mr. O'Connor was underway on his front porch. According to her report, after witnessing the physical altercation between Mr. O'Connor and Sgt. Ryan, Chief Hepburn and Officer Thompson rushed up the stairs to the porch. She read Mr. O'Connor his rights and with Thompson's assistance, she took Mr. O'Connor into custody on the charges he now faces."

"Mr. Hofmann, you seem to have calmed down a bit."

"Your Honor, the defense is digging its own grave. As Mr. Wrightson just said, the other police reports do not contradict Sgt. Ryan's accounting of the events."

"You will have a chance to make your point. Do you have more, Mr. Wrightson?"

"If I may, Your Honor," Wrightson answered.

"Please," she sighed.

"According to witnesses at the scene, Sgt. Ryan's accounting of the events is deceitful in two ways."

"Do tell?" The judge's attitude was condescending. "You are referring to the reports written by a seasoned officer on the police force."

"I understand that. However, the least critical interpretation we can give to the inaccuracies in his report is that his memory of the events is faulty or perhaps he was just careless with the facts."

"Go on."

"Chief Hepburn's account and the neighbors who witnessed the events concur on the following two fallacies in Sgt. Ryan's report: First, Sgt. Ryan did not read the Miranda warning and, second, Chief Hepburn was the officer who arrested Mr. O'Connor. While not materially affecting the outcome of the events at Mr. O'Connor's residence, such discrepancies call the credibility of the motivation for selecting Mr. O'Connor as a suspect into question."

"Tell the court about the witnesses."

"As soon as the uniformed police officers Ryan and White arrived at Mr. O'Connor's residence, several neighbors on the normally quiet Elm Avenue took notice. We have interviewed seven of them. The police have talked to at least two of the same individuals from whom we gathered information. It should be noted that the prosecution has not included their names on the list of potential witnesses."

"That does not sound good." The judge turned to the prosecuting attorney. "Mr. Hofmann, as you know, the defense must be given the opportunity to depose anyone you intend to put on the stand."

"Of course, Your Honor. We have not found any of the bystanders to be informative or, for that matter, very reliable. If something changes, the defense will be the first to know."

"Really, the first, Mr. Hofmann?"

"Figuratively speaking. I mean after yourself, of course."

The judge sighed audibly. "Not much room for figuratively speaking in a court of law, Mr. Hofmann," she said more to herself than to him.

Wrightson said, "Perhaps, the reason the witnesses are not considered to be reliable is their testimony contradicts the police reports."

More sputtering emanated from Morris Hofmann.

"Does the prosecution have an intelligible comment?" the judge asked.

Attorney Yoder rose from his seat just in time to extricate Hofmann from his agitated state. "Your Honor?" He asked to be recognized.

"Yes, Mr. Yoder." Judge Fitzgerald looked down at her notes to be sure she had his name right.

"We will provide concrete justification for including or excluding input from individuals at the scene at a later time. However, we can assure the court that the prosecution's motive is certainly not to hide contradictory statements."

"That is good to know. I will look forward to hearing about your interviews with the other witnesses, Mr. Yoder."

"Shall I continue? Your Honor," the defense attorney asked.

"Please try to wrap it up, Mr. Wrightson."

"Alex Montoya was among the first neighbors to observe the events at Mr. O'Connor's residence on Saturday morning."

My response to the name must have been noticeable. Everyone turned to look at me.

Montoya was a bothersome neighbor with whom we had a strained relationship. He was not someone I thought would ever come to my defense.

At the moment I heard the name in court, I realized that the mysterious individual among the witnesses to my arrest was Alex Montoya. He had to be the neighbor who was shielded from my view under the hooded sweatshirt. He was standing with the crowd across the street when the police took me away.

Chapter 49 . Harassment is not friendly.

After I punched the police sergeant and knocked him down on that fateful Saturday on Elm Avenue, I looked at the faces of the neighbors and gawkers who were witnesses to the ignominy Diane and I suffered on our front porch. I hoped they were siding with me against the zealous, overbearing jerk who had injured my daughter.

The crowd had grown larger. They were all focused on us except for the tall figure with his features obscured by the hoodie that shrouded his face. There was something familiar about him but I could not put my finger on it. Perhaps, he did not want to be recognized.

When Officer Thompson backed out of our driveway and drove swiftly up Elm Avenue, I was suffering the humiliation of handcuffs in the back seat of a police car. I kept my head down and tried to avoid eye contact with any of my neighbors but he was there in my peripheral vision.

Now, on Monday morning in the courtroom, the identity of the mysterious observer was suddenly revealed. Attorney Wrightson said his name.

Alex Montoya was a tall, athletic man who moved in two doors down and across the street from us about ten years ago. Our relationship was friendly at first. In fact, overly friendly.

He would show up uninvited. He would join me in the garage for a beer that turned into two or three or four bottles until his wife sent their eight-year-old son to get him for the second or third time.

Some days he would be lingering in the garage when I got home in the evenings. I was never too keen for his phony friendly attitude but I did like watching a game with him in front of the huge TV screen upstairs in the barn.

Alex could talk intelligently about baseball while we enjoyed an afternoon game televised from a major-league baseball park. It helped to mute the sound and discuss the play like sports fans who knew something about the game. We both disliked the inane chatter inflicted on the viewers by the usual team on FOX Sports.

Lydia did not care for Alex Montoya. She didn't trust him. She told me he was more interested in her than in me. She considered many of his comments to constitute sexual harassment.

I did find his suggestive remarks to be off-putting. His flirting with Lydia right in front of me was offensive but I laughed it off until one day when it was not funny.

On a Sunday afternoon, Alex arrived uninvited as usual. He joined me on the bench in the backyard where I was keeping Lydia company while she worked in the garden.

"Don't leave me alone with that creep," she whispered in my ear.

I agreed but I was still not taking him too seriously. Lounging on the bench on a hot summer day with plenty of beer to drink had dulled my senses.

"Get yourself a beer, Alex, and have a seat."

"Thanks, I believe I will." A moment later, he leered at Lydia and said to me, "Isn't it a great day for gardening with the little woman."

"Yeah, sure," I mumbled.

Alex strolled over to get a bottle of beer from the cooler. He ambled back across the garden and sat next to me on the bench. Lydia was following right behind him.

"You grab me like that again and I will chop you in half," she shouted in his face.

I did not see what happened. In fact, I was a little too sloshed to be able to react in any sort of supportive way.

Lydia picked up the axe from the cord of wood stacked next to the garage.

"Hey, come on. I'm just being friendly," Alex laughed. He stood up and hurriedly stepped backwards toward the driveway.

"I'll show you friendly," Lydia shouted louder than before. She moved in a menacing fashion right at him with the axe raised up off her shoulder.

"Ah, little honey, my negrita, you are not going to smack me with that for just a little tickle," he smirked. He said the word smack with his lips puckered for a kiss.

Alex Montoya totally misjudged his angry adversary. His too cocky response was not smart certainly not when spoken to such an armed and dangerous woman. Lydia raised the axe over her head and swung at her target like she was splitting wood for the fireplace. He lurched to one side. Panic showed on the man's face.

The axe glanced off his shoulder. The momentum of her swing carried it to the ground where the blade took a divot out of the pavement right where he had been standing. Lydia lifted her weapon of choice as if to continue the attack.

Alex Montoya turned and ran for home never again to venture into our yard or darken the large barn doors on our oversized garage.

Chapter 50 . The prosecution's arguments were flawed.

Attorney Wrightson continued to argue the case for the defense in the courtroom. He said "Alex Montoya was out for some exercise on Elm Avenue at about 8:45 in the morning on Saturday. He was directly across the street from the driveway at O'Connor's residence when he saw Mr. O'Connor go into his garage. Some time later, Mr. Montoya chose to walk back over to say hello just to be neighborly."

I thought to myself just to be neighborly certainly does not sound like the Montoya I know.

"What do you mean by some time later? Can you be more specific?" the judge asked.

"Mr. Montoya is quite certain about the timing of the events that morning. He believes he was on the sidewalk across the street on his way toward the O'Connor residence just two or three minutes after ten o'clock."

"Go on."

"He decided not to proceed when he saw the police at Mr. O'Connor's front door. Mr. Montoya told me he stood there watching not to be nosy but out of concern for his neighbor. He observed Mr. O'Connor come from around the far side of his house and across the lawn toward the porch. He said that he had a clear view from his location on the sidewalk 140 feet from the police car parked in the street across from the O'Connor residence."

"He was that precise, 140 feet?"

"Yes, Your Honor. I asked him about that. Mr. Montoya said he knows how far away he was because the lots for the houses on his side of Elm Avenue are all 140 feet wide. He was standing at the midpoint of his next-door-neighbor's lot and the police cruiser was at the midpoint of the next lot."

The judge just shook her head. "All right then. Continue please."

"Alex Montoya is an interesting personality. He can give you detailed information about many things that you might not have asked for. The lots on the other side of the street are not as uniformly cut and Mr. O'Connor's is one of the widest at 175 feet."

With raised eyebrows, the judge remarked, "Too much detail is better than too little."

Wrightson continued, "Mr. Montoya walked up closer to the police cruiser where four others from the neighborhood had gathered. All five including Mr. Montoya observed the entire episode. We have spoken to all of them plus two more who came later. They heard the conversation with the police and witnessed the beating taken by Mr. O'Connor's daughter. They also saw the physical interaction between Sgt. Ryan and Mr. O'Connor."

"Who interviewed the neighbors?"

"Investigators from my office, Wrightson and Associates."

"I see." The judge nodded for Wrightson to continue.

"The witnesses agreed that Sgt. Ryan did not read Mr. O'Connor his rights. They said Officer White started to but he was interrupted before he could get out more than a few words. He stopped short when he tried but failed to catch Diane O'Connor before she fell to the floor."

"As I understand it, Ms. O'Connor refused medical attention," the judge observed.

"That is correct. Diane O'Connor suffered bruises on her forehead and painful lacerations to her face but she did not consider the injuries to be life threatening. She is a tough young woman who put concern for her father ahead of her own welfare."

"I understand. An admirable reaction." The judge's appreciation for Diane's actions was sincere.

Morris Hofmann's groan was audible. He rolled his eyes at the judge when she looked his way.

"Are you surprised by a daughter coming to the defense of her father, Mr. Hofmann?"

"No, Your Honor." His simpering voice cast doubt on the sincerity of his answer.

"Go on, Mr. Wrightson," the judge said.

"Sgt. Ryan's treatment of Mr. O'Connor's daughter was brutal. Mr. Montoya saw blood on the young woman's face. The reaction of the neighbors was that someone had to stop Officer Ryan and they cheered Mr. O'Connor's actions."

"Didn't Sgt. Ryan suffer a concussion?"

"There has not been a definitive diagnosis. However, Sgt. Ryan did exhibit symptoms of a concussion."

Attorney Wrightson took a step forward and said, "Your Honor, I do not see how the impulsive reaction of a father in defense of his daughter falls to the level of assault." He spoke in a quiet voice. His words and manner created a solemn moment in the courtroom.

From the look on her face, I believe Judge Anne Fitzgerald was giving thoughtful consideration to Wrightson's comment. However, she did not allow the sentiment to affect the serious tone of the proceedings.

She asked, "Mr. Hofmann, how do your respond to Mr. Wrightson? Did the grand jury consider testimony from any of the neighbors?"

The judge's question was for the prosecutor. However, Attorney Wrightson interjected. "Pardon me, Your

Honor. The witnesses told us that they had not spoken to anyone from the prosecutor's office. Two of them said Officer Thompson talked to them. They felt he was listening to what they had to say but they agreed that he did not take notes."

The judge looked surprised. She was silent for a long moment before recovering. Judge Fitzgerald admonished, "A well-placed interruption, Mr. Wrightson, but courtroom rules apply to you as well as to the prosecutor."

"Sorry, Your Honor." Wrightson looked down at the floor and took his seat next to me. I could feel the confident satisfaction with how he had taken control of the conversation.

Mr. Hofmann rose up to answer the judge's question. He spoke only a few words. "The grand jury found the statements by the police to be sufficiently compelling to issue the indictments, Your Honor."

Later that day when we had adjourned to an attorney-client conference room, I questioned Elmer about Hofmann's response. He explained to me that the answer was actually well put.

"How can that be?" I asked. "Hofmann did not explain how the grand jury could render a decision without hearing what the witnesses on the street had to say."

"Members of a grand jury do not have to hear all of the evidence. They are not passing judgment, guilty or not guilty. They are only deciding if the DA has sufficient evidence for the case to be brought to trial. Hofmann answered the question exactly right for the prosecution's purposes. He said the grand jury was given the police reports, which are generally the most objective and reliable sources of information."

"Not so much in my case."

"True. However, even if they had statements from all of the witnesses, the DA would have led with the police reports when asking the grand jury for the indictments."

I said, "So, Hofmann avoided getting egg on his face in the courtroom today. He did not admit to any shortcomings in their presentation before the grand jury. He mentioned only what they did right."

"Correct again, Ted. You catch on fast. Hofmann sidestepped the question by not putting on the record that the DA's office had neglected to evaluate input from potentially important witnesses. In the prosecutor's haste to rush to trial, their people have conducted a rather shoddy investigation so far. We have called them on it. Hence, they are likely to be more careful in the future."

"Why did the judge let Hofmann get away with a half-truthful answer to her question?"

"She did not. Anne Fitzgerald is an experienced magistrate. She simply decided not to pursue the issue at that moment but she won't forget it."

Chapter 51 . Justice must be blind.

After Morris Hofmann told the court that the grand jury found the police reports to be sufficient for the indictment, Judge Fitzgerald decided to drop the topic and move on to other items on the agenda for the proceedings.

She said, "I believe we have heard enough for now about the assault charge and the timing of the Miranda warning. Mr. Wrightson, what is your objection to the inquiry at the O'Connor residence on Saturday morning?"

"Your Honor, with very little to go on, the police focused exclusively on Mr. O'Connor. By their actions at his residence the next morning, they had preemptively tried and convicted Mr. O'Connor of the crime."

The judge objected. "If true, such misconduct by members of the Batavia Police Department would surprise me," she said.

"I agree that their actions were not what we have come to expect from our police department but evidently it happened on this occasion. The witnesses mentioned earlier have substantiated the unruly behavior that is certainly unusual for the police in our town."

The judge asked, "Are you referring to the witnesses for whom the prosecutors 'will provide concrete justification for including or excluding'?" To use Attorney Yoder's own words in her question was an oblique criticism of the prosecution.

"Yes, Your Honor," Wrightson concurred. He continued, "To put my client at the scene of the crime without saying how that could be true is disingenuous. The prosecution's case rests on the fact that Mr. O'Connor's credit card was used to purchase fuel from one of the pumps at the service station but they have nothing to indicate that he entered the convenience store and murdered Mr. Hennigan."

"Not so disingenuous, Mr. Wrightson. Credit-card records seem reasonable enough," the judge said.

Wrightson answered, "Yes. I don't disagree, Your Honor. The credit-card data would naturally give investigators names of individuals who might have been on the premises around the time of the murder. However, Mr. O'Connor should have been regarded as one of four equally likely suspects.

"The time stamps on the credit cards show that his transaction was the second of four that evening. Two of the purchases occurred after the charge on Mr. O'Connor's card. There could have been more than four cars at the pumps. However, the District Attorney's office has not made the defense aware of any cash transactions."

"Your point seems to be that the record of transactions at the fuel pumps is insufficient for a conviction. I accept that. However, the information is admissible."

"Understood. Your Honor, the credit-card invoice indicates the defendant bought gas at the service station but that is all. It was Mr. O'Connor who told the police that he went inside. His statement came before he had heard that it was a crime scene and prior to the Miranda warning. There is no admissible evidence that Mr. O'Connor entered the convenience store."

The judge turned to the prosecutor's table. "Is that correct, Mr. Hofmann?"

Without answering the question, Hofmann spoke in a whiney voice. "The credit-card evidence is as real as anything. In answer to the defense attorney's innuendos, we are not trying to be obscure about anything. No cash transactions were recorded on the pumps at the service station."

"That was not my question, Mr. Hofmann. Do you have admissible evidence that Mr. O'Connor entered the convenience store at the time Mr. Hennigan was shot?"

"Yes, we have a witness. Elliot Shaw saw Mr. O'Connor inside the store. Mr. Shaw's name is on the list of witnesses for the prosecution," Hofmann said.

Always on the offensive, he added, "The defense attorney has the list with Mr. Shaw's name."

"Mr. Wrightson, what about the eyewitness who saw Mr. O'Connor inside the store?"

"The defense has not been informed of such testimony from an eyewitness," Wrightson confessed.

"No reason that you should have been before now. Elliot Shaw is a witness for the prosecution. Be sure to take his deposition. The court regards Mr. Shaw's testimony to be significant."

"Yes, Your Honor."

"Mr. Hofmann, can you make Elliot Shaw available this afternoon or soon thereafter?"

"OK, we'll try," Hofmann agreed. "I would like to add that the prosecution does not accept the claim that Mr. O'Connor's statements are not admissible. The credit-card transaction gave the police reasonable cause for approaching Mr. O'Connor at his residence. The defense attorney's attempt to cast doubt on his client's actions is disingenuous to use his word."

"The court acknowledges your position regarding the legality of Mr. O'Connor's arrest. What else, Mr. Hofmann?"

"There is no doubt that Mr. O'Connor went inside the convenience store. In addition to the witness, we have other evidence regarding Mr. O'Connor's activities at the service station."

Mr. Hofmann stopped talking. He glanced at Attorney Wrightson and looked back at the judge.

"Please explain." The judge shook her head in response to Hofmann's attempt to execute a dramatic pause.

Morris Hofmann replied, "The team of investigators lifted Mr. O'Connor's fingerprints from the food counter and other items at the scene."

The judge said, "The fingerprint evidence is admissible. The court has heard enough about whether the defendant entered the store. The position of the prosecution on the topic is understood. What about the others who bought gas with credit cards at the time of the shooting?" Judge Fitzgerald asked the obvious question. "Has the prosecution cleared all three of the other credit-card customers?"

"We have interviewed two of them. Both said they were alone in their cars when they stopped for gas and they left without going inside. We have not spoken to the third customer as yet."

"Any reason to suspect the veracity of the individuals who said they did not enter the convenience store? Taking a suspect's word for it is usually not enough."

"We have found no connection that could link either of them to the victim or provide the kind of motive that Mr. O'Connor had. Only Mr. O'Connor admitted entering the convenience store where the body was found. His actions that evening and at his house the next morning and his history with the victim are incriminating."

"I see. Could the credit-card customer you have not talked to be a suspect?"

"We do not believe so. The name on the credit card is Joan Ingleton. She has not answered her phone or responded to knocking on the door to her apartment.

Her landlord said she might be visiting her grandchildren but he does not know where they live."

"I presume you will be talking to Ms. Ingleton."

"Yes, of course. The landlord said she is expected back before the end of the week."

By the look she gave him, the judge did not care for the dismissive "of course" in Mr. Hofmann's answer. It was not the first time during the proceedings that she found the way he addressed the bench to be off putting. It would also not be the last time.

After a shake of her head and a sigh of exasperation, she asked, "Mr. Hofmann, can you answer the question regarding the justification for searching Mr. O'Connor's property on Saturday morning?"

"Yes, first, the liquor bottle that Mr. Wrightson referred to was dusted in the police lab. It had Mr. O'Connor's fingerprints on it. Second, early Saturday morning after the officers who conducted the investigation at the scene of the crime returned to the station, Police Chief Jennifer Hepburn convened a standard evidence-review conference. They considered all possibilities and drew up a list of objectives."

"Who were the participants in the police review?" The judge interrupted.

"Officers Thompson and Angela Dunning were there. They were on duty Saturday morning and the two of them conducted the investigation at the scene of the crime. In addition, the evidence-review conference included the medical examiner, the county sheriff, Officers Ryan and White, and Chief Hepburn. Their names are on the list of witnesses for the prosecution."

"Thank you. Please continue, Mr. Hofmann."

"Chief Hepburn concluded that Theodore O'Connor was a person of interest. She sent Officers Ryan and White to talk to Mr. O'Connor at his residence. When they got there, it was evident that the house was occupied but no one would come to the door. The exigent circumstances justified a search of the premises. The police acted with prudence and careful consideration but, even if their decision is judged to be hasty, any evidence in the yard would be in plain sight."

"Explain the chronology for me please, Mr. Hofmann. Did the police officers search the premises before Mr. O'Connor answered the doorbell?" Judge Fitzgerald asked.

"Yes, they did. Officers Ryan and White approached the O'Connor residence and rang the doorbell. When no one answered the door, they searched through the bushes in front of the porch and peered into the house through the windows. They did not go around to the backyard or look in the garage. Mr. O'Connor refused to let them into the house. A search warrant for the entire premises was obtained after he was arrested."

"Yes, I know. I signed it. What was found in the house?"

"As expected, Your Honor, Mr. O'Connor did not bring the murder weapon home with him."

"In other words, they found nothing. There does seem to be something to the accusation that you have tried and convicted the defendant before the trial, Mr. Hofmann."

"The DA's office is convinced that we have the person who committed the crime."

"Hmm," Judge Fitzgerald mused. "The validity of the indictment seems to hinge on the accuracy of Sgt. Ryan's report, which has been contradicted by witnesses and called into question by inconsistencies in statements from other police officers. Did you intend to interview the witnesses from the neighborhood, Mr. Hofmann?"

"Yes, Your Honor. We will make it a priority."

"A priority for the DA's office now but perhaps not before the defense raised the issue regarding conflicting testimony from other witnesses?" the judge asked.

"That's correct." Mr. Hofmann was looking sheepishly down at the floor.

"All right," the judge sighed. "Mr. Hofmann, I would like to hear more from the prosecution before I rule on the defense's objection to the indictment."

"Thank you, Your Honor." Hofmann's tone was obsequious.

I could swear the judge rolled her eyes at him again.

"Your Honor," Attorney Wrightson asked to be recognized.

"Yes, Mr. Wrightson."

"Your Honor, Mr. O'Connor should be released on his own recognizance between court hearings," Attorney Wrightson said.

"Objection!" Mr. Hofmann hollered. "The defendant is a murder suspect."

"He is a suspect only on the basis of a very shaky indictment," Wrightson replied.

"The murder charge and the assault on a police officer are very real. Mr. O'Connor should be held without bail." Hofmann spoke in a belligerent tone.

"Are you asking me to set bail, Mr. Wrightson?"

"Your Honor, I believe Theodore O'Connor can be released on his own recognizance. I can personally vouch for the fact that he is not a flight risk."

"The DA's office does not agree," Mr. Hofmann said.

Chapter 52 . Evasive answers are equivocation.

Judge Fitzgerald was looking toward the table for the defense. She seemed to be sizing me up as if she were about to say something to me. Attorney Wrightson was standing next to me. So, I stood up too. The judge's gaze did not waver.

Across from us at the table for the prosecuting attorneys, Mr. Hofmann sat slumped in his chair waiting to be asked for his argument regarding Wrightson's petition for my release.

An associate from Wrightson's firm appeared at his elbow. I was startled by her sudden arrival. Elmer was not surprised. I think he must have been expecting her. Cynthia de Vries handed him a manila folder. He looked inside and handed it back to her. She whispered something to him and he answered her.

Attorney de Vries walked around behind me to the next seat at the table for the defense. She put a hand on my shoulder as a signal that I should sit back down. Wrightson was already in his chair.

The judge was ready to proceed. "What do you have to say, Mr. Hofmann?" she asked.

The prosecuting attorney answered, "It has already been established that the defendant was present at the scene of the homicide on the night that it occurred. The witness, Elliot Shaw, saw him there at the time of the shooting. Mr. O'Connor has not denied being there and he has admitted entering the premises."

"I believe we can accept that Mr. O'Connor was at the service station. What about inside the store?" The judge looked at Wrightson who shook his head no.

"Your Honor." Attorney de Vries stood up.

"Yes, Ms. de Vries." The judge seemed to be acquainted with the attorney who was assisting with my defense. I found out later that, when she was still in law school, de Vries had won a coveted position to clerk for Judge Fitzgerald.

Attorney de Vries held up the folder and said, "According to the information provided by the District Attorney's office, Mr. Shaw saw Mr. O'Connor and his car at one of the fuel pumps in front of the store. Mr. Shaw did not assert in his written statement that Mr. O'Connor entered the convenience store itself. Mr. O'Connor admitted entering the store in a statement that was part of the improper interrogation on Saturday. Our position is no evidence putting Mr. O'Connor inside the convenience store is admissible at trial."

"Duly noted," the judge said.

"Thank you, Your Honor." Attorney de Vries sat down.

Hofmann just shrugged as if he saw no significance in de Vries's argument.

"You may continue, Mr. Hofmann."

"Thank you. There was bad blood between Mr. O'Connor and the victim. Indeed, on one occasion Mr. O'Connor attacked Matthew Hennigan and threatened to kill him."

I hunched down and leaned forward in my chair. The defense attorney on my left let out a swoosh of air. I turned to face her. Cynthia de Vries gave me an astonished look.

The defense attorney on my right stiffened noticeably in his chair. The report an altercation between Hennigan and myself that came to blows was clearly news to Elmer Wrightson.

He looked at me with a questioning expression. I shrugged and grimaced. He turned away. I could see the muscles tighten in the back of his neck.

"What do we know about the dispute between the defendant and Mr. Hennigan?" the judge asked Hofmann.

Mr. Hofmann said, "We have two witnesses who overheard the argument. They said Mr. O'Connor was very angry. They stood by watching not knowing if they should stay or flee from the defendant's wrath. They observed no one else in the parking lot where it happened at Allen's Diner. The witnesses saw Mr. O'Connor punch Matthew Hennigan in the face. They saw the victim fall to the pavement. They heard Mr. O'Connor threaten to kill him."

"Who are the witnesses?"

"Elliot Shaw and Phyllis Todesco. The latter name was recently added to the list of witnesses for the prosecution. Mr. Shaw was already on the list. The new information was provided this morning to the court and to the defense."

"Have you talked to Shaw or Todesco about this incident, Mr. Wrightson?" the judge asked.

"We have not," he answered without offering an explanation.

The judge studied Elmer Wrightson for a moment. When it was clear he had no excuse to offer, she said, "Go on, Mr. Hofmann."

"There are inconsequential differences between the versions of the incident as reported by the two witnesses. We know from their testimony that the defendant fought with the victim and the defendant threatened to kill the victim."

"Allow me to decide if the differences in the two versions are inconsequential, Mr. Hofmann."

"Yes, Your Honor. Ms. Todesco told us that Mr. O'Connor kicked Mr. Hennigan when he was down. Mr. Shaw said he did not. He stated that Mr. O'Connor acted like he was going to kick him but he held up when Mr. Hennigan yelled and squirmed away. Both witnesses agreed that, after he hit him, Mr. O'Connor threatened to kill Mr. Hennigan. According to Ms. Todesco, he leaned over the man on the ground and shouted, 'You should be shot.' Mr. Shaw thought he said, "I'll kill you for that.'"

"Did the witnesses say what the fight was about?"

"In both statements, Mr. O'Connor was quoted as saying that Mr. Hennigan's cruelty was a terrible thing. That he had hurt an honorable man who deserved better. Ms. Todesco said O'Connor used the name Hector for the person Hennigan had victimized. Mr. Shaw said he did not catch the name. We sked him if it could have been Hector and he did not think Todesco was right. The two witnesses agreed that Mr. O'Connor yelled at Mr. Hennigan that what he had done was intolerable. They both quoted him as using the word intolerable."

The judged asked, "Did you interview Mr. Shaw and Ms. Todesco separately?"

"Of course." There was a hint of disdain for the question in Hofmann's voice. He added with emphasis, "Neither witness was even aware that we were talking to the other." Once again, Hofmann's attitude could not have sat well with the judge.

Morris Hofmann paused as if waiting for her approval of his protocol for interviewing witnesses.

Without giving him the satisfaction, she asked, "Anything else?"

"Yes. In his own words, we have Mr. O'Connor threatening to kill Mr. Hennigan but there is more than the heated argument to support the conclusion that Mr. O'Connor is guilty of taking Matthew Hennigan's life."

"Let's hear it please. Or, are you dragging this out for dramatic effect?"

"No, Your Honor. I'm just trying to make a point."

The judge gave him a look of exasperation. Without saying anything, she held out both hands, palms up in a get-on-with-it gesture.

"Late in the afternoon on the day of the shooting, there was a fifth of bourbon on the counter in Hennigan's convenience store. The bottle was about a third full. Mr. O'Connor picked up the container and, according to a witness, he took three or four swigs and took the bottle with him."

"The name of the witness, please."

"Yes, Your Honor. It was Mr. Shaw. The bottle was the same brand and size as the empty container that the police showed to Mr. O'Connor the next morning in his front yard. The police laboratory lifted Mr. O'Connor's fingerprints from the bottle. They also noted that the lettering on the price tag on the bottle indicated it came from the liquor store right next door to Hennigan's service station. That would be Nora Package Liquors."

Mr. Wrightson was again startled by the unexpected. He turned to look at me or rather glare at me with anger in his eyes. He mouthed the question, "A liquor bottle with your fingerprints?"

De Vries whispered to me, "How did we not know about these things?"

"May we have a moment, Your Honor?" The defense attorney asked.

"Did this last piece of news take you by surprise, Mr. Wrightson?" the judge asked. "Perhaps, the defense was also not aware of the combative relationship between the defendant and the victim."

Without responding either to the judge's question or to her comment, my attorney said, "Your Honor, the defense requests a brief recess."

"Denied. There is no room on the court's schedule for a recess at this time no matter how brief. In the future, Mr. Wrightson, be prepared to adequately represent your client. Please try to be fully informed before this case goes to trial."

I could feel the seethe in his voice when Elmer Wrightson answered, "Yes, Your Honor."

If it were possible for smoke to billow from an angry attorney's ears, it would have filled the courtroom.

Chapter 53 . The petition to dismiss was denied.

In light of the disturbing accounts of the contentious relationship between the defendant and the victim, the motion to dismiss the charge of premeditated murder is denied," Judge Anne Fitzgerald pronounced.

I could not turn to look but I knew the sound of Eileen's sobs. I had not heard the likes of it since her maternal grandfather died. I also knew the strength of my wife's character. Lydia would not show her disappointment to any of the onlookers. Diane's reaction was quiet too. She was becoming more and more like her mother.

The disappointment was not as devastating for me as it was for my family. Attorney Wrightson had advised me that a decision to dismiss was not likely. He had explained that there was very little about my circumstances that the judge could use to justify summary dismissal of the murder charge. Even though there were serious questions about the prosecution's case against me, only the discovery of gross discrepancies would allow her to dissent from the District Attorney's decision to seek a conviction.

The judge continued, "The motion regarding the assault charge will be taken under consideration. To release Mr. O'Connor pending trial dates is also a matter for further review. In the meantime, the defendant shall remain in custody."

Judge Anne Fitzgerald said, "Mr. Hofmann, the prosecution has some work to do. Talk to the witnesses who were in the neighborhood on Saturday morning and come back with a convincing argument for the validity of the indictment. You need to establish the credibility of the police reports. While hardly optimal, the court can accept minor discrepancies if you can provide reasonable explanations. However, there seem to be some significant disagreements in the various accounts. Do you understand my problem with your case?"

"Yes, Your Honor."

"Let's see. Today is Monday. There is a trial starting in here at one o'clock. It is likely to take the rest of the week but I will squeeze you in prior to the proceedings on Wednesday morning. Is two days enough time, Mr. Hofmann?"

"I believe so."

"All right. This will take a bit more thought. As I mentioned, we need to clear the room for another hearing that is due to start in a few minutes. Join me in my chambers. The defendant will remain in custody for the moment. We are in recess until Wednesday morning at nine o'clock." She stood up. "Mr. Wrightson, we shall discuss the question of bail."

"All Stand," the bailiff called but the order did not seem to be necessary. We were already on our feet.

Judge Anne Fitzgerald stepped down from behind the bench and strode out through a concealed door to the right of the imposing tall desk at the front of the courtroom.

De Vries said, "Elmer, I will go back to the office to continue with the items on our list."

"Sure, do that," Elmer answered in a disgruntled tone of voice. He said nothing to me.

The uniformed officer who had escorted me into the room was standing at my side. He took my arm and ushered me toward the side door through which we had entered prior to the morning's proceedings.

I watched Janet Bread follow Wrightson and Hofmann through the same exit that the Judge had taken. John Yoder, the second attorney at the prosecutor's table, was the last to join the group. His presence had hardly been felt during the morning's proceedings. He had participated just once.

I turned to look back at my wife and children. Lydia gave me a small wave. I blew her a kiss and tried to smile. She smiled back and returned the kiss. Her gesture was heartening. It engendered a sense of relief.

Mine was an emotional rollercoaster unlike anything I had previously experienced. To be incarcerated for unruly behavior is traumatic. To be arrested for murder is much worse. I had to turn away to hide the tears in my eyes.

As the deputy guided me toward the door, I saw that Mr. Yoder had come back into the courtroom. He looked a bit dejected. Evidently, he was not needed in the judge's chambers.

Chapter 54 . Prison guards were escorts from the courtroom.

The exit through the side door opened to an interior hallway adjacent to the courtroom. It led to the deliberation room for the jury in one direction. About fifteen feet the other way was a holding cell where prisoners waited on their way to or from a session before the judge. I had been confined in that cell a few times myself.

While still at the table for the defense, I had to suffer the humiliation of restraints reattached to my wrists. I left the courtroom, walked past the holding cell to the elevators, and headed back upstairs. The jailhouse was on the fifth and sixth floors of the municipal headquarters in Batavia. Judge Fitzgerald's courtroom and her chambers were on the fourth floor.

To my surprise, one of the two guards spoke to me when we got on the elevator. "Sorry about the handcuffs, Mr. O'Connor, but we gotta follow the rules."

"Yes, I know."

"You clocked Ryan pretty good. That som-a-bitch had it coming."

"What?" I laughed.

"Billy told us what happened."

"Billy?" The reference to Officer White caught me off guard.

"Yeah, Billy White. He's a good cop."

"Oh," was all I could think to say.

"We ain't allowed to talk to you but that Ryan is an arrogant jerk. He can be a real asshole sometimes."

The other guard snorted, "Sometimes, Denny? Ya mean all the time."

"Shh," Denny laughed.

They took me to the attorney-client conference room on the fifth floor and waited outside the door. Half an hour later, my lawyer walked in.

Chapter 55 . The defense attorney cannot tolerate equivocation.

Elmer Wrightson entered the conference room in a quiet fury. He collapsed into the chair across the table from me and sat there looking down at the floor. The silence dragged on toward awkward.

When it was too much for me to endure, I said, "I know you asked for the recess to talk to me about a couple of surprises in the courtroom."

Attorney Wrightson rose to his feet. He leaned toward me over the table and shouted, "A couple of surprises! Is that what they were? No! They were much worse than that. Your surprises were misrepresentations of the truth that a defendant on trial for murder fed to his attorney. What the hell were you thinking?"

I squeaked out an answer. "I was hoping my problems with Hennigan would not come up. I was afraid, if I told you that I took a swing at him one time, you might think the worst and decline to take the case."

In an even louder voice, Attorney Wrightson rejected my excuse. "I'll tell you what would make me decline to take a case. Deceit by a client would make me run as far away as I could go." He stood there glaring at me. He was breathing hard.

"I'm sorry."

"The reason I requested a recess was not to ask you about your so-called surprises but to tell you that I was going to petition the judge to allow me to resign from your defense."

"Are you going to resign?" I shuddered. Elmer's chilling words scared me.

"You're lucky the request for a recess was denied. It gave me a chance to cool off."

I said, "Thank you. I don't know how my family and I can repay you." I could not detect that he had cooled off.

"Your family, of course, is the major reason I cannot drop your case. I am doing this as much for Diane, Eileen, and Lydia as for you."

"I know."

Attorney Wrightson stood with his back to me and arms folded across his chest. When he finally turned to face me again, he asked, "What was your fight with Matthew Hennigan about?"

"Did you know Angel Hernandez?"

"Yes, what does he have to do with anything?" The annoyance in Wrightson's voice was still loud and clear.

"It was Hennigan who ratted out Angel Hernandez to the Immigration and Customs Enforcement."

"Oh, I wondered what happened to the Hernandez family. Iola and Angel were clients. She came to me first to get help for him with ICE. They just disappeared before I got a chance to look into their situation." Elmer was finally speaking in a calm voice.

"We were close to their family. Eileen and Diane looked after their children."

"Now that you mention it, Señora Hernandez told me you were friends."

"Diane was teaching Christina, their eldest, how to drive."

"Christina's mother was worried about that too. I advised against it," Attorney Wrightson said.

"Angel Hernandez worked with me at the Batavia Service Center. He was a very good man with a beautiful, young family."

"So, when you learned that Hennigan betrayed the Hernandez family, you attacked him?"

"It was not premeditated. I bumped into Hennigan at a school function that he sponsored at Allen's Diner. It was a few months after the family disappeared. I do not recall how it came up but I said something about Angel Hernandez to Hennigan and Shaw. I told them I wondered how Angel and his family were doing. Hennigan blurted it out. He thought it was funny. He was laughing about it. I clocked him a good one and he fell down whimpering that he was sorry."

"Did you threaten to kill him?"

"My exact words were, 'I could kill you for that, you evil bastard.' My empathy for an immigrant from Mexico is what made Hennigan laugh as if the Hernandez family amounted to nothing. That's when I lost it and let him have it. Hennigan was such a psycho that he thought nothing of reporting an illegal alien no matter who would get hurt but I never meant that I could kill him."

"Do the witnesses have it backwards? You threatened Hennigan before you hit him?"

"That's right. I yelled at him. He laughed. I hit him. He went down. I did not kick him."

"It is difficult for me to believe that you thought it was all right not to tell me about this."

"The hard feelings did not last. The next time I saw him at a baseball game, he didn't say anything about it and neither did I. It was as if it never happened."

"All right," Wrightson sighed. "The case against you is more serious than I hoped. We have to face the fact that the prosecution has a strong argument that you had motive." Wrightson sat back down across from me. His solemn expression made him look tired. It worried me.

"I'm scared, Elmer. I try not to think about it but what happens to me if I'm found guilty of murder."

"We will face that challenge when and if we must. We are, of course, making notes for an appeal, which will be filed immediately. Otherwise, I refuse to worry about a bad verdict before it's necessary. It takes too much energy away from the work we need to do for the trial. I recommend you take the same approach."

"I'll try. I'm sorry I didn't tell you everything before."

"So am I. However, it only means that my job is more difficult than I had anticipated. Even so, the burden of proof is on the DA's office and, as I see it, their case is still weak."

"I'm relieved to hear you say that but witnesses heard me threaten to kill Hennigan. He wronged a dear friend of mine."

"True. However, motive is not proof."

"What else do they need."

"A lot. They don't even have the murder weapon. Although I do not believe the prosecution has enough for a conviction, it would be a mistake to take an acquittal for granted. Juries can be capricious."

"Shouldn't the District Attorney have seen the weaknesses in their case?"

"It would seem so. However, they did not which means your question needs to be addressed. Why is the DA pressing the case against you? The explanation I will use in court is the police ensnared an ambitious prosecutor in their witless vendetta against a vulnerable suspect."

"Alcoholism and a history of arrests make me vulnerable. Striking a police officer is the motivation for their vendetta."

"In a nutshell, I think that's about right."

"We need to prove I didn't do it."

"No. That is not correct. We only have to refute the prosecutor's arguments that you did do it."

"Yes, I understand that."

"It would help if we could suggest that Hennigan had enemies. Are there reasons the victim was likely to be an object of enmity from others?"

"Hennigan was a hard guy to like. He had an icy demeanor with little empathy for anyone's problems. In fact, it was easy for me to believe that he betrayed Angel Hernandez. I just knew it was true the instant he laughed about it. So, yes, I think there were probably a lot of people who did not like him."

"We want more than an unpleasant or even a nasty disposition. I would like to find other incidents that made Hennigan an obvious object of hatred. We have to intensify our investigation into his background, friends, and associates."

"There is clearly someone out there who wanted him dead," I stated the obvious.

Wrightson said, "My firm has an arrangement with an independent detective agency which specializes in investigating personal histories. I'll have an associate talk to them. Also, I have cleared another name with the judge. We know a private investigator who could be very helpful and effective. Let me think about it."

"OK.," I said.

Although I did not know it at the time, my attorney was referring to Janet Bread. She had just presented herself to the judge in chambers at the conclusion of that morning's session.

Elmer leaned back with his hands behind his head just looking out into space.

"What are you thinking about?" I asked.

"Just trying to put the pieces together." The enigmatic attorney was someone I could not read very well at that moment.

Finally, he said, "Right now, I need you to review with me everything that happened at the convenience store on Friday evening. Given the revelations in court today, it's clear that you left me with a foggy idea about your relationship with Matthew Hennigan. I am particularly unhappy that your deceit was intentional. I hope you recognize it was a mistake. Have you been equivocal with me about other matters regarding what happened last Friday?"

"No," I insisted.

"Good but we must go over everything again. Judge Fitzgerald was correct. You should expect a competent lawyer to be better prepared than I was this morning."

"It wasn't your fault."

"Tell that to the judge." The irony was quite evident in Wrightson's steely tone.

"I'm sorry," I said again.

"I want to know anything and everything about Friday evening. If it comes to mind, you tell me. If it seems trivial or inconsequential, you tell me. Only I will decide if it is or is not important."

"OK," I agreed.

"Good," he repeated. Elmer Wrightson was talking down to me but I was in no position to object. "Fitzgerald is exacting and not given to overlook deficiencies in a defense attorney's representation of a client. Although it is of little consolation right now, the prosecutor is held to a similar level of high standards."

Chapter 56 . The defendant must fill in the gaps.

"Tell me about your fingerprints on the liquor bottle?"

"There was a Jim Beam bottle, a fifth, on the counter next to the popcorn machine at Hennigan's. I was too embarrassed to mention it to you before. I did not want to admit to you that I was tempted by it."

"Were you?"

"I don't know. Fortunately, the temptation was void. I might not have taken sip even if there had been anything left but it was empty. There is a fact of life that I know in my gut to be true. Just a taste is an oxymoron. There is no such thing for an alcoholic. I picked up the bottle from the counter at Hennigan's, realized it was empty, and tossed it into the trash."

"Where?"

"In the barrel with a black plastic liner that is always there at the end of the counter."

"Was the trash can empty?"

"It has a swinging top and I didn't look. Actually, when I pushed the bottle in, I heard it thunk to the bottom of the can. I remember thinking that I was glad it didn't break."

"OK, there could have been some debris in there but not much," Elmer conjectured.

"It had to have been emptied recently. The barrel is usually overflowing with garbage by late in the day."

"I suspect someone saw you with that bottle. How certain are you that no one else was in the store?"

"I was very sure at the time. I looked down every aisle and no one answered my hello. I figured whoever was on duty might just be in the lavatory. The door is always closed whether the room is occupied or not. There is just the one restroom for men or women. You have to knock before trying the knob if you need to use the facilities."

"What about the office?"

"The lavatory is to the right down the center aisle and the office is to the left. I could see through the office windows in the door and in the wall that it was completely dark in there."

Elmer said, "I presume, if someone were in the lavatory, they couldn't have seen you. Maybe not been able to hear you either."

"There is one more thing."

"Something else you decided not to tell me before?" Elmer yelped. He was tired and exasperated.

"Well, you have me second guessing everything. I thought I had already told you the important details until things went awry in the courtroom this morning."

"All right. What is it?"

"The whole time I was inside, my car was still parked at the pump where I filled the tank. I had not bothered to move it. I was not paying close attention to it but I did look out when I heard another vehicle pull in. Whoever it was would have used another pump. A little while later I noticed the car was gone. Maybe it was Elliot Shaw and that was when he saw me."

"There were no cash transactions and his name was not on the list of credit-card payments. It had to be one of the other two purchases made after yours."

"Maybe it was Shaw just returning from an errand and not there to buy gas."

"OK. If it was Elliot Shaw, wouldn't you expect him to come inside?" Elmer asked.

"I don't know. Is it possible he was aware that trouble was afoot?"

"I obviously need to depose the man. There is clearly more to the prosecution's interrogation of Shaw than in his signed statement which does not say he saw you in the store or observed the shooting."

"I am trying to think of other ways he might have seen me at Hennigan's."

"So am I," Elmer said. "You seem pretty confident that he was not hiding inside the store. Maybe he was in his car at a pump or in a parking space. Perhaps he was next door at Nora's. In any case, Shaw has things to say that could be helpful to us. It will be up to me to drag it out of him."

"Shaw could have shot his boss over a labor dispute of some kind," I suggested.

"That would have occurred to the police, of course. For some reason, they don't think so."

I said, "You know what? There is something else."

"Really? Something more?" Elmer exclaimed. His exasperation was showing again.

I just sighed before explaining, "Now that I think about it, the door to the lavatory was not shut tight. It was slightly ajar. It doesn't always close completely on its own."

"Was the light on?"

"No, it was dark in there."

"You're sure?"

"Yes. I walked partway down the center aisle to listen for any sound but I stopped when I saw the door was open a crack and the light was off."

"If someone was in there in the dark, could you have seen them?"

"Not if they backed away from the narrow opening."

"All right. Are you coming up with anything else?"

"I don't think so. No one answered my hello when I walked in. I waited around for a while. It occurred to me that Matt or Elliot could be in the office or the restroom but, as I said, I checked and concluded no one was there. That's when I decided to give up and go home. It seemed to me that whoever was on duty must have left the premises."

"Enough for today. We have a ton of material that has to be whittled down into concise statements for the hearing on Wednesday morning. The judge will be considering the requirements for your release pending the trial and she will indicate her preference for the schedule. In this case, the term preference is a euphemism for the judge's non-negotiable decisions about the dates."

"When do you think we might have to go to trial?"

"Probably not for a while which is disappointing but there is a bright side if you can call it that under these conditions. It is difficult for a judge to deny bail when there is a long delay."

Chapter 57 . The attorney's advice was helpful and sobering.

My parents came to see me during the regularly allocated time slot late Monday afternoon. My lengthy session with Attorney Wrightson concluded not long before they arrived.

"Sorry we were not in court this morning," Mother apologized.

"The entire ordeal is just too much for us," Dad said.

"It's OK. I hate putting you through all of this. In fact, it is probably better if you were not there."

"We are getting old, you know." Dad smiled. Or, was it a grimace? "We will do whatever we can. If it is important for the case, we can show up at the trial if we have to."

"That's right," Mother agreed.

"We can ask Elmer when and if you should be there and for how long," I said.

"We will do what is needed. We will." Mother's voice was shaky. She looked at Dad and stood up to leave.

The sad look on his face told me that they had done what they could just by coming to say hello. I thanked them again and repeated how sorry I was for this new burden.

"I've been arrested before but this time I didn't do it."

"We know," Mother said. "Oh, I almost forgot, we brought you the newspaper. Your father said they wouldn't let us bring anything in here but they said it was OK. So, I was right." She gave Dad the I-told-you-so look. Her attempt to give me a cheerful smile didn't really work.

Mother handed me that morning's copy of the New York Times and they walked out without looking back. I supposed that they couldn't.

Diane came in with Eileen in the middle of the day on Tuesday. They brought lunch, a Reuben sandwich from the deli.

"Wow, my favorite sandwich. Thank you. They do have food in here you know."

"We figured jailhouse fare cannot be too good for you," Eileen said.

"Or, even edible," Diane made a face.

"Thank you."

We were all quiet for a couple of minutes but nobody squirmed. A moment of silence just seemed right.

The visitor's room in the Batavia city jail was not like anything that you see in the movies. We were in a fishbowl atmosphere with a glass wall and a large window in the door. The guard's office was right across the hall. They could watch our every move but did not seem to be paying us any attention.

Everyone had to pass through a metal-detector on the way in from the outside but there was no bullet proof glass with intercoms that separated visitors from inmates. We could talk to each other face to face. We were in an unadorned, grey room sparsely furnished with straight back chairs and a large metal table. There were no listening devices or TV cameras that I could see.

"How are you two taking all of this?" I asked.

"We are staying home and away from everybody for a while. Just reading or watching a movie. We are mostly trying not to think about it. Not to worry, Dad. We will have a big party for you when it's all over," Diane said.

"Nicole is coming over for a little while this afternoon. She is a good friend and she is completely on my side." Eileen was sure of her best friend's loyalty.

"I called my nosy boss and asked for a few days off from work. She couldn't say no," Diane said.

"Of course not, you're way too important," Eileen chided her big sister.

"Watch it or you can walk home."

"Da-a-ad, ever since she learned to drive, Diane thinks she's the boss."

I just smiled.

Diane explained, "Mother said we should lay low for a few days. We can figure out what to do as time goes by."

Before I sent them on their way, I told Diane and Eileen how much I loved them and appreciated how lucky I was to have such wonderful daughters.

When Lydia came to see me late in the afternoon on Tuesday, I said, "I really appreciate the great job you did raising the children."

"They're yours too."

"They brought lunch for me. How does my family circumvent jailhouse rules?"

"When Elmer Wrightson tells people how things are going to be, no one in this town thinks to contradict him," Lydia stated what was quite true in our community.

"I heard that," Elmer laughed. He walked in with Diane and Eileen in tow. Janet Bread was with them too.

"Oh, did we know you would be back this evening?" Lydia looked startled.

I said, "Lydia, I did not get a chance to tell you that I asked my attorney to explain to all of us what to expect. I asked my parents to join us this evening but they said they are not up for it."

Just then there was a knock on the door almost on queue. Elmer released the latch and Officer William White stepped in.

"What are you doing here, Billy?" Diane spoke in a slightly breathless voice.

Officer White answered the question by speaking to me. "Mr. O'Connor, your folks called and I offered to drive them here and escort them in. I can come back and drive them home when they are ready."

Mom and Dad came into the room. After a moment of confusion, Diane ushered them to seats next to each other at the table across from Lydia and Janet. Eileen and Diane took protective positions on either side of their grandparents. I was at one end of the table and Elmer remained standing.

"Thank you very much, Officer White." Attorney Wrightson said. "We will be sure they get home. You do not need to come back." He held the door open and Billy left us alone.

"Thank you for coming, Mom and Dad," I whispered to them.

"Hello, Mr. and Mrs. O'Connor. I was about to tell the family about what we should expect during the legal proceedings ahead of us," Wrightson said.

Lydia spoke to my parents. "Mom and Dad, I'm glad you came. We are probably not going to like what Elmer has to say but I think it would be worse for us to be surprised by unpleasant events."

Both parents nodded their heads. Her words could not be reassuring for my folks but Lydia was right. They needed to hear it as much as any of us.

"There are things that you have to be prepared for," Elmer began. "To state the obvious, to be charged with murder is horrible and traumatic. It will take time and endurance for us to get through this nightmare."

Eileen gulped back a sob.

"I'm sorry, Eileen," Attorney Wrightson said. "Listen, Ted, everyone, there is no point to sugar-coating our predicament. In the best-case scenario, we can expect the ordeal to last for a few weeks, possibly longer."

"How is my family supposed to manage this mess?" I asked.

"There is only one way, Ted, and that is to plow through it one day at a time. To begin with, Diane, Eileen, and Lydia, just stay home out of sight for at least the first week. The same advice applies to you, Mr. and Mrs. O'Connor."

"And after that?" Diane presumed an assertive role.

"You must not give up and hide out for ever. If you do, you allow the bad guys to win. We cannot let that happen. As difficult as it might be, all of us have to go back to our lives as usual."

"How do we handle nosy friends?" Diane asked.

"The best way to keep from constantly thrashing out the bad feelings is to keep the circle of friends you talk to as small as possible. The five of you, Mrs. and Mr. O'Connor, Lydia, Diane, and Eileen, may be as large a group as you need. When you want to talk to someone about a bad day, seek out one another. If that is not enough or when you start to get on each other's nerves, be very careful about choosing someone else to confide in. Even well-meaning friends and co-workers might not be able to keep your confidence. How did you put it, Diane, nosy friends? Nosy friends can be terrible gossips."

Eileen spoke up, "My friend, Nicole, came over today. All she could talk about was if I thought my dad is a murderer. She is not my best friend anymore."

"I'm afraid that is exactly the right example. Even well-meaning friends can be hurtful. There may come a day, Eileen, when you want to forgive Nicole but she is not a good person to talk to right now."

"Not now, Not ever!" Eileen avowed.

"You can also talk to me or Aunt Janet. You can consult with any of us on your legal team. There will be one or two more attorneys in my firm coming up to speed on the case. Some of you have met Cynthia de Vries."

"I think she is nice," Eileen said.

Attorney Wrightson continued, "A viable alternative to trusting a best friend, who might turn out to be unsympathetic or not such a good friend, is professional counseling. When you need someone to talk to about personal matters, I strongly recommend scheduling meetings with a clinical psychologist. Call Katherine Chavis in my office if you need a name."

"Good advice." Janet Bread affirmed. "Thank you, Elmer. Listen everyone. As my cousin Lydia knows, you can talk to me whenever you want but, from my experience, I can tell you that professional counselors can be a great help."

Wrightson said, "All right, the first thing on my list was to advise you to hunker down behind closed doors for just a week or ten days. After that, you must live your lives as normally as possible. When people ask how you are doing, just say you are OK or you have good days and bad. Do not discuss details. If the person persists, be insistent that you cannot talk about it right now.

"The rest of my agenda for this evening is to let you know about the legal proceedings just ahead of us. Tomorrow's session will begin promptly at nine o'clock in the morning.

"I will start by casting doubt on the authenticity of the evidence and the DA's case. I will press the issue particularly hard with respect to the charge of assaulting a police officer. However, the judge has already ruled against dismissing the murder charge and she really can't reverse herself on that decision.

"I will ask the court to release Ted on his own recognizance. The prosecutor will object. If the judge turns down the motion, she can set bail in which case we will have to figure out how to cover the specified amount. The Eighth Amendment to the Constitution prohibits excessive bail but it does not say that the judge must release a suspect on bail.

"Once again, the prosecution will object but they do not have an irrefutable argument against us. The primary reasons for not setting bail are that the defendant is a flight risk and that the defendant poses a risk to himself or others. I do not believe the judge is disposed to believe either argument. However, released on bail is not total freedom. There will be conditions.

"They are out to get my son," Mother sighed.

Elmer tried to reassure her. "No, please don't think that way, Mrs. O'Connor. An important thing to keep in mind is that bail while awaiting trial is not punishment for the crime. It cannot be. Remember innocent until proven guilty. Bail is a monetary assurance that the accused will show up for subsequent proceedings. It is not a fine."

I interrupted with questions. "What sort of conditions? How much liberty will I have? Can I go back to work?"

My attorney gave answers. "The first of the two common conditions for release while awaiting trial is periodic reporting to a court-designated representative. I will offer an associate in the firm. Another possibility for a person whom the judge can accept is the group leader for your AA meetings if he is willing. Your AA sponsor is not appropriate because his first priority is to keep your confidence."

"Why is that a problem?" I asked.

Mother answered my question. It should not have been surprising that she knew how recovery was supposed to work. She said, "Your sponsor is there to help you solve problems yourself not to report you to authorities for any transgression."

"Rosemary is an expert on these matters. She has attended many Al-Anon lectures." My father rescued Mother from the chuckling in the room.

"You made a good point, Rosemary," Janet Bread said.

Elmer Wrightson continued, "The second common condition for your release, Ted, is travel restrictions. You will not be able to leave town and there may well be a curfew requiring you to be home by a certain time every evening with only court-approved exceptions.

"The judge can allow you to go back to work. The Batavia Service Center is a possibility but you might not want to force the issue at the public school."

Attorney Wrightson continued to do the talking. "A strong argument for your release, Ted, is the delay between now and the date for a trial. Her calendar is open to the public. Cynthia De Vries checked it out. She could not see how Fitzgerald could fit us in for preliminary sessions in less than two weeks. We should know more by tomorrow when the judge is likely to be ready to dictate the schedule. Any more questions?"

No one said anything. We just sat in glum silence.

"OK, everyone," Elmer said. "Do you need me to say more or is that enough for tonight?"

Diane spoke up. "When will all the court sessions be over?"

"Nothing is certain but I can tell you about both extremes. The trial could go quickly and it might be all over by the end of the month. Or, jury selection, fact gathering, objections, replies to objections, et cetera could drag on and it could take until the end of the year."

"What if Dad goes to jail?"

"That is not going to happen. Don't even think it." Elmer Wrightson categorically denied the possibility.

The silence that returned to the room was not as glum as it had been.

Wrightson saw that we were looking to him for more. He said, "We could talk about what might happen further down the road but it would be idle speculation. I will try to meet with all of you like this as often as necessary and whenever there is new information to be shared with you.

"Oh, one other thing. I should have mentioned Detective Bread's role at the beginning of our meeting tonight. Janet has agreed to come on board at the firm to investigate issues related to the case. In particular, it is very important for us to get much more information about Matthew Hennigan and his life in Batavia. The court and the prosecution have both been informed that she is joining our team. The judge has signed off on the arrangement."

"What did Hofmann say?" I asked.

Janet replied, "That man objects to everything. He will never be happy."

Attorney Wrightson put his hand on my shoulder. "Now we should all get some rest. I will see you in the morning, Ted. The rest of you go home and try to get some sleep.

"Mr. and Mrs. O'Connor, your presence in the courtroom may well be useful in the future but not so much tomorrow. Do not feel that you should show up in the morning. We need to conserve your energy for when your support is important."

Mother started around the table to give me a hug but Elmer stopped her.

Janet held up her hand to hold me back too. "Stay there. We don't want to rile the guards." They were looking in from the open door watching while my visitors exited the room.

"It's OK, Mother. They want to be sure that you don't slip me some contraband," I joked.

"Exactly!" Janet Bread was serious.

Elmer explained, "A hug can be OK one day and not the next. Some of the guards are more uptight about the rules than others."

Lydia went home and I tried to sleep but it was hard. Notwithstanding all of the attention that I was getting from my parents and family, time in jail was a heavy burden. My wife told me her nights were fitful as well.

My confinement in the city jail was interminable. The hours and minutes crawled by from one set of visitors to the next and from court session to court session.

Chapter 58 . On Wednesday morning, the judge held the bail hearing.

The proceedings began in the usual fashion on Wednesday morning. It was exactly nine o'clock when the bailiff called us to our feet. The judge entered the room and climbed the stairs to her place on the bench.

The Honorable Anne Fitzgerald made her decisions known. She said, "I have reviewed the police reports regarding the incident in front of Mr. O'Connor's house. I have read the statement submitted over Mr. Alex Montoya's signature. According to the attorneys for the defense and for the prosecution, the views of the other witnesses are in essential agreement with the testimony from Mr. Montoya.

"I have noted a number of inconsistencies among the various versions from the witnesses. In my judgement none makes a substantial difference. The indictment for first-degree murder stands. However, nothing from the conversation between the police officers and Mr. O'Connor on Saturday morning is admissible at trial. The existence of an empty liquor bottle with Mr. O'Connor's fingerprints will be admissible at trial.

"Finally, I am inclined to take into consideration the claim that certain actions by the defendant were the natural impulse of a parent in defense of a daughter.

"Mr. Hofmann, does the prosecutor have anything to add before I rule on the motion to dismiss the charge of assaulting a police officer?"

"Your Honor, I spoke to Police Chief Jennifer Hepburn this morning. The Police Department does not care to join in the assault accusation against Mr. O'Connor. She assured me that the victim of the attack was on board with the decision." Morris Hofmann answered the judge with a clear lack of enthusiasm in his tone.

He continued, "Without their support, it would be difficult to establish the assault charge even though an impartial jury might well have found the defendant to be fully culpable. Hence, the District Attorney has decided not to pursue the matter at this time."

"The court accepts the motion to dismiss the charge of assaulting a police officer. Dismissed," Judge Fitzgerald pronounced with the pound of her gavel on the desk.

Elmer Wrightson let out a sigh of relief.

I was unsure. I whispered, "What does he mean by 'not at this time'?"

Elmer answered me in a similarly low voice, "Hofmann might prefer to take up the matter again later but he cannot. The judge dismissed the charge. The DA cannot bring it up again. It's over."

"Mr. Wrightson do you have something to share with the court?" The judge interrupted our private conversation.

Without missing a beat, Attorney Wrightson rose to his feet and said, "There is the matter of releasing Mr. O'Connor on his own recognizance."

"Can you add justification to the motion?"

"Mr. O'Connor's first priority is to seek full exoneration in court. In addition, he has family and meaningful employment in Batavia. Hence, he is not a flight risk. As a respected citizen of his community, there is no reason to suspect that Mr. O'Connor would be inclined to skirt any conditions imposed on his movements."

"Does the office of the District Attorney have any objection?" The judge turned to Hofmann.

"Indeed, we do," he shouted. "He assaulted a police officer and he is accused of murder ..."

The judge interrupted, "Mr. Hofmann, the assault charge has been dismissed. To bring it up again might well constitute contempt for this court's decision."

"OK, sorry Your Honor." At best, it was a snippy apology from Mr. Hofmann.

The Honorable Fitzgerald held up her hand. "Mr. Hofmann, please address this court in a respectful manner."

The truculent Morris Hofmann answered in a less obnoxious tone. Evidently, the message had seeped in that he might be testing the limits to the judge's patience.

He said, "The defendant has been charged with an horrendous crime. He has a sordid past with several arrests for crimes and serious misdemeanors. Such criminal behavior is a strong indicator of a flight risk. He is a threat to the safety of members of our community. The defendant should be confined until trial."

"Mr. Wrightson, how do you answer the prosecutor's objections?"

"Your Honor, Mr. O'Connor does not deny the difficulties he had earlier in his life. However, the behavior that Mr. Hofmann referred to is ancient history. We have statements attesting to Mr. O'Connor's character from the group leader of the Alcoholics Anonymous chapter that he has attended for over seven years and from his employers."

Judge Anne Fitzgerald looked over at me for a full minute and announced, "The defendant shall be free on bail until trial."

"Mr. Wrightson and Mr. Hofmann, join me in chambers to discuss the terms and to look at my calendar for the schedule."

The bailiff called, "All rise."

The judge stood, descended the steps hidden behind the bench, and left through the exit on the back wall.

"So, what now?" I asked Attorney Wrightson.

"They will keep you in custody while we arrange bail. I have to get back there immediately to make sure nothing happens behind my back." He was hurriedly gathering up papers from the table. "It is never a good idea to let the prosecutor have the judge's ear without being there to refute his assertions especially when it is Hofmann spewing nonsense."

Morris Hofmann was already on his way to the judge's chambers a few steps ahead of the always-knows-how-to-keep-the-advantage Elmer Wrightson. He left me at the table for the defense but he did not leave me alone.

The same two men as on the previous occasions escorted me out of the courtroom, back up the elevator, and into the attorney-client conference room. They parked me at the table without removing the handcuffs and took up their usual posts outside the door.

The wait to hear from my attorney lasted longer than usual. It seemed like hours until the guard called Denny finally opened the door.

"Your lawyer is not coming here. We are supposed to take you downstairs," he said.

Chapter 59 . The defendant's past was slow to let go.

The prison guards escorted me down a level to the booking desk on the fifth floor. Attorney Wrightson was there waiting for me. My papers and things from my dreary, cold cell were on the bench against the wall.

"You are free on bail until trial," Elmer said.

"How much was the bail? Who posted the bond?"

"We can talk in private after we are out of here. Come this way." Wrightson pointed to the window where I could pick up my personal belongings as if I did not know the way.

"Thanks, Denny. Thanks fellas," I said to the two guards as they removed the handcuffs.

My wallet, belt, and keys were already on the counter. I picked them up without saying anything to the expressionless clerk standing across from me inside his cage.

Wrightson and I passed through the double locked passageway that separated the jail from the outside world. We walked to the public elevators and rode them down to the building's main entrance. He stopped in the courthouse lobby a few steps away from the temporary freedom for a man awaiting trial for murder.

"You go ahead. Diane will pick you up at the curb. I'll see you in the office." Wrightson turned around and walked back toward the elevators.

Diane was there at the bottom of the courthouse steps. She said, "Mr. Wrightson wants us to go directly to his office building. He will meet us in the conference room. Mom told me to drive you over there."

"Where did she go? What happened to the reporters who were in the courtroom?"

"Mr. Wrightson had us wait for him in a private room for lawyers and witnesses. When he got there, he told us you would be free to go until the next court session. He said the press would think that you were not getting out when they saw Mom drive away. Then, he left us to go see you."

On the way over to Wrightson and Associates, I said to Diane, "My horrid past will not let go of me. I am sorry that I was not a better father to you and Eileen from the beginning. Sorry that my past has thrust the family into another crisis."

"Don't think that way," Diane spoke to her father in a firm tone of voice.

I said, "I just wish the judge could have seen the foolishness in all this and dismissed the murder charge."

"This is just a brief, temporary setback. You will be exonerated and we will have our lives back in no time."

"Did Elmer Wrightson tell you that too?"

"He did give us a pep talk just now before he went off to see you. He was optimistic about the case but I guess he didn't say it would be over in no time. I added that part."

"I hope you're right."

"This whole thing is unreal. They can't possibly keep it up."

"Thank you, Diane. When will we awaken from this nightmare?"

Chapter 60 . On Wednesday afternoon, the defense met at the firm.

Diane drove directly onto the entrance ramp for the Executive Level in the parking garage under the Monroe office building. She took a card from her purse and inserted it into the reader to gain admission at the gate.

She descended the turns on the tightly curled entrance to the lowest level and parked in a numbered space next to Lydia's car. We walked to the elevator. Diane entered a code and pushed the Up button.

The young woman saw my puzzled expression. She explained, "The people who work for Wrightson and Associates think of everything. They are very competent. Ms. Chavis was with Mr. Wrightson when he came to see us in the conference room at the courthouse."

"Ah yes, Katherine Chavis, not one to exhibit much empathy."

Diane agreed, "Yes, that's the one. After his pep talk, Mr. Wrightson left the room and Ms. Chavis took over. She told us where to park and where to go in this building."

"Is that how you got the pass card for the garage?"

"Yes, Ms. Chavis had one for Mom and a second one for me. She used a Sharpie to write space numbers and the elevator code on the case." Diane held it up for me to see.

I said, "She is a capable assistant. Elmer relies on her pretty heavily. Katherine Chavis is in charge of keeping the office running."

"She did say she knows you."

I replied, "She should. I've been here often enough. In friendlier times, I could stop by to visit with Elmer. Some days, the firm would bring in a working lunch. If Elmer himself had the time, he would call me to see if I wanted to join him."

"Nothing like a free lunch."

"As true as that might be, the point is there were times I was welcome here even when I was not in trouble with the law."

"Good to know, Dad," Diane chided.

Without acknowledging her sarcasm, I said, "I think Chavis does a good job. She has been with the firm a long time, from the beginning I think. Back when I could come and go as Elmer's friend, she learned what I liked in my coffee and anticipated lunch requirements and everything. Even so, she was never very friendly."

Diane pushed the button in the elevator for the sixth floor. "Chavis said for us to go to the Yukon Conference Room and that Mr. Wrightson would be joining us. Mom and Eileen should be there already."

We found the meeting room and went in. Lydia stood up to give me a hug. We sat next to each other in two of the leather conference-room chairs at the table.

"How could they suspect you would shoot a friend like Matthew Hennigan?" Lydia asked.

"An erstwhile friend, at best," I answered.

"What do you mean?"

"It was Hennigan who ratted Angel Hernandez to ICE."

"You never told me that."

"I would have some day, Lydia, but it has been too painful to talk about Angel and his family. So, I just haven't mentioned it."

Elmer Wrightson entered the room. Janet Bread was with him. She took the chair on the other side of Lydia.

Diane and Eileen badgered both Wrightson and Bread with pleas to find a way out of our ordeal.

Elmer slumped into the conference-room leather chair at the foot of the table. "We will do the best we can to put it all behind us."

"We know you will, Elmer. Thank you," Lydia said.

Diane and Eileen visited with Aunt Janet across the table from us while Elmer talked to Lydia and me. "I told you that de Vries thought the trial would not start for another ten days or so."

"Right, I remember," Lydia said.

"Well, things have changed. The judge has pushed back the rest of her schedule. The case goes to trial on Monday."

Lydia reacted, "Wonderful. I mean getting it over with is good. Isn't it?"

"Sure. There are trade-offs but getting it over with should be good."

"I was afraid we would have to wait weeks for a trial," Lydia said. "Elmer, what do you think the judge's decision to hurry things up means?"

"I can't be certain of her reasons. It might just be expediency, meaning it is the logical organization of the court's calendar. The judge has a reputation for efficiency. Anne Fitzgerald is always very business-like. One thing we are sure about is we do not have a lot of time to prepare."

"Oh, how bad is that?"

"Bad and good. Cynthia De Vries reviewed the issues with me. We considered asking for a delay. However, the prosecution has the same constraints as we do and we believe the quick turnaround hampers them more than it will hurt us."

"Why would that be, Elmer?" Janet Bread came around the table and sat in the chair next to me. She had been listening with one ear to the conversation with Wrightson while talking to Diane and Eileen.

He explained, "We can speed up our preparations by bringing in extra help and it won't be just anyone. We have a well-qualified individual who can be of immediate assistance. The DA can also dedicate more resources to the case but they will have to rely on junior-level assistant prosecutors to help with the leg work. They do not have whom we have."

"You are referring to Cynthia de Vries," I asserted.

"No, I wasn't. She is already on board. There is another member of the firm who is more qualified than de Vries or myself. He has more experience than both of us put together. Ted, do you remember meeting Arthur Rhinehart. He is a senior partner at Wrightson and Associates."

"Yes, you introduced us when he joined the firm. You said he came from one of the top partnerships in New York City. I asked you why he would want to work for you but I did not get a good answer."

"As you may recall, a serious response was not called for. You challenged me about Rhinehart with a load of sarcasm in your voice. Admittedly, however, you asked a good question. Arthur has ten years of seniority on me as a criminal defense attorney. He enjoyed success with some high-profile and challenging cases. Why would someone like that want to work for my firm in our town? He told me he was tired of the long hours and wanted to slow down. He found out about us because we needed help with the expanding workload at my firm. I posted the opportunity in the Law Reviews. He saw the announcement and called me up."

"Evidently, he liked what you had to say."

"Yes, he did. It did not happen immediately but the match looked good and here we are. Arthur moved to Batavia to join the firm."

"Can he help me?"

"De Vries and I went to dinner with him last night. We laid out your case and he agreed to join the team."

"Does he think there's enough time to be ready by Monday?"

"He does. Arthur is scripting a draft of my opening remarks even as we speak."

"Will he have a role in the courtroom?"

"We'll see. Maybe not. Arthur thinks the appearance of a high-powered New York City lawyer might not go over well with a small-town jury."

Wrightson continued, "The preliminaries will take most of the morning on Monday with jury selection continuing through Tuesday. The prosecutor and I will make opening remarks to the jury on Wednesday morning and the prosecution will begin presenting its case immediately after that.

"Given the scope of the presentations that we have outlined for the judge and the short list of witnesses, she expects the prosecutor to finish quickly and the defense to wrap up by the middle of the day on Friday. She wants to hand the case over to the jury for their deliberations before the weekend."

"Wow. It makes my head spin," I said.

"Mine too," Wrightson agreed.

Janet Bread said, "While Rhinehart does his research on issues regarding the law, there is more investigative work for me to do."

Lydia looked at Elmer. "Can Janet help?"

"Oh, unquestionably!" His response was quick and certain. "We have some very good investigators on retainer at the firm but no one with the reputation and competence of Detective Janet Bread."

"Wow, I didn't know my cousin was that great," Lydia muttered.

"Are you telling me that Ms. Bread has not told you how good she is?" Elmer joked. The woman was standing right at his elbow.

Janet came back at him with a quick retort. "No, of course not. I am far too modest about my unparalleled abilities."

"Sure, you are," Wrightson said. "All right, I have asked Janet to visit with you, Ted. I am going back to the office. De Vries and I are organizing material for the debate in court. Rhinehart will be joining us."

Elmer spoke up to make sure he had everyone's attention. "All of you should go now. We need the time to work with my client for a bit. He can join you at home later."

"Thank you, Mr. Wrightson," Diane said.

"You are welcome. Diane and Eileen, how are you two holding up?"

"We're OK," Diane answered. Eileen nodded.

"Lydia, please keep the conversation going with Diane and Eileen as you know best. Can you make sure Ted's folks and your mother remain informed as well?"

"I believe the three of us will drive over to see Ted's mom and dad right now," Lydia said.

Chapter 61 . Conditions were imposed.

L ydia told me to hurry home. She guided our daughters toward the door. All three hugged me on their way out. Janet Bread remained seated.

"You coming?" Eileen asked her.

"Of course, you're putting me up. Remember?"

"Not now, Eileen," Lydia said and pushed our nearly full-grown brood out of the room.

Elmer said, "Ted, the best defense would be to discover who really did kill Matthew Hennigan. The second best is to redirect the suspicion away from you and toward others. Who else might have a motive? Cheated business associate? Jilted lover? Jealous husband?"

"That's the kind of gossip I don't pay much attention to," I said.

"That's OK. Just give us what you know. The firm has investigators who will do the muck raking."

"We need you to help us understand why you are a suspect," Janet said.

"That's right," Wrightson confirmed. "Ted, talk to Janet about Friday night, about your interactions with Hennigan, and about everything in your history that might cause the police to focus on you. She will be looking for anything we can use in your defense. As I said before, I need to get back to the office. While the two of you are talking, Cynthia and I will work on other preparations for the trial."

Janet asked, "Are you referring to the lawyer at the table with you and Ted during the hearing?"

"Have you not met Cynthia de Vries? She is one of the sharpest new associates in the firm," Elmer said.

"No, I haven't but glad to hear about her and about Arthur Rhinehart." Janet approved.

"There are restrictions on your release, Ted, that it behooves me as your attorney to tell you about."

"Yes?" I smiled at Elmer's convoluted language.

"It is more than just not leaving town. You must be home by ten every evening. You can go to work or just consult at the Batavia Service Center during the day. You can attend church. You must stick to your regularly scheduled AA meetings. I am to let the judge know when and where the sessions are held and I am supposed to provide her with contact information for the group leader and your sponsor."

"I have business cards for both at home."

"Bring them in tomorrow."

"Am I allowed to go out to eat?"

"Yes and no. The judge didn't say and I didn't ask. If I have learned anything as a defense lawyer, it is do not disturb a favorable outcome by bothering the judge with questions about details. It gives her or him the opportunity to reconsider. So, the answer is yes. She did not explicitly prohibit dining out and I believe it would be all right with her. But, no, it could hurt our cause. I want you to keep a low profile.

"We will be asking a jury selected from this community to render a not-guilty verdict at the conclusion of your trial. For you to be seen enjoying life would not sit well with friends or sympathizers of Matthew Hennigan. A picture of you in the newspaper enjoying dinner with your family or with friends or worse seeing you on TV would not be good."

"I understand. It was pretty much a rhetorical question anyway. Whispering among the people at the next table in a restaurant would make me uncomfortable. Lydia and the children would hate it."

"Ask me anytime you have a question or if you are unsure about what you are allowed to do. We could talk more now but I am anxious to get to work. Janet, he's all yours." Elmer hurried out of the room.

Janet started our conversation by telling me, "There is an optimistic angle to the judge's decision to expedite matters that Elmer did not mention. I have not said anything to Lydia or to my two nieces because I didn't want to get their hopes up but I can tell you. Typically, an impartial judge will hurry a case to trial if she is inclined to believe the charges against the defendant are weak. Lengthy proceedings are not fair to the accused if he is not guilty."

"Good to hear if the judge really is on my side."

"None of us should let your hopes soar too high. Fair treatment of the defendant is only one of the factors affecting a judge's scheduling decisions. However, in my opinion, a little optimism promotes diligence. We work harder when we have faith that the effort will bring about a favorable outcome."

With that Janet Bread got more serious. "Let's just start talking about issues that may or may not be related to Matthew Hennigan and see if useful details start coming into focus."

"All right. Maybe, I know something that will help."

"I am counting on it. Can we start with what you know about an interesting observer in the courtroom last Friday. He had red hair and he was wearing a maroon shirt that clashed with his rust-colored tie. Did you notice him?" Janet Bread asked me.

"Yes, I know him. His nick name is Rusty for obvious reasons. I've forgotten his last name if I ever knew it. He is one of the guys who liked to join us after the games. I was pleased to see him show up in the courtroom. I like him. He's a good guy."

"Could it be Rusty Higgins?"

"Yes, of course. I knew that."

"Ted, his real name is Brian Hill, age 53. The man known to you as Rusty, is a drug dealer and an enforcer for organized crime. He served five and a half years of a ten-year sentence for armed robbery before he was paroled 18 months ago. Agents for the DEA, that's the Drug Enforcement Administration, believe he has returned to his old profession."

"I know what the DEA is."

"All right, sorry."

"No problem. Knowing the meaning of DEA might not be something to be proud of."

With just a nod, Detective Bread continued, "The DEA hired me to assist with the investigation of Brian Hill's current activities. After I found enough evidence for the judge to revoke his parole, the narcotics agents lost track of him."

"Was it a total surprise to see him here in the courtroom?"

"Yes, something like that. Discovering Brian Hill in Batavia triggered questions in Washington. Revoking his parole was no longer the objective. The DEA agent in charge believes there is more to learn by leaving him on the outside and keeping him under surveillance."

"What is a convicted racketeer doing here in Batavia?"

"The FBI has a theory about that but I would like you to tell me what you know rather than the other way around. What can you say about the man?" Janet Bread said.

"Rusty knew Matthew Hennigan. They seemed to be friends."

"Interesting," Detective Bread said. "Tell me about it. What was the nature of their friendship? Could they have been involved in the local drug trade?"

"We knew that Rusty had connections but they seemed fairly innocuous. All I ever heard about were small amounts of marijuana. Hennigan never took a puff even if he was right there while a roach was going from hand to hand around the group with Rusty. I don't see how their relationship could have had a lot to do with drugs."

"You said they were friends. What was the connection?"

"I can only speculate about that. Hennigan invited lots of different people to our games or just to outings at the park. Maybe Rusty stopped at his store and they got to talking. It's happened that way before. Someone new to the area would stop to buy gas at the station and find themselves invited to join us at the park. The fact that Matt and Rusty were acquainted might not mean anything."

"I'm not buying that, Ted. It would be too much of a coincidence for my liking. I suspect Hennigan's relationship to Hill is worth investigating."

"All right but there is very little that I can contribute on the topic."

"OK but you can tell me more about Hennigan himself."

Chapter 62 . Righteous does not mean right.

Matthew Hennigan found it hard to be pleasant with anyone. I never cared for him very much but I am not comfortable speaking ill of the dead just because I did not like him."

"Noted. However, under the circumstances, you need to speak the truth," Janet Bread insisted.

"I guess so. Let me just say that he was disdainful of those who did not live up to his standards. He could be preachy and righteous. From the way he talked, I don't see him involved in anything illegal."

"How about his personal relationships?"

"Before Elmer left here to go see Cynthia de Vries, he asked about jilted lovers. I don't know about anything like that. I have not heard any rumors that would tarnish his reputation as a loyal family man but, as I said, I don't participate in gossip that much."

"Your denial of his involvement in unlawful activities did not sound convincing. Do you think there could have been a darker side to the man?"

"In my opinion, he was a bit of a prig. He was righteous but not morally right."

"What does that mean? Are you saying he was phony or hypocritical about his principles?"

"Yes, I think so. He believed that charity was a virtue. However, in my cynical view, he had little sense of what it meant to be charitable. He believed in paying it forward but the progression of doing a favor after receiving a favor need not go further than himself."

"He sponsored the baseball team and contributed funds to programs at the high school."

"Business expenses that kept a steady stream of cars at his service station and convenience store," I opined.

"Interesting. What else can you tell me? Would you say he was a difficult person or vengeful?"

"He was certainly a difficult person to like. You have got me denigrating him more than I intended but he was quite self-centered. He could nod his head and seem to listen when there was something worrying you but he wasn't paying attention. Hennigan was either doing the talking or he was not interested in the conversation."

"None of that says vengeful."

"I guess not but I did not want to cross him. I always had the feeling that his testy disposition might turn a civil conversation into an unpleasant encounter. I wasn't afraid that he might take a swing at me. He did not have a fighter's build or the physical strength."

"All right. I get the picture. Let's move on. What else can you say about Rusty? What did you like about him that made him a good guy in your mind?"

"I was unaware of his criminal background when I said he was a good guy. Now that you have told me about his history, I would like to back pedal on my assessment. Obviously, I haven't known him that long given that he was in prison until recently. I don't think any of the local guys were very well acquainted with him either."

"I understand. Just give me your thoughts about him."

"He was easy going with us, learned our names, joined in the conversations about baseball. He could chat a bit about politics."

"What about drinking or drugs?"

"I was aware that he might join some of the guys at Harry's Pub after an event at the park but not often I don't think. Mostly, he would hang around a while and leave before most of the crowd. He never got obnoxious like many in our rowdy crew."

"You are correct that you do not know him very well. His charisma is a façade. Before he was sent away, Mr. Hill was ruthless in his dealings with colleagues in the syndicate who offended him as well as with rivals in the criminal world. He is a psychopath without the slightest remorse for his victims."

"That is a frightening thought given all of the time we spent with him. You make it sound like he could have turned on any one of us at the slightest provocation."

"I don't believe he posed a threat to any of you. To be sure, he is well trained with combative talents comparable to a Green Beret. He should be feared and handled with care. However, he is also a disciplined and smart soldier in the cartel that he serves. He does not act rashly."

"Rusty or rather, Brian Hill, was one of the visitors from out of town who usually had a few joints in his pocket to share with my teammates."

"Was he selling?"

"No, they say he was not a pusher. I don't have first-hand information because I am not allowed to hang around after we are done playing."

"Not allowed? Who's stopping you?"

"You know. AA rules."

"What have you heard?"

"Rusty might shake a little weed from a baggy onto a paper for one of the guys to roll a fresh joint. He would accept money for it but he didn't have a supply for sale."

"Maybe not at first but it is an approach that dealers can use to line up new clientele," Detective Bread said.

"He gave the appearance of a laid-back guy unburdened by weighty concerns. He was there to relax. He might take a couple of puffs and pass a roach around but that was it."

"What about the baggie of marijuana? Could it have been as much as half a kilo?"

"No. I don't remember seeing it first-hand but Clutch told me it was less than an ounce or two. Also, he was careful with it. If there was anything left on a roach, he would snuff it out and save it in his pocket."

"Nice to know he was frugal." Ms. Bread's tone was sarcastic.

Part V

Answers and Interrogation

I believe great people do things before they are ready.

– *Amy Poehler, <u>Yes Please</u>*

Chapter 63 . Family nostalgia was therapeutic.

Could Janet Bread be harboring doubts about me? I did not want her to get the wrong idea from my comments about the availability of marijuana among old friends.

I said, "You understand, in all of this, I was just an observer. I never touched any of Rusty's supply."

"Oh, no. Of course not." Janet's expression was an all-knowing smirk as if she were reluctant to take my word for it.

"Thanks a lot," I replied.

"Ted, you have told me only about the soft stuff. Did you try other drugs in the past?"

"Ah, well, yes. I sniffed a little of the white powder a few times. Are you asking me about recently?"

"I am probing for anything you can tell me that might be interesting."

"I have taken nothing since the beginning of my recovery. With my history, I would be in a ton of trouble if I even took a puff or got a whiff. I guess it is ironic for a man on trial for murder to be worried about getting caught for something like simple possession."

"It would be more than ironic. Give me the details."

"Lydia is your cousin and confidant. Hasn't she told you everything about my shortcomings?"

"No. I picked up hints over the years about your troubles. But, Lydia has always been loyal. She could never be critical. Whenever I asked, everything was fine."

"She deserved a better man than I."

"Now, that is not entirely true. Lydia and I were playmates as children, confidants in high school, and long-distance telephone friends during our college years. I never saw her happier than when she fell in love with you."

"Wow."

"Do you remember that I was the Maid of Honor at your wedding?"

"Of course I do."

"There was a moment that gave me pause one day that week before the ceremony."

"Was it something you want to tell me about now?"

"I'm not sure if I do. We were all having fun at a party about a week before you tied the knot. Alcoholic beverages were flowing freely. It seemed to me that you had consumed a few too many. You were standing between us holding Lydia close with your left arm and me just as close with your right. I was worried about the bottle of beer in your hand dangling over my shoulder. We were laughing and enjoying the moment. You let go of me to take a swig. Do you remember the occasion?"

"I remember the party and that I was a little out of control with all of the excitement that day."

"More than a little, I think. You had to hold onto Lydia to steady yourself. The bottle slipped from your hand. Fortunately, I caught it before it hit the floor. Otherwise, we would have been sweeping up shards of glass."

"Thanks for the save. I've blacked that part out."

"Lydia shrugged out of your grasp and pushed you away. 'Don't be such a knucklehead,' she said. You stumbled off laughing. 'Yeah, I guess I've had enough,' you said."

"I'm sure that was true," I agreed.

"It was a solemn moment right then. I heard Lydia say, 'He won't drink so much after we are married.'"

"What did you say?"

"Nothing. She did not seem to be talking to me but just to herself. She was reassuring herself."

"All I can say to you now, Janet Bread, is those times are way back in the past. They are bad memories never to be repeated."

"I want to believe you. Lydia does. She believes in you."

I said, "As time went on, we saw less and less of you after the wedding."

"My career was just taking off. So was Lydia's. Still, for the first few years, we talked a lot. We were all together for family reunions in Savannah. You were there too. However, as the years rolled by, the cordiality between Lydia and me tapered off. I chalked it up to the evolution of life that adults must go through. All the same, it made me sad for the loss."

"I can tell you that Lydia always held you close in her heart. She would tell the children stories about the fun you had together as children. I guess I should have known how much she missed you but such things did not occur to me. The self-obsessive nature of alcoholism clouds a person's judgement. That is one of the lessons taught to us in AA meetings."

"Lydia told me over the holidays just last year about the time she took the children to Paris. It was not until then that I came to appreciate the heartache that she suffered. We did not talk much about the trip. Rather, our conversation was more about the depth of her appreciation for your efforts to overcome addiction."

"Lydia is the best thing that ever happened to me."

"Her words exactly except she said it about you."

"Thank you for saying that. As far as I was concerned, our relationship was serious from the first day we met. I guess it showed when I talked about her. Mother was anxious to meet Lydia. She was excited that her only son had found someone he could settle down with. She talked to Lydia on the phone and they made plans for a weekend here in Batavia. As things turned out, however, we wound up visiting Lydia's folks first. She took me home to meet the family for Thanksgiving.

"It was Lydia's junior year at the University. Both grandfathers were there. I enjoyed my conversations with them. I remember asking Grandfather Aaron about the unorthodox naming convention his daughter had implemented for you and your brothers. He was unphased. Just shrugged it off."

"That's Papa."

"I don't remember the specifics but it was clear that Grandfather Jacob was very concerned about me being good enough for his granddaughter. Actually, both grandfathers talked to me about responsibilities. I had a hard time telling them apart."

"They were best friends their entire lives."

"Harmony in the grocery business?"

"Not hardly! They quarreled all the time. The family joke was they couldn't agree on what to charge for a can of beans or on the time of day. The bickering made other people in the family nervous and uptight but not Lydia and me. We thought it was funny. We saw their banter as just for affect but who's to say."

"I think you and Lydia probably had it right."

Janet smiled. After a thoughtful pause, she said, "We were devastated when our grandfathers passed away. They died the same year. Jacob went first with his wife at his side. They called it pneumonia but it was really old age. Aaron went just six months later. They had lived a long time. Jacob and Grandmother MaryBeth were married for nearly 65 years. She is still going strong, alert and spry. We believe she will make it to a hundred and ten!"

Both of us stopped talking, lost in thought for a while.

Chapter 64 . Who would kill Matthew Hennigan?

Janet broke the silence. "Do you think reminiscing was what Attorney Wrightson had in mind when he left us with instructions to work on ideas and strategies for the trial?"

"No. He was hoping you would discover alternative theories about Hennigan's murder by interrogating me."

"I believe you are correct and we have made some progress."

"Have we really? Did you have an agenda in mind?"

"Indeed, I did. In fact, we have been working our way through it."

"Are you telling me, the spontaneity in our conversation has been nothing of the sort?"

"Not exactly. I'm saying a free-flowing discussion was the plan. My approach to interviews with witnesses is to look for significant facts that might pop out of a casual conversation about the event and about the people involved."

"Have you found anything useful by talking to me today?"

"Perhaps." Detective Bread gave an enigmatic shrug.

"What?"

She did not answer my question. After a pause, she said, "We are not just hoping for information, Ted. You and I have a well-defined objective. The defense attorney does need specifics."

"I don't know what else to tell you."

"We should just keep talking," Janet said. "I need to hear more about your history. We have covered a lot of ground but I believe there is more that you can give me. What else is there about your past that might be used against you? It is important for the defense to be prepared for anything that might come up at the trial."

"The fact is it took me a while to shake the immaturity of youthful irresponsibility. Growing up took longer than it should have. I couldn't see any problems with my easy-going attitude and late-night partying but I was wrong. Self-induced crises were threatening the integrity of my marriage and family. Am I giving you too much information?"

"Maybe not. Keep going please."

"Finally, one day, I knew I had to make a change. Serious introspection and the support of my wife and parents helped me turn my life around. The irresponsible behavior is behind me now. I am a recovering alcoholic and reformed addict. I have not touched a drop or used drugs in seven years. I have the AA coins to prove it."

"Assuming they were not obtained fraudulently."

"Ouch, that's harsh but, don't worry, I can take your cynicism." My answer was meant to sound light-hearted but it was tinged with remorse.

"Sorry to be so tough but it is part of my job at the moment. Have you ever stumbled? Has anyone seen you stumble? The questions are legitimate because, as you know, recovery is fragile."

"I've heard that. Over and over again, actually. I have not stumbled and I am determined that I never will."

"OK, good."

Shall I go on?"

"Maybe. Is there a point to your rambling about what a good boy you are now? Or, doth you protest too much?"

"Is it your keen wit or your sharp tongue that my wife loves about you?"

"I am sure it's both," Janet Bread answered without relaxing her serious expression. "Just keep talking."

"After staying away from everyone associated with my previous life, my sponsor allowed me to rejoin the AAU baseball team on a trial basis. He agreed on condition that there would be no parties after the games and not after the practices."

"What do you mean by allowed? Your sponsor does not have the authority to stop you."

"No, but it is very clear that you must treat your sponsor's advice almost the same as the rule of law if your recovery is to be constant."

"Who is your sponsor?"

"Rabbi Ephraim Lamm. He teaches classes at the Bayit Midrash Synagogue. He's a pretty young guy for an old-fashioned name like Ephraim. We call him Ram. He agreed to let me rejoin the team but he said we had to let him play too. It was a terrible mistake."

"A terrible mistake?"

"The guy can't hit, catch, or throw but he rams full speed ahead after everything."

"Is he sincere about your best interests?"

"He's a very good and dedicated sponsor. Overly dedicated at times but probably exactly what I needed. He was by my side, in my face actually, nearly every moment at the beginning of my recovery. It took a while for both of us to become confident that I required less attention."

"It sounds like he was tough."

"Did you see the beard and bald head in the courtroom? Lydia told me he was there."

"No but I couldn't keep track of everybody from where I was sitting."

"Neither could I, of course."

"I do not intend to talk to Rabbi Lamm because I won't try to compromise his integrity as your sponsor."

"I believe Ephraim has the strength of character to not tell you anything even though it would all be good."

"Who was the neighbor Elmer mentioned in court? The one who remembered details about the events on your front porch."

"Are you referring to Alex Montoya?" The feeling came back again that my inquisitor was testing how forthright I could be. Detective Bread surely had his name in her notes if not in her head.

"Yes, that was the name," she agreed.

"He lives a few houses down and across the street. We have not had much to do with him in a long while. There were some unpleasant interactions between us. Lydia finally chased him away and told him never to come back. Can you believe it? Lydia threatened Montoya with an axe!"

"I remember hearing about that," Janet said. "Lydia called and asked for legal advice. She told me about the incident in your back yard. She was afraid of retaliation. I called in a favor from a retired FBI agent who lives in the city not far from here. He made sure Alex Montoya would leave you alone."

"So, you already know about Mr. Montoya. What else can I tell you?"

"Does Montoya come to the baseball games? Does he join the gatherings after a game?"

"No. As I said, I don't have anything to do with him anymore."

"What is his relationship with Rusty?"

"None that I know of."

"Have you ever seen Rusty at Montoya's house or in the neighborhood."

"No."

"You're not much help," Janet Bread laughed.

"Sorry."

"OK. That's enough for now. If you think of anything else to tell me about these guys, let me know." She stood up to go.

"Thank you, Janet, for anything you can do to help."

"You're welcome. I know you are not guilty and that you are staying the course with your recovery because Lydia told me so. I'll be staying with her at your house for a few days or for as long as she needs me."

"I am happy about that. It could mean a rebirth for your friendship."

"Perhaps, our friendship only needed a reawakening. You should go home now." Janet Bread walked with me to the sixth-floor elevators and used her key to summon the express car. She reached in to push the button for the subbasement level.

"I do not have a car here."

"Diane is waiting for you on the Executive Level of the garage." Janet stepped back into the hallway but held the door open with her left hand to tell me, "I will come over later. Tell Lydia not to wait up for me. It could be very late."

The elevator dropped quickly and slowed suddenly at the bottom. I stepped out and spotted Diane in a space across from where she had parked before. I climbed into a dark blue, late-model Impala with my daughter at the wheel.

"Hello, Dad," she said. She put it in gear and crept along at a garage-appropriate speed around to and up the exit helix to the street level."

"Nice car," I said.

"Katherine Chavis picked Mom and me up earlier today and took us to get a rental car. People will start recognizing it as ours soon enough but Ms. Chavis said they want our own vehicles to be anonymous after all the notoriety subsides."

"Who is paying for it?"

Diane gave me a look. She countered with a rhetorical question. "Who is paying for any or all of this?"

I just shrugged.

"Mom said we are supposed to go right home."

"Thank you for coming to get me. I know all of this chauffeuring must be cutting into your social life."

"Aw, what the heck," Diane replied. "Just think of all the conversations starters I'll have when this is over."

"Give me an example." I said.

"Sure. 'Hey there, boyfriend, did you know my father was arrested for murder?'"

We both laughed at her good humor.

"Seriously, Dad, you can stop apologizing. Just think of all the things you had to do for Eileen and me growing up. It was not always convenient."

"Maybe not but you have become a young woman for a father to be proud of."

Chapter 65 . The trial began on Monday.

The jury selection for the trial proceeded according to schedule. The judge defined the rules for the selection process and heard both attorneys' views on her instructions for the jury.

Monday turned into a dizzying day of motions, objections, and decisions flying around the courtroom. The ground rules were finally in place by the end of the afternoon session and court was adjourned for the day.

Voir dire began first thing on Tuesday. The court settled on seven women and five men plus one male alternate. It took all morning and part of the afternoon.

The jurors were chosen from a county-wide pool that included much of the city adjacent to Batavia. I was acquainted with just two of them and a few others looked familiar. Wrightson told me he was happy with the results.

After a brief recess, both sides were invited to make introductory remarks on Tuesday afternoon. We were ahead of schedule.

"My name is Elmer Wrightson. It is my job to defend Theodore Christopher O'Connor against criminal charges." My attorney began speaking in a calm, reassuring voice to the jury.

"My client has been charged with first-degree murder. It was a crime he did not commit. The District Attorney filed the charge against Mr. O'Connor because a witness said he was at the scene of the crime at about the time it was committed. The DA has made a huge mistake. My client just happened to be in the wrong place at a bad time.

"Mr. O'Connor did not kill Matthew Hennigan. Someone else did. There were others who came and went from the scene at the time of the shooting. The police decided my client had to be the guilty party because they had dealings with him in the distant past. The last unpleasant incident was over seven years ago. It should have been forgotten. It has no relationship to the victim and does not define who Mr. O'Connor is today."

Morris Hofmann introduced himself to the jury as the prosecuting attorney. He insisted I had to be the guilty party. No one else had the motive. No one else went inside the store. No one else threatened to kill Matthew Hennigan.

Judge Anne Fitzgerald ended the day with instructions for the jury to come back on time early the next day. She told them, "Be prepared to be sequestered for the rest of the week until the end of the day on Saturday."

Chapter 66 . Witnesses took the stand on Wednesday.

The presentation of the evidence began on Wednesday morning. Mr. Hofmann brought witnesses to the stand to testify against me. During cross examination, my attorney tore into the prosecutor's case like a fierce tiger after its prey.

Phyllis Todesco was the first witness for the prosecution. According to her, I knocked Mr. Hennigan down and kicked him. Elliot Shaw was next. He saw me punch the victim but he was sure that I did not kick him. Both of them heard me threaten to kill him.

One of them said the incident occurred in late April of 2019. The other thought it could have been as long ago as March.

Before the first witness left the stand, Attorney Wrightson asked, "Ms. Todesco, according to your testimony, there had to be bad blood between Mr. O'Connor and the victim. Is that correct?"

"Yes, sir."

"You heard Mr. O'Connor threaten to kill Mr. Hennigan after he knocked him down. Correct?"

"Yes."

"Could it have been the other way around?" Are you sure he knocked him down first before threatening to kill him?"

"Yes, I'm sure."

"What did he say? Mr. O'Connor's exact words please."

The defense attorney did not keep Phyllis Todesco on the stand for long but his questions made her squirm.

"I don't remember the exact words. He just said he was going to kill Matty."

"Did he say I will kill you or I will shoot you?"

"I think it was one of those, yes."

"You think it was but maybe not quite. Could he have said I would like to kill you or I wish you were dead?"

"No. Mr. O'Connor threatened to kill Matty."

"Mr. Hennigan was a respected business owner in Batavia. Was he a good friend of yours?"

"Objection! The witness's relationship with the victim is irrelevant."

It was not the first of Mr. Hofmann's loud protests and not the last. He dished them out to the point where they became tiresome for everyone in the courtroom. After a while, the jury would turn toward him in anticipation of the next outburst even on the rare occasions when he passed up the chance.

"Your Honor, the jury should know if Ms. Todesco was certain about Mr. Hennigan's identity," Wrightson said.

"I will allow the question."

Wrightson did not wait for the answer but asked another question. "Ms. Todesco, you used a familiar name for Mr. Hennigan twice now as if you had a very friendly relationship. Have you always called him Matty?"

"Objection!"

"Sustained."

"That's all for Ms. Todesco," Wrightson said.

When Elliot Shaw took the stand right after Todesco, prosecuting Attorney Hofmann had two lines of questions for him. He started by asking for Shaw's version of my altercation with Hennigan. It differed in some ways from what Ms. Todesco had told the jury.

Hofmann continued with questions about what happened at the service station. He said, "Mr. Shaw, tell the jury what you saw on the night Mr. Hennigan was shot."

Shaw replied, "I was at the cash register at Hennigan's, when Mr. O'Connor drove up to buy gas."

"When was that?"

"It was on Friday evening. I don't know the exact time but I think it was getting dark."

"Were you working alone?"

"Just at that time. Mr. Hennigan had been there earlier but I saw him leave. He came back later and left again. I figured he might return before closing but sometimes he leaves it up to me."

"What happened next?"

"You mean after Mr. O'Connor got there?"

"Yes, that's right." Hofmann sighed.

Exasperation with his own witness did not seem to me to be good prosecutorial technique in front of a jury. Elmer told me later, "That's Hofmann for you."

Elliot Shaw said, "Mr. O'Connor got out of his car and started to pump the gas for himself. He didn't need me for that and I had to go to the bathroom. Mr. Hennigan wants me to lock the doors when I leave the cash register unattended but he wasn't there and I figured I'd be quick.

"I hurried to the bathroom at the back of the store. I didn't turn on the light or even close the door tight because no one was there to see me. A minute later, I heard the front door chime. I looked out and Mr. O'Connor was there. When I saw him looking at the bathroom, I backed up so he wouldn't see me in the dark. The door is supposed to close on its own but sometimes it stays open a crack and you have to pull it shut."

"Why not come out to greet the customer to see what he needed?" Mr. Hofmann asked.

"I guess I was embarrassed that I was using the bathroom with the door open."

"What happened next?"

"I stayed real quiet for a while. I was waiting for Mr. O'Connor to leave. After a long while later, I heard Mr. Hennigan shout 'No! Don't!' Then there was a loud gun shot. I was so scared, I couldn't move."

Hofmann said, "It must have been frightening. Please go on, Mr. Shaw."

"Mr. O'Connor turned off the lights and I heard the door chime again when he left the store."

"Are you certain it was Mr. O'Connor?"

"Yes, sir. No one else was in the store."

"You mean no one else besides you and Mr. Hennigan."

"Oh, yes. Mr. Hennigan must have been in his office. I didn't know he was there."

Hofmann said, "What did you do next, Mr. Shaw."

"I didn't hear anything for a long time. Finally, I just left the store and went home."

"What about the body on the floor."

"I didn't see Mr. Hennigan there until Saturday morning when I came back to open up."

"What about the gun shot? Did you report it to the police?"

"I didn't have to. Two policemen arrived when I was on the way to my car. A customer coming out of the liquor store had heard it and called 911 on her cell phone."

"Did you let the police back into the convenience store?"

"I was about to but they decided the whole thing was a false alarm. They were talking to the people who heard the shot at the liquor store and I told them that I was in the bathroom when I heard it."

"Did you tell them the gun was fired inside the store?"

"Yes but I was pretty shook up. I said I thought it was in the store. They told me to wait next to my car while they talked to the other people."

"Did you tell the police that Mr. O'Connor was there?"

"Yes, I told them I saw Mr. O'Connor and Phyl Todesco. They took down their names but I don't know if they talked to them."

"Did you mean Phyllis Todesco?"

"Yes, Phyllis. People call her Phyl."

"What happened next?"

"After a while, one of the cops came over and told me I could go and not to worry about it. So, I put it out of my mind and went home. The police were getting ready to go when I drove off. It was not until the next morning that I realized what actually happened."

"Thank you, Mr. Shaw."

Chapter 67 . Cross examination was important for the defense.

Attorney Elmer Wrightson stood up, walked over to the witness stand, and came back to the table for the defense. He was evidently putting on a show for the witness. He finally began his cross examination with a question "Mr. Shaw, are you aware that perjury is a serious crime?"

"Objection!"

"On what grounds?" Judge Fitzgerald asked.

"The witness is not on trial," Hofmann said.

"Questioning the veracity of this witness is important for the defense. There are differences between the testimony of Ms. Todesco and Mr. Shaw," Attorney Wrightson said.

"Overruled."

"Do you know that the penalty for lying to the court in a murder trial means jail time?"

"Objection! Badgering the witness."

"What is your point, Mr. Wrightson?" the judge asked.

"Your Honor. Mr. Shaw should know that prison time is dangerous for a witness who perjures himself to protect criminal elements."

"Enough of that, Mr. Wrightson. The objection is sustained!"

"Mr. Shaw, you said and a previous witness agreed that Mr. O'Connor threatened to kill Mr. Hennigan after he knocked him down. Is it possible the events occurred the other way around? We just need you to tell the truth."

"I suppose."

"In other words, first Mr. O'Connor got angry and threatened him. Mr. Hennigan just laughed and then Mr. O'Connor punched him in the jaw. Correct?"

"Yes, I remember now. That is how it happened," Elliot Shaw said.

"How long did the argument last?"

"I'm not sure. Not long. They were standing across the parking lot when I came out of the restaurant right behind them. I did not pay attention until I heard shouting."

"You did not see how the fight started. Correct?"

"Yes."

"Could Mr. Hennigan have insulted Mr. O'Connor or threatened him or hit him first?"

"I don't know. I was just coming out of the restaurant."

"Thank you, Elliot. It's good that you remembered now. The jury and everyone in court appreciates hearing the truth. No perjury. No life-threatening jail time."

"Objection!" Hofmann shouted.

"Sustained!" There was irritation with the defense attorney in the judge's voice. "Please, Mr. Wrightson," she admonished.

The judge put a stop to Wrightson's line of questioning but it seemed to have already had an effect on Shaw. He appeared to be rattled. His hand trembled when he brushed hair back from over his forehead.

"Mr. Shaw, you were in the lavatory with the lights off at the back of the convenience store when you heard the gun shot. Is that correct?"

"Yes."

"How did you react? Did you rush out to see what happened?"

"No, I was too scared. I kind of collapsed in the corner and waited for him to go away."

"About what time did you hear the gunshot?"

"It was at eight-thirty."

"Exactly at eight-thirty or maybe eight-thirty give or take fifteen or twenty minutes?"

"No, not that much. It was eight-thirty give or take maybe five minutes."

"Mr. Shaw, you testified under oath a few minutes ago that you did not know what time Mr. O'Connor drove up to one of the self-serve pumps. Yet, now you are quite certain of the time when you heard someone fire a gun. How can you remember one but not the other?"

"I don't know why but I looked at the clock when I heard the shot."

"What clock? Is there a clock in the lavatory?"

"No." Shaw snickered. "There is a clock up on the wall behind the cash register."

"Let's see. How did that work?" Wrightson turned away from the witness and said, "You were looking out of the lavatory in this direction." He pointed forward with his left hand. "The cash register and the clock are out of your line of sight over in this direction." He gestured to the right with his other hand. Wrightson looked back at Shaw over his right shoulder and said, "You must have stepped out of the lavatory to see it. Correct?"

"No. Maybe I just looked at my watch."

"You are not wearing a watch now."

"I don't always wear my watch."

"Is it possible, Mr. Shaw, that you are just guessing at the time from the what the police told you or from when you got home?"

"No." Shaw's voice fluttered. "It was 8:30."

"Interesting that you could tell the time on an invisible watch in a dark lavatory."

"Objection!"

"Sustained."

"Mr. Shaw, did you wait in the lavatory until after someone turned off the lights in the convenience store?"

"Yes, that's right."

"How long did you wait after the gunshot? Did the lights go off right away after the gunshot?"

"Yes, almost right away. Maybe five minutes after the gunshot."

"Mr. Shaw, you heard the gunshot at eight-thirty give or take five minutes and the lights went off five minutes later. So, the lights were turned off and you heard the door chime when the killer left the building no later than 8:40 PM. Is that correct?"

"Yes, it is..'

"Could it have been 8:45 PM or 8:50 PM?"

"No, it was 8:40."

"Did you see the person flick off the light switch?"

"No, I couldn't. You have to go into the office to turn them off."

"How did the person who turned off the lights get out of the store in the dark?"

"I don't know. Maybe he had a flashlight."

"Was it too dark to see anything?"

"It was pitch black."

"How did you get out? Did you have a flashlight with you in the lavatory?"

"No, I didn't. There was some light through the windows from the lights over the parking in front of the liquor store."

"So, it wasn't pitch black. Right? Surely, enough light to see a body on the floor."

"Objection! The witness has already said he did not see the body."

"That was not my question. Was there enough light for someone to see the body?"

"Overruled."

"No, I didn't see the body. It was pretty dark. Maybe I just crawled on the floor to the door. I don't remember."

"Of course, you don't remember because it did not happen the way you described it. The lights were still on when you walked out of the lavatory and out the front door."

"Objection!"

"Sustained."

"According to your testimony, Mr. Hennigan must have been in the office when you left your post to go to the lavatory but you did not know he was there. How was that possible? You saw him leave earlier in the evening. How could you not notice that he had returned?"

"If it was busy, he might have come in through the door from the liquor store and gone into his office without me seeing him."

"That is an interesting suggestion we have not heard before, Mr. Shaw. Is it possible someone else came in and went into the office either with Mr. Hennigan or by themselves?"

"No, I don't think so. I didn't see anyone."

Wrightson sighed audibly. "You did not see Mr. Hennigan go into the office but he must have been there. You did not see someone else go into the office but she or he must not have been there. Correct?"

"Yes, I think so."

"Mr. Shaw, you testified earlier that you told the police you saw Mr. O'Connor and Phyllis Todesco at the service station on Friday night. Did Ms. Todesco come into the convenience store?"

"Yes."

"Was she there at the same time as Mr. O'Connor? Before or after?"

"It was before. She left just before Mr. O'Connor drove up."

"Why was Ms. Todesco there?"

"Objection! There is no point to this line of questioning."

"Ms. Todesco's name was mentioned in Mr. Hofmann's direct questioning of this witness. The defense needs to establish her relevance."

"Overruled."

"Why was Ms. Todesco in the store?"

"I don't know. She went right past me into the office."

"Did she say anything to you?"

"She said, 'Hi, El,' when she came in. That's what she calls me, El."

"Is that because you call her Phyl?"

"No, I call her Mrs. Todesco. Mr. Hennigan calls her Phyl. Or, I mean he did call her Phyl."

"You said Missus. Is Phyllis Todesco married?"

"Yes."

"I see. Did Mrs. Todesco say anything on her way out?"

"She asked me where Mr. Hennigan was."

"I said that maybe he went out to eat."

"Why did you mention Ms. Todesco's name to the police in the first place."

"I thought she might have seen Mr. O'Connor or gone to see Mr. Hennigan."

Attorney Wrightson stood in front of the witness looking right at him. Elliot Shaw squirmed under his glare.

"May I have a glass of w- water?" Shaw's voice broke as he spoke.

Attorney Yoder slipped out of his chair next to Hofmann, handed the witness a bottle of water, and hurried back around to his place at the prosecutors' table. Shaw struggled to unscrew the cap. It took several tries.

Without waiting, Wrightson continued, "Elliot Shaw, the court needs the truth from you. Is it possible that someone else could have been in Hennigan's store on Friday evening?"

"I don't know. Maybe."

"Could the other person have been in the office or hiding in the lavatory with you?"

"No. I can't say that."

"Objection! Mr. Wrightson is badgering the witness beyond all reasonable norms for the defense."

"Your Honor, the defense maintains that it is not unreasonable to explore weaknesses in the testimony of this witness."

"Overruled."

The bottle cap came loose and water splashed out on Shaw's hand. He nervously lowered his arm to hide his wet sleeve inside the witness stand.

Mr. Wrightson did not let up. "Why can't you tell us if there was another person in the lavatory with you? Has that person threatened you? Mr. Shaw, is that person here in the courtroom right now? The one who was in the lavatory with you when you saw Mr. O'Connor in Hennigan's convenience store?"

Every member of the jury followed Elliot Shaw's eyes when he glanced up at the spectators. He quickly looked down at the floor. "No, he's not here. No, there was no one in there with me."

"Objection!" Hofmann interrupted Shaw. "Your Honor, the defense attorney is making himself into a witness for a story of his own creation."

Elmer Wrightson did not argue. He just shook his head.

"Sustained."

Wrightson continued, "Mr. Shaw, when Mr. O'Connor drove up to one of the fuel pumps, it was about quarter after seven o'clock. How long had you been at the station?"

"I started work at four o'clock."

"Was Mr. Hennigan there?"

"Yes, I took over at the cash register when I got there."

"When you take over at the cash register, doesn't Mr. Hennigan usually go home?"

"Not right away. During the week, Mr. Hennigan goes home about five o'clock and leaves me to close up at ten but on Fridays he stays longer."

"How much longer?"

"It depends on how busy we are."

"How late did Mr. Hennigan stay on the Friday when Mr. O'Connor came into the store?"

"I'm not sure. He was in and out and, after a while, I didn't see him. As I said before, I think he must have been in his office."

"Mr. Shaw, you said Mr. Hennigan was not there when you saw the defendant drive up and you left your post to go to the bathroom. Was that wrong?"

"No but now I think maybe he was in the office."

"You were alone in the store except maybe Mr. Hennigan was there too. Correct?"

"Yes."

Attorney Wrightson walked away back to his chair at the table for the defense but he wasn't done. He turned to face the witness again.

"Mr. Shaw, how many times did you hear the door chimes at Hennigan's on Friday night? It was more than three times. Wasn't it?"

"No, just three. Or, no. It was just two. I think."

"The door chimed when Mr. O'Connor came in and again when he left. It chimed every time Mr. Hennigan came and went. How many is that? Did the door chimes ring four times, five times?"

"No. I don't think so but I don't always pay attention or count all of the times."

"It must have chimed when the killer came in or was he already in the lavatory?"

"No. He wasn't there." Elliot Shaw was not looking at Wrightson. He seemed to be scanning for someone among the spectators.

Wrightson sat down.

Mr. Hofmann stood at the prosecutor's table. "Mr. Shaw, just forget all that stuff about perjury. The door chimed just twice, once when Mr. O'Connor came in and again when he left. Correct?"

"I guess so."

"Yes or no, Mr. Shaw," the judge instructed the witness.

"OK, what is the question?"

Hofmann rephrased, "Mr. O'Connor was the only other individual in the store. Correct? Yes or no? Don't let Mr. Wrightson's talk of perjury bother you. You are not going to be charged with perjury."

"Objection!" Wrightson stood up. "Your Honor, is the DA's office offering the witness immunity from perjury charges in exchange for his testimony against the defendant?"

"Mr. Hofmann?" the judge queried.

"No. Of course not. No more questions."

"Proceed with the next witness, Mr. Hofmann."

Officer William White took the stand.

Prosecuting Attorney Morris Hofmann said, "Officer White, please tell the jury about the physical evidence found by the police."

William White took the stand, he looked over at Attorney Elmer Wrightson before he began to answer the prosecutor.

"The police took a liquor bottle into evidence. The crime lab found the defendant's fingerprints on the bottle. When we showed it to Mr. O'Connor at his residence, he denied knowing anything about it." His statement sounded carefully rehearsed.

Chapter 68 . The timing was inconsistent.

Attorney Wrightson was startled by Officer White's response. He muttered under his breath so quietly that only I could hear his voice, "What was that?" Wrightson straightened up and stared at the witness.

Officer White seemed to nod at Attorney Wrightson before looking away. It occurred to me that he might have been signaling for follow-up questions. By Wrightson's reaction, no heads-up was necessary. He was focused and listening intently.

Hofmann asked, "What kind of liquor bottle? Tell the jury please." The prosecuting attorney was sharp enough to have noticed the nonverbal communication between White and Wrightson.

Officer White turned toward the jury when he answered, "It was an empty fifth of Jim Beam with markings that indicated it came from Nora Package Liquors."

Hofmann continued, "That would be Nora's next door to the convenience store where Mr. Hennigan was shot. Correct?"

"That is correct. The two establishments are connected by an interior door that allows customers to proceed directly from one into the other."

"Where would a customer find a fifth of Jim Beam in Nora's, if you know, Officer White?"

"The shelves with the bourbon in Nora Liquor Store are just inside the entrance from Hennigan's." William White was careful to use the exact name of the liquor store. There is no apostrophe-s.

The prosecuting attorney proceeded to have Officer White tell the jury everything that happened after the police received the call from Elliot Shaw at six o'clock on Saturday morning.

When he finished, Mr. Hofmann asked, "Did Mr. O'Connor resist arrest?"

"Not technically, no."

"What does that mean, not technically?"

"Mr. O'Connor was very angry. He did not come quietly with the arresting officers. However, he has not been charged with resisting arrest."

"Would you say he did not make it easy for the arresting officers to take him into custody?"

"In a way."

"Yes or no, Officer White."

"Yes, he did not make it easy on the arresting officers."

"Thank you, Officer White."

Attorney Wrightson jumped up and strode quickly across the room to the witness stand. "Officer White, you showed the liquor bottle to Mr. O'Connor at his residence on Saturday morning. Correct?"

"That's correct."

"When you and Sgt. Ryan arrived at Mr. O'Connor's residence on Saturday morning, there was a delay before anyone responded to the doorbell? Did you have to wait long?"

"Yes. According to our official timing it was nearly 16 minutes from the time we exited the police cruiser across the street until Mr. O'Connor walked around from the rear of the house to meet us at the front door."

"Hmm, not a particularly long time if Mr. O'Connor was busy with something in the garage and hoped someone in the house would get the door. Do you agree, Officer White?"

"Perhaps not a long wait from Mr. O'Connor's point of view."

"The official 16 minutes includes the time from starting the clock in the cruiser to ringing the doorbell in addition to the response time for Mr. O'Connor to get from the garage to the front of the house. Correct?"

"Yes, that's correct."

"While you were waiting, either you or Sgt. Ryan found the empty Jim Beam liquor bottle in Mr. O'Connor's front yard. Correct?"

"No, that is not correct."

"Do you mean the empty liquor bottle was not found in Mr. O'Connor's front yard or that someone other than yourselves found the bottle? Officer White, can you please set the record straight for the jury?"

"Yes, I can. Officer Louis Thompson was one of the members of the force who were called to the crime scene early Saturday morning. He found the bottle on the counter next to the cash register in Hennigan's convenience store. He considered it to be physical evidence and handled it according to standard protocol."

"Do you mean the Jim Beam liquor bottle was not found at the O'Connor residence?"

"Yes."

"How did you happen to have it with you to show it to Mr. O'Connor at his residence?"

"Sgt. Ryan directed me to bring it along."

"Officer White, we have witnesses who heard Sgt. Ryan tell Mr. O'Connor that the liquor bottle was discovered in the bushes next to the porch. How can that be?"

"The witnesses are not correct about that. Sgt. Ryan did not tell Mr. O'Connor that the bottle was found on his property. Rather, Sgt. Ryan was attempting to rattle Mr.

O'Connor by letting him think the bottle was found in the front yard."

"That would be good interrogation technique. Am I right? The policeman tries to get suspects to say something incriminating by making them nervous."

"I believe that is what Sgt. Ryan had in mind."

"Something is not right here, Officer White. Sgt. Ryan tried to extract incriminating statements from Mr. O'Connor before reading the Miranda warning and before Mr. O'Connor knew why the police were at his house."

Hofmann called, "Objection! Your Honor, Sgt. Ryan is not on trial. He's not even here. Sgt. Ryan is recovering from injuries suffered in the line of duty."

"Be careful, Mr. Hofmann," the judge warned in a stern voice. "The objection is sustained."

"Officer White, Elliot Shaw was on the stand as a witness for the prosecution earlier today. He got very nervous when I asked him if there was anyone else in the lavatory with him on Friday night. Did you see that?"

"Objection! A policeman is not a psychiatrist who can tell us if someone is nervous."

Wrightson answered, "Your Honor, it is standard police practice to watch for the reactions when questioning a person of interest."

"Overruled."

Once again, the defense attorney changed course with a different question. "Officer White, according to the police reports, the lavatory where Mr. Shaw was hiding was swept for fingerprints. What did they find?"

"Nothing. There were no fingerprints on anything. The room had been wiped clean."

"Interesting. Why was the lavatory swept for fingerprints in the first place? What were the police looking for? Did the police suspect that there was someone else in there with Mr. Shaw? Perhaps, the real killer?"

"Objection! The defense attorney is insisting on a line of testimony of his own making."

"Sustained."

"How do you explain the lack of fingerprints in the lavatory? Mr. Shaw was in there but he certainly would not have wiped it down that night. Would he?"

"Sgt. Ryan asked him that. Mr. Shaw told us he had just cleaned the room on Friday morning."

"Did no one use the facilities for the entire day? How about Mr. Shaw's fingerprints while he was hiding in there?"

"Mr. Shaw said he must not have touched anything."

"Officer White, according to the police reports, the manager's office and storage space in the convenience store were also dusted for fingerprints. What did you find? Was the office wiped clean?"

"No. The investigators found fingerprints in the office."

"Were the defendant's fingerprints found on anything in the office? Perhaps, on the light switches?"

"No."

"Whose fingerprints did you find in the office?"

"The deceased fingerprints were everywhere."

"Any others?"

"Mr. Shaw's fingerprints. There were prints that could not be identified either because they were not clear or they were not in the database."

"Do you remember names that were in the database?"

"Phyllis Todesco's fingerprints. Prints from the FBI database for Brian Hill. Officer Louis Thompson's fingerprints."

"Ms. Todesco is the witness who referred to Mr. Hennigan as Matty. Correct?"

"Objection!"

"Sustained."

"A police officer's prints? Why were Louis Thompson's prints found in the office?"

"Officer Thompson told us he and Mr. Hennigan were friends."

"What can you tell us about Brian Hill?"

"According to the FBI, Mr. Hill was recently released from a federal penitentiary. There are no outstanding complaints against him. We do not know why he was in Batavia. We understand he was acquainted with Mr. Hennigan."

"Did you interview Mr. Hill? Did you look for him?"

"No."

"No reason to look for an ex-con when the police already decided who did it. Correct?"

"Objection!"

"Sustained."

Mr. Wrightson switched to another topic. "Officer White, according to the credit-card records at Hennigan's filling station, Mr. O'Connor stopped there for gas on Friday evening. Is that correct?"

"Yes."

"This is a copy of the receipt. The timestamp is for 7:17 PM. Is that correct?"

"Yes it is."

"Can you tell which pump Mr. O'Connor used?"

"It says pump number 3 on the receipt."

Let me show you another receipt and ask you to read the details to the jury."

"Objection! The defense attorney is taking us on a fishing expedition. There is no point to his line of questioning."

"The line of questioning does have a well-defined purpose. The timing of the events on Friday is shown on the receipts, which the prosecution marked as exhibits for the trial," Wrightson pointed out.

"Overruled."

"Officer White, what do you see on the second receipt?"

"Joan Ingleton paid $23.19 for regular gas at 8:23 PM on Friday at pump number 3."

"The same pump as the one used by Mr. O'Connor. Correct?"

"Yes."

"Officer White, according to the police reports, there were two phone calls from a cell phone to the house phone at Mr. O'Connor's residence. The cell phone is registered to Lydia H. Kingston. This is a copy of the record from the cell phone carrier. The timestamps for the two calls are 6:58 PM and 8:04 PM. The first call lasted four minutes and the second one took 19 minutes. Do you see that?"

"Yes, that is correct."

"Do the police have any reason to dispute the fact that the first call was from Lydia Kingston to her daughter and the second call was from Lydia Kingston to Mr.

O'Connor, which would put the defendant at home in his residence from before eight o'clock? Yes or no, please."

"Objection! Any speculation about the identity of the persons on the phone call is hearsay."

"Sustained."

"Officer White, Mr. Elliot Shaw testified that he heard the shot that killed the victim at eight thirty give or take five minutes. Do the police have any reason to dispute the time of death?"

"No."

"No more questions," Wrightson said.

"The prosecution rests its case," Mr. Hofmann said.

Judge Fitzgerald adjourned the proceedings until after lunch.

At 1:20 PM, Attorney Wrightson said, "The defense calls Joan Ingleton to the stand."

"Objection! Ms. Ingleton is a prosecution witness who was not called to testify."

"Ms. Ingleton is on the list of witnesses for the defense as well as for the prosecution," Wrightson said.

"Overruled."

"Ms. Ingleton, according to the credit-card records at Hennigan's filling station, you bought gas there on Friday evening. Is that correct?"

"Yes."

"This is a copy of the receipt. The timestamp is for 8:23 PM. Is that correct?"

"I don't remember exactly what time I was there but that sounds about right."

"Did you go into the convenience store?"

"Objection! Joan Ingleton is not a suspect."

"The defense is establishing the timeline for the events on Friday evening. We are not accusing Ms. Ingleton of wrongdoing."

"Overruled." The judge's sigh of exasperation was audible.

"No, it was late and I needed to get home. I had to leave early on Saturday for a trip to see my grandchildren."

"Was the convenience store open?"

"Oh, yes."

"How do you know?"

"Well, because I bought gas. The pumps have to be off when the store is closed. Also, the lights were on like they always are at Hennigan's at that time. Otherwise, I would not have stopped for gas."

"Thank you, Ms. Ingleton. No more questions."

There were no questions on redirect from Mr. Hofmann.

"You may step down, Ms. Ingleton," the judge said.

Attorney Wrightson said, "The defense calls Mary Gallagher."

The name caught me by surprise. Clutch hired Mary Gallagher as a part time employee to help around the garage when she was still in high school. She used to come back to work for us during the summers while she was in college. I did not know why she was testifying for the defense.

"Have you been in the stands for the AAU baseball games this summer?" Attorney Wrightson asked the witness after she was sworn in and took the stand.

"I do not believe I have missed one yet. I am a baseball fanatic and our team is about as good as it gets in Batavia." Ms. Gallagher added a rueful, "Unfortunately."

I saw a few of the jurors chuckle at her commentary along with the twittering from the courtroom pews.

"Have you observed Mr. O'Connor and Mr. Hennigan at the baseball games?

"Yes, they are both almost always there."

"Amost always?"

"Ted O'Connor plays second base and bats second or third in the lineup. He is always there. Mr. Hennigan shows up probably nine times out of ten just to watch." Mary Gallagher gulped back a gasp. "I guess I should say, used to show up for almost all the games."

"Sadly, yes. Please go on Ms. Gallagher."

She took a deep breath and said, "Mr. Hennigan usually did not stay for the entire game. He would talk to the players and do some coaching but leave before it was over. From what I could tell he knew the game pretty well. He sponsored the team in Batavia. So, he must have loved baseball too."

"Have you observed interactions between Mr. O'Connor and Mr. Hennigan?"

"Yes. They would talk to each other at every game. I have observed them talking throughout the season."

"How about recently before Mr. Hennigan died?"

"Mr. O'Connor went down swinging on a pitch well out of the strike zone in the first inning of the game a week ago Wednesday. It had to be just before Mr. Hennigan died. It was not a good at bat. He took off his helmet and banged it down in disgust. He walked back past the dugout over to the bleachers and sat down next to Mr. Hennigan. I heard him ask, 'What did you see?'"

"Do you mean Mr. O'Connor was asking Mr. Hennigan for coaching advice?"

"Yes, that's right. I was sitting in the bleachers not far from Mr. Hennigan. He told Mr. O'Connor that he was pulling his head up on the pitch. Mr. O'Connor came back and talked to Mr. Hennigan again after his next at bat. As I remember, he lined out to first."

"Did you see animosity between them?"

"No, just the opposite. Mr. O'Connor put his hand on Mr. Hennigan's shoulder and said, 'Thanks' before he ran back out on the field. A few minutes later, Mr. Hennigan got up and left. I stayed for the whole game." Mary Gallagher bragged.

"No more questions," Mr. Wrightson said.

Mr. Hofmann asked, "Just answer yes or no, Ms. Gallagher. Would you say Mr. O'Connor and Mr. Hennigan were buddies?"

"No. I can't really say that."

"Just yes or no, please. Would they go out to eat together or go for a drink?"

"Not that I know of."

"Thank you. That's all."

"You may step down, Ms. Gallagher," the judge said.

"The defense rests, Your Honor," Attorney Wrightson said.

"Nothing on redirect, Your Honor," Attorney Hofmann said.

The judge sequestered the jury for the night on Thursday and adjourned the proceedings until Friday morning.

Chapter 69 . The deliberations began on Friday.

The jurors were bussed to the Hampton Inn in Socorro. They walked around the corner to the family restaurant for their dinner on Thursday evening. Breakfast was served at the same three tables in the morning before the bus took the members of the panel back to the courthouse.

The prosecution took the floor first at 9:00 AM on Friday. Morris Hofmann began by telling the jury, "Disregard all of the nonsense that Attorney Wrightson spewed out about how the police focused on Mr. O'Connor because they disliked him. Do not be fooled by the defense attorney's attempts to rattle the witnesses.

"The Batavia policemen are well-trained professionals who arrested Theodore Christopher O'Connor because they had reason to believe he murdered Matthew Hennigan in cold blood. The prosecution has proven that the police were correct beyond a shadow of a doubt."

Mr. Hofmann went on at some length to review the testimony and to claim motive was established by witnesses and the defendant was the only one with the opportunity. He did not bring up the liquor bottle as physical evidence.

Elmer Wrightson spoke next. He started by talking about the topic that Hofmann omitted.

"An empty liquor bottle had been left on the counter next to the popcorn machine. It happened to be the container for a fifth of Jim Beam. A fingerprint found on the bottle belonged to Mr. O'Connor. What does that tell us? My client picked it up and threw it in the trash. Why did he bother?"

The defense attorney asked and answered his own questions.

"He was just trying to be helpful. It was an empty bottle that did not belong there. It was in the way of scooping popcorn into a bag. Did my client intend to take a sip of bourbon from the bottle and discarded it when he realized it was empty? The answer to that question makes no difference. He threw the bottle into the trash can and left the building more tidy than he found it.

"The police tried to rattle Mr. O'Connor by showing him the empty liquor bottle when they confronted him at his house the next day. Their tactic didn't work. Mr. O'Connor could not be intimidated because he is innocent of the crime.

"The bottle was retrieved from the trash in the convenience store and planted next to the cash register. Someone saw Mr. O'Connor pick it up and throw it away. They made a clumsy attempt to plant evidence that would tie my client to the crime scene.

"The killer must have been watching. Very likely she or he was inside the lavatory with Elliot Shaw. Evidently, the police thought so. Why else would they dust the restroom for fingerprints? We know what they found."

Attorney Wrightson stood looking at the dozen individuals seated in front of him. It was a dramatic pause orchestrated by an accomplished, experienced attorney who knew how to pull it off without being too obvious.

He broke the silence in a quiet, serious voice. He said, "They found nothing! The room had been wiped clean of fingerprints. No fingerprints at all in a public lavatory seems a bit strange, doesn't it? The cleaning service would have left fingerprints on the door handle, the walls, the faucet, or somewhere. Even the toilet brush had been wiped clean.

"There was an altercation between Mr. O'Connor and the deceased approximately a month or more ago. The two witnesses are not sure exactly when it happened. They disagree on important details. Did the victim provoke Mr. O'Connor? Did Mr. O'Connor actually threaten to kill Mr. Hennigan or was it just angry words that anyone of us might have said but not really meant in response to an insulting comment? The witnesses could not be sure of what they saw. It was dark and late in the parking lot at a family restaurant here in Batavia where no alcohol was served.

"Members of the jury, the most telling indication that no real motive existed for Mr. O'Connor to kill Mr. Hennigan is that they were seen interacting on friendly terms on several occasions since their argument. They were on the sidelines chatting between innings at a baseball game, in which Mr. O'Connor was competing. The last time was just two days before Mr. Hennigan was slain. Does that sound like motivation for murder? Not to me.

"I agree that the Batavia Police Department is staffed by well-trained professionals. I also think that any miscarriage of justice is abhorrent to them. However, this time, they rushed to judgment in their enthusiasm to solve a crime with an answer that was simply too easy for them. In fact, it was also too simple to be correct. The police convinced themselves of the verdict in advance which allowed the prosecution to gloss over their reasons for dusting the lavatory for fingerprints?

"Someone wiped the lavatory too clean to be believable. It was not the defendant. It was the real killer who was hiding his or her identity.

"Mr. O'Connor threw an empty bottle into the trash, helped himself to a bag of popcorn, and left the place the way he found it with the lights on and the front door closed but unlocked. Except for the stray empty bottle thrown into the trash, the store was neat and tidy the way it always is when he arrived and it was still that way when he left.

"We heard Elliot Shaw say that he saw Mr. O'Connor in the store. He also said that he heard the gun shot but did not see who pulled the trigger. That much was true. The rest was the talk of a very frightened man. We saw how scared he was on the stand when I pressed him for answers.

"Someone killed Mr. Hennigan in the convenience store on that Friday evening but it was not Mr. O'Connor.

"The timing does not work. Officer William White confirmed the time of death to be approximately 8:30 in the evening. Mr. O'Connor was home with his daughters by about 7:30. We have phone company records to prove he talked on the land line in his house to his wife, who was out of town on business, for nearly twenty minutes between eight o'clock and eight-thirty. The testimony that he was in the convenience store for all of that time is clearly false.

"Ms. Ingleton bought gas at 8:23 at the same pump that Mr. O'Connor used. He was gone before she got there. The lights were still on and the convenience store was still open and Mr. O'Connor had already gone home.

"Mr. Hennigan was shot by somebody else who turned off the lights and locked the door later in the evening."

Elmer Wrightson concluded with, "Members of the jury, I firmly believe that a not guilty verdict is the correct decision. Thank you."

Was 12:30 PM on Friday.

The judge decided that catered courthouse fare in the deliberation room was the right course of action. She took the next twenty minutes to explain the instructions for the jury regarding the law as it applied to the facts of the case. At 1:00 PM, the panel filed out of the courtroom to consider the merits of the case against me and the value of the arguments presented in my defense.

Two hours later, with no indication regarding the outcome, we were called back to our places in the courtroom. The not guilty verdict was announced at three o'clock on Friday afternoon.

"You are free to go, Mr. O'Connor," the Honorable Anne Fitzgerald said.

To my surprise, Morris Hofmann came across the aisle to the table for the defense. He shook hands with my attorney and said, "Congratulations, Elmer." Without looking at me or speaking to anyone else, he picked up his briefcase and walked out of the room.

Elmer Wrightson shook hands with me. He hugged Lydia and each of our daughters. I believe I saw a tear in his eye when he said, "I am glad it's over."

We walked out of the front of the building together and down the courthouse steps. My lifelong friend stood next to me on the sidewalk while I took deep breaths of the air of freedom. We shook hands again and I went home to my family.

Our celebration was both heartfelt and subdued. It was a great relief to be exonerated but it was also greatly discomforting to have been accused of a horrendous crime.

Someone took the life of a man in our community. Although not easy to like, he had many years ahead of him and no one had the right to deprive him of his future.

Chapter 70 . It was an unfinished solution.

Friday afternoon at our house seemed unreal. The nightmare that had disrupted our lives was over. People closest to our family dropped by to express their relief for me.

Was it relief that I felt or anger or something else? It had not had time to sink in.

Within the span of three weeks, I had gone from contented father and husband to murder suspect to exonerated but still living under the cloud of an unresolved accusation.

Our visitors shared stories and pleasantries. Clutch and Melissa came over just to be there for me. Elmer Wrightson stopped by. I told him to stay as long as he liked and he did.

Neighbors brought food as if I had just come home from the hospital and needed their kindness. None of us put it into words but the similarity seemed very real to me.

Friends offered assurances that life could and would return to the way it should be for me and my family. Principal Mansfield told me that I was welcome back at the school. She visited briefly with Diane and Eileen before saying goodbye to me and Lydia.

The only police officer to join us at our house that afternoon was William White. He stepped forward to shake my hand.

"I am really sorry that you had to be put through all of this," Billy said.

"So am I, Billy. So am I."

Officer White arrived with his mother and stepfather who welcomed me back and offered best wishes for the future.

Billy's sister came too. He and Margaret sat on the couch with Lydia and Eileen for a few minutes. I was trying to observe the young adults without being too obvious. When Billy had to leave, he squeezed Diane's hand on his way out the door. Though not a lip-reading expert, I know he whispered, "I'm sorry."

"Are you OK, Diane?" I asked. She seemed very serious, almost sad after he left. I was fiercely afraid that Mr. White had broken her heart.

"Daddy, Billy is worried that you are angry about his testimony for the prosecution. He is afraid that you cannot forgive him."

"Diane, it is exactly the opposite. Mr. Wrightson knew an arresting officer had to be called to the stand for the prosecution. He told me he was angling for Officer White as the best option for the defense. Elmer predicted it would be Billy because the prosecution's case would not stand up to an appeal if they had Sgt. Ryan testify against me."

Diane quipped, "Ryan would be obviously biased because you and I beat him up on our front porch." It had been a while since I had heard her funny chortle.

"Yes, that's right, of course." I let her assessment go uncontested.

"Seriously though, if it were not for Officer White's honesty and integrity on the witness stand, the outcome could well have been different. It took guts to admit to the failings of an investigation performed by his own police department. There can be no hiding it from his comrades in blue."

"I am happy and relieved you feel that way," Diane said.

"Well, I do. Billy has grown up to be a fine police officer. He is a man to be admired. You can tell him I said so."

"I believe I will."

"I'm afraid to ask, Diane. Is everything all right between you two? I saw how hurt you looked when Billy left just now."

"Hurt? Not at all. It's just that there is something I need to tell you." Diane's somber face had returned.

"What?" I sighed.

"Daddy, Billy wants to ask you for my hand in marriage. Mom and Eileen already know but I have been waiting for the right time to talk to you."

"What a quaint way to put it."

"Billy is an old-fashioned guy. That's why I love him."

My answer was a bear hug for my wonderful daughter.

Roger and James were standing nearby. I did not realize they were listening in until James clasped me on the shoulder. They were among the several friends and neighbors who knew about Billy and Diane before I did.

"What? How did that happen?" I asked. It was feigned indignation. How could I harbor resentment along with the good feeling in my heart for my oldest daughter's happiness?

Diane said, "In the midst of all the recent turmoil, I needed to talk to someone outside the family. When I saw Roger and James walking by one morning last week, I knew just the right people."

The two of them were apologetic. I told them not to be. "I greatly appreciate all of your contributions to the well-being of our children. It takes a village to raise a daughter like Diane."

James said, "We did a damn good job too."

They were very pleased that I was free and back home. They knew all along that I "was too good a man to be guilty of such a heinous crime." They brought two casseroles, lemonade, and soft drinks. They did not stay long.

Before the end of the afternoon, it became even more obvious that Diane's obtuse father was among the last to know about her hopes for the future. Bill White, my friend from AA and Billy's biological father, came to the house by himself to wish me well.

"I've not been in your house since I fell off a roof," he joked. "Perhaps, we will be seeing more of each other in the future."

"That might well be," I answered.

Janet Bread was greeting and visiting with our guests. She had to be there. After all, she was living in our guest room.

"Don't worry, Ted. I have not moved in permanently." She gave me a hug.

"You, Janet Bread, may stay as long as you like."

"Would you step into the den to talk to me for a minute?" she asked. Detective Bread wanted to hear more about Matthew Hennigan.

"Did his business seem to be thriving?"

"Yes, his was the only store in town after seven o'clock in the evening," I said.

She pressed on with another question. "Hennigan was quite generous with his support of civic activities. Did he have another source of income?"

"Not that I know of."

"How about Elliot Shaw? How did he support himself?"

"I think he just worked at Hennigan's."

"OK, thanks. That's all. Go back to your family."

"Janet, you are family and more. It is great to see how much Lydia enjoys having your company. As for myself, you are a lifesaver." It was to be a prophetic comment though I hardly knew how much so at the time.

Janet said, "If there is more I can do, I will. It is I who appreciates the chance to do something for Lydia and for you and the lovely Diane and Eileen."

"Wait a minute," I said. "What do you mean by if there is more you can do? You have picked up something that might be significant. Haven't you? What are you working on?"

"Nothing definitive yet," Detective Bread said. "I'm still wondering about Brian Hill. What was he doing here?"

"I think I have told you everything I can about him but I'll be happy to answer more questions if it would help."

"Thanks, Ted. I am going in to Wrightson's office for a while this afternoon. I have work to do there and some phone calls to make. I may want to talk to you again sometime tomorrow."

"This is all very mysterious, Janet."

She smiled. "I try to be that way. It keeps life interesting. Tell Lydia that I may be out late again."

"She's right over there talking to Diane but I'll give her the message if you wish." We were standing at the door between the den and the living room.

A little while later, I noticed Janet was gone.

That evening, it was just the four of us sitting around the kitchen table grazing on the leftovers from what people had brought to the house.

"It is kind of like old times. Isn't it? Can our lives ever be the same again?" Lydia asked.

"We are older and wiser now." Of all people, it was Eileen who said it.

323

"Are you happy for me, Dad?" Diane asked.

"Immensely so!" I responded with no hesitation.

My grown-up little girl gave me a big hug. "Thank you, Daddy."

Lydia was quiet. I sat there gazing at her.

Finally, she said, "I am not going back to Cardinal Energy. I have signed on at TDBank as an outside contractor to do financial consulting for their customers. No more long hours and no more traveling for business."

"That would be wonderful for us," I said. "You know Elmer's mother is a big honcho at TDBank."

"Yes, I do know that. She is the reason I got the job. She told me about the opportunity when I ran into her at the bank about a year ago. I've been mulling it over ever since and I went back to see her again last week."

"Can you be happy with such a change? Won't it be a huge letdown for you?"

"I am very much relieved and content with the idea. The ups and downs at Cardinal Energy have always been stressful but lately it has become even more so. The board of directors is planning to take the company in a new direction."

"But, you are on the board. Did you fight the changes?"

"Yes, I am on the board. No, I did not fight the changes. Going in a new direction was my idea. The plans are actually mostly mine. The company has been stagnant for too long and we need to take on new challenges. There are business opportunities that a company as strong as ours should be taking advantage of."

"Wouldn't you like to be part of the implementation of your plans?"

"Not really. I've talked to the CEO. She would put me in charge if I asked her to but we agree that it will be a tough job best handled by the new people some of whom I hired."

"No one can do whatever it will require as well as you," Eileen piped up.

"Of course not." Lydia enjoyed the adulation of her children. Our eyes met and I could tell she believed the compliment was true.

"Agreed," I said.

"I could do the work. However, it would mean more responsibilities and longer hours to see the plans through to completion. Alternatively, I can hand the task off to new talent at the company. One of them is a woman I recruited from DTE Electric. She has built up her credentials there for the past ten years since getting her MBA from Columbia."

"Same as you, Mom," Eileen said.

"Right except there are differences. She did her undergraduate work at the University of Dayton."

"No! Not an Ohio school," Diane exclaimed.

"Afraid so."

"Something else worries me a little, though," Lydia said.

"Are you going to be at home all the time micromanaging my life?" Eileen was only half kidding.

Her mother ignored the question. She said, "Janet has prevailed upon me to consult for her agency. They have a sporadic need for someone to examine the finances of a company when there is reason to suspect improprieties. She does not have a particular case for me right now but the opportunities arise often."

"What did you say?" I asked.

"I told her only if the investigation is interesting and intriguing." It was said with a rueful smile. Lydia added, "I couldn't say no."

"Wow. Will we be having another criminal investigator in the family?" Diane wondered. "You will be putting members of the mafia behind bars for tax evasion just like Eliot Ness. Can Eileen and I join your team? We will be the famous Batavia Untouchables."

Eileen said, "I don't know if I like that idea. The famous part sounds good but it could require serious work. I would rather drop out of school and stay home to watch the soaps on TV." Our youngest daughter had the knack for lightening the mood.

The silly chatter was enough to break up the party in the kitchen. I went to work at repackaging the salvageable items in refrigerator dishes. Lydia reorganized the shelves to fit everything in.

The girls remained oblivious to any requirements for them to chip in. Diane reached around her mother for a bottle of seltzer which she shared with her little sister. They went into the dining room and sat at the table to be out of our way. We tacitly agreed to let them be. It was nice to see our daughters chatting like friends.

Lydia and I adjourned to the den a bit later with our own glasses of seltzer over ice to continue the serious conversation about our future.

Part VI

Search and Interview

If there's a book that you want to read but it hasn't been written yet, then you must write it.

– Toni Morrison

Chapter 71 . The investigator went dark.

It was nearly five o'clock the following morning when I woke up with a bad feeling that something was wrong. My wife was not on her side of the bed. When I got down the back stairs into the kitchen, I found Lydia at the table with a visitor. It took me a minute to recognize him as a family friend.

"Ted, this is FBI Agent Irving Ronan. I don't know what is going on. Janet did not come home last night." Lydia's voice broke. She braced herself on the table and started to get up but couldn't.

She said, "Listen, the coffee might be done. Do you want a cup, Ted? Irving, the coffee is ready."

"Janet didn't come home here?" I asked. "What are you talking about?"

"Oh, I don't know what I'm saying. Irving, can you explain what is going on to my husband?" Lydia snuffled.

"Hello, Ted. I have been hearing good things about you."

"Thanks, Irving. What brings you to town? I don't remember when we saw you last. It's been years," I said.

"I am here to answer a summons from Janet Bread. As I believe you are both aware, she is a private detective who works for the Drug Enforcement Administration. Her firm actually has agreements with both the FBI and the DEA."

"We know all that but Janet came here as a supportive friend for Lydia while I was on trial for murder."

"Did Janet tell you about us and the trial?" Lydia asked.

"Yes, she has been checking in with us all along," Agent Irving Ronan said.

"What do you mean?" I asked. "Was Janet keeping you informed about something? I thought she was here just to see us. Was she also on an assignment that we were not aware of?"

Ronan said, "We had nothing to indicate a connection between the crime you were accused of and anything we were working on. When she left our office in Washington last week, Janet gave only personal reasons for coming to Batavia. She took leave from her work on a racketeering case just to be here with you."

"Janet was my emotional support," Lydia mumbled.

"Right. That's what she told me." Irving confirmed Lydia's feelings for the matter. "However, a man we have been looking for showed up in the courtroom. Janet Bread spotted him among the spectators. Brian Hill was there at the preliminary hearing on Monday two days after you were arrested, Ted."

Ronan looked down to consult his notes. "In the afternoon on the same day, Janet questioned you about the stranger in the courtroom. You told her his name was Rusty Higgins."

"I did not remember his last name right away but I knew she was referring to Rusty."

"I've met Rusty," Lydia said.

"Oh, really? In what capacity?" Ronan sounded alarmed.

"Just to speak to him at Ted's baseball games," Lydia explained.

"Good. Don't cross him. The man is a dangerous hombre. He is physically powerful, quick, and very clever. He is as tough to handle as any criminal you can imagine. To relax in his company or assume you have the advantage is a mistake that you will make only once."

"Wow. I never would have guessed." Lydia shivered. Irving's warning made both of us uneasy.

"The DEA had Mr. Hill under surveillance for months but he slipped away over a year ago. No one knew what happened to him until he showed up here. Janet Bread called the FBI office in Washington, D.C., to alert us to Hill's whereabouts. She talked to you about him and initiated additional conference calls with us. We discussed the implications for the racketeering investigation.

"I reviewed related cases in this area of the country. We spoke again late on Tuesday and talked for a while before calling it quits for the night."

"Why didn't the FBI and the DEA send agents to pick him up?" Lydia asked.

"We considered it. However, FBI Senior Agent-in-Charge Irene Cleary concurred with the DEA that it was important to find out what Hill was doing here. Cleary asked Janet to investigate."

"Just on her own?" I asked.

"No. They needed a surveillance team. Bread agreed with Cleary that using local talent for surveillance would be less conspicuous than FBI suits in this small town. Janet reported back later that she had found the right people to do the job. The DEA and the FBI assumed a watch-and-wait approach that has not yielded clues regarding Hill's activities."

"Until last night?" I asked.

"That's right. Yesterday afternoon, Janet let me know you had been acquitted. She had just talked to you again about Matthew Hennigan and about the possibility of connections between him and Brian Hill. She was working in office space at Wrightson's firm. The last time I spoke to her was late yesterday evening."

Lydia said, "She told Ted that it might be late. So, we didn't wait up."

"At 11:43 last night, Detective Bread sent an emergency message to our alarm account. After that, she went dark. When the agent in the office called her back, she didn't answer. He tried several times before waking me up at 12:20 in the middle of the night."

"You got here fast," I noted.

"I commandeered a transport out of Andrews and came as quickly as I could."

"Commandeered?" I wondered out loud.

"Detective Bread's firm has priority status with the United States Army Ordnance Corps. You do know who Janet's mother is. Don't you?" Ronan asked.

Lydia answered for me, "The highly decorated United States Army Colonel Helen Kingston."

Stories about her cousin's family were well known to the children and me.

"Two other agents are waiting to hear from me before they decide if it is necessary for them to join us here," Irving Ronan said.

"What is going on?" Diane asked. She had come down the front stairs and was standing in the doorway from the dining room.

Her younger sister appeared right behind Diane. Eileen said, "All of the commotion down here woke me up." The irritation in her voice was quite evident.

"Sorry to disturb your beauty sleep," Lydia said. She swallowed hard to hide the quake in her voice. "We have a surprise visitor from out of town. Mr. Irving Ronan is a friend of Aunt Janet's. Just say hello and you can both go back to bed."

"I think I will," Eileen pronounced. She turned to leave back through the dining room but did an about face. "Wait. Are you Uncle Irving?"

"Yes I am and proud of it." Irving Ronan smiled.

"I'm Eileen and she's Diane."

"I've heard your names many times but don't worry. Let me assure you that not everything Aunt Janet has told me about you is bad." Uncle Irving clearly had the knack for putting our youngsters at ease.

"Now, go back to bed," their mother repeated. "You can visit with Uncle Irving in the morning."

"OK, good," our younger daughter agreed and started to go again but stopped abruptly. Eileen performed another pirouette in the dining room and ran all the way into the kitchen. The girl rushed Uncle Irving to give him a big hug before finally departing for more sleep.

"It is very nice to meet you too," Uncle Irving said.

"G'night," she called from the front stairs.

The older daughter did not follow her little sister out of the room. Diane suspected that our early-morning rendezvous had a more serious purpose than a social call. The tremor in Lydia's voice might have given it away. Without asking permission, she pulled out a chair and took a seat next to her mother at the kitchen table.

"Should Janet Bread be here too?" Diane asked. "I noticed the door to the guest room is ajar. I don't think she is in there. Is she in trouble?"

Ronan leaned back and looked at Lydia. Uncle Irving did not know how much to tell our almost twenty-year-old little girl.

I decided she should know about our alarming quandary. "Diane, FBI Agent Ronan is here because Detective Bread sent him a message late last night. She did not say what she wanted. When the FBI tried to respond, they were not able to get through for details. Agent Ronan flew in early this morning to investigate. We have still not heard back from Aunt Janet."

"Do you think something bad might have happened to her?" Diane shuddered.

Agent Ronan answered, "Not necessarily. My policy is to assume everything is under control but also to be prepared for problems. The FBI protocol is to wait for her to make contact. We must not get panicky because we need to keep a clear head."

Agent Ronan stopped talking. His demeaner suddenly changed. "Did you hear that?" he asked. "Shhh." He held up a hand for quiet.

Diane echoed my answer, "No. What?"

"It came from the driveway," Lydia whispered. She pointed to the side door.

With startling agility, the wiry Irving Ronan slipped out of his chair and moved up against the wall between the door to the pantry and the exit from the kitchen to the mudroom.

He spoke quietly, "No one knows I am here. I left my rental in a parking lot on Central Boulevard and walked over in the dark."

Lydia had heard the footsteps in the driveway. Irving had sensed an interruption was coming. The FBI agent motioned for us to move to the opposite side of the kitchen toward the living room. All of us waited expectantly for signs that we had company.

Chapter 72 . Another visitor arrived at the kitchen table.

The family residence faced south on Elm Avenue, which ran mostly east and west. The driveway was along the east side of the house from the street to our barn-like garage.

As shown in the Figure, there were four ways in and out of our eat-in kitchen. A full-sized door separated us from the living room, which served as a combination great room at the front of the house.

A picture window looked out from the living room onto the wide porch that stretched across the front of the building. The main entrance with its double-wide oak doors was adjacent to the window.

The rectangular library or den was on the east side of the living room. A half bath was located off the den in the front corner of our house.

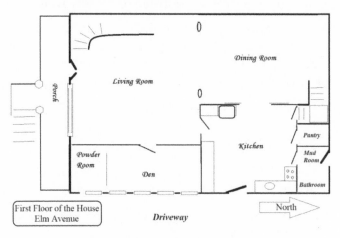

First Floor of the House
Elm Avenue

Driveway

North

First Floor Plan

Looking up from outside in the driveway, you could see that the lavatory window matched the row of four windows well above eye level in the den.

On the west side of the living room, a broad elegant staircase rose from just inside the front entrance up to the bedrooms on the second story.

Polished pillars straddled the opening between the living room and the dining room. A pair of sliding doors, which were seldom closed, separated the kitchen from the dining room to complete the circle on the first floor from kitchen to living room to dining room to kitchen.

The three doors on the north side of the kitchen were for the back stairs to the second floor, the walk-in pantry, and the mudroom with an exit to the backyard. A three-quarters bathroom at the back corner of the house was attached to the mudroom. There were two stairways to our full basement. One was under the staircase in the living room and the other through a door at the back of the dining room.

I was beginning to suspect Irving and Lydia were mistaken about hearing anything when there was a rap on the side door from the kitchen to the driveway.

"Are you expecting anyone?" Agent Ronan was looking at Lydia. His suit coat was pushed back to reveal the weapon on his right hip. The strap on the holster for his gun was undone and he had a grip on the handle.

"No." Lydia backed a step away from the door. "Who's there?" She called.

"It's Elmer Wrightson," was the answer.

I let out a sigh of relief and hastened across the kitchen to let him in. "Hello, Elmer. Is something wrong?"

Agent Ronan was not ready to relax. He asked Wrightson, "Are you alone?"

"Yes. Who are you?" Wrightson backed up a step. He appeared to be ready to turn and run.

"Come in, Mr. Wrightson. My name is Irving Ronan." He did his own introductions. "I'm one of the FBI agents who was on the conference call with you and Janet Bread last night."

"Yes, I recognize your voice," Wrightson said.

"Elmer, why are you here at this hour?" Lydia asked.

He looked at our oldest daughter. "Are you OK, Diane?" Wrightson's voice trembled. His complexion was ashen.

"Yeah, sure. I'm fine. Why?"

"Did you encounter any trouble yesterday? Any strangers approach you?"

"No. I didn't notice anybody. Why are you asking?" Diane was getting anxious. "You're scaring me."

Eileen reappeared. "You're scaring me too." She stumbled into the kitchen from the dining room.

"Elmer, what are you talking about?" Lydia sounded angry.

Chapter 73 . The intruder's intentions were a mystery.

Wrightson did not answer Diane, Eileen, or Lydia. He came back with another question instead. "Where is Janet Bread?"

Agent Ronan was reluctant to give anything away. He asked, "Why are you concerned about Diane's welfare or about Detective Bread?"

"Someone broke into my condominium last night and left this file on the kitchen table." He held up an oversized tan envelope. The flap at the top was hanging open.

I reached for it. "What's in it?"

Elmer pulled it back. He said, "There are threatening photographs in here. I'm not sure you want to see them."

"I'll take it." Irving Ronan fished gloves out of his suit-coat pocket. He took his jacket off and hung it on one of the kitchen chairs.

The strap over his gun was snapped back in place. The leather holster was attached to his belt just behind his right hip. His matter-of-fact manner about the concealed weapon added to the aura of the FBI agent's authority.

Ronan pulled on the gloves with one swift motion after another and accepted the envelope. Wrightson gave it up readily and pulled another chair up to the table. He squeezed in between Diane and me.

Irving Ronan was standing across from us. He slid a manila folder from the envelope, held it in front of him, and paged through the contents. The rest of us sat, watched, and waited for him to say something.

"Have you notified the police, Mr. Wrightson?" Ronan asked.

"Yes, I called from home. The dispatcher said they would send a patrol car over to my house but they did not seem to be taking me seriously. I am not on their favorite-persons' list right now."

"A criminal-defense attorney seldom is. The police need to catch the lawbreakers. Your job is to refute the charges," Ronan agreed.

I could see that the folder contained several 8" by 10", black and white, printed photographs. I looked over at Lydia. Her face showed no emotion.

After a patience-challenging hesitation, Agent Ronan said, "Take a look but don't touch. We need to check for fingerprints other than yours Mr. Wrightson."

Elmer said, "I was careful to handle them on the edges."

Ronan spread three photographs on the table for us to see. The first was of Diane standing by the car in the subterranean garage below the building that housed the offices of Wrightson and Associates. The second was of Diane and me in the car. It showed our faces through the windshield as she drove onto the ramp toward the exit to the street.

In the third photograph, Janet Bread was seated in a straight-back chair at a black metal table. Her attire was the same as yesterday. She was wearing the dark slacks of an FBI agent with the coffee stain from yesterday on her white shirt.

No restraints were visible but her hands were behind her back and the table covered her ankles. Her stoic expression gave no indication that she was under duress. The picture was taken some time during the night. The ones of us were from the previous Wednesday.

Elmer put his arm around Diane and put a hand on my shoulder. He said, "The pictures of you two scared me."

Chapter 74 . Backup errs on the side of caution.

The two photographs of Diane and me were taken in the garage on the Executive Level under the Elise Monroe Office Building. Obviously, someone had been watching for us.

I reminded my daughter of the circumstances. "Diane, you picked me up in that rented car in the picture on Wednesday after the bail hearing. You drove us from the courthouse to Mr. Wrightson's office. I stayed at the firm all afternoon to answer questions. These pictures were taken at the end of the day. Did you see anyone in the garage when you came back for me?"

"People but no cameras."

"The first picture is just of you standing next to the car. The second one shows both of us through the windshield on the way out of the garage. I guess I was too wrapped up in my problems to spot anyone taking pictures. In fact, I don't remember seeing anyone at all."

"I saw people before you got down there. Three maybe four individuals came out of the elevators ahead of you. They went to their cars and drove off. No one seemed to pay any attention to me. I think there was just one car that came into the garage while I was waiting for you. I watched the driver, a man, go across to the elevators."

"The man who walked over to the elevators, did you see him go in and the doors close behind him?" Agent Ronan asked Diane. He was paying close attention to our conversation. The others in the room were listening to us as well.

"No, Uncle Irving. I remember thinking it was taking a long time for an elevator to get there but, when I looked back later, he was gone. I presumed the elevator doors had finally opened and closed."

"Could you describe him?"

"Not very well. He did seem familiar but there was nothing distinctive about him. He turned in my direction while he was waiting and looked right at me. That's when I stopped watching him. He might have been wondering about me sitting there in our rented car."

"Do you know if he actually pushed the button to call for an elevator?" Ronan asked.

"Not really. Why wouldn't he?"

The FBI agent explained, "It's a common ploy. Pretend to be waiting for an elevator, force the person you are stalking to look away, and dodge out of sight."

"That's a scary thing to say, Irving. Do you think someone was stalking Diane?" Her mother asked.

"Lydia, I am not the one saying it. These photographs are."

Irving Ronan noticed Lydia's look of dismay.

"Lydia, you have a right to be worried but, so far, all we have are pictures in an envelope. We must not overreact," he said. "A threatening gesture to be sure. However, whoever took the pictures has yet to tell us what they want."

"Irving, it seems more serious than a gesture," I said.

"Perhaps but maybe not much more. If whoever took the pictures meant to do harm, they had the opportunity right then in the garage with few people around. We must not minimize the potential for danger but we should not exaggerate it either."

"I understand," I said. From the look on her face, Lydia did not agree.

"Diane, can you tell us anything else about the man at the elevator?" Irving Ronan asked.

"Not much. As I said, he did seem familiar. He looked like any of the attorneys or businessmen in Mr. Wrightson's building on the way to their office. One thing a little different was the large briefcase on a strap slung over his shoulder."

"Did it seem to be heavy?"

"Yes, I thought so."

"It could have contained a camera bag," I suggested.

"Do you think you would recognize the man from a book of mug shots?" Ronan asked.

"Maybe. I don't know. I could try."

"OK, Diane. Thanks," he said. "I will see if we can get a package sent over for you to look at."

"Is my family in danger?" Diane asked the question that was nagging her mother and me.

"My presence gives you some protection." Uncle Irving smiled at Diane and tapped the holster on his hip. "I can hold off an army with this thing."

The look on her face told him that our daughter was grown up enough to be frightened not thrilled by the thought of an exciting shootout.

FBI Agent Irving Ronan appeared to change his mind about making light of our situation. He said, "Nothing has happened yet but, rather than just sit and anxiously anticipate trouble, we should get prepared for the possibilities."

I asked, "Should we ask the police to provide protection for us here at the house?"

"Sure, we can but I am not particularly worried about defending ourselves against intruders during the day. It would be likely that they would be noticed. Whomever we are dealing with is more cautious than that. The burglar snuck into your place, Elmer, under the cover of night."

Wrightson replied, "Rather than hang around here watching over us, the BPD could be catching the culprit who broke into my house."

Lydia said, "The police should find out who took those pictures."

"Yes," Agent Ronan agreed. "We need to know the nature of the threat posed by the photographs. The police might be able to identify the backdrop in the picture of Janet Bread."

Diane spoke up, "Agent Irving, I think I can get through to the police. Would it be OK for me to call Officer William White and tell him about those creepy pictures?"

"Yes, please do. I presume Officer White is someone you know in the Batavia Police Department," Ronan said.

"Yes, he is. "

"Diane, the police are already on notice. They should be aware that something is afoot because I called them this morning," Wrightson said.

"I'll tell Officer White about that. I'll use the phone in the den." Diane shrugged her way out of the kitchen.

Lydia looked at me with a bemused expression. I returned the look along with a knowing shrug.

Lydia explained to Uncle Irving, "William White used to live down the street when he was a little boy. He is now on the Batavia police force. Diane has been rather coy about her interest in him until recently. They just got engaged."

"That's wonderful," Uncle Irving exclaimed.

When Diane returned, everyone looked toward her for a report. She said, "Officer White was not there. Officer

Angela Dunning is another friend of mine. She told me that Sgt. Ryan and Officer White were not working today. She took the message that we wanted someone to come here. She said Officer Thompson was on duty but I do not know who that is. He must be new."

I said, "Diane, you should remember him. His name is Louis Thompson. He was one of the four cops who were here on the Saturday morning when I got arrested and you got shoved into the wall on the porch."

"Oh, is that right? I guess I never noticed him. Was he with Chief Hepburn?"

"Yes."

"Well, I still wouldn't know him if I saw him. I was hardly aware of the other cops. I remember it was Officer White who helped me get up off the floor after Sgt. Ryan knocked me down."

"What you mean is you only had eyes for Billy," Eileen teased.

"No, stop that."

I said, "Diane, Thompson was the one who pushed me down into the back seat of the cruiser."

"Of course, I do remember that. I only saw his back when I stopped Eileen from slugging him. I never saw his face."

"I did," Eileen exclaimed. "He looked mean and ugly."

"Diane, what was the bottom line on your conversation with the Officer Dunning? When can we expect to get some help from them?" Agent Ronan asked. His equanimity in the midst of the uncertainties seemed to be wearing thin.

"Oh, sorry. Officer Dunning took the message. She didn't say how long it might take them to respond."

Agent Ronan pulled a phone from his suit pocket and tapped numbers onto the screen. "I need to check in with the office in Washington," he said.

When someone answered on the other end, Irving Ronan started talking. "Irene, have you heard anything from Janet Bread?"

After a pause, he said, "No news here either. Let me fill you in on a local development and you can decide if you need to send another agent or join us yourself."

Agent Ronan walked into the dining room to talk to the agent in charge. He sat down at the table. Their brief conversation was not audible from where I was sitting next to Lydia.

Ronan stood up again and came back into the kitchen. "Yes, I agree. We should arrange for local backup. Would you call Jennifer Hepburn, the chief of police in Batavia, and ask for her help?" Another pause. "Having the request come from you might be necessary. We need their full cooperation." Pause. "OK, Thanks." He hung up.

Agent Ronan explained to all of us in the kitchen, "That was FBI Section Chief Irene Cleary. My instructions are to take the threat implied by the photographs very seriously. Also, she is quite concerned about Janet Bread. She will make a phone call to the BPD to hasten their cooperation. I suspect Agent Cleary will be joining us here before the day is out."

"FBI Agent Ronan, how much trouble are you expecting?" Lydia addressed him formally. A litany of concerns flowed from her lips. "I'm feeling in the dark about the potential for harm but you have dealt with many difficult cases. What do you make of these photographs? Are we in danger? Has Janet been kidnapped? Are members of my family next? Is there something we should be doing to protect ourselves?"

"Lydia, I do have a lot of experience but I can't be certain about the level of the current threat. My gut tells me we should be getting ready for trouble."

"Janet says you are never wrong."

"That is high praise coming from Ms. Bread. However, the only reassurance I can honestly offer all of you is we will be taking appropriate precautions."

"By getting help from the police?" I asked.

"Yes and by learning more about whom we are dealing with. The Batavia Police Department might be able to get a book of photographs sent over for Diane to look at," Ronan said.

Just then, the side door opened. Everyone jumped. Diane could not hold back a shriek. The woman at the door dropped her purse and tripped into the room.

Chapter 75 . The good servant is tantamount to family friend.

Lydia jumped forward to steady the startled visitor on the doorstep into our kitchen. "Oh, Alena, I'm so sorry to scare you. We have unexpected guests and I forgot you were coming to help clean the house this morning."

On the recommendation of a neighbor, I had hired Alena C'de Baca a number of years ago to help with household chores. Lydia was away a lot. I was not keeping up on my own.

Ms. C'de Baca has been a constant in our lives for so long now that it is hard to remember the time before she became a well-loved member of the family. Without waiting for directions, Alena undertook all sorts of chores from laundry to cooking and baking to cleaning. In years past, she even helped the children with their homework.

The woman became invaluable soon after she entered our lives. Lydia appreciated her ability to see what needed to be done and do it. It was not easy for me to admit it back then but Alena quickly learned that part of her job was to make up for my deficiencies.

Regardless of her competence, Alena was bewildered by the confusion in our kitchen. To be greeted by serious and worried people was not what she could have expected early on a Saturday morning.

Lydia said, "You are here really early. It's not even six in the morning." She pointed to the large, decorative clock on the wall over the doors to the dining room.

"Oh, I can come back," Alena whispered. "My husband dropped me off early because he has to drive into the city and my car is not working. I was going to wait outside until six o'clock but I saw the light and heard you. So, I decided to come in. I have another job on Monday but I can try to come some afternoon next week."

"Don't let her leave," Agent Ronan said just to me.

"No, no. Don't go, Alena. We need your help today," I insisted.

She hesitated and looked around at the crowded room and at me. "I didn't know you would be here Mr. O'Connor. Are you OK? I am glad you are not guilty. We have been praying for you at church."

"Oh, Thank you. I appreciate the prayers and your kindness," I said.

"We pray for Mr. Hennigan and his family too. You know sometimes his cousin comes to our church."

"No. I did not know that, Alena. Mr. Hennigan was a good citizen in our town and I would never wish him any harm. I hope we will all be free of the shadow his death has cast over us very soon."

Alena relaxed a little. She came the rest of the way into the kitchen. Lydia reached around her and closed the kitchen door.

"An FBI agent is here to help find out who did kill Mr. Hennigan. He is Irving Ronan."

He smiled at Alena and acknowledged her with a wave. Ronan moved back into the dining room to answer his phone.

"My attorney is here too," I said.

"Yes, I know Mr. Wrightson."

"We have not had anything to eat yet today," Lydia said. "I know it is early but I am starting to feel lightheaded. Can you make breakfast for us?" My wife was looking pale and wan.

"Oh, yes, I will." Our capable and accommodating domestic helper was happy to have something to do.

Lydia said, "You can let the cleaning go until next week, Alena. Our plans for today are up in the air. We are not sure what we will be needing. Please help with breakfast and maybe lunch too. And just see what needs to be done. Thank you."

Alena gave Lydia a bright smile. Relief from the uncertainty replaced her anxious expression. The family had come to understand that Ms. C'de Baca enjoyed the independence of taking charge. She was a proud woman who liked to be appreciated. She took an apron from the pantry and opened the refrigerator.

A moment later, Alena turned toward all of us and said, "Out of my kitchen, please. Not you, Dee. And where is Eely?" Alena used her preferred nicknames for our daughters. She had cared for them on many days since their early childhood. "I will be wanting some help," she explained to Diane.

Chapter 76 . Effective investigations require a capable police force.

Elmer and I stepped out of the kitchen and into the dining room. Lydia followed right after us. Irving was seated on the other side of the table. He gave us a please-be-quiet wave of his hand and continued talking into his phone.

"We should go to the den," Lydia whispered. She led the way across the living room toward the study where we tried to make ourselves comfortable in spite of our worries. In addition to the easy chairs and leather couch, the furnishings included a writing table and Lydia's nice mahogany desk. The family knew it as her's because Lydia always used it more than I.

In hardly a moment, Irving caught up with us. He said, "My first inclination is to make things appear as normal as possible around here. That's why I did not want the cleaning lady to come in and then leave immediately after arriving."

"Do you think someone is watching the house? What should we do about it, Irving? Can you make some sense of our situation?" Lydia pleaded.

"No, Lydia, I cannot make sense of the situation. We do not yet know enough to explain the motivation of the intruder at Elmer's house. To worry about the unlikely possibility that someone is watching us here is to err on the side of caution."

"Do we sit idly by in the meantime? My beloved cousin's life may be in jeopardy," Lydia fretted.

"We are definitely not sitting idly by." Agent Ronan was a bit put off by the question. "I've initiated the organization and planning process. I have asked for assistance from the police. I have just spoken again to Senior Agent Cleary in our Washington office. She will be arriving here as quickly as she can arrange transport. Another agent may be coming with her."

Elmer detected the edginess in the FBI agent's voice. He said, "Lydia, I think Irving knows what he is doing. We are going to get the help we need from the Batavia Police Department and from whomever is on their way here from Washington." His words had a calming effect on Lydia and on me.

Irving Ronan said, "That's correct, Elmer. However, I do not know what we can expect from the police in Batavia. Whom do you know and trust on the local force?"

Elmer Wrightson replied, "Chief of Police Jennifer Hepburn is quite competent and beyond reproach. In addition, there are several savvy, honest officers in the department. Hepburn has made it a priority to improve and develop a professional police force since she took over a few years ago."

"Good, I would like you to call Chief Hepburn and ask her to assign two detectives to work with us here at O'Connor's house."

Elmer said, "OK, yes, I can do that. But, did you hear me say that the Batavia Police Department is small? They have no full-time suits on the staff. All of the detective work is handled by uniformed officers, which is not to say the department suffers for it. Starting with Chief Hepburn herself, they do insightful detective work."

My diplomatic friend Elmer Wrightson noticed me squirm at his high praise for the police. "Of course, Ted, I don't mean the BPD never makes mistakes, even the gross error in your case."

When he saw the quizzical look on Ronan's face, Wrightson explained, "Oh, sorry, Irving. BPD is how we refer to the Batavia Police Department around here."

"I got that, Elmer. I was wondering about the BPD mistakes. Should we be wary that they might let us down at some key moment?"

Wrightson explained, "There is an officer on the force who can be antagonistic toward suspects. Ted has had more than one run-in with him."

I answered Ronan's worried look, "He shouldn't be a problem for us now. I'm not worried about him. If anything, his attitude could be an asset in the face of a serious threat."

"Good. Whatever talent the BPD has we can use," Agent Ronan said. "I don't know if it will be enough."

"Maybe not. It is a small force," Wrightson said. "Irving, the FBI has access to many more resources than we have in Batavia. So, you should feel free to take the lead."

Ronan replied, "Agent Cleary told me that Chief Hepburn plans to take the reins herself. As she sees it, Batavia has jurisdiction and the FBI will be cooperating with the police department."

"Are you expecting problems?" Elmer asked.

"Cleary doesn't think so. She could detect no indication that Jennifer Hepburn would feel we were stepping on her toes. In fact, she feels a sense of rapprochement with the chief. Hepburn told Cleary the BPD would be grateful for the FBI's expertise."

"Shall I call her now? I will ask Chief Hepburn for all the help she can give us." Elmer reached for the phone on Lydia's desk.

"Good. See if she can recommend additional resources," Irving said.

Elmer replied, "I have an idea about that. I will ask Chief Hepburn to alert the county sheriff to the possibility that their assistance may be required. He is another well qualified policeman in our community."

Elmer dialed the number for the police department and asked for Chief Hepburn. "Would you tell her to get in touch with Elmer Wrightson right away?" He dictated the number off our desk-top phone. "Please, it's important."

He hung up and said to Irving, "She is out of the office on a call but they will contact her."

Irving said, "While we are waiting to hear back, I have some questions about your residence and your office building, Elmer. What surveillance devices do you have in place?"

"Nothing at home other than good neighbors. We try to keep an eye on things for each other."

"And your office building?"

"A few of the other occupants of the Elise Monroe building have put up cameras but I haven't paid much attention to the issue. One of the tenants has been pestering me to invest in a building-wide system. I just have not gotten around to it. The truth is I have not seen it as a high priority."

"Until now?" Ronan asked.

Wrightson looked chagrined. He tried to rationalize the low level of protection in his building. "I couldn't see that video monitors would add significantly to what we already have. There are security guards at night. Admission through locked doors is limited day and night. We have receptionists and trusted maintenance staff in the building at all times. Installing surveillance cameras has seemed like an unnecessary expense. Batavia is hardly a high-crime city."

"Well-placed cameras are a low-cost complement to any security system. They deter crime as well as catch scofflaws," Ronan explained. "Why are the tenants coming to you to ask for monitors? Is it your decision?"

"I am the president of the real-estate company that owns the building. We have not installed a system yet but we will now. What do they say about hindsight?"

"It can be expensive." Lydia filled in the missing words for Elmer.

Ronan said, "For now, we have to work with what we've got. Perhaps, the cameras belonging to the tenants picked up something useful. I would like you to go over there and talk to the tenants. See if anyone saw something last night and find out if there is anything on their surveillance cameras. For your safety, I want a security guard to go wherever you go. Precaution is the best policy in the face of unknown threats."

Eileen pushed open the door to the den. "Alena is about to take a heap of scrambled eggs off the stove. You should come while they're hot."

Chapter 77 . Nourishment was required.

There was a mad dash from the den into the living room, around the furniture, and through the door into the kitchen.

Eileen had to jump out of our way. "I guess everybody's hungry. I made a ton of toast," she boasted.

We assembled at the kitchen table where Diane poured coffee into every upturned cup. The toast, sausage links, and bacon began to disappear at a rapid pace. The mountain of scrambled eggs became a mole hill in a matter of moments. Diane moved quickly to brew another pot of coffee. Finally, Lydia sighed and leaned back in her chair.

"Are you feeling better now?" I asked.

She nodded.

Everyone jumped when the doorbell chimed. Evidently, ample nourishment had not quieted our nerves.

Agent Ronan took the lead into the living room. Alena felt it was her duty to greet guests. Diane followed her through the door but returned immediately. She waved at me to follow her and pushed passed everyone to get to the back stairs.

Alena returned to announce, "Police are here."

Alena and Eileen remained in the kitchen while the rest of us made our way toward the front door. I figured I could check in with Diane a bit later.

The drapes were pulled to the sides and we could see the two uniformed officers through the front picture window. Wrightson identified them for Ronan as members of the Batavia Police Department.

"How did they get here so fast?" Irving Ronan asked Elmer Wrightson under his breath. "I thought you didn't get through to the police?"

Elmer answered, "I only left a message. Chief Hepburn was supposed to call right back." He looked at his watch. "It has been about twenty minutes."

Ronan acknowledged, "Longer than I thought. Twenty minutes is more than enough to get from anywhere to anywhere else in Batavia. Did you tell the dispatcher that it was urgent?"

"Maybe but I did not say where I was. My powers of telecommunication are usually not that great. The dispatcher said Chief Hepburn was out on a call. Evidently, that meant she was on her way here."

Lydia opened the door to invite the officers into the house. Jennifer Hepburn came in but the police chief motioned for the patrolman to remain outside on the porch.

Louis Thompson was in his mid to late forties but he was new to the Batavia Police Department. Chief Hepburn brought him on board only recently. He did not seem to mind being relegated to the outdoors. He went over to the table on the porch and sat down in a chair facing the street with his back to the window. Officer Thompson pushed Eileen's elegantly hand-painted no-smoking placard to one side and lit up.

The last time Hepburn and Thompson were at our house, they were there to arrest me and cart me off to jail in a police cruiser. My reaction to the reappearance of the same two police officers prompted an anxiety attack that caught me off guard.

The urge to retreat was overpowering. I stepped back into the dining room and slumped into a chair. I tried to force myself to relax but it felt like I couldn't breathe.

Lydia noticed my distress. She sat down next to me at the dining room table. "Are you all right, Ted?"

"Yeah, I guess. It's just that to see cops on our porch again gave me quite a jolt."

"I understand." She put her hand on mine. "It's OK. The trial is over. There will never be a challenge that you and I cannot overcome. You are safe here now."

Lydia's reassuring touch reminded me of how lucky I was. From time to time during my troubled years and all through the subsequent good years, something would happen to give me pause. I would stop and try to analyze our relationship. What did love at first sight really mean? In my youth, I had met and dated other beautiful, nice, attractive women. My relationship with Lydia, however, was something quite different. For Lydia and me, the initial attraction transitioned into best friends and soul mates.

When I would ask Lydia what she thought, she just chuckled and smiled. She was amused and a little perplexed at my need to explain us. Evidently, for her, we were just meant to be.

We sat a few more minutes at the table in the dining room. I took several deep breaths and regained control of my nerves. My wife took my arm and we joined the others in the living room where Attorney Wrightson was introducing FBI Agent Irving Ronan to Chief Jennifer Hepburn.

Chapter 78 . The police heard the FBI's suspicions.

Chief Hepburn said, "Agent Irene Cleary called from her office in Washington, D.C., this morning. She said you asked her to contact me, Agent Ronan."

"Yes, I did."

"She told me there were two issues you wanted me to be aware of. A suspected surrogate for a crime boss was spotted among the spectators at Mr. O'Connor's trial and a private investigator working on a criminal case for the FBI has disappeared in Batavia."

"Did she fill you in on the details?" Ronan asked.

"No, she didn't. Agent Cleary did not want to spend much time on the phone. She had a plane to catch. We agreed that I could get more information from you and she would tell me about the FBI's interests once she got here. She did say that it was Private Detective Janet Bread who had gone missing."

"I asked her to call you because I thought an official request from Senior Agent-in-Charge Irene Cleary would carry more weight than it would from an FBI field agent."

"An interesting ploy, Agent Ronan, but I don't believe it was necessary." Hepburn paused a moment before continuing. "Cleary also told me that the FBI and Ms. Bread had reason to believe the Hennigan murder and the interests of organized crime in this area might be related."

"That's correct," Ronan said.

"I confess that I am not seeing the connection."

Ronan explained, "I was Section Chief for the northern district of the FBI's Alexandria office. I am mostly retired now but there are pieces of my old case load that are still unresolved. Agent Cleary asked me to stay on in Washington to assist with an ongoing racketeering investigation. I could not decline. The case is pretty significant."

"Are you suggesting there's a link between your racketeering case and something going on in Batavia? If so, I would certainly like to know about it?" Chief Hepburn said.

"All we have are conjectures," Ronan answered. "Shall we sit down in here?" He beckoned Hepburn to follow him into the dining room. "Elmer, join us if you will."

As soon as she saw them sitting there in the dining room, Alena put a tray with coffee, cream pitcher, sugar bowl, and coffee cake on the table within their reach.

"Thank you, Alena," Ronan said.

Hepburn looked up and smiled.

All three, Jennifer, Irving, and Elmer, picked up a cup and took a piece of the pastry.

Alena asked, "Should I bring coffee to the policeman at the table on the porch?"

"That would be very nice. He is waiting out there for me," Chief Hepburn answered.

The conversation continued in the dining room out of ear shot for Lydia and me. We were served our coffee at the table in the kitchen. Eileen and Alena were chatting and keeping busy at the counter behind me.

Ronan briefed Hepburn on the racketeering case in which Brian Hill was involved. He went on to explain that, after the trial was over, Janet wanted to talk to me again about Brian Hill, who was known in Batavia as Rusty Higgins. Janet had questions for me about Hill's relationship with Matthew Hennigan.

"Were Bread and O'Connor still at the courthouse?" Hepburn asked.

"No, they had returned here to the house. His folks and a few friends came over to help the family unwind at the end of Ted's ordeal. After talking to Mr. O'Connor, Detective Bread returned to her office at Wrightson's firm to make phone calls and to search for files in the FBI archives that she could reach from there."

Ronan told Hepburn about the previous night's conversations with Janet Bread. The first was a telephone conference that included Wrightson and Bread in Batavia while Cleary and Ronan himself were on the other end in Washington. Detective Bread initiated the call to discuss her plan to uncover local activities that involved the cartel's henchman Hill.

Wrightson explained to Hepburn that he was in on the call just to say he could recommend a local detective agency for some follow-up work on the surveillance team's observations. There were four interactions with locals that Janet thought looked interesting. She needed identification of the participants.

Irving said, "I believe we have covered everything that Elmer and I know. Bread and Cleary talked again late last night. Cleary is on her way to Batavia now. She can tell us about their conversations when she gets here."

"Good. I would like to talk to her."

Elmer said, "Did you get the message that I tried to reach you this morning?"

"No."

Ronan said, "Elmer was calling you to request protection for the O'Connor family."

"Protection from what, Agent Ronan? What is threatening their safety here in Batavia?"

Ronan told Hepburn about the stranger in the garage under the Monroe office building. Also, she had not been made aware of the photographs and the break-in at Wrightson's home.

They were still talking in the dining room when Diane came down the back stairs.

"Did you need to tell me something?" I asked.

"Yes, I do."

Before Diane could say more, Chief Hepburn interrupted, "Mr. O'Connor, where are the photographs that the intruder left in Wrightson's house?"

The folder was in the den on the desk. Lydia led the way. The rest of us followed. Diane remained in the kitchen with Alena. So did Eileen.

I did wonder what Diane wanted to say to me but I put it off again. "I'll come find you," I said.

I hurried after everyone else into the den. Agent Ronan handed a pair of gloves to Chief Hepburn. She took the three photographs from the manila folder and examined them one at a time.

Chapter 79 . The intruder's identity was the enigma.

"There is little doubt these pictures were meant to be threatening, Mr. Wrightson," Chief Hepburn said. "I can see why you hurried over here to warn Mr. O'Connor and his family. Perhaps, you should have called the police as well."

"I did call the police. I reported the break-in even before I noticed the envelop left on my kitchen table. The dispatcher said the BPD would send a car out to my house first thing this morning but I did not hang around. In the panic of the moment, my greatest concern was for the safety of the people in the photographs."

"The dispatcher's name?"

"It was Elizabeth. I think."

Hepburn agreed. "That's right. Elizabeth Stewart was on the over-night desk. Was anything else disturbed at your residence?"

Elmer said, "As I told Ms. Stewart, there was nothing missing as far as I could tell."

"Did you call us back after you saw the pictures?"

"No, I guess I was so relieved to see everyone was all right when I got here that I did not call the station again. Also, of all things, I found an FBI agent watching over the family."

"Yes, that is interesting. Agent Ronan, what prompted you to come here so quickly?" Chief Hepburn asked. "Bread had been missing for only a short time and you had not seen these photos."

"Good point. Hearing that a consultant had fallen off the grid for just a few hours is generally not a serious concern for the FBI. It would customarily take more than that for an agent to drop everything in Washington,

D.C., and rush here to Batavia. However, I was concerned for Detective Bread's safety."

"I'm not sure why," Chief Hepburn said. "I have met Janet Bread. I am aware that she is Lydia Kingston's cousin and she was in town to support the family during Ted O'Connor's trial. Ms. Bread came by the office as a courtesy to introduce herself when she got here. She wanted me to know that a licensed-to-carry professional was visiting our community. I appreciated the heads-up."

"Was it necessary?"

"Notification is required by a local ordinance but not everyone complies. Detective Bread left me with the impression that she was not in Batavia on any sort of official business that could be of interest to the police."

"You heard her correctly. Lydia's cousin came to Batavia strictly for personal reasons. It remained that way until she stumbled onto something of interest to the FBI. After several conference calls, we concluded that her observation in the courtroom might point to a connection between the O'Connor case and a racketeering investigation."

"All right, thank you for clearing up a few matters for me," Chief Hepburn said. "Detective Bread actually did return to my office to say things had changed and there was a problem she needed to investigate. She said it might not amount to much but she wanted to check it out. Bread asked me where she could find reliable personnel for stakeout duty. I referred her to the county sheriff."

"Did she give reasons for the stakeout?" Ronan asked.

"At that time, I trusted her to provide me with details if and when I had the need to know."

It did not seem to bother anyone else but I wondered why Chief Hepburn qualified her answer. Did Bread enjoy her trust then but not now?

Agent Ronan said, "Detective Bread called in a coded alarm from Batavia late last night. We were not able to reach her for an explanation. Her circumstances were sufficiently alarming to justify a quick trip to see if she needed assistance. She was observing the activities of the paroled convict Brian Hill."

"You did say that Mr. Hill is potentially very dangerous. Do you think Detective Bread got careless and Hill figured out she was on to him?"

"No. That did not occur to me. Bread is far too careful to reveal her interests to a suspect. It could be that Brian Hill went after her because he was overly wary of his circumstances. It is also likely that something or someone tipped him off that she had noticed him."

"Why would that be likely?"

"Hill took advantage of a network of inside connections before he was arrested. We believe some of the contacts survived his incarceration. Hill had been serving a lengthy sentence for criminal behavior that was less serious than several crimes for which he has not yet been convicted if you know what I mean."

Hepburn answered, "I do. You are implying the FBI had not found sufficient evidence to convict Brian Hill of the truly serious felonies but you could put him away for lesser crimes."

"Right. It was the Eliot Ness syndrome. They couldn't get Al Capone for extortion and murder so they put him in prison for income tax evasion."

Lydia was finding the conversational tone to be lacking sufficient urgency. She broke in to complain, "Jennifer, my cousin might be invincible in the family lore but we are actually very worried about Janet right now."

Agent Ronan waited for Lydia to express her concern before backing up her point. "Hill does have a history of violent behavior. Last night, just a week after she spotted him in the courtroom, Detective Bread suddenly disappeared. She is still AWOL this morning. It is not too much of a leap to suspect that Hill might have reacted by kidnapping Janet Bread."

The suggestion gave me the chills. I sat looking at Irving Ronan with a sense of disbelief. Was it not he who had warned us about Brian Hill earlier in the day? Janet Bread could be in the grasps of a man 'as tough to handle as any criminal you can imagine.' What chance did she have with such a psychopath? I thought to myself how could Ronan speak of the matter in such a calm voice?

Chief Hepburn said, "If your speculations are accurate, there could be an urgent need for a rescue operation."

"Agreed. However, the situation calls for due deliberation. There are no solid leads to Bread's whereabouts. We only have Brian Hill's interest in the trial." Ronan said. "The premise we are working under is Hill came here to meet Hennigan and something went awry."

Hepburn suggested, "Could Hennigan have had knowledge or assets of interest to Hill and Hill's associates?"

"Exactly what we are thinking. Hill came up empty when he tried to get what he needed from Hennigan."

"Then, why would he kill him?"

"Bread told us her theory. She thinks Hill concluded that Hennigan handed off the assets to Ted O'Connor on the night of the shooting?"

"As the detective who is new to the game, I do not have answers, at least not yet," Hepburn said.

Agent Ronan said, "We are hoping that, by working together with the BPD, we can solve the mystery surrounding Brian Hill's business in Batavia and the disappearance of Janet bread."

"Where do you want to start? I am open to suggestions," Chief Hepburn said.

"The identity of the intruder at Mr. Wrightson's residence, might help answer all of our questions."

Hepburn nodded in agreement. "It would certainly be a good start."

Chief Hepburn stood up. "Let me check on the police officer who accompanied me here. I will call the station from the car to see who is available and make some assignments. I will ask the dispatcher to call in the off-duty officers."

Jennifer Hepburn went out the front door and spoke briefly to the man on the porch. She proceeded to the cruiser to radio for the requested assistance. Officer Thompson stood up when she came out and remained there watching her from the porch.

Lydia pushed open the screen door. "You can come in if you wish."

He said. "No, thank you. I will wait here."

His stone-faced response gave me the chills. Maybe, I was too sensitive. He did not seem to bother Lydia.

"OK. Suit yourself," she said and closed the front door.

"Do you know what Diane wants?" Lydia asked me. "She whispered something to me in the kitchen about talking to you or Irving."

"I know. She waved at me earlier. I will go see what's bothering her in a minute."

Chief Hepburn came back into the house. She announced, "Help is on the way. In the meantime, let's try to get organized. We need a plan for locating Janet Bread and getting an explanation for her mysterious disappearance. Do we agree that she might have some of the answers to the investigation of criminal activities in my town?"

"Yes, I believe that's right," Ronan said.

"Review the circumstances for me, please. Where was she last seen? Who spoke to her last?" Chief Hepburn asked.

Chapter 80 . A cloud of suspicion adheres to unsolved murder.

"No one has heard from Detective Bread since she sounded the alarm at 11:43 last night," Agent Ronan repeated.

Attorney Wrightson said, "I saw her when I waved goodnight on the way out of my firm's building late yesterday evening. It was after ten o'clock. She was sitting at the desk in the office for visiting attorneys. The space was assigned to Detective Bread when she was assisting with the preparations for the O'Connor trial."

"Why did you give her an office? Was Janet Bread's purpose for being in Batavia actually more than a family visit?" Chief Hepburn asked.

"Not at first and it had nothing to do with Brian Hill in Batavia," Attorney Wrightson answered.

"What then?" Hepburn demanded.

"I've known Janet Bread for many years. I met her before she graduated from college. I've been aware of her reputation as an investigator since the beginning of her career. When she showed up two weeks ago to visit her cousin Lydia, I asked for her help with O'Connor's trial. Naturally, the arrangement had to be approved by Judge Fitzgerald. Of course, the DA's office was informed as well."

"OK. Whatever Bread's original motivation for coming to Batavia, it does not change our current priorities." Chief Hepburn let the matter go but I wasn't sure that she was fully convinced by Elmer Wrightson's explanation.

Wrightson continued, "Janet attended the hearings prior to the trial. She worked with our client almost every afternoon. Her contributions helped us achieve the acquittal on the murder charge."

"I'm convinced justice was served," Hepburn said.

Chief Hepburn's comment answered a question that was worrying me. Did the police still think I shot Hennigan? That I had gotten away with murder? It was a relief to hear Chief Hepburn acknowledge and even affirm the not-guilty verdict. Could her comment mean my family would soon come out from under the cloud of suspicion hanging over us?

Ronan said, "Although Brian Hill might well be in violation of his probationary terms, the DEA agent in charge said not to pick him up. He agreed with Bread and with the FBI that there could be something going on here. He asked us to keep an eye on Mr. Hill."

Elmer Wrightson said, "Ted was found not-guilty. The verdict was, of course, a great relief. Detective Bread was very pleased with the outcome. However, the unsolved murder was unsettling for her."

Lydia spoke up. "It is unsettling for all of us. It is something that has to be resolved not just for our sake but for the sake of the entire community."

Chief Hepburn asked, "How convinced are you that the disappearance of Janet Bread is related to her obsession with the connection between Hill's interest in the court case and finding Hennigan's killer?"

Agent Ronan answered, "It is highly likely. Whoever authorized or committed the murder grabbed the tenacious Bread because she was getting too close."

"Reasonable."

Ronan continued, "There are two potential sources of leads. Who was the intruder at Wrightson's residence? Did Bread leave clues at Wrightson's law firm where she was last seen working late into the night on Friday?"

Chapter 81 . A skilled, experienced police detective was required.

Police Chief Jennifer Hepburn said, "Mr. Wrightson, I will send a team of BPD officers to your condo. They will stop here for the keys on their way." She held out her hand. "Where should they look?"

"They might not need these." Wrightson handed Hepburn a set of keys. "I tried to close up but the latch is broken on the back door. It had been forced open. The folder was left just inside on the kitchen table. There are seven buildings in the condominium complex. Each of the structures consists of three or four two-story town houses. Every unit has two or three deeded garage spaces underneath. Building Six is on the left of the main driveway and mine is the end unit."

"Yes, I know the place quite well, Mr. Wrightson. I have attended neighborhood-watch and public-service meetings in your clubhouse on a number of occasions."

"Of course. I've seen you there. The intruder may have gone no further than the kitchen. Perhaps, into the dining room or adjacent parlor but I did not hear anything and, as far as I can tell, nothing was disturbed. So, I don't think he roamed about much." After a pause, he added, "or she."

"We will look for fingerprints in obvious places. We will also talk to your neighbors. Let's hope they can tell us something."

"The couple in the adjacent condo are early risers, to which I can attest all too well. They are not always very quiet. They might have seen or heard something this morning."

"We will be sure to talk to them."

"Good. I know they will try to help if they can."

Irving Ronan said, "Elmer, the incident at your condo is important but the Monroe building has a higher priority. We need to find any evidence that Detective Bread or her abductor might have left behind. The tenants' surveillance tapes could be helpful."

"Half the businesses keep weekend hours. So, many will be on site today. I will go over there and talk to them right now."

Hepburn said, "Good but you must not go alone. It is possible that the person who invaded the privacy of your home might decide to sneak into your firm's offices."

Ronan asked, "Does the Batavia Police Department have a skilled, experienced detective who can conduct a thorough investigation in Mr. Wrightson's office building with his assistance?"

Chief Jennifer Hepburn answered, "Without question. The police department is small in number but our investigators are very well-trained."

Agent Ronan said, "In addition to providing for your protection, Elmer, a good detective can spot clues that might be overlooked by the untrained eye. We need to know if there is any evidence of foul play. We are looking for anything that can give us information about what happened to Janet Bread."

Chief Hepburn said, "I believe you are all acquainted with the policeman waiting for us on the front porch."

"Quite so," I muttered.

She ignored me and continued, "Officer Louis Thompson remained out front to watch for anyone indicating an inordinate interest in our presence here. I have been watching for his signal and nothing has caught his attention. I spoke to him when I went out to the car to call the station. He confirmed that all was quiet."

"I would expect whomever we are dealing with to be too clever to get caught snooping around here," Ronan said.

"You could be right," Hepburn agreed. "I will ask Officer Thompson to accompany you to your office, Elmer. I am confident of his abilities. He came to the BPD with a reputation for excellent investigative skills. He was highly recommended by his commanding officer in the Chicago Police Department. He is very solid with the fundamentals. He ranked near or at the top of Chicago's handgun-accuracy qualification exams every year since he joined the force as a cadet."

It was Lydia who thought to ask, "Is the fact that he can shoot straight important in Batavia?"

Chief Hepburn just shrugged in response.

"Sorry, but isn't the BPD a bit of a letdown for a man with such credentials?" Ronan asked.

Was Hepburn's response to Irving's putdown a little defensive? I could not be sure. She said, "We might not have everything Chicago has to offer but Batavia is not a bad place to live. Thompson needed to get away from his home on the South Side for personal reasons, which I accepted as true and reasonable."

"None of our business, of course. His competence is what's important," Wrightson said. I can grab my brief case and go right now."

"There is something else before you go. No one has asked why Officer Thompson and I came here this morning."

"I had not forgotten about that particular detail," Agent Ronan said. "What brought you here?"

"A witness who testified against you at your trial, Mr. O'Connor, was found dead this morning. Elliot Shaw was killed with the same caliber bullet that as Mr. Hennigan."

Lydia sank onto the couch across from her desk. "What a nightmare," she moaned.

"He was shot just before closing time late yesterday in a convenience store at a service station in Santa Rosa, New Mexico."

"How did he get there? Where was he going?" Wrightson asked.

"He may have been running away from something or somebody," Hepburn conjectured. "He took a midday flight on Friday into Will Rogers World Airport, Oklahoma City, under a false name and rented a car. It had to have been a marathon drive."

Ronan asked, "How did you make the connection?"

"Shaw was carrying two passports."

"I take it one of them tied him to us," Wrightson said.

"That's right. The state police investigated after noticing a car had been left for hours in front of the darkened filling station. We have no definitive explanation for his actions which brings me to the reason Officer Thompson and I came here this morning," Chief Hepburn said. "We were looking for Janet Bread. We need to talk to her about the execution of Elliot Shaw."

"Why Janet Bread?"

"She was seen with him at Allen's Diner immediately after his testimony in court on Thursday. She took him there for a late lunch and they talked for 45 minutes or so. Do you know why, Mr. Wrightson?"

"She did not tell me about her plans with Mr. Shaw. I can only conjecture that she was probing for information. It seemed to us at trial that he was hiding something," Wrightson said.

Hepburn continued, "They were seen together again on Friday. He seemed to be waiting to talk to her. The last reported sighting of Mr. Shaw in Batavia was with Ms. Bread outside the courthouse prior to the morning's session. She spoke to him for five or ten minutes before going in to observe the proceedings. Mr. Shaw did not attend the session. He was killed late last night and Ms. Bread disappeared about the same time. The obvious question for me to ask myself is why? Is she on the lam?"

"Do you seriously suspect that Janet Bread might have followed Mr. Shaw across the country and shot him in a gas station in New Mexico?" Agent Ronan asked.

"Of course not, Irving. She was here at the time. We are only investigating the possibilities. For the moment, Ms. Bread is just a person of interest. At my direction, Officer Thompson constructed a scenario for the execution of Mr. Shaw. His narrative included a credible argument that implicates Ms. Bread."

"Does his scenario involve Hennigan's murder?" Wrightson asked.

"Yes, it does. Bread could be complicit in both executions. From the testimony that you dragged out of Shaw, Mr. Wrightson, it became clear that an element of organized crime had seeped into our community. Mr. Hennigan may have been caught up in a dispute over a drug deal gone bad. According to Thompson's scenario, Janet Bread was sent here on a clean-up detail. She convinced Mr. Shaw to run and let her controller know where he was going."

"As you might have guessed, I find the so-called scenario to be preposterous," Irving Ronan said.

"Agent Ronan, are you certain that Bread is not here and she is not expected here?" Chief Hepburn asked.

"Yes, absolutely." His response was unequivocal.

"OK, good." Hepburn accepted his answer.

"I think I get it now," Agent Ronan said. "Officer Thompson was not consigned to the porch to watch for just any suspicious onlookers. He was put there to catch Janet Bread coming or perhaps sneaking away from this house. How good is my conjecture, Chief Hepburn?"

"Partially correct but not entirely," Hepburn admitted. "I did want him to be on the lookout for Ms. Bread. I also wanted to be unencumbered by his presence while I discussed the matter with you, Agent Ronan."

"Do you mean that you wanted to keep us unaware of your suspicions until now and Thompson might have given them away?"

"That's right. I did not want you to become defensive with what you might say about Ms. Bread."

"What have you concluded?"

"Based on everything you have had to say about Detective Bread, I believe Thompson's scenario is likely to be just a reasonable concoction from details that fit the circumstances. However, all possibilities must remain on the table until the mystery is solved."

With that, Chief Hepburn dispatched Officer Thompson with Attorney Wrightson to the Monroe office building in their cruiser leaving herself without a ride at our house on Elm Avenue.

Part VII

Research and Betrayal

Without the heart-stopping moment between the noise and the splendor, the beauty of the fireworks would mean nothing at all.

– Marilyn McGrath,
All You Know on Earth

Chapter 82 . Mug shots would not be necessary.

Moments after Wrightson's departure, as if on cue, Officer Angela Dunning took Thompson's place on our front porch. I could see a police car in the driveway but not if anyone else had arrived in it with her.

Chief Hepburn noticed that I was peering out the front window. "Mr. O'Connor," she said, "we need our best officers to investigate the burglary at Wrightson's house. I have assigned the task to Officer White. He is good but still green. I am asking a senior officer to go with him and to take charge."

"What are you telling me, Ma'am?"

"I know this may be a problem for you. However, as gruff and bull-headed as he may be, Sgt. Ryan is very good at ferreting out the kind of information we are looking for. We need his help today. I wanted you to know that he will be on the job and you may be forced to interact with him."

"Thank you, Chief Hepburn. I appreciate the courtesy. No explanation would have been necessary even if I were inclined to take umbrage with your decision. Given my history, I am in no position to complain."

"Your history should no longer be an issue. I will not be an apologist for ill-mannered members of the force. Overzealous police work will not be tolerated. Sgt. Ryan knows it and it won't happen again."

That my past history should be forgotten was the second time in a matter of minutes that Chief Hepburn had said the right words of encouragement for me. My family and I would not live forever under a cloud of suspicion.

Irving Ronan pulled Jennifer Hepburn back to the matter at hand. He was holding the folder with the photographs and told her, "I will send these to the FBI lab to be dusted for fingerprints."

Chief Hepburn objected. She insisted that the BPD was more than competent to take care of the matter locally and more quickly.

Agent Ronan acquiesced without hesitation, "Good. If you have the facilities, please do dust for prints. The sooner the better."

Chief Hepburn took the folder from Ronan and hastened down the porch steps. She climbed into the back seat behind Sgt. Ryan on the passenger side. Officer White was at the wheel. They would be dropping the chief off at the station on their way to Wrightson's residence.

As soon as they were gone, Diane raced down the front stairs into the living room. "Where is Mr. Wrightson?" she demanded.

"He went back to his office to see if Janet left any clues that can help the police find her," I explained.

"Uncle Irving, you and Mr. Wrightson questioned me about the man I saw in the garage when I was waiting for Dad." Diane gasped for a breath. "You said you were going to get a photo album for me to look at. Well, I won't be needing it. It was the police officer on the front porch who came over here this morning with Chief Hepburn. He was not in uniform but I am certain he was the one waiting for the elevator in the garage under Mr. Wrightson's office building."

Lydia gasped. The color drained from her face. "That was Officer Louis Thompson, the policeman you could not remember when we talked about him before."

"I know that now," Diane said. Her gaze shifted from her mother to me and back. "What's the matter? When Alena and I went to answer the doorbell, I saw him through the window. So, I ran back into the kitchen and up the stairs to hide. I was afraid he would notice that I recognized him. What did I do wrong?"

"It's not you," I said. "The worry is Mr. Wrightson. He and Thompson left here together in a police car ten or fifteen minutes ago. Chief Hepburn sent them to search his office."

Diane rationalized, "I couldn't tell you before now. I didn't know if I should say anything in front of Chief Hepburn and that policeman was always right outside the window."

"You did good, Diane. Your instincts to be careful were exactly right," Agent Ronan said.

"What about Mr. Wrightson?" She pleaded.

"We need to warn him of the potential danger if he doesn't already know. Ted, would you use the desk phone to call his office. You can say we are wondering if he and Thompson have discovered anything about Janet. Try not to say anything that could alert Thompson to our suspicions. Listen for signs of distress."

I sat down in the desk chair and reached for the phone.

Ronan asked, "Lydia, is your work phone handy? Ted is using the desk phone and I need mine to call the office in Washington."

"Yes, Cardinal Energy just gave me a new cell phone for work issues. It is a significant upgrade over the old one."

"Do you have Chief Hepburn's cell phone number?" Ronan asked.

"No," Lydia said. "It's not like you can look up a policeman's number in the phone book."

Lydia reached into the top drawer on the left side of the desk. I rolled the chair out of her way.

"Here it is," she announced.

"Call the police station and have them radio Chief Hepburn. She needs to know our suspicions about Thompson. Tell her we are mounting a rescue operation for Wrightson. She should come back here if she will."

"I'm on it." Lydia stepped back and dialed 911.

I called Wrightson's office. The administrative assistant answered on the first ring.

"Hello, Katherine. What are you doing there on a Saturday?" I was surprised to hear her voice.

"I'm often here on weekends to help the partners in our firm with their backlog." Katherine Chavis sounded a little huffy that I should question her dedication.

"Is Mr. Wrightson there?" I asked.

"He has not come into the office yet today, Mr. O'Connor. May I take a message?" She recognized my voice.

"Please tell him to call me as soon as he gets there."

"I'll give him the message, Mr. O'Connor." It sounded like she might just stick a note on a nail for him to find.

"Katherine, I do need to talk to him. If you get Mr. Wrightson on the phone, ask him to contact me right away."

"I understand. I'll see to it that Mr. Wrightson gets your message." Her assurances made me feel a little more confident.

I told Irving and Lydia that Ms. Chavis said Wrightson had not shown up yet. Both acknowledged that they understood. There was nothing more to do but wait.

Chapter 83 . More FBI agents arrived.

Agent Ronan hung his suit-coat jacket on the tall mahogany clothes tree next to the door. Without a coat to cover it, the holster with his sidearm was visible on his right hip.

"Hallo, Mr. O'Connor." Alena was at the door to the den. "There is someone here to see you. They came to the kitchen door."

I looked across the desk at Ronan. He motioned for me to stay where I was. He loosened the strap on his holster and moved over next to Alena. She stood stock still.

He flipped the cover off his cell phone. "I will check to see how far out Agent Cleary is."

"That won't be necessary," Irene Cleary and another individual were already there right behind Alena.

Irving put his phone away and reattached the strap over the gun in his holster. He exclaimed, "I'm glad to see the two of you. We are facing a potentially threatening complication."

He turned to us and said, "Lydia Kingston and Ted O'Connor meet Irene Cleary and Rohit Kumar."

Ms. C'de Baca scurried away back toward the kitchen. "Thank you, Alena," I called after her.

Agent Cleary said, "We knocked on the back door. Alena wouldn't let us in until we introduced ourselves and showed her our ID's. When she saw we were FBI agents, she yelped, 'More people for lunch!'"

"Uh-oh, Was she mad?" I asked.

"Didn't seem to be. She was smiling."

"Good. We certainly don't want Alena to quit on us right now. She is preparing lunch for all of us," Lydia said.

"That would be good. Rohit and I have not had much to eat yet today. We were in a hurry to get here," Irene Cleary explained.

"OK, we can eat as soon as it's ready."

"Where are your girls?" Agent Ronan asked me.

Agent Kumar answered, "Eileen and Diane showed up while Ms. C'de Baca was interrogating us. She told them to stay there and help her in the kitchen."

Agent Ronan got back down to business. "Ted, keep trying to get through to Wrightson. If Ms. Chavis gets irritated by the hassle, we can live with it."

He asked, "How are you doing, Lydia?"

"I've got the dispatcher on the phone now."

"Good. Leave a message for Hepburn about Diane's encounter with Thompson. Let me brief Cleary and Kumar on our situation."

"Elizabeth, we need to find Chief Hepburn." Lydia was speaking into the receiver.

"What's the threatening complication?" Cleary asked.

Chapter 84 . To unravel a mystery requires new revelations.

FBI Agents Ronan, Cleary, and Kumar gathered around the small conference table by the bookshelves in the den.

Lydia stepped into the living room to finish her conversation with Elizabeth Stewart at the police station. She came back into the den and sat down with the three of them at the table. I remained across the room in the chair at the desk.

Irving Ronan said. "As you know, Janet Bread did not come home here last night."

"Of course, that's why we are here." Irene Cleary sounded a little cranky to me.

Ronan ignored her. He continued, "No one has seen Janet since late last evening when she was working in her office at Wrightson and Associates. Attorney Wrightson told me that, after the conference call with Janet and the three of us in DC, he was ready to be done for the day. He thought Janet would call it quits as well. However, she was back on the phone presumably with one of us when he left her there on his way out of the building."

Cleary interjected, "She could have been talking to me, Irving. I had several conversations with Janet last night. She told me that, earlier in the evening, Attorney Wrightson had sent out for Chinese and got a dish for her. She said he left shortly after that."

"Yes, I was still there with you for that call." Irving chuckled, "Janet didn't particularly care for the cashew-chicken over fried rice but she ate it. She said she was desperate."

Cleary took a breath and sighed. "Well, OK, you're right. You were still there but I talked to Ms. Bread at least once more after that. Get on with your story, Irving." She sounded impatient.

When Lydia asked Irving about Irene Cleary later that day, he shrugged it off, "Oh, that's just how she is. Irene hates to waste time. It is especially difficult for her if she herself is the source of the distraction." Evidently, it was rare for Irene Cleary to stray off track with any non-essential details like Chinese food for dinner.

Cleary's tendency to be brusque left Irving unphased. Rohit Kumar's reaction was different. It was obvious that his crusty boss made him uncomfortable. Rohit had not been around her long enough to become as inured to her curt responses as Irving was.

Irving Ronan continued the briefing for Cleary and Kumar about the day's developments. He explained that he was already here at our house when Attorney Elmer Wrightson arrived and that the police showed up shortly thereafter.

He said that Wrightson was in a panic. He considered the photographs left in his condominium by the intruder to be very alarming.

Kumar said, "Tell me about the photographs."

Ronan repeated, "Janet Bread was a captive in one of the images and the other two were surveillance photos of Diane and of Diane and Ted O'Connor."

"May I see the photographs?" Cleary asked.

"Chief Hepburn took them to their lab to dust for fingerprints."

Agent Cleary did not look happy about losing control of the chain of evidence. She said, "I do want to see them. There might be something in the photograph of Bread that could give us a hint to her whereabouts. Was she sending a signal of any kind?"

Ronan said, "I couldn't see anything but you should certainly examine the image yourself."

"I believe I will even though you are probably right. You do know what to look for."

Diane came into the den and sat in the side chair next to me at the desk. She whispered that Alena no longer needed her in the kitchen.

Ronan returned to his description of the day's developments for Cleary's and Kumar's benefit. "When they arrived this morning, I assumed the police came here to talk to Elmer Wrightson. I figured they wanted to question him about the break-in at his residence but they didn't even know about it. They were here for a different reason.

"Chief Jennifer Hepburn and the patrolman with her were investigating the murder of one of the witnesses in the O'Connor trial. Elliot Shaw was executed last night. The BPD officers were not looking for Wrightson. They wanted to talk to Janet Bread."

"Why would that be?" Kumar asked.

Ronan explained, "Janet Bread is a person of interest because she met with Mr. Shaw here in Batavia on more than one occasion in the days before, during, and immediately after the trial. Janet was the last one seen with him before he disappeared over night."

"That sounds fair enough." Agent Cleary agreed that the police were proceeding in a logical fashion.

Ronan said, "Perhaps, but it's a misdirection of their attention. They should not be spending resources on investigating Janet Bread."

"Of course not." Cleary agreed.

"If Janet Bread had been here, the BPD might have taken her into custody. Chief Hepburn told us they thought she could be complicit in Shaw's murder. Naturally, we did our best to dissuade her of the notion. She did seem to be listening but we can't be sure."

"I see," was all Irene Cleary could say.

Ronan continued, "Diane O'Connor picked up her father at the Monroe office building a week ago on Wednesday. It was the day of the preliminary hearing. It was also when the photographs were taken of the two of them.

"There were several individuals coming and going into and out of the garage where Diane was waiting. She took notice of one person in particular, a professional-looking male in a suit and tie who seemed to be lurking by the elevators longer than usual."

Uncle Irving turned toward the desk where we were sitting and said, "Diane, please tell Agents Cleary and Kumar what you saw."

"It was the BPD policeman who was here this morning with Chief Hepburn. He was in civilian clothes when I saw him in the garage but I know it was the same man," Diane said.

Agent Ronan clarified, "That would be Officer Louis Thompson. He left here about an hour ago with Elmer Wrightson in a police car."

"Have you tried to get through to Attorney Wrightson again?" Ronan asked me.

"No, I'll do that now." I picked up the receiver from Lydia's desk and dialed the office. Unlike the first time I called, it took several rings before Katherine Chavis answered the phone.

"No, Mr. Wrightson has not come in yet today. He does not arrive before noon on Saturday."

"Oh, OK, thanks," I said but I knew better. Why would Ms. Chavis volunteer a false comment? Elmer was well known for getting an early start especially on a Saturday.

"Unph," I heard Katherine wince.

"Are you OK?" I asked.

"Yes, yes. I'm fine. It was nothing." Her voice squeaked.

"Please ask Mr. Wrightson to call me when you see him. I do need to talk to him but I don't want to bother him at home."

"OK," Katherine answered. The connection went dead.

Something was wrong. I reached over to put the phone back in its cradle.

"Hey, listen. We may have a problem," I tried to break into the conversation.

Ronan held up his hand to stop me from interrupting. He was still talking to Cleary and Kumar.

Chapter 85 . Irregular performance belied devotion to duty.

Agent Ronan was explaining the chronology of the morning's events. Officer Thompson drove off with Wrightson in his car just before Chief Hepburn left to return to the police station. It was not until after she was gone that we became suspicious of Thompson after she was gone.

"Agent Ronan," I insisted on being heard. "I think Thompson is holding Wrightson and Katherine Chavis in Wrightson's office."

"Did you talk to him?" Ronan asked.

"No, Chavis answered the phone again just now but her business-like manner was gone. She was hesitant with her responses. You said to listen for signs of distress. I believe I heard her wince in pain as if struck while she was talking to me."

Ronan explained to Cleary and Kumar, "Katherine Chavis is the administrative assistant in Attorney Wrightson's office. I fear the worst is happening. Thompson is holding Wrightson and Chavis in the firm's offices."

The desk phone startled me. It rang with my hand still resting on the receiver. I snatched it up.

"This is Chief Hepburn. Is Agent Ronan there?" She asked before I could say hello.

"Yes, he is; plus, two more FBI agents came to the house right after you left."

"Are they right there? Put me on speaker."

I flipped the switch on the telephone base and replaced the receiver.

"Chief Jennifer Hepburn is on the phone," I announced.

"What am I hearing about your suspicions regarding Officer Thompson?" the police chief demanded.

"We have reason to believe he is the one who took the surveillance shots of Theodore O'Connor and his daughter. Diane O'Connor identified him as the suspicious individual she saw in the garage at the Monroe office building," Agent Ronan said.

"I am on my way back to join you right now. I would like to hear what you've got. I hate to think Thompson might be tainted. However, it could explain recent anomalies in his behavior."

"Like what?" Ronan asked.

"I am pulling up to the curb. Open the front door."

Ronan left the den and returned with the chief of the Batavia Police Department. "Jennifer Hepburn, I would like you to meet FBI Agents Irene Cleary and Rohit Kumar." Irving Ronan did the introductions.

"After talking to you on the phone, I feel like I already know you, Agent Cleary. Nice to meet you Agent Kumar," Chief Hepburn said.

Cleary said, "Yes, Chief Hepburn, I'm the one who called you from DC this morning to ask for your assistance. What were you about to tell us about Officer Thompson?"

"Please call me Jennifer. The unquestioning confidence that all of you have in Janet Bread's integrity got me wondering," she said. "So, I reviewed Thompson's report implicating Detective Bread. Upon reflection, it seemed to me to be a bit of a stretch."

Irving Ronan said, "I am absolutely certain about Janet Bread's character."

Hepburn continued, "I have had occasion to wonder about Officer Thompson's performance on the job. There have been unaccounted for periods of half an hour or more when no one knew where he was. Each time, he had lame excuses like traffic or not feeling well. I chalked it up to a bit of laziness that we could live with but perhaps something else was going on."

Cleary asked, "Jennifer, could Thompson be a mole in the police department? An unexplained absence from duty occurs when a warped agent reports to his handler in the organization? Thompson's behavior is typical of a cop who has been compromised."

"I don't like it, Irene, but I'm listening."

"The three of us, Kumar, Irving, and myself, were in a conference call with Janet earlier in the week. We were in DC and she was in her office in Wrightson's building. We were talking about Brian Hill known in Batavia as Rusty Higgins."

"I have been briefed on the investigation regarding Mr. Hill," Hepburn said.

"Janet told us she had arranged for a deputy sheriff to track Hill's movements."

Chief Hepburn said, "The sheriff told me Detective Bread had enlisted the help of a deputy whom I happen to know. He is very competent. I believe she got a good man."

Cleary replied, "Bread got the names of several deputies from the sheriff. They have been watching Brian Hill for about ten days. They observed interactions with several individuals. Janet took names. She was looking into some of their backgrounds."

"Last I heard nothing had materialized," Irving said.

Cleary continued, "Detective Janet Bread called me back a little after ten last night. She said that Wrightson had just left the building."

"The timing agrees with what Wrightson told us this morning," Irving said.

"Understood. Both of you had gone home too." Cleary gestured toward Ronan and Kumar. "Janet told me that, on one of the days of the trial, the deputy on surveillance duty observed a meeting between Hill and an officer in the Batavia Police Department."

Diane asked, "Who was it?" The young woman was conflicted about the BPD. Her friendship with Officer White made her feel protective. But, who could forget the nasty encounter she had shared with me on our front porch?

Cleary acknowledged the question with a nod of her head but continued talking without answering. "Last Wednesday afternoon, two days before the verdict, Hill drove from the courthouse to the Monroe office building. He left his car on the street and went inside through the main entrance. Moments later, the same police officer came out and got into a sedan in the small lot in front of the building. He was in uniform but the car was not a BPD vehicle."

"Hill went in. A policeman came out. That doesn't mean they were together," Ronan interrupted.

"Let me finish," Cleary said. "The deputy reported that the policeman drove into the entrance for the two public levels of underground parking. Thirty minutes later, the two men exited the building."

"Could the timing of their visits have been coincidental?" Diane asked.

"It is certainly possible," I said, "There is a variety of businesses in that building. People will even go there just to eat in the ground-floor bistro."

Cleary replied, "The deputy told Janet that they left through the front entrance and drove off together in Hill's car."

"OK, not a coincidence," I said.

"It seldom is," Ronan agreed.

"Who was the cop?" I asked.

"Janet identified him from the deputy's photos as Officer Louis Thompson," Cleary said.

"This is the first I've heard any of this," Ronan said.

"Right. You and Kumar had gone home by that point."

"Is Thompson's car still there in the Monroe parking garage?" Lydia was completely tuned in to the conversation.

Cleary answered, "As far as we know it is. Detective Bread suggested they might have been planting the vehicle there as an escape valve from a planned enterprise in the building. In any case, the deputy's observation was enough for Janet to decide to focus her attention on Officer Thompson."

"This could be bad. Thomson is now in that building possibly with one or more hostages. Do we know what he and Hill could be up to?" Lydia worried.

Irving answered, "We were already confident that, right after he was paroled, Hill had reconnected with the crime syndicate he used to work for. Thompson must be involved in a conspiracy of some kind with Brian Hill."

"There is more you need to hear, Jennifer." Cleary continued, "In our conversation last night, Detective Bread told me about questionable aspects of your officer's background. In particular, there are FBI files on Chicago Police Lieutenant Louis Thompson that were not accessible to Janet."

"Can we get them?" Agent Kumar asked.

"I told Janet that I would try. We ended the conversation with plans to talk again this morning."

"Only something happened to prevent that." Lydia's voice was not much more than a whimper.

Cleary said, "I was able to discover some pieces of information about Thompson. However, I could not see the charges in a sealed indictment that had mysteriously been dropped by the United States District Court in Illinois last September. No one would say anything about it until I got through to the wife of Thompson's ex-partner who would only talk off the record. She is very bitter about it because her husband is doing eight to ten and she blames Thompson. Twenty-two kilos of cocaine disappeared from an evidence locker in a neighboring precinct. Lieutenant Louis Thompson and his partner were implicated. Only the partner is doing time."

Chief Jennifer Hepburn said, "There appears to be no question that we have a bad apple in the Batavia Police Department. I hired him based on what I considered to be sufficient vetting. However, this is not the time to rationalize my mistake."

"I agree." FBI agent Cleary sympathized with the police officer.

Chief Hepburn went on, "There are two people, possibly more, who could be in imminent danger. We should take action now but we must proceed with caution. I don't want my town to be permanently scarred by collateral damage."

"You're right, Chief Hepburn. We need a strategy that minimizes the risks for hostages who might be in jeopardy," Senior Agent Cleary said. "Mrs. O'Connor, do you have a large easel or a corkboard or blackboard that we can use for designing an action plan? Also, can we assemble in a larger space?"

"Um, yes, OK," Lydia answered. "Let's go in the living room." She pulled a packet of multi-colored erasable markers from her desk and led the way out the door.

"My wife's name is Lydia Kingston," I whispered to Agent Cleary.

"Oh, sorry," she answered without appearing to be apologetic. However, she did not repeat the mistake.

Lydia instructed her daughter, "Eileen, you're the tall one. Take the paintings off that wall and stack them out of the way in the den."

"Do you have tape and paper we can use to cover the wall?" Cleary asked.

"No. Write with these erasable markers right on the wall. The interior decorating in here is years old."

Lydia, scrunched up her face and looked at me. She knew how hard I had worked on the color scheme and the paint job. It was the kind of meticulous finishing work that I did not relish.

I signaled that I understood with a shrug. Lydia was right that it had been a while but I thought my paint job still looked pretty good.

Chapter 86 . The living room wall was a bulletin board.

Our living room was about to become the war room for a police action. A wall of smooth plaster would be Agent Cleary's canvas for designing a multi-faceted criminal investigation. Of all the colors in the pack, she chose one of the blackest markers.

It was immediately clear that the senior FBI agent knew how to take charge. Without any hesitation, Irene Cleary started the first column on the left side of the large open surface. She wrote

- Janet Bread held captive
  Location unknown

just above eye level.

The copyrighted color 'Soft Sunshine Yellow' laboriously applied to our living room wall was no longer clean. Erasable or not, I knew the print left by the markers would never be completely gone.

Agent Cleary added entries to the first column.

- Held under duress by Thompson:
  Katherine Chavis
  Attorney Wrightson
  in Monroe building

- Brian Hill, a.k.a., Rusty, in the wind

- Shooting victims:
  o Hennigan, 2 weeks ago, Batavia
  o Elliot Shaw, yesterday, New Mexico

"If Thompson is still in the building, it means he has not gotten what he came for yet," Chief Hepburn said. "My best guess is Wrightson is buying time but Thompson knows he cannot afford to be patient for too long. Does the FBI have a theory?"

Agent Cleary started another list of items to the right of the first column of notes. She wrote

- Connection to Mendoza cartel

I interrupted. "What does the Mendoza cartel have to do with anything?" I asked.

"It's a mystery to me too," Chief Hepburn said.

"We can talk about that in a minute," Irving put us off. He said, "We need to keep track of everyone involved."

Hepburn dictated names while Cleary wrote them on the wall:

- Present and accounted for:
  - O'Connor daughters
  - Domestic helper
  - Lydia Kingston, Ted O'Connor

- At Wrightson residence
  - Sgt. Ryan, Officer White

"We should add to this list when we know more," Chief Hepburn said.

"Help me with the assignments," Cleary said.

Chief Hepburn stepped forward and took the marker from Cleary. She started a third column under the heading

- Action Items

to the right of all the notes already on the wall. She said. "As I see it, we have three urgent issues."

Hepburn underlined the column heading and wrote:

- **Action Items**
  1. Track down Brian Hill
  2. Rescue Janet Bread
  3. Capture Thompson
     - No collateral damages

Agent Ronan said, "In answer to your question, Jennifer and Ted, the Mendoza cartel has been doing business in human trafficking and drug smuggling across the border from Mexico into New Mexico and Arizona. We believe Brian Hill has been working for the cartel."

Agent Kumar added, "The Mendoza cartel continues to do business all along the border with Mexico from Antelope Wells, New Mexico, west to the Buenos Aires National Wildlife Refuge in Arizona and beyond that all the way into the Tohono O'Odham reservation."

I said, "I know that area, not first-hand but I know about it. A good friend, a mechanic at the garage where I work had to flee from his home in the Mexican state of Sonora. Soldiers in the Mendoza cartel had threatened him and his family. He took refuge here in Batavia until ICE chased him away. He and his wife taught us a lot about the geography of that part of the country. We have lost track of my immigrant friend and his family."

"What was his name?" Cleary asked. She picked up another black marker and added the information:

- Connection to Mendoza cartel:
  - Brian Hill
  - Louis Thompson
  - Angel Hernandez?

"Some time before he was killed, Matthew Hennigan tipped off ICE about the Hernandez family," I said.

"That does make it interesting," Irving replied.

My guess is the two victims were cartel executions." Cleary added their names:

- Connection to Mendoza cartel:
  - Brian Hill
  - Louis Thompson
  - Angel Hernandez?
  - Hennigan, Shaw

"Does everyone agree with the action items?" Cleary asked.

"Yes. Perhaps not in that order," Agent Kumar weighed in on the crucial issue.

"How would you put it?"

"Attorney Wrightson, staff member Katherine Chavis, and others in the Monroe office building are the most vulnerable. Janet Bread can take care of herself."

"What?" Lydia gasped. "You can't just abandon her."

"No, Ms. Kingston, I do not mean to suggest that," Kumar said. "Rather, we can depend on Detective Bread to help from the inside while we mount a rescue effort from the outside."

Cleary said, "In fact, Action Items 2 and 3 cannot be dealt with separately. Detective Bread was last seen in the Monroe office building and we believe Thompson is there with Wrightson now.

"We should begin by concentrating our efforts on the office building. Chief Hepburn, how much support is available to us for launching a floor-by-floor search and rescue in the building?"

"I have called in all the off-duty officers but we are a small police force. You can only count on six of us. Here are two of our officers now."

A BPD cruiser was coasting to a stop behind Hepburn's car at the curb.

Chief Hepburn said, "Our office administrative assistant and radio dispatcher is Elizabeth Stewart. The two uniforms are Sgt. Claire Winters and Officer Padraic McGuire."

The new arrivals were led by dispatcher Stewart into the living room.

Cleary added Stewart's name to the board:

- Present and accounted for:
  - O'Connor daughters, Diane, Eileen
  - Domestic helper -- Alena
  - Lydia Kingston, Ted O'Connor
  - Elizabeth Stewart

Chief Hepburn said, "I talked to the county sheriff. He and three deputies are on their way from Socorro."

"They are already here," Stewart said. "They are waiting for instructions at the station. The sheriff told me he can muster a dozen more officers but it might take them a while to get to Batavia."

Cleary squeezed more items into the center of the chart on the wall.

- 3 FBI agents
  Officer Dunning, Chief Hepburn
  Sgt. Winters, Officer McGuire
  Sheriff deputies

"Where else can we go for additional personnel if we need more help?" Cleary asked.

Sgt. Winters volunteered, "There is a security agency in Socorro. The company has contracts for buildings and businesses throughout the region. Also, they cover special events locally and in the city. Some of their agents are licensed to carry."

"Do you have their phone number?" Cleary asked.

"I can find it," Diane volunteered. She was standing next to Claire Winters. The police sergeant was the older sister of one of Diane's high school classmates in our small town. Diane went into the office and came back with a printed Batavia directory.

"I found Socorro Elite Security Services. Is that the one?"

Yes it is," Winters confirmed.

Diane read the number to Eileen who wrote it with obvious self-importance on the wall below the words

- Security agency

that Agent Cleary had just put there.

Chief Hepburn said, "Elizabeth, put in a call to Socorro Security now please. Ask if they have agents available for immediate assignments. We will need a dozen or more. Eileen wrote their phone number on the wall."

Elizabeth Stewart said, "I already had it. I know the guy at the front desk."

"Yes, of course you do." Hepburn was aware that Elizabeth had a relative employed as a security guard. She just did not remember where.

The police chief hardly had a chance to turn around before Elizabeth had an answer. She said, "Chief Hepburn, my nephew answered the phone. He said they can send a hundred security guards on the spur of the moment. He was exaggerating but I know they tap into a large pool of agents."

War Room Notes and Map

- Janet Bread held captive
  Location unknown

- Held under duress by Thompson:
  Katherine Chavis
  Attorney Wrightson
  in Monroe building

- Brian Hill, a.k.a, Rusty, in the wind

- Shooting victims:
  o Hennigan, 2 weeks ago, Batavia
  o Elliot Shaw, yesterday, New Mexico

- 3 FBI agents
  Officer Dunning, Chief Hepburn
  Sgt. Winters, Officer McGuire
  Sheriff deputies

- Connection to Mendoza cartel?
  o Brian Hill
  o Louis Thompson
  o Angel Hernandez?
  o Hennigan, Shaw

- Present and accounted for:
  o O'Connor daughters, Diane, Eileen
  o Domestic helper — Alena
  o Lydia Kingston, Ted O'Connor
  o Elizabeth Stewart

- ## Action Items

1. Track down Brian Hill
2. Rescue Janet Bread
3. Capture Thompson
   No collateral damage

- Security agency
  555-4321

N

Monroe Bldg.

Wrightson's condo

BPD station

Central Blvd.

O'Connor-Kingston residence

Elm Ave.

Columbia St.

Wrightson's parents

O'Connor's parents

Part VIII

Arrogance and Desperation

Cowards die many times before their deaths; the valiant never taste of death but once.

— *William Shakespeare,* Julius Caesar

Chapter 87 . The senior FBI agent rode with the police chief.

The police and the FBI agents were preparing to depart for their mission at the Elise Monroe Office Building but Chief Hepburn did not want to leave my residence unprotected. Security guards would be needed for the operation center on Elm Avenue.

The chief of police said, "Elizabeth, call Socorro Elite Security back and ask for personnel to ensure the safety of everyone here. They should start right away and be prepared to provide round-the-clock coverage."

"We need armed guards. Am I right?"

"Yes. They should be prepared for armed and dangerous."

"Also, one of the culprits could be in uniform," Elizabeth said.

"That's right, Elizabeth. Very good point! Make sure the guards on the protection details know what to expect."

Elizabeth dialed the number.

Hepburn interjected, "Guards will also be needed at Wrightson's residence."

Elizabeth upped the request for personnel. She said, "Thanks nephew" and hung up.

Hepburn explained, "I consider it to be unlikely but the intruder could return to Mr. Wrightson's residence. If anyone arouses suspicion, they should be held for questioning. We are not protecting human assets at his house. So, once the guards have supervised the repairs on the broken door and secured the premises, they can leave. You can ask them to come back here for new assignments."

"Chief Hepburn, I'm worried about Ted's folks and Elmer Wrightson's too," Lydia said.

"OK, Elizabeth, add two more locations to the list for Socorro Elite. Are you sure they can handle it?"

"I believe so. What account should I use for all of this?"

"Put it on 'General Services.'"

"OK. Our credit should be good," Elizabeth Stewart said.

Chief Hepburn rolled her eyes. "We'll worry about the city council's reaction after they see the expense report. In the meantime, Elizabeth, we cannot cut corners. I believe we could be dealing with serious threats from a sophisticated criminal organization."

"I understand."

Senior FBI Agent Cleary said, "We have an account number that will cover at least part of the costs. Elizabeth, remind me later to give it to you. There is money in the FBI's budget for the Mendoza investigation. Chief Hepburn and I can talk about the funding issues later. You don't need to worry about it."

"OK. Thank you."

FBI Agent Ronan asked, "What do the numbers look like for launching a floor-by-floor, search-and-rescue effort in the office building?"

Chief Hepburn answered, "There are the three of you. Sheriff Dennis Quan is standing by with several deputies at the BPD station. He said he can muster a few more depending on our needs. Finally, I am counting seven police officers including myself."

I stepped into the conversation to contribute what I could. "It will take a long time for so few people to look in every room of that building. I know it pretty well and there are many places where Thompson could be hiding with Wrightson and Chavis."

"We can get more security guards from SESS," Elizabeth Stewart volunteered.

"SESS?" Hepburn asked.

"That's what my nephew who works there calls it. SESS is an acronym for Socorro Elite Security Services," Ms. Stewart explained. She pronounced the abbreviation the way it is spelled.

"There is a limitation on the numbers," Ronan said. "Flooding the place with a large search-and-rescue team will take organization that we don't have time for."

"I believe Sheriff Quan is up to the task," Hepburn asserted.

"Let's see what he has to say." Agent Ronan asked Lydia to call Sheriff Quan on the speaker phone in the den. Kumar, Hepburn, and Cleary gathered with Ronan around the desk. Lydia and I sat across the room on our new Osler Cleo chairs. Elizabeth Stewart took a seat on the sofa.

Sheriff Quan answered the phone. He agreed that a sizeable force would be needed to search and evacuate the office building. He said, "Another deputy just walked in. We now have eleven women and men here at the station."

Chief Hepburn said, "The Batavia police officers are all on standby and we can count on a dozen or more personnel from Socorro Elite Security Services."

The sheriff suggested a small-team approach that was familiar to his staff. Hepburn said the Batavia police officers had the same training.

The details appeared to be new to the FBI agents. However, the sheriff was aware that some of the security guards at SESS were well acquainted with the process.

The Sheriff said, "Let me give you a quick introduction. For the small-team approach, squads of half a dozen soldiers or, in our case, police officers are assigned one of three responsibilities which are contact, backup, or lookout. First, two members of the team lead the way. Second and third, the others provide backup and watch for trouble approaching from their surroundings."

Chief Hepburn said, "The responsibilities within a group are the same whether entering, searching, and evacuating a room inside the building or interviewing and clearing an evacuee who is coming out of the building. Remain vigilant and attentive to the mission. Cover for each other. Be alert to your surroundings and, of course, be safe."

"It's a military-style operation. I've heard of it before," Kumar said. "Pay attention to your particular responsibility but stick together in your squad. Follow your team leader's directions throughout the operation."

Sheriff Quan said, "I can assemble the small teams with a mix of the individuals who are trained in the method. I will designate group leaders. They will be ready to go by the time you get here."

Kumar spoke again. "I will get to work on assembling the book. In fact, I already have the data for several pages."

Quan said, "I guess you have heard of the small-team approach before, Agent Kumar. For the benefit of those of you who may not know, the book contains names and instructions for identifying persons of interest. It is an essential tool for the squads intercepting the evacuees as they leave the building."

Chief Hepburn turned to give instructions to the BPD dispatcher. "Elizabeth, we are going to evacuate the Monroe office building by brute force. Please get back in touch with SESS and ask for twenty additional armed security agents. Have them meet you here for instructions."

The two of them left the den to look over the items on the living room wall.

Hepburn said, "Sgt. Ryan and Officer White should be finished with Wrightson's residence by now. As soon as the contingent from Socorro Elite Security gets there, Ryan and White should return here. Give them a full briefing on the details."

"Where do you want them?" Elizabeth asked.

"Sgt. Ryan should go to the station to work with us on the staffing assignments. The sheriff can use his help with training and deploying the search-and-rescue teams."

"And Officer White?"

"Tell both of them to join us at the station as soon as all of the residential locations are secure."

"Yes, Ma'am."

"Make sure all of our recruits understand what is at stake." Hepburn waved her hand over the war-room notes on the wall. "Brief everyone on the details of our operation. Cover the private residences first and then send everyone else to Sheriff Quan at the BPD station."

Elizabeth Stewart answered, "The personnel for our location here are already on their way from Socorro Elite Security." She was holding a state-of-the-art cell phone for police work the size of a red brick. "They are recruiting additional forces as we speak."

Still not satisfied that we were completely secure, Hepburn said, "Elizabeth, the O'Connor family might be perfectly safe here but we can't be sure. I'll have Officer Dunning remain here with you until you are certain that you have adequate protection in place."

"Irving, you should stay here with the family until the protective detail arrives," Agent Cleary said.

He replied, "I'll follow you to the station as soon as I can."

Hepburn said, "Elizabeth, it is not likely that the senior O'Connor's will be disturbed. However, you should send two reliable security guards to stay with them just in case. Wrightson's folks are a different matter. They could be used as leverage against their son. Make their protection a first priority. Just ask if you are unsure about anything. Do you think you know what to do?"

"Yes, I believe so. Overkill on protection details is better than the opposite." Elizabeth's confident response was all Chief Hepburn required.

After hesitating for only a moment, Elizabeth grabbed a marker and drew a box in an open space on the wall and started writing. She sketched a rough map of the geographic locations that needed security guards.

Eileen was standing nearby. She seemed in awe of the dispatcher's self-confidence. "How did you know what to do?" she asked.

"I don't," Elizabeth answered. "We have never had anything like this in Batavia before. I'm making it up as I go. Do you have thumb tacks and sticky notes?"

"There's a pad of Post-It notes on the desk." Eileen pointed toward the door to den. "I'll go look for the tacks." She ran to the kitchen to search through the junk drawer and returned with a box of push tacks that I didn't know we had.

Elizabeth Stewart started writing names on the notes and securing them to the wall with the tacks. She put separate tags for White and Ryan at Wrightson's condo.

Tags labeled for Officer Angela Dunning and for the members of my family were pinned to the Elm Avenue location on the hand-drawn map. Kumar and Wrightson were placed at the BPD station and the Monroe office building, respectively. It was the beginning of a blizzard of notes that added a pin-cushion effect to our marked-up living room wall.

"We can move the tags from place to place when their assignments change," Elizabeth explained to Eileen.

"Are you ready?" Hepburn asked Cleary.

"Yes. Let's go."

Alena and Diane hurried out of the kitchen. Each was carrying two large grocery bags. "Take these with you," Alena instructed. "It is time for lunch. You need to eat. There's some for sheriff and deputies too."

Diane said, "Chicken-salad sandwiches, chips and soft drinks. Sorry. We only had diet Coke."

"Thank you. You are a life-saver, Alena. You too, Diane." Chief Hepburn was very appreciative.

"Ride with me?" Hepburn asked Cleary.

"Yes." Cleary handed her keys to Ronan and told him, "My car is around the corner on Columbia Street."

Once, they were in the police cruiser, FBI Agent Cleary asked, "Jennifer, what is your assessment?"

"It won't be a cake walk but I believe we are as ready as we can be. The war-room description of the situation that you sketched on the living room wall has given us a clear picture. I have confidence in Elizabeth Stewart. She is quite capable of allocating assignments to the available staffing."

"What about the on-site organization?" Cleary asked.

"Sheriff Dennis Quan is very competent. I trained him myself. He joined the BPD after a stint in the Army. He was with us less than two years before deciding to run for sheriff. I'm still mad at him for leaving and taking one of our best recruits with him. The young man is now a top-notch deputy. I would not be surprised if he is at the station with the sheriff now."

"How do you want to handle it when we get there?"

"If you agree, you and I will lead the first wave into the building. Maybe four to six individuals including the deputy and Officer White if he gets here by the time we go in."

"A total of four might be right for the first group. We want a streamlined evacuation process without panicking the occupants of the building."

"Sheriff Quan can stay at the station to organize the troops into small teams to search the building and to intercept and clear everyone who leaves."

"Good. We need to get started quickly on the inside. However, the exterior perimeter has to be secure before we go in."

Chapter 88 . The police action was search and evacuate.

Rohit Kumar was already at the station when Hepburn and Cleary arrived. He told them, "Obtaining up-to-date blueprints was straightforward for such a recent renovation."

Agent Ronan walked into the station just a few minutes behind Cleary and Hepburn.

"How's everything at the house?" Hepburn asked Ronan.

"Well organized. Elizabeth was setting up procedures to vet and dispatch the security personnel. Even before you left, she had selected two or three of the best to keep there with her to protect the O'Connor family. Officer Dunning took them with her to survey the premises. One was posted in the garage. Another will watch the back of the house and the doors into the kitchen."

Hepburn asked, "How are the numbers looking? Will we be getting any more help here?"

Ronan nodded. "Yes. As soon as Dunning got back from inspecting the place with the security guards, Elizabeth put her to work checking identifications and credentials. There had to be six or eight individuals waiting on the front porch. It was time for me to get out of the way. How can I help here?"

"I presume you are the other two FBI agents," the sheriff said. "I've already met Rohit Kumar."

"Yes, sorry." Chief Hepburn introduced Irving Ronan and Irene Cleary to Dennis Quan.

"Are we ready to begin?" the sheriff asked.

Agent Cleary answered, "Yes, I believe so. Jennifer and I will go into the building first and direct traffic from inside the main entrance. Is that OK?"

"Yes. Sounds good," Sheriff Quan agreed.

Cleary continued, "Irving, will you supervise the activities in the plaza in front of the building? Dispatch each squad to where they are needed inside or outside the building. We will let you know when we need more help on the inside. Please queue up teams to come in when called for."

"All right. I'll be ready."

"Good. Yours is a multi-tasking assignment. So, it will get hectic on the outside. You will need to supervise the interviewing at the main entrance and make sure no one escapes through the emergency exits or the driveways from the garages. You will have to be on all sides of the building at once."

"I understand, Irene. We will do the best we can with the personnel we've got."

"OK, Sheriff Quan. Let's get the ball rolling. This crowd of security agents is anxious to get to work," Cleary said.

The sheriff addressed the women and men waiting outside the BPD station, "You all know who I am, Sheriff Dennis Quan. You have your instructions for searching and evacuating the Elise Monroe Office Building. FBI Agents Irving Ronan and Irene Cleary will be joining the effort."

Ronan and Cleary each took a step forward and waved to acknowledge their introductions.

Quan continued, "Our job is to evacuate the entire building in a quick and efficient manner. Speed is essential. Taking the suspects by surprise will reduce their opportunities to offer resistance."

Hepburn said, "I believe most of you know me. I am Chief Jennifer Hepburn of the Batavia Police Department. Agent Cleary and I will set up a command post inside the main entrance to the building and supervise the evacuation from there. Before entering the building, each team will get its assignment from Agent Ronan or Sgt. Robert Ryan of the BPD."

Agent Cleary announced, "We are looking for one or more persons of interest, possibly armed and dangerous. We intend to funnel all occupants out through the main entrance where you will check their identification as they leave."

Sheriff Quan said, "FBI Agent Rohit Kumar is here now with copies of the book for the teams that remain outside to intercept and interrogate the evacuees."

Kumar had assembled what was referred to as the book. It contained a sheet with a picture and particulars for each of nine possible suspects. Pages 1 and 2 were for Brian Hill and Louis Thompson. The next seven pages included two of Thompson's former cronies in Chicago and five of Hill's known associates in the cartel. There were also two pages of FBI boilerplate on how to watch for suspicious behavior.

Chief Hepburn said, "The building has two emergency exits, one each on the north and south sides. There are three levels of parking under the building. The access points in and out of the garages are on the north and west sides. We must block the driveways and cover the side exits. No one should be allowed to leave without going through you. It is Saturday but there could still be as many as a hundred individuals in the building."

Agent Kumar let his presence be known with a mixed metaphor, "Study the pages in your copy of the book. Scrutinize every individual as they leave the building. We believe there are fewer than half a dozen culprits among the many in the building which means your odds are no better than a racetrack trifecta in a haystack."

The sheriff ignored the perplexed expressions and set the operation in motion. "Let's get to work."

Chapter 89 . Evacuation of the building was chaotic.

Jennifer Hepburn said, "Dennis, please send Sgt. Ryan and Officer White forward to assist us as soon as they get here."

"We're here now." Ryan was standing right behind her.

"Oh, good. Bob, work with Irving Ronan to help with the team assignments. Billy, with me."

Chief Hepburn and Senior Agent Cleary led the way into the Elise Monroe Office Building. A deputy sheriff and Officer William White came in right behind them.

The main entrance cut an angular piece off the southeast corner of the first floor. The enclave for the four elevators was straight ahead of them in the center of the vast, open-concept floor plan.

It was obvious to everyone who saw them make their entrance that the four officers were on a mission. Hepburn, White, and the deputy were in uniform. By association, the dark suit typical of an FBI agent gave Cleary away as well.

It was past time for lunch but there was still a number of patrons and servers in the restaurant. The eating area occupied the full quadrant of the main floor immediately to their left. The tables were partitioned off by a decorative, waist-high paneling of polished hardwood.

The L-shaped open kitchen and bar were constructed against the north and west walls of the quadrant. Gleaming stainless-steel hoods over the stoves were visible beyond the top of the high, pass-over counter for the wait staff to pick up plates of food or glasses of liquor. The establishment served as a luncheonette during the day and as a bistro at night.

Chief Hepburn broke through the murmur of the sound of people visiting and eating at the tables. She called out in a loud voice, "Everyone must evacuate the building immediately."

The startled crowd stopped and looked toward the contingent of officials. It was like watching a freeze-frame movie.

Hepburn raised her voice again. "There is a potentially lethal threat in the building that must be taken seriously. Form a single line and go out through the main entrance. Once outside, you must identify yourself to one of the uniformed officers. They will guide you to safety."

A few individuals began to cooperate. A man sitting by himself tucked his newspaper under his arm and headed for the exit.

A woman with three children, one in a stroller, frantically started herding them toward the door. It was not going smoothly for her. She knocked a plate and glass off the table. The plate broke and the milk spilled. The tallest of the three, maybe five or six years old, bent over to pick up the pieces.

"Just leave them." His mother's voice was stern. The youngest of her toddlers began wailing aloud. The deputy sheriff caught the stroller before it tipped over. He steadied the woman and ushered her and her brood in the right direction.

Hepburn responded, "Do not panic. Move quickly and carefully toward the main exit. Show identification to the officers outside the door. They will make sure you get out safely."

A waiter looked our way but did not stop what he was doing. He continued toward one of the tables on the far side.

Chief Hepburn recognized him. She shouted, "Anthony, that means you. Put down those plates and immediately come this way. Everyone, move now. Your lives may depend on an orderly exit as quickly as possible."

The door to the stairwell just past the restaurant opened. Someone looked out and quickly jumped back. He pulled the door closed.

Hepburn spoke into her radio, "Irving, we have suspicious activity. Someone might be escaping through the emergency exit from the north-side stairwell."

A chef continued to work at the grille with his back to us. The classic tall white hat was on his head. The dark sports jacket under his apron did not fit expectations for someone in food service.

"Hey you at the stove, did you hear my evacuation order?" Hepburn yelled.

The man hesitated a moment before turning to face us. The spatula in his hand was not a spatula. It was a gun. The long knife in his other hand was a long knife. He found the sheath for the blade on his belt and took aim with the handgun.

With elbows on the food-service counter, he fired several shots at the contingent of security forces. The female customer with the stroller screamed and dropped to her knees. She wrapped her arms around her little ones and pulled them down next to her. She was unharmed.

A bullet tore through the neck of the sheriff's deputy standing next to her. His lifeless body fell to the floor.

"Thompson, drop the gun!" Hepburn screamed.

He turned and ran toward and out the door into the same north-side stairwell.

Chief Hepburn and Agent Cleary were aiming their weapons but could not return fire. Too many civilians were still inside.

Hepburn spoke again into her radio. "Irving, are Sgt. Ryan and Sgt. Winters there?"

"They are already on their way in. We heard the shots. Officer McGuire is coming in too." Irving Ronan's answer crackled back on her radio.

"Good. Send in two of the search teams and hold the rest for the moment," she replied.

A contingent of armed security guards and sheriff's deputies came in with sidearms in their hands. Sgt. Ryan, Sgt. Claire Winters, and Officer Padraic McGuire were right behind them.

Ryan said, "The shooter might be going down to the garage. The sheriff found one of our cruisers parked on the Executive Level."

"Watch the side doors but do not follow," Irene Cleary gave the order to the officers in the group.

"Jennifer, I'll go down the south stairwell after Thompson if you will come down on the north side. Give me a head start. OK?"

"Agreed." Chief Hepburn gave another order. "Sgt. Winters, take charge of the evacuation of the main floor only. Do not proceed with the upper floors until you hear from us. If anyone comes down the elevators or out of the stairwells, escort them out the front entrance to be identified."

Claire Winters nodded that she understood.

"With me, Sgt. Ryan," Hepburn said.

Agent Cleary ran toward the symmetrically placed stairwell on the south side of the main floor. Officer White went with her.

They ran down the first flight of stairs. Cleary listened at the steel door. She held White's arm. "I'll check it out. You stay here."

Officer White said, "It's two more flights down to where the cruiser is parked."

Cleary answered, "Thompson must know we found it. I believe he has a different escape vehicle on one of the first two levels."

She pushed open the door to Garage Level I. They heard the sharp cry of a woman's voice. Irene Cleary followed the sound into the garage.

Officer White stopped the door from closing completely with his boot against the frame. He watched Agent Cleary move across to the other side of the middle row of parking spaces where he lost sight of her. The tension was so great he could hardly breathe. His body shook with trepidation.

Many seconds passed. Officer White heard Agent Cleary shout, "Stop right there. On your knees. Drop the gun. Put your hands behind your head."

William White knew what he had to do. He ducked down and pushed his way into the garage. He located Cleary again. She was aiming her weapon with both arms straight in front of her. Her target was off to the right out of his line of sight.

"Drop the gun now," she repeated in a louder, commanding voice.

The growled response was mostly unintelligible. White heard the words, "Back off or she's dead." The voice was familiar but different. There was a cold hard edge to the words.

"Drop your gun," Cleary repeated.

An instant later, the sound of a single gunshot rang in Officer White's ears. He heard a wild yelp of pain. The sound sent trembles through his body.

He watched Agent Cleary lower her weapon. She started walking in the direction she had fired. White hurried after her. She strode the full width of the garage and leaned over a motionless form to feel for a pulse.

When Officer White caught up, she had already holstered her weapon. He kicked Thompson's gun to the side and said, "I'll call an ambulance."

"That won't be necessary." There was a tremor in her voice. Billy thought Agent Cleary sounded sad.

Chief Hepburn came in from the other stairwell with her gun drawn. Sgt. Ryan was with her.

Cleary said to Hepburn, "I'm very sorry it had to end this way. Officer Thompson could have been a fine policeman."

Hepburn acknowledged the feeling. "I am sorry too."

Cleary repressed her feelings of regret and said, "The fact that he was still in the building means Wrightson should be here."

"What about Katherine Chavis," Ryan asked.

It was Chief Jennifer Hepburn who answered Sgt. Ryan's question. She had inferred the details of the showdown between Cleary and Thompson the instant she entered the garage.

"Right there." She pointed to the administrative assistant, a trembling bowl of Jello plopped on the floor next to the open door on the passenger side of a dark sedan. "Thompson was trying to use her as a hostage to make his escape."

Cleary nodded in agreement.

Billy helped Katherine Chavis to her feet and stood there holding her. The competent, confident middle-aged woman could not stop shaking.

Billy White asked, "Should we look for Mr. Wrightson? Do you think he's OK?"

"He's alive, no reason to kill him," Cleary said. "I don't believe Thompson got what he wanted. He would have been under orders to keep Wrightson alive until they did."

Katherine Chavis made a sound only Officer White could hear.

"Where is he, Ms. Chavis?" Officer White whispered in her ear.

"Mr. Wrightson was tied up in the Yukon conference room," she squeaked.

White relayed the message. "The Yukon conference room is on the sixth floor."

"Let's find him." Chief Hepburn took the initiative. "Sgt. Ryan, organize the effort. We are looking for Wrightson and any other victims. Get the floor-by-floor, room-by-room search going in earnest. Top two floors first because that's where his law firm and conference rooms are located. If not successful, go to the remaining floors next. Victims are not likely to be in the garages. We will look there last."

Sgt. Ryan remarked, "There could still be active threats in the building."

"That's right. Use the multi-squad approach that the sheriff has organized."

Dennis Quan said, "You've got it." No one had noticed that he had joined the group of officers in the garage.

Sgt. Ryan headed for the stairs. Hepburn called after him, "Bob, tell everyone to be careful. Thompson's cohorts are armed and dangerous. Whoever was helping him is probably gone by now but we can't be sure."

Agent Cleary joined the cautionary refrain. "Chief Hepburn is right, Sgt. Ryan. Agent Ronan has already detained three individuals with criminal backgrounds when they were forced out of the building from the restaurant or one of the lower floors."

'I know," Ryan answered. "We have not established a connection but they could have been working with Thompson and there might be more."

Chapter 90 . Indominable meant more angry than frightened.

Officer White pulled away from Katherine Chavis. He patted her on the arm and started for the stairwell after Sgt. Ryan. He knew it was his responsibility to accompany his partner.

Chief Hepburn said, "Billy, stay here a minute. We are going to need statements from you and Ms. Chavis about the shooting."

"It was reasonable and necessary force," Officer White asserted.

"I know."

Sheriff Dennis joined the conversation. "We have to do this by the book. I would love to handle the investigation but I cannot. We just lost a young deputy upstairs and I believe that is the murder weapon." He pointed to Thompson's gun.

Cleary said, "The situation is complicated even further because the perp was a police officer."

"A police officer in my department which recuses me as well," Chief Hepburn said. "Officer White, you must assume temporary custody of the physical evidence. Hand it over to the state police as soon as possible. They will need to do the official investigation. The District Attorney will take jurisdiction."

"Thompson's sidearm should go in an evidence bag. Officer White kicked it aside but no one has touched it," Cleary said.

William White used a pen through the trigger-guard loop to pick up Louis Thompson's gun. He turned to look at Irene Cleary. "How about yours?" he asked.

"You will need my weapon as well but not until we have finished searching the building and rescued Elmer Wrightson," Agent Cleary said.

Chief Hepburn nodded her acceptance of Cleary's reasoning. "Also, we have not yet found Janet Bread," she said.

Locating Wrightson did not take long. Two deputies with guns drawn stepped cautiously into the receptionist's vestibule for his law firm. Sgt. Ryan and two more security guards fanned out behind them.

As soon as he heard the police announce themselves, Wrightson started hollering. Sgt. Ryan found him taped to a chair in the adjoining Yukon conference room.

"The bastard took off with Katherine Chavis. You've got to save her." Wrightson's voice was shaky and hoarse.

"We found her," Ryan said.

"Is she OK?"

"Unharmed physically but very distraught."

"Oh no. Poor woman," Elmer sighed. His anger was exasperated by his own tears. "Can you get this fucking tape off of me?"

"Yes, sir, I'm trying." One of the deputies was pulling at the aluminum, sheet-metal tape holding Wrightson's wrists to the arms of the chair.

"Well, try faster."

"Sir, this stuff will take flesh with it if we are not careful." One of the other deputies left and came back with a pair of scissors.

"That might not work very well." Officer White had just arrived. "It's too dull." He pulled his Optinel Carbone pocketknife from a pouch on his belt and slit the tape along each forearm. He carefully followed the seams on Wrightson's jacket.

427

While Officer White worked to free Wrightson's bonds, Sgt. Ryan pulled a chair up close to the man and put a hand on his shoulder. "Mr. Wrightson, we need your help. Was Officer Thompson working alone?"

"I don't know. Ask him."

"He's deceased. Agent Cleary had no choice." Ryan said to the suddenly attentive attorney.

"Oh, I see."

Officer White finished cutting through the last strips of tape around Wrightson's chest and legs.

Sgt. Ryan had to grab hold of him when he struggled to stand up. Wrightson's awkward balancing act with the remnants of the silvery tape all over the front of his suit gave the impression of the stumbling tin man from the Wizard of Oz.

"It will be difficult to get that stuff off your clothes," the deputy offered. "They might be ruined."

Wrightson shrugged out of his suit jacket and, in a moment of anger and disgust, he threw it on the floor by the waste basket. He looked with dismay at the tape stuck to his pants below the knees.

Sgt. Ryan said, "You can change clothes later, Mr. Wrightson. The BPD and sheriff deputies are searching the building. We need to know what we are looking for."

"I heard Thompson on the phone. He was in the next room. He had me all taped up and Chavis was handcuffed to that chair."

"Was he talking to an accomplice in the building?"

"I couldn't make out all the words. I think he was mostly doing the listening. I heard something about meeting him somewhere. Katherine Chavis might have gotten more but maybe not. She was frightened out of her wits. Both of us were."

Bob Ryan asked, "Billy, will you see if Ms. Chavis is in any shape to give us some help."

"I will." Officer White pocketed his knife and left the room.

"Mr. Wrightson, the building is surrounded. We are checking the identification of everyone who leaves. Close to fifty so far. Does that sound right?"

"I can't remember the details right now. My head is swimming," Wrightson complained.

Ryan helped him into another chair turned away from where he and Katherine Chavis had been uncomfortably bound. "How many people should there be in the building at this time of day?"

Wrightson answered a slightly different question. "The building is not fully occupied. There are vacancies on the third and fourth floors." The reliably eloquent Attorney Wrightson could not assemble his thoughts. "Hell, I don't know. It might be the fourth and fifth floors. My firm occupies all of the seventh and eighth," he misspoke. The building was just seven stories tall.

Sgt. Ryan pressed him. "Should there be more than a hundred, less than a hundred in the building today at this time?"

"Oh, yeah. I remember. Dot told me we reached a hundred occupants a couple of weeks ago or months. Is Dot all right?"

"Dot?"

Wrightson mumbled the words, "Chavis told me we needed someone in our real estate business with all of the new tenants coming and going. She hired Dorothy to help keep track. Her last name is Croix."

"Is Dorothy Croix here somewhere?"

Wrightson didn't answer. His head lolled to one side.

"Elmer, Elmer," Ryan yelped. "Stay with me." He dropped down to his knees and cradled Wrightson's head against his shoulder.

"I'm here. I'm here." Wrightson was indignant but had no right to be. The back of his head felt sticky to Ryan's right hand. It was matted with blood.

"Oh shit!" Ryan yelled, "Deputy, call Chief Hepburn. Tell her we need an ambulance fast. Attorney Wrightson may have suffered a concussion."

Wrightson lifted his head and smiled a silly grin at Ryan. "Really? A concussion? He clocked me pretty good. Didn't he?"

"Tell me what happened." Ryan knew to keep Wrightson talking.

"Thompson told me to open the safe." Wrightson was slurring his words. "When I said no, he threatened me with that heavy award thing that I have on my desk. Dot tried to stop him. She shouldn't have."

"What did she do? Where did Dot go?"

"He clobbered her and, when I shouted at him to stop, he said, 'Open the safe or I'll kill her.' So, I opened the safe and then the filthy jerk hit me anyway." Elmer shuddered, "My head hurts."

"Where is Dorothy Croix?" Sgt. Ryan was getting panicky at the thought there might be another victim.

"Who? Oh yeah, you mean Dorothy." Wrightson tried to focus. "She was sitting on the ground over there by the window and I sat here to open the safe."

Wrightson was losing coherence. He turned to point at the floor under the window as if he thought he was in his office.

"You mean the safe in your office?"

"Oh, yeah, in my office."

Chief Hepburn entered the room through the side door from the sixth-floor hallway. Several well-armed sheriff deputies escorted a woman and a man pushing a gurney into the conference room. All of them were wearing bullet-proof vests.

Ryan moved aside to let the EMT take over. She lifted Elmer's eyelids and examined his irises. With a deft motion of her scissors, she cut Wrightson's shirt sleeve off his left arm while barking out orders.

The two attendants moved fast. In less than ten seconds, Elmer's arm was a pincushion of needles. A blood-pressure cuff was wrapped around his right biceps. One of the tubes into an entry point on his arm was taped in place for intravenous medication.

While the medics were at work, Sgt. Ryan took Mark Silas, the deputy who had come up with him, aside.

He said, "Mark, you heard Attorney Wrightson mention the name Dorothy Croix. He called her Dot. We haven't found her and there may have been other victims in the firm's offices."

"Yes, I know."

"Get some help and double down on the search for anyone who might still be injured or sheltering in place in this complex of offices for Wrightson's firm. We are looking for other lawyers, clerks, receptionists, even clients who might have been here for appointments. Can you do that? Just remember we have to be careful with every individual we come across."

"Yes, sir." Deputy Silas lifted his radio and started talking to Sheriff Quan. He asked his supervisor for help.

Although their assistance was hardly necessary, Hepburn, Ryan, and a deputy reached in to help slide Wrightson from the chair onto a stretcher. They lifted him onto the gurney with the bottle for the IV strung overhead on a pole.

The EMT whispered to Ryan, "Nice catch. It's a serious concussion but I believe he is going to be all right." One of the armed deputies held the door for her and they sped off down the hallway toward the elevators.

"I don't feel like it was a nice catch." Ryan said to Hepburn after they were gone. "With all of my training for concussion protocol, I should have spotted the problem more quickly."

Hepburn shrugged and patted Ryan on the back. "The way I see it you saved Wrightson's life. Now might also be a good time to tell you that you have done a masterful job of organizing the evacuation."

"As good as your golden boy Sheriff Dennis?" Ryan gave her a sheepish smile.

Hepburn just nodded. She stepped back to answer her phone. "Yes, I understand. Thank you for letting us know."

She turned to Ryan. "One of the search teams found Dorothy Croix in the north stairwell. They got her into an ambulance right away. That was the hospital on the phone. She didn't make it."

The tears in his eyes might be expected even for a tough, no-nonsense police officer with years of experience. He was totally exhausted from the intensity of the day's operations.

Chapter 91 . The ominous threat hovered in the air.

"Brace up man, we've got work to do." Chief Hepburn hid any indication that she too might be feeling the pressure.

"Can't the paperwork wait till tomorrow?" Ryan knew that good police work meant reports had to be filed as quickly as possible while the details were still fresh in your memory. However, it was not the paperwork that Hepburn was referring to.

"We need to get back to the station and check in with Agent Cleary. She is heading up the effort to locate Detective Bread. The other FBI agent who came from Washington with Cleary has been developing leads."

'That would be Rohit Kumar." Ryan reminded Hepburn of the name.

"Right, thanks. He believes there were others in the building late yesterday evening who might have seen something."

Ryan asked, "Could Bread still be here in the building? Sorry to say it but it would not be hard to stash a body somewhere in this place. Old renovated buildings always have secret compartments and hidden cavities behind new partitions."

"You make a point that could not be dismissed out of hand. However, we have building blueprints from the contractor and the city inspector."

"Were we able to examine all of the details?"

"It turns out that Elizabeth's recruiting talents exceeded expectations. After she hired a dozen security officers from Socorro Elite, she started getting phone calls from volunteers."

"Qualified and licensed to carry?" Ryan asked.

"Qualified, licensed, and she told them they had to bring their own vests. We didn't have enough to go around. Elizabeth said she verified credentials carefully."

"She thought of everything. We are lucky to have such a competent dispatcher in the department."

"Indeed, that is very true but you don't know the half of it. We wound up with an abundance of riches in terms deputies and security guards crawling all over this place. Elizabeth is starting to send some of them home. She brought in two supervisors from Socorro Elite to help with the debriefings which she insists are absolutely necessary before anyone leaves. I think they are all going to get Christmas cards from her this year."

"Isn't Elizabeth Jewish?" Ryan said.

"Oh, maybe. In any case, my point is, Sgt. Ryan, Elizabeth is convinced that no rock has been left unturned. There are no unexamined hidden cavities left in this building."

Sgt. Ryan accepted the conclusion. "We must turn our attention to finding Detective Bread somewhere else."

"Yes, let's get on with it."

Officer White met Chief Hepburn and Sgt. Ryan on the main floor when they exited the elevator.

He said, "Agent Ronan left a while ago to check on the O'Connor's and to talk to Elizabeth. He said he would look in on Mr. Wrightson on the way. Agent Cleary is out front in the BPD police van. She has been on the phone with the FBI in Washington. Also, I overheard her talking to Helen Kingston."

"Oh, good. Cleary thought to call Colonel Kingston. She should be kept informed about her daughter. Have we got anything new on Janet Bread or Brian Hill?"

Officer White said, "Yes but it's good and bad news. Recall that, when we first entered the building this morning, there was suspicious activity at the south-side stairwell next to the restaurant."

"Of course, I didn't get a good look but it was definitely a male. I alerted Agent Ronan immediately to watch for him at the south-side exit. There is an outside door on the first floor from each stairwell. Did they catch him?"

"That's what I am trying to tell you. They made the identification while we were upstairs with Mr. Wrightson. It was Brian Hill. Unfortunately, he got away."

"How?" Sgt. Ryan gasped.

"The sheriff's deputy who was leading the team reported that they stopped an unassuming character at the south-side exit. The man said he was just following our orders to evacuate the building. He seemed legit. They were about to let him go when one of the security men noticed he was carrying."

"Didn't they recognize him?"

"Not then. They took his weapon and detained him for further questioning. He had identification and he had papers for the gun. He was completely cooperative at first. Unfortunately, he overpowered the junior deputy assigned to escort him to the police van. He had martial arts training that caught the officer by surprise. He snatched back his gun, papers, and ID. Before anyone could react, he was gone."

"How did you identify him?"

"He introduced himself by another name which matched his driver's license. However, the deputy and police officer who questioned him are not in agreement. They jotted down different spellings of his name. We now know who he was but not his current pseudonym."

"Ah, too bad."

"It may not matter. He has probably changed it by now anyway. Agent Ronan sent the three of them, the two who checked his ID and the one who tried to escort him to the van, over to the station to look at mug shots. I'm told that is how they got the positive identification."

Hepburn, Ryan, and White exited the office building and walked over toward the police van.

Chapter 92 . Car and fugitive were hidden in plain view.

After visiting with Elmer Wrightson at the hospital, Agent Ronan went to the O'Connor residence to check on the family. He wanted to see them in person to tell them about Elmer's condition and to let them know the doctors were confident there would be a full recovery.

Irving Ronan said, "He was admitted to the hospital but Elmer will probably be released tomorrow morning. I know you are anxious to see him but you must not go out of the house. I want you to remain here with the security guards at least another day. Visitors might not make much sense anyway. Elmer was asleep when I left him."

Lydia asked, "Is there still a present danger for us here?"

"Hopefully not. Brian Hill escaped our grasp at the office building but I don't believe he will risk coming here. I think he has undoubtedly left town."

"What about Janet?"

"We have not found her yet."

"Oh, dear," Lydia gulped back a sob.

"Detective Bread knows how to take care of herself. I am confident that she is perfectly fine. When she shows up, Janet will have a good explanation for all of us."

To my ear, Irving Ronan did not sound very confident.

"OK, I have to go," Ronan said. "I am going back to the police station to see what Agent Kumar has come up with. He is attempting to track down Brian Hill and look for Janet. I will check back with you later."

Irving Ronan stopped at the station to check in with Rohit Kumar. They talked for a few minutes. Ronan agreed that the possibilities held some degree of promise. He left Kumar alone to follow up on the leads and walked over to the Monroe office building.

The sheriff was there with a dozen of his deputies. They were gathered at tables in the otherwise closed-up restaurant. Several Domino Pizza boxes were scattered in front of them. Every two-liter, soft-drink bottle had been drained dry. Crushed paper cups and crumpled napkins completed the messy collection.

Agent Ronan sat down with them. He said, "Sheriff Quan, I had a chance to meet two of your deputies on the way over here this morning. They impressed me with their dedication and knowledge of police work. Ah, there's one of them now."

A tall, clean-cut young man in an ill-fitting, protective vest was coming toward them from the front entrance. Ronan waved to him. "Hi, Joe, how are we doing?"

"It's Josh," he said. "The building's clean. I think we are about to wrap things up."

"Sorry, Josh. I'm terrible with names. It was a pleasure to meet you and thank you for your good work."

"I didn't do much but I was glad to help." He took off the vest and slumped into a nearby chair." One of the other deputies slid a pizza box toward him.

Josh pushed it away. "Thanks but I've had enough. I ate half a pizza before Sheriff Denny sent me to get the car."

The sheriff pointed to the boxes. "Irving, there might be one or two pieces of pepperoni left. If I had known you were coming, I would have saved some Pepsi for you."

"Thanks anyway, Dennis. How are things going here?"

"We decided to stick around just to talk for a while. We have been reminiscing about the loss of one of our own today. Harrison Fraley was a smart, dedicated deputy sheriff. We were discussing plans for what to do about a memorial."

Agent Irving Ronan said, "Allow me to assure you that the Federal Bureau of Investigation will do everything we can to honor Mr. Fraley's memory. The Sheriff's Department made the ultimate sacrifice in the line of duty today.

"Every one of you performed honorably. You did a great job. Sheriff Quan and all of you should know that the assistance you provided was invaluable. The Sheriff's Department has reason to stand proud.

"Although we knew Mr. Fraley only briefly, I speak for Agents Cleary and Kumar as well as for myself when I tell you we know from experience how you feel right now. We will contribute what we can to his memory and at his memorial. I will participate personally if you want me to."

"Thank you," Dennis Quan said.

"If there is anything we can do, please let me know."

"We will. For now, I believe our work here is about done. I have to hang around until Chief Hepburn locks up the building."

"I'm going out to the BPD van right now myself. Shall I tell her you are ready for her?"

"Sure. Two of my deputies have agreed to watch the place for the night until Chief Hepburn turns it back over to the tenants in the morning."

Chapter 93 . The neighborhood canvass needed helpful residents.

Irving Ronan sat down in the BPD van across from Irene Cleary. Half an hour later, Jennifer Hepburn and Robert Ryan squeezed in next to them at the tiny table.

Cleary said to the police officers, "Irving was just telling me he and Rohit Kumar have developed some leads."

Ronan said, "That's right. Recall that three individuals interacted with the man who got away from us this morning. I sent them over to the BPD station for a debriefing. We were hoping we could get an ID from the two of them who checked his driver's license or from the deputy who tried to escort him here to the van."

"Tried but failed," Ryan interjected.

Ronan continued, "Rohit showed them a series of surveillance photographs. Irene, you know how Rohit operates. He put the three of them at separate desks and mixed up the photographs. He got a definitive identification. The man who escaped the deputy's grasp was Brian Hill."

"Ugh," Ryan groaned. "The sheriff told me about that kid. Talented but green. Worries too much about doing the right thing. He was acting too polite which is the reason Hill got away."

"Hill might have escaped anyway," Cleary said.

"The deputy who let him get away was anxious to return here. He said it was the sheriff's orders. Rohit took the other two out on the streets to canvas the neighborhoods. Five of the extra security guards at the office building went with them," Ronan explained.

He continued, "All of the commotion around the police station and the Monroe office building had people watching out their windows. They were happy to talk to the deputies. Although there was a lot of chaff mixed in the wheat, Rohit found one individual who had an observation that seemed right."

Cleary held up her hand to stop Ronan. She said, "Let's go talk to Agent Kumar."

On the short walk from the police van at the Monroe office building to the BPD station, Agent Ronan continued to fill the others in on what had been discovered.

"A resident of a house over on Princeton Street said there was a car that did not belong parked at the curb in front of his house last night. When it was still there this morning, he went out to look it over. It was a late model, dark blue almost black BMW sedan. He did not know the year but it looked pretty nice to him. A little while later, he noticed the car was gone and he forgot about it until the deputies came around asking questions."

"Over on, did you say Princeton Street? That's a few blocks away. How did they happen to find the witness?" Ryan asked.

"OK, let's go in," Ronan said. They had arrived at the station.

Agent Kumar provided the answer to Ryan's question. "We could not knock on every door, of course. So, we fanned out on foot and stopped people we found on the street. One of them said she had just seen someone matching our description of Hill. He was jogging in that direction."

"You mean toward Princeton Street," Ronan said.

"Yes, she remembered the man because he wasn't dressed for it. Leather loafers not running shoes and slacks not sweatpants. We used her directions to focus on the next few blocks."

"How lucky. You found an observant individual in the middle of a Saturday in Batavia," Ryan said.

Kumar explained, "When a resident on Princeton Street saw us walking down the middle of the road, he came out to see what was going on. He told us about a car that had been left overnight in front of his house."

"License plate?" Ryan asked.

"Unfortunately, he did not get the registration. He said it was out-of-state. He thinks Louisiana. He apologized for not writing down the number."

"It would have been nice but very few would have," Cleary volunteered.

Kumar continued, "More than one resident commented on the car. It was not a vehicle that belonged to any of them. The couple living across the street said they watched a woman stop to inspect the car early this morning. The husband said it was just a jogger going by.

"The wife said she was definitely not a jogger. She said, after looking it over, the woman turned around and walked back the way she had come. A jogger wouldn't do that. The two of them did agree that she was wearing dark blue slacks."

Chapter 94 . The psychopath's objective was a certain package.

Four security guards stayed back at the house with the O'Connor family when the FBI agents and police chief left that morning to go to the BPD station.

Lydia went into the den to ask, "Why so many on guard here, Elizabeth?"

"I actually don't know. Perhaps, it is because Chief Hepburn is not entirely sure about the nature of the threat that we are facing," Elizabeth explained. "She told me there is no evidence of anyone out there but someone could be watching the house."

"OK. I guess the extra caution is reassuring. It is better to be safe with too many guards than not enough."

"There is one other thing. Chief Hepburn is afraid, if Alena leaves, she could be followed. Can you keep her here without alarming her?"

"I'll talk to her," Lydia said.

Alena said, "Oh, I would be happy to stay and help with everything. The police chief said I couldn't leave. Don't worry about the money. You don't have to pay me. I just want to take care of my friends. You're family to me."

"We will pay you, Alena."

"No, no. It's not necessary besides I feel safe here. If I go home, someone might follow me."

So much for not alarming her. Alena clearly understood that some kind of trouble was brewing.

"We want you to be safe too, Alena."

"Also, I want to do my part to catch whomever killed Mr. Hennigan."

Lydia nodded and smiled. There was no hiding anything from the astute Alena.

I called my parents to see how they were doing. They assured me that everything was fine but their questions were worrisome.

My father asked, "How long will this siege go on?"

When it was her turn on the phone, Mother said, "The fine young man who is here for our security is very competent."

"Is there just one man there with you?"

"Yes. There was another one but he needed to leave. Family matters. We told him he should go. Nothing will happen here. Our neighborhood is very safe."

When I got off the phone I told Elizabeth that I wanted to go see my folks.

"You really should not be going out. Are you worried about their safety? We have two good men at their house with them."

"No, one of them left."

Without hesitating for even a second, Elizabeth gave an order. "Andre, go over to the senior O'Connor's house immediately. Call me as soon as you get there to confirm that everything is OK. I will let the sheriff and the chief know."

"Shall I take the deputy's car in the driveway? Where do they live?"

"Yes. Ted, go with Andre to show him the way."

Diane ran out with us. "I'm coming too. I can help with Grandma and Grandpa."

We were on our way before Elizabeth Stewart had a chance to object.

Andre talked to the remaining security guard when we got to my parents' house. He called Elizabeth and told her, "Everything seems fine. Douglas said there has been no trouble. I took a walk around the block and nothing looks suspicious. What do you want me to do?"

When Andre hung up, he told me that Elizabeth said he should stay at my parents' with us at least for the time being.

"Do we know why the other guy left?" I asked.

"Elizabeth checked. There was nothing about a family matter that she could find," Andre answered.

"Is she worried?"

"Maybe she is too suspicious. I don't know Elizabeth very well. Do you?"

"We've known her a while but not well enough to say if she is an alarmist," I replied.

"She did tell me not to worry your folks but we should remain vigilant," Andre said.

It was after three o'clock in the afternoon when the conversation with my father in the living room was suddenly interrupted. My mother walked in from the kitchen.

She said, "Ted, there's a gentleman at the back door who wants to talk to you. I don't think he is one of the security men."

A familiar-looking individual came in behind her. Brian Hill had Diane by the arm as if he were an usher guiding her to a seat in the theater. The terrified look on her face gave lie to his jocular greeting. "Hi, Ted. We need to talk."

I turned to look for our security guards.

"The protection detail has chosen not to participate. They have been confined to the garage. I wonder how much time those poor boys have before the exhaust gets to them."

"Did I hear you start my car?" Mother asked.

"Yeah, I did. Actually, there are two cars in there. I got both engines running. You have a pretty nice Mercedes-Benz sedan, Mr. O'Connor," Brian Hill said.

"That's my car," Mother told him.

"Oh, is it? The Park Avenue is nice too. You both foolishly left your keys on a hook inside the kitchen door."

"What do you want, Rusty?" I asked. He had a maniacal look that I had not seen before.

"I think you know what I want, Ted."

"No, I don't."

He slid a satchel from his shoulder onto the recliner across from me and pulled a firearm from the holster attached to his belt at the small of his back.

He shoved the two women toward Dad on the couch. Diane landed sitting down but Mother fell to the floor.

When Dad reacted, Rusty cracked him across his forehead and whirled toward me. The view down the barrel of his gun took away my urge to attack.

Mother was crying. Dad was bleeding. I rose up engulfed in fury. Rusty's firearm was a few inches from my nose.

"Please don't try anything stupid, Ted. Can you see that I mean business?"

I helped Mother up onto the couch next to my father. I put a hand on Diane to hold her down. Our eyes met and I could see the rage.

Rusty took a spool of cord from his satchel and whipped it around Diane and her grandmother. He cinched it tight lashing them together. He took a switch blade from his pocket and flipped it open next to Diane's ear.

"Sit there, Ted." He pointed to the straight-back chair next to the end table with the house phone. He cut the rope, came back around the couch, and tied me down too.

He did not need to restrain my father. I could see that Dad was breathing but not conscious.

"What did you do to my father? He needs medical attention."

"Naw, he's a tough old bird. He'll last at least till morning." Rusty let out a raucous laugh. "It's just a little bump on the head, Ted. Dad will be fine unless you choose to be uncooperative. In which case, who knows?"

"Tell me what you want?"

"Let me tell you how I know you know what I want." The gun was back in my face.

"Please do."

"Matthew Hennigan had been hiding from us for quite some time when Elliot Shaw found him a few years ago."

"Hiding from whom?"

"La Familia, of course."

"The Mendoza cartel?"

"Cartel is not a good word. We are a family business."

Father groaned and gasped for air but he didn't try to get up.

Rusty glanced in has direction without showing any sympathy. It was the look of a psychopath.

He continued, "We did not do anything about Hennigan for a long time because we couldn't. He had a file with lots of important names and information about our operations in this country."

"You killed him," I accused.

"Not back then. I wanted to take him out but Señor Mendoza had a soft spot for him. After all, Matty had been a good soldier. The family was sure he would never betray El Patron by releasing hurtful information."

"I'm guessing you did not agree."

"That's right. I knew it would happen. Matty got greedy. Even El Patron knew that blackmail must not be tolerated. You see what I mean?"

I couldn't answer. I just shook my head.

"Are you still not cooperating, Mr. O'Connor? Perhaps you are willing to sacrifice your daughter." He grabbed Diane by the hair and held the gun against her temple.

"Let go of me, you asshole," Diane hissed.

"Watch your language. It's not ladylike," he laughed. Rusty raised his hand to strike her but held up. "No, I am too smart for that. I can't punish you yet. You know why?"

Diane jerked her head away without answering.

"If I hit you, I might have to shoot your father and I won't get what I want. I should save you for last anyway. Perhaps, your father will be more cooperative if I put grandfather out of his misery."

He held the switch blade up for me to see and moved around behind the couch toward my father. The blade drew a few drops of blood from the unconscious man's neck.

Mother shouted, "Stop it!"

"What do you say, Ted? Will you give me what I want?"

"Yes, yes. How do you know I've still got it?" I did not know what he was taking about but I had to say something.

Just then there was a loud bang and a flash of light outside the picture window. It startled all of us including Rusty.

He quickly regained his composure. "That would be my new friend telling me to hurry up. I told Alex Montoya to monitor the police frequency on my radio. You want to know how I know about you, Ted?"

"Sure."

"Elliot Shaw was my lookout for Hennigan at his store when you stopped for gas last week. He was working that night and he was supposed to call me when Hennigan showed up. Elliot was sipping a little whisky to help his nerves. He always had a bottle of Jim Beam hidden in the locked supply closet in the lavatory. He did not want customers to see him drunk so he hid when you came in but he forgot his bottle on the counter. He watched you from the lavatory until you gave up and left."

"I threw the bottle away. It was empty."

"Elliot was happy that you did because Hennigan would have seen it. He walked in immediately after you left."

"Hennigan was there to close up the shop. Elliot dialed my number from the store phone by the cash register like he was supposed to. When I got there, he told me about your visit. I thanked him and sent him home."

"He made up everything he said in court."

"With a little coaching from me. After he left, I tried to persuade Hennigan that it was in his best interests to tell me what he had done with his files. The lavatory provided a sound-proof and hidden location for my interrogation. The lights were on in the store. He declined to cooperate. So, I shot him. For the sake of La Familia, we have to set an example that betrayal cannot be tolerated."

"You executed him before he gave you the files."

"I had to. The dope rushed at me like he thought he could take me down. Things got a little messy. I had to clean myself up in the lavatory.

"From our conversations at the park and afterwards, I already knew about Hennigan's relationship with Elmer Wrightson. When that fool Louis Thompson found that the files were not in the safe in his office, he called me and we figured out that Wrightson entrusted the package to you."

"I don't have them with me."

"Of course not. The files are at your house or somewhere else. It makes no difference. You will go get them and bring them to a place where your daughter and I will be waiting."

"Where will that be?"

"Come on now, Ted. You know better than that. You will have to wait for that information."

The expression on Rusty's face suddenly changed.

"Ah ha!" Diane glared at him. "The security guards got free."

It was the sudden quiet that startled him. The rumble from the car engines had ceased.

"No, they did not get loose. They couldn't have. It must be a signal from Montoya. What is that idiot doing?"

"It's not Alex Montoya you have to worry about, Mr. Hill, but you're right he is an idiot." A calm female voice spoke from the hallway.

"What the hell?" The belligerent Brian Hill snarled.

"The police are on the way, Mr. Hill. I've called for an ambulance. The two men in the garage are pretty sick. Were you going to leave them there to die?"

"What do you think?"

Janet Bread walked into the living room. In a cool, hard voice, she said, "It's over, Mr. Hill. Drop the knife. Toss the gun over by the fireplace."

"You're joking," he snarled. He put a bullet in the wall where she had been standing.

The sound of the blast made Mother shriek.

Brian Hill grabbed the rope that tied Mother to Diane and jerked the two of them up off the couch. The knife was back in his hand. He cut the rope and pushed Mother away. He pulled Diane close and crouched behind her to hide from Janet's voice.

Janet spoke again. "You are running out of time, Mr. Hill. Let go of the woman. Get down on your knees and put your hands behind your head."

"I've got a hostage and I'm leaving now," he shouted. Brian Hill had Diane by the throat with the muzzle of his gun at her temple.

"Let her go," Janet said. "It's your last chance."

Brian Hill wasn't listening. He pointed the gun at Mother. "Back the Mercedes out of the garage. Leave it in the driveway and step away. I am going out the front door."

"You are wrong, Mr. Hill. You are not leaving."

Hill answered, "Stay out of my way or I'll kill the girl."

He was interrupted by the sound of sirens.

He shouted at Mother, "Get the car now."

"OK, I'm going," Mother cried. "Where are the keys?"

"I have them." Janet Bread was standing up again. She held up a key ring in her left hand.

"Toss them over here," Hill demanded. He pointed at the floor with the gun.

The car keys landed at Mother's feet. She scrambled to pick them up. She pleaded, "Let him go. He'll kill my granddaughter."

Our obstinate daughter had a different suggestion. "Shoot him, Detective Bread." Diane tried to twist out of his grasp.

I shouted, "Diane, don't rile him. The psychopath will have no qualms about hurting you."

"Damn right." He pulled Diane tighter against his side and leaned over me. Brian Hill growled in my face. "I'll be back another day to deal with you." It was a false threat.

The bullet from Janet Bread's gun struck him between the eyes.

Chapter 95 . The house belonged to the medical examiner.

"Where have you been, Janet Bread?" Diane was indignant with her cherished aunt. She jumped to her feet. "The whole world has been looking for you. We thought you were dead!"

Detective Bread gave no answer. She was standing over me. She rolled Hill's body to the side. I could still feel the sting from the spray of cartilage in my scalp and across my forehead. She grabbed my face with her bare hands and felt for wounds. She wiped human detritus off my head and neck.

She said, "I don't feel anything. Are you OK?"

"I think so."

"Stand up." Janet slipped a knife from a sheath on the calf of her right leg and cut the rope that bound me to the chair. She helped me to my feet. She shook me by the shoulders. "You're good. Go get cleaned up and get a wet washcloth for me." She gave me a push and dropped down in front of the couch to examine my father. Mother was holding up his head and whispering to him.

The living room was suddenly crowded with medics, police officers, and FBI agents. I had to thread my way through them toward the kitchen. A woman in uniform took my elbow and guided me to the sink.

When I got back, an EMT was hovering over my father. Janet Bread got out of his way. He had to jostle Mother to one side. He lifted Dad's lids to shine a flashlight in his eyes. I handed Janet a warm wet towel and she wiped the blood from her hands.

The attendants loaded Dad onto a stretcher. I went next to him and took his hand. His grip was firm. He said, "We got him, son." I had to laugh. The old man was claiming some of the credit for himself. He was going to be all right.

They rolled him out to the ambulance. Mother got in with him and they drove off with sirens blaring.

"The old coot is gonna love talking about today," I said.

"Dad, this is serious," Diane admonished.

She held me by the arm as we looked down the street to see the ambulance swing around the corner on the way to the emergency room.

A voice from behind us said, "Excuse me please."

We turned to see that a large white van with Office of the Medical Examiner printed on the side had pulled up in the street. We stepped aside to let an attendant push a gurney up the driveway toward the house.

Officer Angela Dunning said, "The ME will need a couple of hours to process the scene before you can go back in. Let me give you a ride to the police station."

She loaded Diane and me into the back seat of a BPD cruiser. It struck me that it could be the same car in which I was carted off to jail not that many days ago. The disquieting thought landed on top of many traumatic minutes. Diane quelled my uncontrollable shuddering with her arm around my shoulders.

Dunning explained, "Chief Hepburn has asked everyone to come to her office for a post-mortem on today's events. She wants to review the details while they are still fresh in your memory."

Diane asked me, "Can you do it, Dad? Will you be OK?"

"Yeah, sure."

When we got to the police station, Lydia and Eileen were already there. The four of us sat together on the couch in Chief Hepburn's office. We just held onto each other too numb to talk.

Sgt. Ryan and Officer White walked in and sat down at the police chief's conference table.

Billy said, "I'm glad all of you are all right."

Diane glanced up at him and looked down again. I could feel her sigh.

Chief Hepburn said, "Detective Bread and Agent Kumar are in the bull pen at Sgt. Winters' desk. They are setting up a conference call with a senior DEA agent in Washington. We will convene a discussion of today's events when they are ready to join us."

Sgt. Winters knocked on the open door to the chief's office. "Chief Hepburn, Agent Kumar has the DEA on the phone and they are waiting for the three of you."

"Lydia and Ted, you are welcome to make yourselves comfortable here or go out to get something to eat. Please be back in an hour." Chief Hepburn walked out of her office. White and Ryan hurried after her.

Diane and Eileen agreed with Lydia agreed that another location would be preferable to our current situation. Each of us picked out items from the counter in the hospital cafeteria and carried our trays to Dad's room.

I took a detour on the way out to look in on Elmer Wrightson. I found him with a visitor. Cynthia de Vries and Janet Bread were there. Katherine Chavis was huddled up in a chair under a blanket looking cheerful but pale. I told them I couldn't stay. Chief Hepburn was waiting for us at the station.

Bread said, "Tell her I'll be right there."

Chapter 96 . Participants achieved closure with a post-mortem conference.

When we got back to Chief Hepburn's office, she told us the conversation with the DEA agent had been quite revealing. "We can tie up the loose ends as soon as Janet Bread returns. She should be right back. Did you see her at the hospital?"

"Yes, she was visiting Elmer. She said she was coming."

Elizabeth Stewart stuck her head in the door. "Chief Hepburn, did you call me?"

"Have everyone join me in the conference room."

"Sgt. Ryan and Officer White are already there. Did you want anyone else?"

"See if you can find Angela Dunning and Claire Winters. You should be there too. Please take notes and contribute as needed."

We reassembled on the hard-back chairs around the large Steelcase table in the room across the hall from the chief's office.

It took a while for everyone to get there. Janet Bread was the last to arrive. She said, "Sorry to keep you waiting. I stopped in to see your father, Ted. He was joking with the hospitalist who was there to check on him. One of them thinks Roger Maris should be in the Hall of Fame. The other does not. I thought it wise not to voice my opinion. I think your Dad is going to be all right. Your Mother is with him."

Agents Cleary, Ronan, and Kumar took places at the conference table. From what we could see of their faces, relief and fatigue were evident everywhere.

Chief Hepburn said, "I believe everybody who can make it is here. I did not ask Katherine Chavis to join us. She is really shaken up after this morning's ordeal. I called the hospital and talked to Wrightson. He should be released in the morning. He wants to leave now but the hospitalist said no."

Before she could finish the sentence, Sheriff Dennis Quan came in with Katherine Chavis and Elmer Wrightson in tow. It was standing room only.

"Elmer, you're supposed to be in the hospital," I said.

"The more I thought about it the more certain I was that I needed to hear Detective Bread's story," Wrightson said.

Ronan helped Stewart roll extra chairs into the room from the chief's office across the hall.

Hepburn said, "Let's start with you, Detective Bread."

Lydia's cousin began to fill us in. "After I spotted Brian Hill at the bail hearing in the courthouse, I talked to Agent Cleary about him. We agreed that he should be kept under surveillance. Chief Hepburn put me in touch with Sheriff Quan." Bread turned to look at him.

Quan said, "The deputies who worked the stakeout at different times included Harrison Fraley. In one of his reports, Fraley wrote that he had seen Thompson speak to Brian Hill on the street after a session in the courtroom. I discussed the issue with Deputy Fraley. I told him it might not mean anything. I figured Hill was probably just nodding to a uniformed police officer. Harrison was not so sure. It seemed to him there was more to the exchange."

Hepburn said, "Unfortunately, Louis Thompson was passing inside information to Hill. He was in on all of our discussions. Brian Hill had Deputy Fraley made almost from the day he joined the investigation."

"You know, Chief, my own faith in Officer Thompson was unshaken until the day the son of a bitch sold us out." Sgt. Ryan could see no reason to mince words.

"Thank you, Bob, but no one is to blame but myself. I hired him. I am sorry I missed whatever might have been there to indicate the man was corrupt. I am most sorry, immensely sorry and saddened about Deputy Fraley. It appears he was targeted. Why him and not me."

"I was there with you when the shots were fired," Agent Cleary said. "Very likely Thompson was aiming to hit both of you. He was a crack shot but your experience saved you. Young Fraley could not get out of the way. He took a bullet for all of us. His sacrifice put the investigation on high alert. We knew then that we were facing a lethal threat in the Monroe office building and elsewhere in Batavia."

"Elsewhere in Batavia is where I was at the time," Janet Bread continued. "Fraley and the other deputies recorded sightings of Hill in various locations in the area. Hill was staying at the Holiday Inn Express under one assumed name. His car-rental agreement from a place in the city was under another name. Rusty Higgins is the pseudonym he was using around town for the last year or more.

"The surveillance team saw Hill hide his rental in plain sight at the curb on a side street not far from the station. When I was sure he was not around, I jogged through the neighborhood and attached a tracking devise to the rear bumper."

"It was near the corner of Princeton Street and Walnut Avenue. Neighbors reported seeing you there," Sgt. Ryan said.

Detective Bread said, "Oh, that's bad. I thought I was more careful than that. Anyway, it was the tracking device that allowed me to follow him to the senior O'Connor's house this afternoon.

"Brian Hill was friendly and nice to the staff at the hotel. Naturally, it got him favored-guest status with the desk attendants, maids, and helpers in the complimentary breakfast room. The man could exude charm when he needed to.

"Another agent, a security guard we got from Elite Security Services, noticed that Hill seemed to be focused on one of the maids in particular. A woman named Rosalie Ortega. Brian Hill spoke to her in the halls. On one occasion, he gave her a small gift. Another afternoon, he prevailed upon her to give him a ride to Allen's Diner where she dropped him off."

"Let me tell you how Ms. Ortega fits in," I said, "Some years ago, a Mexican national named Angel Hernandez was not in good graces with the Mendoza cartel. When they threatened him and his family, they fled to the United States. They found Batavia to be a safe haven but only for a short while. His wife and Ms. Ortega became friends."

Detective Janet Bread resumed her narrative. "Good to know. It means it was not a coincidence that Brian Hill made friends with Rosalie Ortega.

I said, "The cartel had a general idea of where to find Angel Hernandez and he knew it. He also knew that he was of too little interest for them to bother with. However, when he missed a filing deadline due to a government mix-up, ICE came looking for him. Rather than try to get his papers renewed, Mr. Hernandez left town with his family."

Janet continued, "It all makes sense now. Brian Hill intended to extract information from Rosalie Ortega to locate Hernandez whom he would force to help him get back to Mexico. It was part of his escape plan after he obtained what he came here for, a dossier in Hennigan's possession. He believed it contained incriminating evidence about the cartel. Hill would employ whatever means necessary, including killing Matthew Hennigan and Elliot Shaw, to get that file."

"How did Thompson get involved?" Ronan asked.

Detective Bread explained, "Patrolman Louis Thompson was gradually sucked into the business by taking harmless favors now and again which got more and more tempting until he became important to Mendoza's interests in Chicago. The Mendoza cartel owned him. When Brian Hill asked him to come here to assist with a special project, he had no choice. His life depended on it. Also, Hennigan needed the financial support provided by cartel. He had costly obligations. Thompson's son is a junior at Loyola University and the younger boy is graduating from Adlai Stevenson High School in the spring."

"What about his wife?" Ronan interrupted with another question.

Janet said, "A piece of work. A wanna-be socialite who loved the status that her husband's ill-gotten, extra income provided. She had no interest in moving with him for his new job here. She stayed in their home in Chicago."

"Was that OK with him?" someone asked.

"Not so much but I don't really know. Their relationship had little relevance to what was happening here." Janet Bread was determined to keep after her story if we would let her finish.

She continued, "After I visited with you, Ted, in the afternoon at your house on Friday, I went back to the Monroe office building.

"My intention was to follow up on a few leads. As you know from our conversations on the phone, Irene, and Irving, we were not zeroing in on anything conclusive. You were on the call too, Elmer.

"I decided to give up and try again this morning. However, on my way out of the building at about 11:30 last night, I spotted Louis Thompson driving a BPD cruiser out the exit from the upper-level garages. I dropped back and followed him up the street to Harry's Pub. He entered the bar through the back door from the parking lot. I radioed an urgent message for assistance to the FBI office in Washington before entering the establishment myself.

"Thompson was sitting across from Hill at the table in the corner by the rear entrance. I decided to set myself up and let them capture me if they would. I took a step closer and looked around as if letting my eyes adjust to the dim light. 'Care to join us?' Brian Hill asked me. Obviously, it was not a question.

"He took me at gun-point down the stairs into the dungeon-like basement below the bar. No one paid any attention. Hill must have had some kind of arrangement with the staff. He had a key to a steel door on one side of the dank and cluttered lower level."

Sgt. Ryan said, "We have the bartender and a waitress who were on duty in custody. They have admitted that Brian Hill talked them into letting him borrow the room. He was so nice that they couldn't see the harm. He also promised he would make it worth their while. We are not sure if the complicity of either one goes any deeper than that. At least, not yet."

"I might like to have a word with them myself," Janet said. "Hill concocted his scheme right there in front of me in the basement below Harry's Pub. No need to hide anything from me. Thompson had already told him about my investigation. They were sure everyone would look for me in the Monroe office building and not at Harry's when I failed to show up this morning.

"Brian Hill showed me pictures of you and Diane, Ted. He said, they could get to you if I tried anything foolish. Thompson took a picture of me sitting right there at the table. 'For insurance,' he told me.

"Thompson left for the night. He was supposed to report for duty with the BPD early this morning and watch for an opportunity to corner you, Elmer, and extract an item of value. Hill was too guarded with his comments for me to know what he was looking for. I think he did not want to reveal the details to Thompson.

"The third conspirator surprised me. Some while after midnight, Alex Montoya showed up with take-out meals from the Patel Indian Restaurant. He actually had an entrée for me which, by his expression, Hill hardly thought was necessary. They ate first before giving me a turn. Hill was impatient so I had to wolf it down."

Eileen asked, "Was it good? I like their food."

Janet smiled at the question. "I like Indian food too but there were two things wrong with it. First, it was cold by the time I got to it and second I had just had the same dish at Patel's two days ago."

"Did you complain?".

"No, I didn't dare. Hill wouldn't put the gun down until I was back in cuffs. I hardly had time to gulp down the Indian tea, which had gone cold anyway."

"What did you do about, you know?" Eileen whispered.

Janet whispered back, "If you must know, all four of us had to pee in the same 10-gallon pail but, honest, I did not look when they did it." Of course, she said it loud enough for all of us to hear.

Eileen blushed like her own father didn't know she could.

Janet said, "Now you know the whole story."

"No, we don't. Janet, how did you escape?" Lydia demanded.

"The reason Hill and Thompson needed Montoya was to watch me while they went after you, Elmer. Around ten this morning, Hill left the two us alone and did not return. Early in the afternoon, he called to tell Montoya that there was a change of plans. He was needed elsewhere. I deduced that Thompson had been eliminated somehow. Hill gave Montoya instructions to leave me locked up and join him somewhere. I persuaded Mr. Montoya to let me go instead."

By Janet Bread's tone, I could tell that persuaded might not be quite the right word.

"What do you mean, persuaded?" Chief Hepburn looked doubtful.

"It was the kind of persuasion that is best carried out at the point of a gun."

"How did you get loose?"

"A plastic zip tie is not the right kind of restraint to use on someone tied to a steel chair especially if there is a rough edge on the back of the seat."

"Was Brian Hill really that dumb?"

"It was Alex Montoya's solution. Hill was not paying attention."

"Tell us more," Eileen exclaimed.

Detective Bread continued in a serious tone, "When they freed me to eat last night, Thompson hung his handcuffs back on his belt. As soon as Hill ordered me tied down again, Montoya grabbed one of the zip ties that they were using to bind my ankles.

"Alex Montoya is clearly not a professional criminal. Neither Hill nor Thompson would have made the same mistake but it didn't really matter because I already had a key to the handcuffs."

"How did they let you get away with that?" Diane asked.

"The key fits perfectly in your mouth between cheek and gum," Janet explained.

"You had a key in your mouth the whole time." Eileen was astonished.

I said, "Montoya wouldn't tell you where Hill had gone but you found us anyway."

"Fortunately, I had other means for tracking Hill to his destination. I logged into the tracking device on his car and came right to you."

Detective Bread continued, "As soon as Mr. Montoya got off the phone with Brian Hill, I took the gun away from him. I tried to get him to tell me where Hill had gone but Montoya was in an agitated state. He did not react well to failing his assignment to keep me under wraps. He was too frightened of Hill to cooperate with me. I promised that the FBI would provide protection but he said Hill would track him down and kill him the same way he got to Mr. Hennigan. He refused to say where I could catch up with Mr. Hill. So, I was forced to leave him behind alone in the cold, locked room."

"Poor Mr. Montoya," Officer White deadpanned. "He was not at all happy when Sgt. Ryan and I transferred him from the dungeon beneath Harry's Pub to the Batavia City jail."

"Will Montoya testify that Hill killed Hennigan? How about Elliot Shaw?" I asked.

"He might but it won't be necessary. Mr. Hill bragged about both crimes to me," Janet said.

"The New Mexico State Police will be interested in hearing about Mr. Hill," Agent Cleary said. "They arrested a known member of the Mendoza cartel at the border with Ciudad Juarez early this morning. He pulled over on a side street, abandoned his car, and started to cross into Mexico on foot. It was only by chance that a border guard recognized him. They are holding him in Las Cruces. My guess is Hill arranged for the assassin to intercept Shaw on his way to the border."

"What was in the dossier that Brian Hill looking for?" I asked.

Agent Cleary said, "Agent Kumar, please explain."

Kumar said, "Matthew Hennigan was in the DEA's protective-custody program."

"Do you mean there was no dossier for Hill to recover? Hennigan had already turned everything over to the authorities," Attorney Wrightson asked.

"Yes and no. Hennigan's testimony put two of the most egregious offenders in the cartel behind bars for life. However, he did not reveal anything that could be used against Brian Hill. He claimed that Hill was clean. A DEA agent was not so sure. She kept a file on Hill and two years later, the DEA got him on charges that had nothing to do with Hennigan."

"Could Hennigan have been harboring additional incriminating evidence against members of the cartel?"

"Evidently, Brian Hill thought so. However, we may never know. Hennigan claimed that he destroyed all of the evidence that he possessed but there could be a package hidden away somewhere.

Hennigan's wife was devasted by his murder. She has given the BPD and me her full cooperation. Officer Padraic McGuire and I spent yesterday afternoon working with her. He was back at it this morning and I joined him midday.

"Paddy has been a tremendous help and he will keep digging but, at this point, we believe that there is nothing at Hennigan's business or hidden in his home."

Janet Bread resumed speaking and guided the post-mortem conference to its conclusion. "Brian Hill's car was parked around the corner from your folks' house, Ted. The sheriff's car was in the driveway and both garage doors were closed. I could hear car engines running. Finding unconscious security guards handcuffed to the steering wheels made me rather angry to say the least. I opened the doors and switched off the engines before calling for ambulances."

"What about us?"

"Oh, of course, Officer White. I had already called the police when I discovered Hill's car," Janet Bread said.

Sgt. Claire Winters said, "When we arrived, Angela and I saw the garage doors going up. We jumped out of the car and Detective Bread motioned for us to come inside. She said she was going in alone and not to follow her. She told us to create a distraction."

Officer Dunning said, "I ran back to the cruiser for a percussion flare and set it off on the other side of the house outside the living room window. We unshackled the two security guards and dragged them out onto the neighbor's yard."

"When we heard a gunfire, I sent Angela to the front door and I went through the garage into the kitchen. I heard Brian Hill threaten Mr. O'Connor followed by the blast of a gunshot and suddenly it was over. All I can add is Detective Bread was amazing."

Janet Bread interrupted with the final word, "The rest is history."

Epilogue.

Find ecstasy in life; the mere sense of living is joy enough.

– Emily Dickinson

§ The Year 2023 §

Three and a half years later in February of 2023, we hosted a party at our house to celebrate Diane and Billy's second anniversary.

My gallant parents were there. Dad had the permanent appearance of a retired boxing champion. He wore the scar that Brian Hill had impressed upon his forehead like a badge of honor.

Mother said, "The plastic surgeon told him she could fix it but he won't hear of it."

Lydia's cousin came for the occasion and, to everyone's delight, she stayed a week. She could have taken Diane's old room but Janet Bread preferred her usual accommodations. Eileen had already decided we no longer had a guest room. It was to be known henceforth as Aunt Janet's Chambers.

Great-grandmother MaryBeth sent a card with a note written in a shaky hand. "My Very Dear Diane and Bill, Happy Anniversary! Congratulations! Sorry that I cannot be there. The doctor does not want me to travel. Perhaps, you will come here to celebrate your next anniversary with me. Love, Grandma."

Elmer Wrightson brought a gift and stayed the whole time. Roger and James were there too. There was no way they would have declined the invitation.

Billy's mother and stepfather arrived early. Both helped with the preparations. Ever since the wedding, we were in each other's homes for one occasion or another nearly every month.

Billy's biological father also joined us for his son's anniversary party. I believe he showed up for important events as much as he could but I sensed an element of unease in the company of the mother of his children. I could be empathetic. I felt a pang for him. There but for the Grace of God go I.

As soon as the entire audience had assembled, Diane radiated wonderful news. "We have an announcement everyone." She turned toward us old folks, his parents and hers. "Billy and I are expecting your first grandchild in October."

I told Lydia that Diane was looking at her Mother. Lydia smiled at me with the same glistening eyes that mesmerized me when we first met.

Both mothers expressed delight. Aunt Janet did too. They jumped up to hug Diane and each other. I said something inane like, "I hope you have started saving for college."

Later in the afternoon, in a quiet moment, Janet Bread told me, "I have something that might interest you."

She handed me an envelope with an uncancelled postcard inside. It was a glossy picture of an antique John Deere tractor preserved on a platform in front of a multi-bay garage. The sign on the building read, 'Christina Automotive Repair.'

When Lydia saw it, she asked, "Where did you get that?"

Janet Bread said, "When I was attending a hearing in El Paso for the DEA last December, I took a side trip to Las Minitas and visited with some of the folks who live there. An elderly woman listened intently when I told the gathering in her home about a lovely couple from Mexico who lived in Batavia for a while. I explained to them that the family had five beautiful children.

"It made the woman laugh when I said my niece taught their oldest child Christina how to drive. There was a tear in her eye when I told her that my cousin's husband was Godfather for their youngest child Liam.

"Señora Teresita Rosado opened the top drawer of a buffet cabinet where we sat in her living room. She took out this post card and handed it to me. I asked if I could keep it and she said yes. Now, I am giving it to you, Ted."

When we were alone that evening, Lydia and I decided it was high time for us to follow through on a long talked-about plan to rent a motorhome for a vacation just by ourselves.

The perfect opportunity came when we hauled Eileen and all her stuff off to college for her third year at John Carroll University. It was in the middle of August 2023. We continued from there on a leisurely drive through Missouri and Nebraska.

We were sure we knew where to look for an antique John Deere tractor parked in front of an auto-repair shop somewhere along the road. We figured we could be gone for weeks before we had to be back in Batavia to welcome the new addition to our family.

Index of the Initial Occurrence of a Name.

Made in USA - North Chelmsford, MA
1070762_9781689233514
04.06.2020 1539